Robin —

Thank you for helping create this world!

Robin,
Thank you for helping
create this world!

T.J.

This is a work of fiction. Names, characters, places, and incidents either are the product of the author's imagination or are used fictitiously. Any resemblance to actual persons, living or dead, events, or locales is entirely coincidental.

Copyright © 2020 by Travis Betz

All rights reserved. No part of this book may be reproduced or used in any manner without written permission of the copyright owner except of the use of quotations in a book review

Book design by Natasha MacKenzie

ISBN: 978-1-7359971-2-4

**EVERYDAY MONSTERS**

To: piller@humansagainstinhumans.com
Subject: Poisoned and misguided

To whom it may concern,

I believe you corresponded with my parents in the past. If not, then you saw them on the news. Everyone did. The media dubbed them "The Cannibal Couple," and while it's true they did eat portions of their victims, the nickname is lazy and in bad taste (pun not intended). They are currently stuffed into straitjackets, while my older brother, Jordan, and I—he's twenty and I'm eyeballing eighteen—still reside in the house in which eight innocent men and women were caged and killed.

Having read my mother's diary cover to cover and launching my own private investigation, I am convinced that, although mistakes were made on their part, my parents were privy to a group of unsavory individuals that your website calls "a plague of festering evil." I have devoted the "best years of my life" (whoever made up that lie about high school is a serious asshole with no real depth or personality) to uncovering the hiding place of these foul creatures. This has made me an outcast where I live—a tucked-away mountain town appropriately named Rainy Mood, Virginia.

I discovered your business card amongst my mother's things. She needed your help, and now, as circumstance commands, I need it. I have slipped into her shoes—picked up her torch. In their honor, I will eradicate these moon-baked vermin. I am revenge.

You might advise me to fill my heart with love (your website labels you a religious organization), and while I enjoy the sentiment, I'll leave love to the ignorant masses that stumble through life with their necks exposed. It is now my job to protect them. For the good of mankind. For my parents—poisoned and misguided by a plague of festering evil.

I look forward to hearing from you.

Derek Stabbers

# CHAPTER 1

Paxton Hellswood's dinner stood a few yards away, face to the stars, neck vulnerable—a cherry pie cooling in an open window. An unusual-looking young man, his features were slightly off-center, as if he'd been punched in the face as a baby causing everything to develop a micro-measurement to the left. His name was Derek Stabbers. She knew that because everyone knew that. His parents had once painted a gory trail through the streets of her tucked-away town of Rainy Mood. His blood contained the scents of garlic and aluminum.

She gripped the cinnamon-red bark of the river birch tree that concealed her. Tonight was her 100th birthday, and she'd made the decision to walk through Little Horn Woods rather than fly over it. The lush, green thickness made it easy to hide. The trees had twisted personalities—bending, curling, and grabbing—their roots unsatisfied living beneath the dirt, arching in and out of the earth like a sea serpent. A tangled mess to many, but beautiful and complex to Pax. Trees could be trusted; humans on the other hand…

Enamel daggers broke the seal of Pax's lips and turned her sweet, awkward grin into something dangerous. She drowned out the world around her. The crickets, the wind, and the general hum of the universe all faded away as she focused on the rhythm of his heartbeat. Irregular. It would take a bit more time to feed on him due to his spastic pumper, which annoyed her.

Pax considered herself an indoor vampire. She would rather be spread out on her couch like a slug watching the *Space Lion* marathon on TV, but she had promised her family she'd put on non-pajama-type clothing and go out for the traditional birthday hunt—the one time of year they were allowed to drink directly from a human neck. She wasn't afraid of the outside world, she just had no use for it. It had betrayed her plenty in the past. Her couch, however, had never once pretended to be something it was not, and more specifically, had never run a sword through her chest, leaving her to bleed out on a cobblestone street.

The broken images of her past distracted her, for when she refocused on her meal, it had disappeared.

"Where'd ya go, psycho?" she mumbled under her breath. "Just want enough of your fruit punch for a solid buzz."

Pax breathed deep and caught the scent of his blood a few yards off the path—peppered ribeye and buttered asparagus. Her nose crinkled when a pair of invading scents pinched her nostrils—rotting bone and peroxide. She pushed them away, the bitter aromas not strong enough to distract from her goals: to eat, get home, and lounge on the couch until her 200th birthday rolled around.

Like a deadly ballerina with rocks in her slippers, she crept after her meal. Pax found him crouched low, watching a salamander wriggle under a large stone he had upturned. She dug her toes into the ground, ready to attack, drink, and flee. Derek would get lightheaded and blame a wild animal, and Pax would sleep with a belly full of crimson champagne.

She lowered her body in an attack stance, when a tiny chirp caught her ears. Her ravenous grin soured; her slate-gray eyes dropped their focus.

*Shit*, she mouthed and slowly turned her head.

Just behind her, propped up on its hindquarters, stood a fluffy, mocha-colored squirrel—its tiny claws clasped together. Pax hated squirrels. All vampires did. It was rumored—but never confirmed—that these delightful menaces were the trapped spirits of those murdered by the vampires' hunger. Since the dawn of Pax's kind, there had always been three things to avoid: the sun, beheading, and squirrels.

The intruder unhinged its cute little jaws and dug its adorable upper incisors deep into Pax's ankle. The vampire shrieked; the squirrel went in for seconds. Pax flailed about like an air dancer at a car dealership as the squirrel crawled up her torso. The stiff, short hairs of the squirrel's cheeks bristled her neck as it gnawed on her flesh. Was this how it would end for her—rolling around in the bushes in her Monday underwear on a Wednesday night? Who would get all her cool stuff? Who would even appreciate a hundred years of action figures and collectible lunch boxes?

As she contemplated her mental will and testament, the squirrel let out a shrill squeak, and a sharpened point pricked the surface of Pax's chest. She cracked open her eyes and stared down at the worrisome visual of a wooden stake as it wobbled just above her heart and out the back of the very dead squirrel.

"What are you doing out here?"

The voice sounded irritated and far away. Pax wanted to look up, but the ink-black eyes of her dead nemesis had her paralyzed.

"The woods aren't safe."

A hand entered her field of vision and grabbed the stake. It yanked upward; the squirrel stuck to it like a shish kabob. Pax's eyes followed the gored critter to the face of Derek Stabbers. He turned the squirrel over several times, studying it.

"Never seen a squirrel attack someone like that."

Derek flicked his wrist with a sharp snap. The squirrel slid off the wood and cut through the air, a grotesque bend to its body, and landed with a soft thud behind a bush. Derek stepped toward Pax, stake out. She scurried back, bumping her head against a tree. Derek stopped. Pointed at her neck.

"*You're* bit."

She felt the tiny puncture wounds on her neck, the moment drenched in irony. Derek Stabbers, her birthday dinner, had saved her from a throat-hungry creature. A thank-you would have been appropriate, but Pax's embarrassment mixed with a combative nature took control of her tongue.

"You're bit."

Her face twisted in disapproval. Before she could attempt a better sentence, Derek's stakeless hand shot toward her, halting a foot away. She stared up at his short, dirt-smeared fingers and wondered what in God's name he was doing out here this late—because Derek was right, the woods were not safe.

"Fine. Help yourself up." He lowered his hand and turned to leave.

"You poked me," she blurted, confused by her sudden need to keep his attention.

Derek paused, looked up at the moon. She could tell he thought he looked cool. He didn't, but she allowed him to have his hero moment.

"What's that supposed to mean?"

"The stake." Pax fanned two fingers over the tiny dot of blood on her top—just over her heart.

Derek shifted his gaze from the moon to her chest.

"It went through the squirrel's belly and poked me a little. I'm fine, obviously."

Another long, awkward silence floated around them.

"Just say thank you so I can move on."

Pax listened to his muscles tighten around his creaking bones, his heart accelerate. She listened to his stomach squish and his toes brush up and down against each other inside his shoes. The things he said out loud were cold and mean, but the things his body communicated from within were scared and almost sweet.

"Thank you."

"You're welcome."

Derek wiped the squirrel's blood from his stake, placed it securely inside the pocket of his oversized trench coat, then wandered off into the woods. Pax let him go, her appetite suddenly lost to the rather strange encounter. Derek Stabbers had just lived up to his reputation as a chip off the ol' psychotic block. She felt bad for him.

Pax rubbed the tiny mark on her chest, then breathed in long and deep, wanting to indulge in one final olfactory moment with the man who started off as her supper and ended up her savior.

Her eyes watered when a strong, non-Derek odor attacked her nose—the foul scent of wet mushrooms, bile, and halitosis. A rush of hot, rotten air pushed the vampire's hair over her shoulders. Pax suddenly missed the squirrel as she turned to face an even more disgusting animal—a creature she had smelled all along but chose to ignore. Little Horn Woods had two hunters tonight.

# CHAPTER 2

Derek Stabbers's compartmentalized Styrofoam plate had long given up the battle of the food walls. Mystery mixtures of meat and unidentified "vegetables" bled together on the battlefield of school lunch. He shoveled a sporkful into his mouth and instantly regretted it.

He hadn't slept much the night prior. His stupid pounding heart kept him awake. The weird girl in the bushes had upset his entire evening, and the worst part was, he didn't understand why. He'd gone out in those woods to hunt monsters, but his only accomplishment was the murder of a rabid squirrel.

The feeling of being watched chipped away at his spine, as it did every day he spent receiving a mediocre education from Barbara D. Hooker High School, or simply Hooker High. He raised his head from the table and scanned the cafeteria. No one looked directly at him, but the feeling remained.

The cafeteria, like the rest of the school, hadn't been upgraded, renovated or painted since the fifties. As the yellow-and-green tiles on the wall seemed to fade dramatically with each passing year, the light brown tiles that made up the floor grew darker. This depressed Derek, but brighter colors wouldn't mend his soul.

Teenagers were scattered everywhere, yapping on and on with mouthfuls of food, bodies bursting with hormones. His eyes narrowed as they closed in on one student in particular. Lotti Lyons—a self-proclaimed goddess of physical attractiveness. Her natural blond hair was curled just enough, and painstakingly tucked for effect under a black, slouchy-ribbed beanie. She sat at a table full of stunning teenage girl clones who all wore the gray version of the same hat—to a much lesser effect. Every giggle, every frown, every hair flip, and every eye-bat were absorbed, deconstructed, and mimicked by them in hopes of Lotti's acceptance.

Derek pointed his finger at the popular teen.

"Lotti Lyons."

He glanced over at three teenagers sitting at the far end of his table: a freckled redhead, a scrawny geek in a *Space Lion* T-shirt, and a curly-haired dork caught mid-bite of his peanut butter and banana sandwich—all stared nervously at him.

"She's vapid, selfish, and her voice makes me want to plug my ears with bullets," he continued. "And she's hiding something dark, gentlemen. I'm going to find out what."

The boys looked at each other, then back at Derek in his plain black T-shirt and greasy hair.

The ginger of the three spoke first. "Why are you talking to us?"

*Space Lion* shirt spoke next. "If we did anything to offend you, we're sorry."

Followed by the teen with a mouthful of peanut butter and banana. "Please don't eat us."

There was a time, long ago, when Derek would have been considered a harmless geek—an easy target for bullies and prom rejection—but the Stabbers name had been stained in blood. His parents' incarceration changed him both mentally and physically. His hair would no longer part perfectly on the side but hung shaggy above his eyes. Gone were his shirts with colors and collars, traded in for the dark, baggy, and torn. He spoke rarely, but when he did, his words were creepy and cold. Students no longer picked on him, they avoided him.

Derek reached over, grabbed a cookie from the kid with the *Space Lion* shirt, and shoved it in his mouth. There were zero protests. With a smile full of crumbs, Derek stood and made his way toward the table everyone secretly referred to as *hot lunch*.

He wasn't surprised to find a line of guys waiting to talk to Lotti. Never one to push the limits of his reputation, he took his place at the back. Lotti gabbed it up with some handsome asshole. A football player maybe. Behind him waited another equally handsome jerk holding a crumpled piece of paper, rehearsing some poorly composed poem in the name of teenage lust.

After two short rejections, it was his turn. Lotti shook her head and looked up as Derek took a step forward.

"There is no situation in which *we* ever happen, Stabbers." She huffed, tugging at the hair peeking out of her adorable hat.

Derek had no interest in Lotti. It's not that he didn't find her attractive, because she was, but Derek wasn't a hot surface kind of guy. If he were ever to get entangled—and that was a big if—he'd like to know something beautiful slopped about inside the person. Since he had devoted his life to revenge, it seemed a highly unlikely event.

Derek maintained his purposeful, intimidating silence and studied the spoiled brat in front of him. At close inspection she looked tired, but her exhaustion was well-hidden behind makeup. His eyes dipped to her neck, finding a splotch of smeared pancake applied in heavy strokes, hoping to cover something up.

Losing patience, Lotti tapped her fork on the table. "Hey, creep. Everyone else in this school might be afraid of you, but not me, so fuck off."

"And here I was about to ask you on a date," he said sarcastically.

"Great," Lotti replied, "all my organs just threw up inside my body."

Before Derek could add to her insult, Lotti gripped her temples, her face contorted in pain. Derek had seen her do this before. It would immediately be followed with an excuse for her to leave.

"I gotta jump."

Lotti gathered her things and stood. The girl with the glossiest lips and longest faux lashes stood as well. "Want company?"

"Why don't you go on that date with cannibal offspring in my place," Lotti said with more than a touch of frenemy venom.

She brushed past everyone quickly and exited the cafeteria. Derek set his eyes on Lotti's heartbroken friend and gave her a menacing grin.

"Please don't eat me."

Cruising fifteen miles over the speed limit in her retro burgundy Mustang, Lotti stuck to the back roads—tree lines and dirt paths. She did not want to be seen. Derek followed at a safe distance in his shitty Mercury Capri, avoiding potholes that took up more surface area than actual asphalt. Mountains peered down in the distance and always made Derek feel a little claustrophobic—surrounded by rocky giants that trapped his fears and insecurities.

He passed a large boulder tagged by spray paint—initials, hearts, and a few crudely drawn dicks. Derek made a point to look at the bold red letters near the oversized rock's jagged peak: *HAI*. While he never saw them do it, or even asked them if they were guilty, he knew his parents had sprayed those letters.

Derek's heart fluttered. He slowed the car down, gripped his chest, and let out a couple hard coughs. His damaged organ sputtered, then kicked back into its usual rhythm, leaving a thumping in his ears. He ignored the symptoms, put more pressure on the gas pedal, and his rusted transpo caught back up to Lotti.

He'd had a bad ticker ever since he could remember. He didn't need a doctor to tell him, he could feel its betrayal every day—fluttering chest, shortness of breath, and dizziness. He'd be lying to himself if he wasn't a little scared, so he became the world's greatest liar.

Lotti's Mustang pulled off the road and parked at the edge of Little Horn Woods. Derek drove past her and parked over the hill and out of sight. He doubled back on foot, just in time to see the senator's daughter swallowed up by the trees.

Derek had noticed a pattern with Lotti a few weeks back. A sharp pain in her skull would lead to her ditching class for the rest of the day. At first, he figured she suffered from migraines, or she faked the headaches to shop or drink or…whatever a popular girl did when not at school. He reevaluated his theory when he noticed a small amount of blood on her backpack during Latin class. Just above the zipper. A few splotches of red. The next day, she had an entirely new bag.

The woods grew thicker, and Derek knew exactly where she was headed. It was a place he'd been staking out (a pun he proudly intended) for weeks. What business did a self-centered prom queen have with *a plague of festering evil?*

Lotti stormed out of the woods and climbed up a small hill. Derek poked his head out of the tree line, took out his phone, and switched it to camera mode. He fired off a couple pictures of her and made sure to include the Victorian-style mansion in the frame as well.

# CHAPTER 3

Lotti cursed her flip-flops as she tripped up the steep stone steps toward the gigantic tri-level mansion. She stopped briefly to admire her toenails and their new paint job—the left foot showing the growing, segmented body of a caterpillar, with the big toe ending in the head. The right foot's toenails sequenced a cocoon breaking open in four stages, ending with a tiny butterfly on the littlest toe. So. Cute.
*LOTTI!*
Lotti clutched her temples, the voice in her head hot with pain.
"Aw! Fuck! I'm coming," she hollered back to no one.
The house was quiet, as it usually was during the daylight hours. As old and creepy as it appeared on the outside, the inside looked more modern. A tasteful blend of ancient art and touch-finger technology filled each room. The richly painted dark walls gave off a warm and gothic quality that would make a spider question if a web was overkill. In front of her stood a grand staircase that only existed in movies and ghost stories—rising steep and straight, then curling off in two directions like a bifurcated serpent's tongue. Blackout curtains covered the many tall windows, and an oversized golden chandelier acted as a faux sun.
Ascending the stairs, Lotti nearly bumped into Clemencia Hellswood, the matron of the house.
"Hello, Charlotte, dear," she said.

Clemencia was one of the only people who ever called Lotti by her full name. It annoyed her, but one did not correct the head vampire.

"Madam Hellswood," Lotti said in her most respectful voice.

The definition of beauty, Clem's raven hair and china doll skin seemed almost fraudulent in their perfection. Her eyes told the story of centuries—confident, wise, and haunted.

"You're up late," Lotti said. "Or early?"

"So much still to prep for the Company of Wolves."

"You sure put a lot of energy into a party you hate throwing," Lotti said.

Clem gave her an amused look—an ancient, patient stare for a lesser brain. It always made Lotti feel small.

"When you live forever, my dear, even the things that displease you are planned with care."

Science fiction posters from movies Lotti had never even heard of peppered Pax's closed bedroom door. With a defeated sigh, she raised her hand to knock. The door flew open before her knuckles could connect. Pax grabbed Lotti by the wrist and yanked her into the room.

"Bitch!" Lotti yelled, rubbing her bruised skin.

"Take your sweet time, Lotti! I could have been trapped under a boulder in the sun!" Pax said with wild, unslept eyes.

"Then why wouldn't you just telepath, *Trapped under boulder. Daylight. Help,*" Lotti said with great sarcasm.

She knew the tiny vampire hated her, but Lotti hated Pax twice as much. The two had nothing in common except the fact that they were saddled with each other for a very long time.

"You are my shade," Pax said. "When I call on you, you scoot your ass over here on the wind!"

Shade was merely the cheerier term used in place of slave. Vampires considered the sun *the asshole in the sky,* and so they struck a deal with a handful of carefully chosen humans to help them with any needs during daylight hours. After three years of devoted service, the shade—as their reward—would be turned vampire. Lotti had managed to use her father's government connections to bribe her way into one of the coveted spots. Vamps weren't out in the open, but enough humans knew about them to make some back-alley deals from time to time.

"You're not going to enjoy the job I have for you," Pax said, "but I have to be very, *very* clear when I tell you that it's *the* most important thing I have ever asked you to do."

Pax revealed a syringe she'd been hiding behind her back.

Lotti put up her hand in protest. "No way, Pax! You're not injecting me with that shi—"

Before she could finish, Pax stabbed her in the neck, pushed the yellow liquid deep into her bloodstream.

Lotti became immediately groggy. "Bitch…"

The vampire's face blurred out of focus, and everything went black.

Lotti couldn't remember how she arrived back in Little Horn woods, but it didn't matter because she was too busy gawking at a shimmering display between two trees: dozens of white, faceless busts wearing hip, trendy hats.

"Ho-ma-gahd!" Lotti squealed.

The excitable teen pored over the selection like a crazy person trying to decide which delicious bug to eat first. They had all her favorites: A Duelcrastis crimson felt fedora, a Jenny Mo-Mo red-and-gray mixed-yarn beanie, an XOXU charcoal leather ball cap, a Basket Sense concrete jungle floppy rim. Lotti's eyes fell upon the glitter-drunk sign that declared everything:

"Fifty percent off?! Ho-ma-gahd, it's like a dream!"

Lotti's own words punched her in the gut. She suddenly felt sick with realization.

"No…nonononononono."

"You need to see this," Pax said, appearing at her side.

"You stuck me with that damn needle again!"

Lotti steamed, then turned back to the hat sale. It was gone. In its place, a deer took a healthy shit. The woods changed from Lotti's straight and strong dream-trees, to the vampire's dark and twisted ones. Lotti had officially crossed over into Pax's headspace—a practice vampires called *linking*.

Pax pointed to a dark clearing not yet fully formed. Lottie watched as gray smoke filled the clearing with trees, bushes, a dream-version Pax, and…

"Derek Stabbers?" Lotti yelled.

The creepy teenager now stood over the dream image of Pax, his hand held out to help her up.

"Watch with your eyes, not your mouth, Lotti," Pax commanded.

Lotti crossed her arms and huffed, resigned herself to watching Pax's dumb memory play out in front of her.

Dream Derek said a thing or two, but she was barely listening. Then he walked away. God this was dull. She watched Dream Pax take a deep breath, and couldn't help but wonder who would want to linger in the scent of Derek Stabbers? Gross times twelve.

Lotti's focus suddenly grew sharp as something shifted near the bush Dream Pax sat in front of. To her great disgust, a bony black shadow emerged and leaned toward Dream Pax with a low growl. Lotti immediately identified the creature. Nothing good was about to happen.

Dirty yellow eyes with diamond black slits bounced around in a fur-coated skull. A long snout gave perch to a black nose that dripped continuously but remained more a decoration, since the beast in question only breathed out of its jagged-toothed mouth.

"Alfie, I'm trying to hunt," Pax said in the most neutral tone she could muster.

She hated Alfie Bubwyth, the youngest werewolf son of Maker and Jackie Bubwyth—who were brother and sister, and one of the major reasons Alfie's social skills lacked any sense of social or skill.

The Bubwyth farm sat on the opposite end of the woods from the Hellswood estate. The trails Pax took into town went nowhere near it, but somehow Alfie—in his even uglier form as a man—sniffed her out every time.

"I bury ma bone in yer marsh, Pax," Alfie would say out of his six-toothed mouth.

Pax declined his sexual advances every time, but it did little to deter the oblivious beast. Alfie's last attempt to get himself a piece of Pax had come days earlier with a warning attached. A warning that, at the time, she brushed off as an empty threat from an empty head.

"We shuv things togetha, Pax, or I eat yer face."

"Sounds great, Alfie," she had said, already walking away. "Pencil me in for that face eating."

The werewolf growled as thick, puke-colored saliva dripped from its mouth. His right eye dipped toward the ground as if it had lost interest in whatever the left eye focused on. Pax snapped her fingers in front of the gooey orb, and it shot back into place.

"Quit your posturing, Alfie. You know as well as I do that vampire/werewolf violence is against the vampire/werewolf treaty of—"

Before she was able to finish her historical defense, the werewolf pushed forward on its hind legs, stabbed its powerful, wet jaws into her shoulder. Poison from the bite filled the wound. Pax howled in pain, and Alfie howled by nature. Before she could react, the werewolf charged and knocked her hard against a giant pine. She gave him a swift kick to the chest. The wolf arced through the air and landed behind the same bush as the dead squirrel.

"No means no, you furry family fucker!" she hollered.

Pax stood, winced at the pain in her shoulder. The holes left by the wolf bite burned as if someone were dripping acid into them with a dropper. She looked toward the bush—no movement.

"I knock the wind out of you? Good. Maybe next time you'll learn to—"

Before she could finish, the werewolf blasted through the brush—its storming, heartbroken jaws opened wide and aimed at her face. In a moment of pure instinct, Pax grabbed the wolf by the ears and threw its head sharply to the right. The sound of snapping neck bones sent immediate paralysis through her body. The wolf fell to the ground with a terrible, heavy thud.

Lotti shot up on Pax's bedroom floor, heart racing as Pax put away her needle kit labeled with pink alphabet stickers that read: *Lotti*.

"The bite!"

Pax pulled the neck of her T-shirt over her shoulder to show the infected teeth marks leaking puss.

"As you can see, it hasn't healed," she said.

This made Lotti dizzy. Vampire wounds healed within minutes—hours tops.

"Jesus, Pax! You're gonna turn into a werewolf! That's illegal!"

"A werepire," she corrected. "And no, I'm not, and even if I do…I'll handle it."

"The Company of Wolves is tomorrow night," whispered Lotti. "They're gonna chop off your head, and then they'll drain me of all my blood. Pax! Your family is going to drink all my goddamn blood, and some of them are going to eat my flesh! My funeral will have to be a closed casket. Do you know how embarrassing that's going to be?"

The vampire tossed a large burlap sack at Lotti's feet. Several metal instruments clanged together inside.

"Not if they never find out."

Lotti knew exactly what was expected of her, and she couldn't say no. She'd already lost one parent to a noose and a note. If she had to dismember a werewolf to keep her father from meeting the same fate, so be it.

# CHAPTER 4

Having connected Lotti to the mysterious mansion in the woods, Derek decided his time would be better served at home unfolding his plan to eradicate Rainy Mood of immortal Hell beasts, rather than returning to his dead-end education at Hooker High. He was in good spirits until he found access to his own garage denied by three strange cars parked haphazardly in the driveway. He begrudgingly parked across the street, then made his way back to the dark wood two-story he had grown up in.

A nice house, nothing flashy—simple wood walls with a peach-colored brick porch. Deep green pachysandra hugged the front yard and wrapped around to the side, where he could see two of the three medium-sized pine trees he'd helped plant with his parents.

Warm cream and burgundy were the themes inside the house. The dimly lit foyer showed off the living room to the right, the dining room straight ahead, and the stairs to the second level on the left. Picture frames lined the walls of the hallway, all of them empty but two: a picture of his older brother's dog, Blooper, and a picture of Derek and his brother, Jordan, when they were kids, splashing about in a backyard kiddie pool—the only memories that remained of a family torn apart by teeth.

The wall rattled to some of the shittiest douche-rock ever created. Derek let out a gigantic sigh and pulled his way up the stairs toward the source of the auditory foulness. It put him, as he well suspected, in front of Jordan's room. A sign made out of computer paper and black marker hung crooked on the door by a piece of tape: Cocaine Party! No Dereks Allowed.

Knock, knock, knock.

The room answered back.

Clap, clap, clap!

Knock, knock, knock.

Clap, clap, clap!

Derek shouted over the noise. "Jordan!"

Clap, clap, clap!

"Fuck this."

Derek turned to leave, when the door popped open. A naked, rail-thin brunette leaned out and grabbed him by the shoulder.

"Where you going, pizza guy?" she slurred.

Jordan—equally as naked—pushed the brunette out of his way, his perfectly symmetrical face red with sweat.

"This isn't the front door, Pricilla," he shouted, unable to control his volume.

"So, the pizza guy just walked into your house, bro? That's fucking invasion."

A beefy guy (also naked) with a buzz cut and a white-powdered mustache joined the doorframe party. "Who cares how he got in? Let's put this pizza in our faces!" he yelled, also unable to control his volume.

"There's no pizza," Jordan said. "That's Derek."

Confused looks dominated the stoned faces.

"My brother."

"Oooooh," ooohed everyone.

Beefy guy raised a bump of white powder to his nose and inhaled. "Did he bring pizza?"

"I need to talk to you," Derek said.

Jordan pointed to the piece of paper taped to the door. "There's a sign."

"Jesus, Jordan, it's important."

Jordan sighed as if the world were his enemy, stepped out into the hall, and closed the door.

"My kindness has a time limit." He pressed an invisible

button on his invisible wristwatch.

Derek took a deep breath. "I think the government might be involved."

Jordan stared back at him, his coked pupils the size of Junior Mints.

"With Mom and Dad's condition."

Jordan slammed his fist against the wall, adding a dent to the many others.

Derek's heart fluttered. He took a few labored breaths, then settled. Jordan ran his hand over his forehead, collecting beads of sweat that only reformed again a second later.

"Always with the heart thing," Jordan said. "I've half a mind you fake that."

"This girl from my school, Lotti, her dad is a senator. I think he might be funding the creatures that poisoned Mom and Dad. I followed Lot—"

Jordan grabbed Derek by the throat, cutting off his air.

"You defend those cannibals one more time and I'll make your dumb heart do backflips."

It'd been almost two years since their parents were committed, and Jordan hadn't gone to visit them once. Unlike Derek, he didn't buy into their claim that evil forces were responsible for their insanity. Jordan might have even forgiven their horrific actions if it hadn't been for the murder of his best friend—a miniature foxhound beagle named Blooper.

In a town that vilified the children of monsters, the only way Derek knew to survive was to internalize everything. Push all his hate into a private little ball and focus that ball on revenge. Jordan, however, did the exact opposite. He reversed the hate. Spit it all back out at anyone in his way. Friends, strangers, co-workers, and especially Derek. Both brothers were angry, but Jordan's anger made him self-destructive, and Derek had no clue how to reset him back to the factory image.

The bedroom door opened, and Pricilla stumbled into the hall just as Derek's face was turning blue.

"Jesus, Jordan, pay the pizza guy already."

Jordan released his grip but kept his eyes on Derek, his

cocaine smile hanging loose and upside down.

"You're almost an adult," Jordan sneered. "Do some drugs and have some sex before everything starts hurting."

The door closed. Derek stood alone in the hall, his brother's finger marks fading away on his neck. In a minute they'd be gone completely, and Derek would add this memory to his ball of hate.

# CHAPTER 5

Lotti spotted the corpse thirty yards away, a brown-and-peach lump that sat motionless against a rotted-out log. She looked down at the awkward sack of tools Pax had given her and noticed the smiling caterpillar on her big toe had been badly chipped. All this bullshit just to one day have slightly sharper canines.

Lotti had no real interest in becoming a vampire. She loved the beach and her bikini body too much to lose access to the sun, but none of that mattered anymore. Not since her mother hung herself from a tree in the backyard with a garden hose, a suicide note addressed to Lotti pinned to her nightgown. Ever since that day—three years ago and some change—Lotti found herself knee-deep in blood, mud, vomit, and slime.

"You look just like her," her father had said one night—a 9mm in his lap. Lotti had been able to take the gun away, but since then she'd made it her mission to keep her father alive. He was all she had left.

She buried her anger and dragged the sack a few more feet until she could see the unnatural way Alfie Bubwyth's neck rested on his shoulders. His eyes stared straight up to the sky, and it was the first time Lotti could remember seeing them so symmetrical. The morning had turned him human, which made her task all the more disturbing.

The tricky thing with werewolves was that if you didn't chop them up into seven pieces (why seven, she never understood), they'd reanimate on the next full moon. At least with vamps once you detached their head from their shoulders or left them out to bake, it was all over.

Stuffed in the back of the sack, mixed in amongst the variety of saws, she found a bright yellow hazmat suit. Wearing the suit helped a little. It distanced her from the reality of the situation—a thin layer of plastic that protected her totally cute outfit from someone else's coagulated blood.

She picked out the saw she deemed most likely to cut through bone quickly and scanned the body. An arm seemed the best place to begin. With a firm grip, she rested the teeth of the saw just under the armpit.

"Okay. Like carving a turkey. Push through, Lotti. Push through, then find a really good therapist."

She took a couple of big breaths, then pushed the saw forward. Alfie's arm split open, and a generous stream of blood hit the shield of her hazmat suit. Lotti released her school lunch inside the helmet, coating the visor in brown, green, and orange slime. She choked on the stench of her own vomit as she clawed at the suit. The helmet ripped from her head as she breathed in deep.

"Fuck everyone."

For hours she hauled her nightmare around town, doing her best to stay out of sight. She hid the body parts in the darkest corners of Rainy Mood. An arm wrapped up in the hazmat suit went in a shallow grave in the woods, while she tossed the torso, Olympic hammer-throw style, into Dead Cat Lake. She lobbed a leg into the dumpster behind the Puzzle Box (a bar frequented by non-humans) and buried the other arm below the goalpost of Hooker High's football field. A safe place, she thought, as the Hooker High Hornets hadn't scored a touchdown in over twelve years. She left Alfie's other leg just outside a stone mausoleum in Neverwake Cemetery. Lotti knocked lightly, then sprinted away. She got along rather well with the ghoul that lived there, she just didn't want to watch it eat.

With two bags left to hide, Lotti stopped at Saint Chester's, the old, abandoned church once run by one of Rainy Mood's most colorful characters, Chester Bobby. He'd developed a devoted congregation after the kidnapping of a young girl spooked the community toward religious extremism back in the seventies. Chester was well-loved, and to this day no one knows where he vanished to, or why he poisoned the communion wine—no one but the thirty-odd ghosts still trapped within the church walls.

The building had been boarded up for decades. On a haunted scale from one to ten, most people would say "I don't give a shit what number you pick, I'm still not going in there." That's how haunted it was. Lotti figured this would be the perfect place to hide the head.

The doors were locked, but she knew (as all vamps and shades did) about the loose window board in the front. She pushed it off the nail it rested on and crawled through.

The inside was a cobwebbed mess. Beams of sunlight shot through holes in broken stained-glass windows to highlight the dust and debris of the forgotten church. Overturned pews, broken candles, and shredded hymnals added to the apocalyptic aesthetics. If there was a God, he hated this place as much as anyone. Lotti, however, found it peaceful. Honest. Ugly on both the inside and out.

She passed through rooms and corridors until she found an old wooden bench with a removable top. Inside were stacks of dusty hymnals and a large black spider that had claimed them for his own. Lotti pushed the books together, then wedged the severed head inside. The bench was too narrow, and Lotti had to stomp on Alfie's face several times. With an awful squish, it eventually fit.

She dropped the lid down and peered into the bag at the final item. She was almost done, and she knew the perfect place where no one ever went.

**EVERYDAY MONSTERS**

Lotti Lyons entered the immaculate ghost town that was the Rainy Mood Public Library. Endless rows of dusted shelves stood silent and still—soldiers at a funeral. High frosted windows made it impossible to see out, and the green and purple-flowered carpet, while old as dirt, showed permanent vacuum lines. Lotti noted that this place was far creepier than anywhere else she'd been today.

She snaked down the many rows of faded spines and searched for the perfect place to stash the final piece of Alfie Bubwyth. Her eyes fell upon a small grate toward the back of the building—the finish line.

Lotti knelt down, took out her car keys, and used them to twist the screws holding the grate to the wall. They came out easier than she expected. Her mind drifted to the bath she'd be taking later, accompanied by her dad's expensive wine, and a detachable showerhead.

The grate came off and the bag went in. She bounced two fingers off her forehead, saluted the final piece, then replaced the grate and tightened the screws.

"Gold star, Lotti Lyons. Gold fucking star," she said with pride.

She turned to leave, then screamed when she discovered a short, thick-framed teenager blocking her path—arms crossed and eyebrows raised. Jazz Whitley shared the same birth year as Lotti, but that's where the similarities ended—physical and intellectual.

"What are you doing, Char?"

Lotti cringed at her old nickname and grabbed a book off the closest shelf.

"I'm checking out books," she said, her voice up a few octaves.

"Since when?"

"Since books are retro and retro is the rage."

"Whatchya got there?" Jazz asked.

Lotti held the book to her face and read the title out loud.

*The Strain: Get to Know Your Hemorrhoids.*

"You have hem—"

"No!" Lotti re-shelved the book and grabbed another from

across the aisle. "I meant to grab this one."

Reading the title in her head first this time, Lotti relaxed.

"*Nuts for Squirrels,*" she said. "I love squirrels because they're cute. I'm checking this book out."

"Great."

"It is. So you can put that on the front page of the *Hornet's Nest* and suck it."

The *Hornet's Nest* was Hooker High's school newspaper. Jazz had taken over as editor in chief at the beginning of the year and turned it into a hard-hitting exposé of the school, and even the town. Jazz had the talent to sniff out a person's scars and re-open the wounds for all to see, one of the many reasons she had no friends. Nobody dared get close enough to the girl who was always on the record.

Lotti squeezed around Jazz and pushed her way out into what was left of the day. When she arrived at her car, she caught a glimpse of her reflection in the driver's side window. What stared back at her was not the beautiful face of the teenager Rainy Mood knew and secretly despised, but rather a plain-looking girl with ratty hair and a slight acne problem.

Lotti snarled back at the strange phantom in the window with a thousand-dagger stare. She held up her fist and extended her middle finger at the reflection.

"Fuck you, Mom!"

# CHAPTER 6

Pax recognized her original birthday meal even before he opened the door. She could smell his blood and hear the weak, irregular rhythm of his heartbeat. *What are the odds?* she thought.

Derek didn't wait for her to speak. He stepped aside and invited her in. Pax couldn't believe how easy that was. Usually, she had to jump through clever word hoops to get someone to give their permission to enter. Of all the vampire curses, it was the second most annoying.

"Does Marco P. live here?" she asked.

He looked surprised, and she knew right away that Derek was Marco.

"I'm here about the Craigslist ad," she said.

"The ad. Right. I forgot about the ad," he said. "I use the name Marco because, well, because—"

"Because you're Derek Stabbers," she said, finishing for him.

He gave her a small nod. He didn't seem surprised that she knew him.

"You're the weird girl from the woods."

"Squirrel girl. That's what they call me."

Nobody called her that. Why was she acting so dumb?

An intense pain spread through Pax's body. Since the attack in the woods, she felt her organs growing weaker by the hour. She smiled through the sickness, keeping herself upright when all she wanted to do was fall over and die. She needed to keep this reunion brief.

"Can I see it?" she asked.

The basement door opened with a predictable creak, and the light source came from a predicable naked bulb attached to a dirty string. The weak glow did its best to illuminate the cement and wood. Derek pointed to the item in question.

"This is the one in the ad, but if you like, they're all for sale."

Pax found herself looking at eight different cages, all large enough to fit a person.

"Quite the collection," she said.

"They belonged to my parents. I just want them gone, so if you need more than one, I can cut you a good deal."

The cages reeked of human blood, and Pax shuddered at the thought of what happened down here. Innocent townsfolk accused, judged, executed, and eaten based on the deranged idea that they might be vampires—not that it would have mattered if they were. Modern vampires were not murderers despite their portrayal in the arts.

Pax listened to the way Derek's muscles stretched uncomfortably. The way his exhale lingered until he remembered he needed to take in more air. He was getting by the best he could considering the circumstances, and she suddenly felt bad for ever calling him a psycho.

"Nobody died in the one I listed. Just so you know," he said.

His macabre honesty endeared her. She hadn't truly enjoyed a human's company since the night she bled out on the cold, midnight cobblestone.

Pax approached the large cage, opened the door, and looked up at Derek.

"May I?"

He nodded. Pax slipped inside and shut the door. There was just enough room for her to turn in a circle, and a little extra in case she grew a tail.

"My ex-boyfriend stuck me in the chest with a sword," she offered.

His face changed color, and for the first time, Pax saw what she thought was the real Derek Stabbers. An odd little man who desperately craved a connection.

"He stabbed you?"

"Yup."

"With a sword?"

"He was a collector," she said, then off his look, "but I got better. Physically and mentally…well, mostly physically."

Pax rattled the cage with her hands and tested its durability. Derek rubbed his head. He looked uncomfortable.

"You don't go to Hooker High, do you?" he asked.

"Homeschooled," she said, and then added, "I'm Pax."

A sharp pain attacked multiple spots on her body like an iron maiden. The wolf's poison gnawed at her skeleton. Pax doubled over and threw up thick black bile. Embarrassed, she lifted her head, wiped her chin.

"Well that was attractive," she said.

"It wasn't at all. In fact, it was disgusting," Derek said playfully.

It was the first time Pax detected any lightness in him. He had used it to try to make her feel better. She slipped out of the cage and blocked the mess she made.

"An infection. Nothing serious. Just get me some paper towels and—"

"I got it. This basement could use a good mopping anyway."

Derek was oddly sweet for such a tightly wound ball of anger. She didn't enjoy the idea of him cleaning up her puke, but she could feel her body shutting down swiftly. Best she leave before bad things occurred.

"Thirty dollars?" she said.

"Uh…yeah…no. Fifteen bucks. Shitty boyfriend discount."

Pax could feel herself blushing, and it bothered her greatly. She washed any sign of interest off her face and pulled out three ten-dollar bills.

"Thirty. Like the ad said." She added another twenty to the pile. "And twenty for janitorial services."

She leaned over and wrapped her fingers through the checkered metal wires.

"Thanks for the cage, Marco," she said sweetly.

"Do you need some help—" he said, but stopped short when she lifted the heavy cage over her head and ascended the stairs on her own.

~

Derek sat amongst the remaining cages for several minutes thinking about Pax, something bothering him—weird girl he'd never seen before. Alone in the woods. Needs a cage. Stabbed by ex-boyfriend. Super cute. Awkward in a charming way. Dorky but cool. Smelled like honey. Made him smile.

He tried and tried but could not put his finger on what it was that made her different than most. His eyes dipped to the puddle of vomit near where the large cage used to be. Normally he wouldn't linger on the visual of someone else's sick, but for the first time, he noticed the color—black. Not a murky gray or dark beige, but tar black.

Kneeling to get a closer look, he noticed razor-thin swirls of white and red that circled inside the sticky mess—like a diseased, expanding galaxy. Derek had no clue what this was, but he knew for sure what it wasn't: human vomit.

He raced up the stairs and into his dark, depressing room. He locked his door and sat at his desk, dragged a white index card in front of him, and scribbled something on it. Standing, Derek chose a red pushpin from a container full of them and stuck the index card into an oversized corkboard that hung opposite his well-made bed. He stepped back and stared long and hard at what he had just written—*Pax*.

He scanned the rest of the board, a detective obsessed with the pieces. News clippings that headlined missing persons and strange anomalies, handwritten notes, photographs of local haunts, and index cards with the names of those he suspected of evildoing.

His thumb bounced off the space bar of his laptop, waking the computer that displayed his open email account. He hit refresh, but nothing changed. Humans Against Inhumans hadn't responded to his well-crafted letter for reinforcements. As usual, the only person he could count on was himself.

"Fine. I'll save the goddamn world alone."

A new email arrived with a *ding!* His heart fluttered, then sank. It was from Doctor Shawn at the Rough Edges Mental Institution. He often emailed Derek short, cryptic progress reports on his parents. The subject line read: *Your crazy parents.* The body of the email read: *Goats are popping over here!* Derek steamed. He hated Doctor Shawn, not just because his reports never made sense but also because he was a serious creep who got off on the suffering of his patients. If Derek could stake him, he would.

He looked over at a creased and faded photo tacked directly into the wall above his computer. One of those professionally taken photos where everyone's hair and clothes were just right. The position of their hands and eyeline crafted with purpose. Jane Stabbers. Elliot Stabbers. Jordan Stabbers. Derek Stabbers. Authentic smiles in front of a faux "fall day" backdrop.

"I'll save the goddamn world for *you*."

# CHAPTER 7

Lotti lifted her mantis-green party dress over her ankles and ascended carefully in high heels up the manor's suicidal steps. Several other young humans also made the journey, all dressed to impress. The Company of Wolves was a big night for supernatural creatures and a pain in the ass for the shades.

A tension-filled evening where vampires and werewolves dined together to remind themselves about some dumb treaty, made on some long-ago date, that promised peace between two species that hated each other. Last year's dinner had left several scars on Lotti's brain, and no amount of hypnotherapy could wipe them clean. The Bubwyths were the very definition of disgusting guests.

When she reached the front porch, the other shades acknowledged her out of duty, but she knew how they really felt. She had used her father's connections to worm her way into the program—everyone else had been carefully selected. This made her an outsider, and the others never let her forget that. She often felt like the Derek Stabbers of Hellswood Manor.

"Green's not a very appetizing color for a dinner party, Lotti," said a snotty girl in a deep red dress.

Federica Ghioldi. Lotti hated her. She was to the manor what Lotti was to Hooker High—the queen.

"I choose to look *good*, not edible, when serving monsters," Lotti responded.

"You shouldn't talk like that," Ian Thomas Anderson said...

or was it Thomas Ian Anderson? Lotti didn't care. Just one more shade to look down on her.

"One day you'll be one of those monsters," David Urban added as he checked out his helmet of hair on his phone's camera screen. It was a pile on.

"Consider it pre-self-deprecating humor then," Lotti said.

*Monster* was a dirty word around most non-humans. A label created by mortals for things they feared—therefore things they wanted to eliminate. Lotti used the slur often, but never around the Hellswoods.

The house smelled of spiced meat and flowers—two pleasant aromas that would be ruined when the wolves arrived to devour the former and relieve themselves on the latter. Fucking wolves.

Gretel Hellswood bounced gleefully into the foyer, a piece of parchment in her hand. Aside from Pax and Clem, there were four female vampires that lived in the manor: Gwenore Hellswood, an extreme snob with impeccable fashion sense; Zelda Hellswood, the sweet brainiac of the family; Christy Hinter Hellswood, a classic goth vamp all in black; and Gretel, the thicker-framed charmer of the group. Her cute blond hair edged sharply over her adorable plump cheeks, her smile warm and sincere.

Gretel hadn't gone through the shade program, as none of Clemencia's children had. The Hellswoods were vampires made from broken human lives. Everyone knew about Gretel's terrible past because Gretel shared it loudly and proudly.

"My sister was a fractured bitch, you can be sure of that," she would say. "We always knew she was gonna kill us someday. Always staring at us like we were devils. Man, she was a hoot."

In the early 1900s, Gretel's sister, Martha May, was released back to her family from an asylum after having killed and eaten the family dog, and then skipped rope with its intestines in the middle of the street. On Martha May's first night back, she poisoned the tea she served to her family as well as herself. Gretel was the last of her kin with breath in her lungs. Clemencia Hellswood heard that breath from the street.

"You kids ready to serve a bunch of crotch-lickers?" Gretel said loudly.

David Urban looked up from his own image on his phone's screen.

"Isn't that disrespectful to our guests?" he said with an entitled smirk.

Gretel leaned in and gave David a peek down her shirt.

"Way I see it, they're dogs. Dogs lick their crotches. They do it in front of people all the time," she said in her charming Southern accent. "It's like me referring to you as a heartbreaker, David. Facts are facts."

David returned to his image.

"All right, let's assign you shades some jobs," she said as she held up the parchment in her hands. "Lotti, you'll be Maker Bubwyth's pleasure tonight."

Lotti's neck snapped so fast it made her dizzy. "What? That's not cool, Gretel! I was a food scraper last year. I should get promoted."

"This *is* a promotion."

"The hell it is!"

Maker Bubwyth, head of the Bubwyth clan, and the absolute king of gross. An uneducated, drooling mutt, who she caught masturbating under the table at last year's event. Being made a wolf's pleasure meant you were their personal servant for the evening. Waiter, bartender, pillow, and even napkin to a wild animal. A truly horrible, demeaning job that paid in blood, bile, and nightmares.

"'Tis the price you pay for immortality, blah, blah, blah," Gretel said as she trailed off.

Federica Ghioldi gave Lotti a smug grin. It made Lotti feel like a tiny green bug. It was impossible for her week to get any worse. She had to just accept it.

⁂

Pax pressed her forehead against the cage. A drop of sweat fell from her brow and splattered dramatically on the original

EVERYDAY MONSTERS

wood floor. She stared at the salty speck of liquid with a mix of amusement and horror. Vampires didn't sweat.

"Paxton Hellswood."

Pax had been so distracted by the pain she didn't notice her mother enter the room. She stared out from the cage at the matriarch vampire, who folded her arms in judgement.

"I do not have the patience today for whatever movie scene you're attempting to recreate for whatever reason."

Pax was a skilled fuckup, a trait she carried over from her human days. There were many times she wondered if her mother regretted turning her. All of Clem's children died as troubled souls, but it seemed everyone but her was able to better themselves as vampires. Pax wanted to change—to be useful to herself and her family—but mostly she just felt like an extra dash of salt that ruined a perfectly good soup.

"Our guests have arrived," Clem stated coldly. "Downstairs. Five minutes. Fangs in."

Clem glided out of the room. Pax had gotten lucky. On any other night, Clem would have smelled the beast inside her a mile away, but since wolves were already in the house, her scent blended in perfectly. She stepped out of the cage, slapped herself hard across the face, and removed her shirt. She could do this. A quick dinner, then back in the cage. No one the wiser.

As she reached into her closet for a dress, her vertebrae vibrated, popped, and cracked. It rang loud in her ears. The vampire froze, expecting to transform. Instead, her back settled. A false alarm.

"The moon is my friend. The moon is my friend."

~

The dining room reeked of ground chuck in bathwater. Obnoxious cackles smacked the sick vampire in the face as she descended the stairs. Pax gripped the banister and held back a round of vomit. Successful, she gave herself a weak high five, reconfirmed that this would be a disaster, and entered the dining room.

The table was animated, with waving arms and flapping lips. The Bubwyths pounded their meaty, inbred fists as they told loud stories nobody listened to. Shades in masks surrounded the table and illuminated the dining room with handheld candelabras—truly one of the more beautiful and underused rooms in the house. Deep, rich oak dominated. The walls, floors, table, and fireplace all shined from a fresh polish. Three small chandeliers caught the light from the candles and sprinkled a dancing glow over the table and guests.

A sharp pain struck Pax's gut; she fell hard to the floor. A perfect beat of silence passed before the Bubwyths—sans Maker—erupted into childish laughter. Clem urged the fallen vampire to her feet with a sharp look. Too sick to be embarrassed, she peeled her pretty pink party dress off the floor and used the remainder of her strength to push herself into the empty seat between two wolves whose names escaped her.

"Ya fell and it was funny!" howled the female to her right. Her breath reeked of last year's bacon.

Pax felt her fangs pierce her gums. Alfie's poison burned in her like wildfire. Suddenly, Maker Bubwyth stood from his position at the head and punched a fist-size hole in the table, his soup bowl showering Pax's sister Gwenore.

"Alfie Bubwyth been missin' since two night ago," Maker said, accusation ripe on his tongue.

Clem stood from the other head to maintain an equal playing field.

"I don't like your tone, Maker."

"I don't like my kid missin'."

"Then be a better father. Do not enter my home and accuse me or any of my children of breaking the law."

Maker dragged a goopy brown booger from his right nostril with a huff. He wiped it clean on Lotti's green dress as she stood at attention behind him. Pax watched her shade accept the booger with grace but could smell the saltwater build behind her eyes.

"I done walked all over this town today, and my boy Alfie… he was everywhere. The whole gerd-dern town reeks of him."

**EVERYDAY MONSTERS** 49

"Marking his territory," Pax blurted out.

Maker set his suspicious eyes on her.

"Ain't urine," Maker said. "I smell his hide. I smell his blood. How my boy be everywhere at once, but nowhere t'all?"

"Take your seat, sir," Clem commanded. "Your boy is your business, and the mystery of his scent is to be solved by you. Since you're finished with your soup, I suggest we move on to the main course."

Maker stared a moment longer, then sat back down. Pax wished she could appreciate the moment. Clem was in fine form. Sadly, as the moon rose higher in the sky, Pax's organs began to melt inside of her. She clenched her body in an attempt to stave off the transformation.

A number of shades exited the kitchen holding trays slopped over with a variety of meats. The moment the food touched the table, the massacre of good manners began. Someone placed a glass of thick, red giraffe's blood in front of Pax, and she almost knocked over half the table to grab it. The blood poured down her throat and oozed into her stomach. The results were immediate. Warmth folded over her, and she suddenly felt much better. She had just needed sustenance.

Pax sat back, confident she could now control herself. For once she wouldn't ruin things. For once she would—

Her bones shook violently, cutting off the celebration in her head. The moon framed itself in the window—out in all its pale glory. Her body surrendered to it. She slammed her hands onto the table as razor-sharp fingernails pushed her heavily chewed ones out of their fleshy homes. Pax felt her head hit the oak; one by one her vertebrae popped out of her skin like a well-choreographed family of prairie dogs.

One of the best things about being vampire was the tolerance for pain. They could still feel the sensation—a gunshot would hurt in the way a bee sting hurts—but it never crippled them. Ever since Alfie bit her, Pax had become conscious of every ache her body produced. The experience had been miserable, but it didn't hold a candle to the hell that now boiled inside her. It felt like every cell racing through her bloodstream sprouted serrated metal blades—tearing her apart from the inside out.

She cried loudly as her body slapped down on the table—thick brown fur curled out of her flesh. A fowl, speckled tongue flopped from her mouth, and her eyes filled in a dingy orange. Pax could feel her brain give in to a darker, wilder consciousness, one that she would have no control over. Spots of black ate around the sides of her vision as her arms increased in length.

The last thing she saw before it all went dark: the disappointment in her mother's eyes.

~

Lotti's immediate instinct told her to run out the door, vanish to a tiny island, and slowly poison herself with rum. Her feet had other plans as they gripped the floor in stone-heavy fear.

The werepire stood up on its hind legs, extending its arms to display fur-covered bat wings. Unlike a regular werewolf, Pax didn't have ears. Her stomach was hairless, black, and covered in bumps. Until now, werepires had only existed in ancient illustrations. The practice had been outlawed centuries ago due to their powerful and uncontrollable nature (as well as the racist undertones of cross-species contamination).

"I can see yer boobs!" Mazy Bubwyth laughed, pointing at Pax's bare chest.

The werepire clamped her giant jaws over Mazy's head and ripped it clean from her neck. The Bubwyth clan pushed their chairs away from the table and began their own transformations. Maker kept his eyes on the monstrous hybrid as he addressed Clem.

"She kilt my boy!"

Clem rose from her seat. "She was obviously attacked, Maker. Look at her."

"We got laws for this," he snarled.

The Bubwyths advanced on all fours. Pax snarled on top of the table, moon drunk and out of control. She opened her mouth; steam rose from her tongue. A gray wolf crept around her back, ready to pounce and kill.

"Pax! Watch out!" Lotti screamed.

The advance warning allowed Pax enough time to turn the tables. She stepped to the side as the gray wolf jumped on the table, then she buried her teeth into its stomach. Guts spilled onto the polished wood like wet spaghetti.

Pax's sister Christy Hinter shifted in her chair in an attempt to slink out of the room. Lotti watched with heavy heart as the movement caught the werepire's eyes. Surely Pax would recognize her own sister.

The answer was no.

The werepire squeezed its jaws around Christy's neck, and with a single tug, removed eighty percent of her throat. No longer able to hold the weight of her head, Christy's neck flopped to her chest as blood poured down the front of her black dress.

Clem wailed and swung a large silver serving platter at the beast. The werepire dropped from the table and headed for a window. The only thing standing between it and freedom was Federica and David, the candle-holding shades who seemed surprised when their insides suddenly became their outsides. The shades dropped dead, and the werepire crashed out the window—wings extended.

# CHAPTER 8

The front doors of Saint Chester's were propped open like the patient mouth of a hungry crocodile. Derek found this odd. He often scouted the exterior of the decrepit structure, and it had always been boarded up tight. He felt his pockets for the comfort of sharpened wood, but to his dismay discovered them empty. Strange, as he never traveled without them.

Stranger still, he had no memory of making the trip to Saint Chester's, yet here he stood outside the doors of Rainy Mood's most haunted location in the middle of the night—unarmed.

A small wind exhaled from the open door of the church and lifted the flaps of Derek's trench coat. He stood his ground, unafraid of the two shadows that now hovered in the doorway, staring out at him. They hadn't been there before, but now they were. Quiet and still—cloaked in darkness.

Derek's brain throbbed. It wasn't a headache, but more like someone had their fingers stuffed into the folds of his think machine. Uncomfortable, and chilling.

"Who's there?" he said. His voice sounded like it was underwater.

The shadows remained, quiet and still.

Derek considered leaving. They were no doubt teenagers getting drunk or amateur ghost hunters seeking a cheap scare. Whatever they were, Derek couldn't seem to turn away from them. He tried, but something had a tight grip on his ankles.

"What the—"

Two skeletal hands with scraps of flesh clinging to their joints reached out of the earth below, their boney fingers holding Derek where he stood. The sound of shifting dirt caused him to look back up—a strange pathway to the church being formed. Hand after skeletal hand clawed their way out of the ground, like macabre breadcrumbs pointing the way home. The shadows remained, quiet and still.

Derek's heart sputtered. He punched his own chest to let it know he was still in control, then kept as calm as he could. The hands that held him pushed his legs forward, helping him walk directly into the next set of hands. When they released his ankles, the second pair of rotted fingers immediately latched to them. The process repeated, and Derek quickly understood he was being walked toward the shadows that—you guessed it—remained. Quiet and still.

Grip. Push. Release. Grip. Push. Release.

The sounds of old bones rubbing against their own joints replaced the crickets' nightly tune, and the shadows grew closer and closer, until Derek came to an abrupt halt a few feet before them. He felt scared but refused to allow whoever these assholes were to see that, so he fixed his eyes on them and tried hard not to blink.

"You better hope your corpse lackeys don't let go, because both my fists are fully loaded and ready for—"

He choked on his own words the moment the shadows stepped forward into a perfectly placed beam of moonlight. A man and a woman. A mustache for him, hazel eyes for her. Pale faces, slightly parted lips.

"Mom...Dad?"

Derek's heart fell loose in his chest, bounced carelessly down his ribcage, and plopped heavily into his stomach where the acids began to chew it away. It didn't matter this wasn't how the inside of a person worked biologically, because this wasn't real life. He realized this when he sprung awake in his bed.

Heart pounding, brain throbbing, Derek looked around his dark room as shadows reformed from demonic blurs into nightstands, lamps, and a chair. He often dreamt of his parents, but something about this one felt different—urgent.

A cool breeze licked his neck. Derek noticed his window raised, the song of crickets loud in his ear. Hadn't he closed that before bed? He swore he had. The throbbing in his brain faded away.

# CHAPTER 9

Lotti sat in the cafeteria hiding her greasy hair under a super cute lavender trucker's hat with an ironic pink semi-truck on the front. Her gang of glossy-lipped copycats watched her like a hawk. Lotti had yet to take a bite of her lunch, and it was bad form to eat before your leader—the popular girls' version of saying grace.

Last night's disaster played on repeat in her head. Pax had wolfed out in front of everyone, slaughtered a handful of wolves and nearly decapitated her own sister-vamp. The Bubwyths raced out of the manor in canine form, and the Hellswoods followed, only in bat form. Lotti had grabbed a couple bottles of wine and snuck home.

The fact that she was still alive meant Pax was also still alive, a shade an extension of their master. As soon as Pax was caught, however, there would be a double execution. Lotti needed a plan, not for herself but for the sanity of her father. After all, this was her mother's fault. If she hadn't decided to peace out on her husband and daughter, Lotti would have never gotten mixed up in supernatural nonsense in the first place.

She pushed her food aside and focused on the cafeteria tile at her feet. For the first time in all her high school years, she noticed that it wasn't supposed to be brown, it had just never been mopped. Underneath the thousands of meat, soup, and vegetable splotches were small specks of white suffocating in filth. Lotti and the cafeteria tile suddenly had a lot in common.

A thick pair of ankles entered her visual frame. Lotti damn near pissed her pants in anger when she looked up to find Jazz Whitley hovering like a hornet ready to sting.

"How's the squirrel book?" Jazz asked.

"The hell is a squirrel book?" Lotti said, seriously confused.

With all that had gone down, she had completely forgotten about her brush with Jazz. The current situation with Pax required her to wear way too many hats—none of them cute.

"That book was informative and adorable. Can I do anything else for you?"

Jazz produced a yellow folder, dropped it down on the table.

"I thought we could chat about this."

Lotti opened the folder, then immediately slammed it shut. Her hands shook so badly she had to sit on them. The glossy-lipped clones began to circle like jackals.

"Leave," she commanded.

The over-produced teenagers peeled themselves away from their leader, unsure where they would go. After a few failed suggestions, they settled on the only empty table left—still dirty from its previous users.

Lotti brought her hands back to the table and opened the folder. She stared at the high-resolution close-up of the seventh piece of Alfie Bubwyth—his deformed penis. The memory of the three saw tugs she took to remove it came flooding back, and a small amount of vomit crept into her mouth.

"I agree," Jazz said. "That is not an attractive penis. But that's not even my favorite pic."

"Why did you print out actual photos?" Lotti asked.

"Dramatics, girl," Jazz replied as she tossed a separate photo on top of the penis.

Lotti's cheeks bloomed red as she stared at herself in the Rainy Mood Public Library. It was the reason she was the only girl at Hooker High who didn't have a social media account. Like in the reflection of the car window, her face was not the well-crafted beauty with impeccable skin and a brilliant snow-white smile. The photo showed a plain-looking girl whose hair was a shantytown populated by split ends—her skin a minefield of acne long-since exploded. The cheekbones were lower, her jawline wider, her ears attached instead of adorably lobed—the spitting image of her mother.

Jazz was the only person in the entire school who really knew Lotti back when she was Charlotte. The only thing more dangerous than an enemy is an enemy who used to be your best friend.

"Remember that girl? I do," Jazz said. "What's most curious, though, is why she's showing up in photographs after all that plastic surgery daddy paid for. Well, that, and her obsession with day-old cock."

"What's your price?"

"A hug?"

Lotti sneered.

"Actually, I was thinking about running a story in the *Hornet's Nest* this Friday. Give me your thoughts on this headline: *Ugly Lotti Lyons Hides Penis.*"

Lotti had more than enough on her plate with her looming murder, but she certainly didn't need a salacious story like this one ruining her legacy post-mortem.

"I said what's your price, damn it!"

"Give me more on the penis story, and I'll keep your name out of it. Whose was it, how'd he lose it, and why were you hiding it?"

## CHAPTER 10

Pax woke naked and stretched out on a warped church pew, her head on a stack of Bibles. The good books made a bad pillow, and she sat up rubbing her neck. Everything felt sore, but her body was back to normal. Sunbeams filtered through the stained glass around her, and she thought it excellent luck she had passed out in a perfectly shadowed spot of Saint Chester's.

Bewilderment struck her for several minutes as she glanced around the broken nave of the church. Her brain worked overtime as it attempted to piece together the previous night. The cage. Her mother. The Bubwyths. The dining room. A glass of giraffe's blood. Darkness. Nothing beyond that.

Pax licked her lips and scowled. The taste of well-done beef boiled in cabbage water surrounded her mouth and chin. Werewolf blood. A bad enough sign that things had not gone well but made worse when she detected the salted rubber taste of vampire's blood as well. Fuck.

Sudden images flashed in her brain, searing her memories like a branding iron: a dining room table filled with blood and intestines, along with the large chunk of flesh missing from her sister's throat. In Pax's attempt to hide her mistake, she had caused an unforgivable amount of damage to her family, and quite possibly the vampire/werewolf treaty.

Guilt tugged hard at every muscle in her body, pulling her to the tiled floor, where her tears painted circles in the dust. All she ever wanted was to feel like she belonged somewhere. The human world had offered her very little, and the vampire world seemed no glass slipper either. She had spent two lifetimes being an awkward fuckup. The floor was cold and cracked. The perfect spot to lie down and never get up again.

~

Several hours later, Pax managed to push her sorrow-heavy body up and over to one of the windows. She stared out through a gap between two wooden boards, the sun no longer a threat as night had fallen. Her nerves were so tight she could have slid a bow over them to create a little mood music. The trees outside sat motionless in the quiet black, but inside the church, a mysterious breeze somersaulted down the aisle. Bible pages fluttered, and seasick spiders swayed in their webs.

The tiny werepire (as she now officially was) shuddered, the shadows of the dead church telling her to leave. Ghosts creeped her out. They were still largely a mystery amongst supernatural creatures—a being trapped between life and the void. This must have made them irritable, because they always seemed to take it out on all things non-ghost. Pax had sent Lotti numerous head-messages about her location, but her unreliable shade had yet to show up. Best she escape on her own before the dead parishioners decided to materialize.

Pax threw open the giant wooden door and yelped in fear at the faces that stared back in bowling pin formation. Clem was the first to enter, followed by the rest of her brothers and sisters—sans Christy, of course. No one looked at Pax, their eyes busy as they scanned the haunted interior of Saint Chester's. Clem, however, had locked onto her. The matriarch's soft, pink eyes sent dread through Pax's body.

"I don't know where to begin to apologize, Mother," Pax said softly.

Clem caressed her daughter's chin, pulled her close with slender fingers. She planted a sweet yet suspicious kiss on Pax's forehead. Red warning flashes went off in her head, much like the ones on *Space Lion*'s ship. Unfortunately, this wasn't a fan-

addicted science fiction TV series. This was her life…well, her second life.

"Clem, Alfie attacked *me*!" she pleaded.

"I gave you a hundred extra years, sweet child," Clem said. "You wasted every one of them, scared of the view from your couch."

Her words were ice—perhaps because they were true. Pax began to tremble. Clem leaned in close, whispered cryptically in her ear.

"Bon voyage."

Pax's entire body went stiff with fear. The front door of the church cracked open, and a dirty, meat hook of a hand pushed it forward. Maker Bubwyth stepped inside, a mangled, severed arm gripped in his right hand. He raised it by the shoulder bone that jutted from the bicep and pointed it at Pax. The wrist was limp, but the message clear. She didn't need to see the wrinkled yellow hazmat suit in Maker's other hand to know whom the arm belonged to.

Maker spit upon the church's hallowed ground, then tossed the arm of Alfie Bubwyth at the feet of the terrified werepire. The rest of the Bubwyths slinked inside and circled her in wolf form.

"Paxton Hellswood, you have broken the sacred law of the vampire/werewolf treaty of 1943," Clem said, no joy in her voice. "A law that states clearly and without emotion that you are to be eliminated from your second life and shuffled off into the dark unknown."

Pax searched Clem's eyes for any hint of compassion but found only darkness. Clem had chosen the many over the few. Pax opened her mouth to protest, but before a single syllable could roll off her tongue, one of her brothers, Jim Hellswood, slammed a wooden stake deep into the part of her chest that gave her heart shelter.

It is said, in most legends and films, that a stake through the heart is the surest and purest way to kill a vampire. In real life—assuming there is such a thing—vampires' hearts beat like any other mortal, just at a decelerated pace. To stab a vamp in the heart was not to kill them, but instead to paralyze them for the kill that was to follow.

She had only ever been staked once before. Clem had done it a week into her second life. She had insisted that Pax understand the paralyzing effect the unprotected organ risked. Her dear second mother tried to teach her that a vampire's heart, though stronger than any mortals, could just as easily betray her.

Pax gasped as the pointed edge of the wood pierced her blood pump. A thickness shot through her body, like cement poured in her veins—a statue made of flesh. The wolves salivated below her. Pax could feel the foulness of their breath on her ankles.

Maker dropped the hazmat suit and reached outside the church door. His hand returned holding a rusted ax, its dull blade covered in blood from God knows what. The smile on Maker's face told her that he would be her executioner. They were his children, so it was his right. Clem had no choice. To start a war over one tiny vampire who enjoyed sci-fi novels and ironic T-shirts would cause others to suffer.

Maker raised the rusted instrument of death in the air with delight-filled eyes. Pax opened her mouth to let out her final, heroic words.

"Pleeeease don't kiiiill meeeeeeeee!"

The mournful werepire broke down into a mess of saltwater and sobs.

"I…don…wan…die…Clem…God…pleas…"

Clem's voice whispered inside her head: *Be brave, my sweet daughter. Death is not always finite.*

The heavy, dull blade of the ax connected with brutal force, and Paxton's head lifted violently off her shoulders in a single swing. It flew through the air, struck the back of a pew, and landed still on the floor. She could feel no pain, but her fear remained. Within moments her consciousness would be gone.

Her brain raced to find images that would be worthy of her last. A cobblestone street, blood in the cracks, a sword in her chest. She refused to end her second life on the death of her first.

Further back, her mind slapped her with the image of

Christmas morning. She was eight. Rats had cleaned out their pantry, no money for food—plenty enough, however, for her father's whiskey curse.

The bad memory melted to form another. A teenage boy whom she happily gave away her virginity to—who whispered sweet words to her in a cornfield while he removed her undergarments. Muffled snickers hidden in the tall stalks—the audience he'd secretly gathered to watch his conquest.

Every memory that flashed and dissolved was from her life as a human—all the pain, misery, and self-loathing she felt before Clem rescued her. She had died once, then lived another hundred years. All of it wasted. Granted a second chance to shine, to take back the world from those who tarnished it—and all she did was hide.

The dark ate away at the world around her, like a filmstrip melting on the screen. Her life, both of them, held nothing of real value for her. Perhaps this was the best thing that could have happened.

Pax stopped fighting and let her head relax. Her mouth dropped open, and her eyelids loosened. It was over. Mother Death gripped her soul, and the visuals of pain and horror ceased.

Just before the end, her synapses fired off one final image. It would have greatly confused her if she had the time to be confused. The last thing she thought about before she slipped into eternal black—Derek Stabbers.

# CHAPTER 11

Axe Handle only cared about two things in life: his girl and his bed, so both had to be beautifully crafted. He watched the breasts of an insanely gorgeous, raven-haired knockout bounce in hypnotic perfection above him—her head tilted in Oscar-winning pleasure, her lips forming sounds porn stars had not yet invented. A beautiful cherry oak headboard punished the white wall behind it with a merciless beating. It rattled and thumped inside a sparse, undecorated room.

He reached over to the nightstand, wedged a lit cigarette between his fingers, and guided it into his mouth. The smoke brushed the inside of his throat; his exhale drifted high and caught the lazily spinning ceiling fan. Everything was exactly how he wanted it. Nothing could sour his mood.

The woman's hips suddenly tightened. Her face snapped out of her head and spun around into the back of her skull, replaced by a computer screen. A quick blip of light introduced him to the heavily wrinkled face of an elderly woman. Axe turned his head in disgust.

"Am I interrupting?"

The face of an elderly man joined the face of the elderly woman in the tiny screen. Both smiled down at Axe.

"Hello, dear boy!"

Axe snuffed out the butt of his cig and lit a fresh one.

"Bill. Angie. You two just ruined my fucking day," he said, his focus on the robot's breasts.

Bill and Angie Piller were a sweet old couple. The closest thing Axe had to family since vampires wiped out his real one. They also happened to be his employers.

"We've received some inside information that will require your skills," Bill said.

"You know I enjoy killing things," Axe said.

"Can we buy you lunch?"

"You know I enjoy eating things."

"Those cigarettes are gonna kill you young."

"That's the plan."

"Finish up and meet us, Mr. Too-Cool-For-School," she said. "Socket will give you the address."

"Roger."

The screen pushed forward and rotated once more. Socket's warm smile returned. She climbed off Axe and began to scavenge for her panties. Axe watched her fluid movement. It always amazed him how lifelike she was. Before Socket, he'd been downright miserable. He didn't play well with others, and it left him lonely and depressed. The Pillers thought it best to get him some sexy supervision.

Axe didn't know where they got her—the Pillers' pockets and connections ran deep—but he knew she had been created specifically with Axe in mind. Her hobbies included: fucking, sleeping, drinking, smoking, cursing, not talking, and kicking ass—a female version of himself. She made him happy, or at least numb.

However, sometime over the last couple years he noticed a shift in her personality. Unlike Axe, the robot could store every experience in her memory bank. These memories changed the way she looked at the world. She began to question the morality of the missions they were sent on and the intentions of his cheerful bosses. Each passing day she became more of an individual and less a piece of programming, whereas she claimed Axe was just the opposite—becoming more a piece of programming than an individual.

A short "getting dressed" montage later and Axe was ready to rock. Black tennis shoes fed off dark, worn-in jeans held up by a belt decorated in vampire fangs. Not bad for a bottom half. A gray turtleneck under a thin, russet leather jacket finished the top half. Axe slid a pair of designer sunglasses between his ears—a wooden stake and a mysterious square object got filed into his pocket. He gave himself a once-over in the mirror—goddamn.

Socket entered his reflection, wrapped her arms around him, kissed his ear.

"Remember, not every creature is a monster," she said.

Axe looked through the mirror into her protective gaze, then thought about the hollow, lifeless eyes of his family.

"But every monster needs to die."

~

Axe pulled his steel-gray scooter into a front row parking spot of the green and red striped mega-chain restaurant, Wormies. The place looked dead—the lunch rush long over. He killed the engine but remained seated until he finished his cigarette.

When the ember hit the butt, Axe flicked it away, and like a cowboy entering the bad guy's saloon, pushed through the breezeway and approached the hostess stand. A tiny girl in a green and red striped shirt greeted him with just the right amount of flair.

"Table for one?"

Axe ignored her and stepped around the corner into the main dining area, where he spotted nine assholes crammed into a booth talking loudly. Axe had a bad feeling he'd been set up. When he arrived at the table, he was more than a little annoyed to find his worries justified.

He knew all of them through the organization Humans Against Inhumans, or HAI (pronounced "hi"), which was also the group's secret greeting—a greeting that proved problematic in determining who was a member and who was simply saying hello.

"HAI."

"HAI."

"HAI."

On down the line.

Axe considered himself the ultimate lone wolf and had expressed this to his bosses, Bill and Angie Piller, on a number of occasions. The cheery old couple had rescued him from the foster system after a long-faced vampire slaughtered his entire family. Little Axe (Alex at the time) was found hidden under the bodies of his two older sisters and one younger brother. The scent of their blood and guts still lingered in his nose hairs.

Everyone at the Wormies table had a similar grim story about dark creatures that had ruined their lives. The Pillers collected societies broken souls and raised them to be literal warriors of good in the name of God Almighty. The members of HAI all shared the same dream—a world without monsters. Axe was proud to be a part of it, as long as he didn't have to interact with others.

"Lotta assholes at this table," Axe said as he sat down next to a gigantic bald guy with tattooed hair.

A few laughs overpowered the sounds of complimentary corn chips beaten to death by teeth. A gaunt woman with cornrows and a red blindfold over her eyes slammed a hunter's knife into the table.

"Axe Handle, we all thought you quit," she said through poorly applied lipstick.

Axe shot her a dirty look even though she wouldn't be able to see it.

"I came out of retirement to watch you run into walls, Justice."

Justice smiled and attempted to dip her chip in the salsa. She missed by three inches.

"That's no way to talk about your sister, brother."

At the far end of the table sat Cog, HAI's resident teamwork enthusiast.

"I'm here to make the world a better place, Cog. If I talk to you, then I've failed."

Axe had hoped this would be a solo lunch between him and the Pillers. He would not have shown if he'd known it would be a cluster of fucks.

"They found a nest," the Blood Hound said—a noseless man with a silver goatee.

"Ten men for a single nest?"

"Seven men," Arista said, one of the three ladies present.

Axe gave her a nod out of respect. There were few HAI warriors he could tolerate. Arista was one of them. She was a serious badass, dressed in a seashell bra and tight pants made of fish scales—her weapon of choice, a harpoon. The Pillers often sent her out on sea-faring missions to do battle with sirens and krakens. He wondered how much experience she had with vampires.

Day suddenly turned into night. The windows of the restaurant went dark, a thick fabric draped over them from the outside. Many of the warriors jumped to their feet, but Axe remained seated. He never moved unless he had to. From around the corner, thirteen soulless fucks dressed in winter protective gear stepped into the dining area—their teeth out and ready for action.

"What's happening?" Justice asked, truly in the dark.

"Outnumbered," Axe said, a hint of joy.

A tall vampire with spiked hair and hunter-green eyes stepped forward.

"Hi, HAI."

"How did you know we'd be here, creature?" Cog said.

The vampire raised his cell phone.

"One of you tweeted your location," he said, then proceeded to read, "At Wormies with my boys from HAI. Hashtag yuminmytum, hashtag monsterssuck."

Every warrior eye went straight to the largest man in the restaurant. His muscles bulged behind a pathetic piece of fabric he called a shirt; inch-thick veins snaked around his body like rivers on a bumpy map.

"Damn it, Roid Rage," the Blood Hound said.

Roid Rage hung his head in shame.

"Hashtag sorry," he mumbled.

Axe didn't understand social media, but he knew enough to keep HAI meetings secret. Most vamps kept to the shadows, but there were fringe groups who actively sought out members of his organization.

Justice sounded the battle cry. "Let justice be served!"

The *d* on the end of her sentence came out garbled since a large portion of her throat had been torn out of her neck by an agile vamp.

Wormies went apeshit. A dwarf-sized man named Uzi Die-Die double-fisted his machine guns, his fingers white-knuckled on the triggers as a hailstorm of bullets tore through the air, separating a vampire's head from its shoulders.

The rest of the vampires zipped around the dim restaurant, the sun no longer an obstacle. Axe's eyes bounced and scanned each neck rapist, hesitant to attack until just the right moment. A vamp in a *What Would Jesus Do?* shirt lunged over a fake potted plant, her fangs fixed to feed. Axe slid out of the booth, dropped to his knees, and removed the stake from his pocket. Her fingernails dug into his shoulder; her body twisted up and over, landing behind him.

He turned just in time to push back her fangs; they dragged along the surface of his neck in two thin scrapes. The vampire used her super-human strength and leaned forward; Axe felt his bones on the verge of cracking under her grip. He chomped down hard and fast on his own molars and shook a pair of fillings loose. He built a generous glob of saliva around them, and then spit the hunks of silver into the vamp's eyes.

She screamed as smoke poured from her sockets. Axe pulled two attached metal rectangles from his pocket but was cut short when another vampire rushed him. Axe rolled over the table to the other side of the restaurant just as the vampire lunged.

He stepped to the side and buried the wooden stake in the vampire's heart as it skidded past him. The creature came to a stop, every muscle in its body paralyzed. With lightning speed, Axe pulled the metal rectangles apart to reveal a thick piece of piano wire that unrolled from each end. He wrapped the wire around the vampire's neck.

"Do me a favor," Axe whispered. "Tell Satan to suck my dick."

Axe spun in a circle, thrust his wrists down over his own

chest. The wire cut clean through the vampire's neck. Its head bounced off a table and tipped over some salsa.

Axe surveyed the scene. Plenty of dead vamps, but no shortage of lifeless HAI members either. A gory battle that continued to see casualties on both sides. Three good guys (and one awesome guy if Axe counted himself) remained.

The final two vampires duked it out with Nun and Chuck, the Siamese twin brothers. Born with a thick flap of flesh that conjoined them spine to spine, the brothers had made a monster-killing career by literally having each other's back. If Axe actually gave a shit, he'd have to admit it was a tad beautiful watching them work.

Nun…or Chuck…whichever…would slice a vamp's neck wide open with his affixed wrist blades, then the brothers would flip their bodies like well-trained acrobats, and Chuck (on Nun) would knock the vamp's head from its shoulders in a single, devastating uppercut. Too bad they were both mega-douchebags.

Arista arrived at Axe's side, her face streaked in vamp blood. Axe suddenly felt bad he ever doubted her land battle abilities.

"Well, that could have been worse," Axe said.

"Yeah. *We* coulda got killed," Arista said.

She was flirting with him. Maybe he would ask her out. Just for sex of course. He wasn't interested in a relationship, because fuck relationships.

"Well shit, Arista, maybe we should get out of here and—"

A gore-covered fist pounded its way through the back of Arista's head and took her face off like a bad 3-D movie. Axe peered through the giant hole of his sea-faring associate, bits of her brain dangling from the exposed top. The vampire Axe had blinded with his silver fillings stood on the other side, dry blood streaked down her cheeks.

Enraged, with a touch of guilt, Axe reached through Arista's face-hole and grabbed the vamp by the top of the scalp. Nun and Chuck leaped into action, sliced the back of her neck open, and tore out her spine with their combined hands.

Axe let go, and the vamp dropped to the floor, her vertebrae hanging out of her like a strip of wet spaghetti.

"What a show!" said a voice behind them.

Axe turned to find the two flickering white images of Bill and Angie Piller sitting in the booth, projected from a phone on the table. Their holographs sputtered as they put their hands together to applaud the remaining warriors.

"Have a seat, boys," Bill said.

Axe obeyed, as he always did. Nun and Chuck grabbed a couple chairs and sat back to back.

"Terrific job. All of you!"

"Some truly fantastic kills."

Bill and Angie were in good spirits even with seven members of their highly trained team dead at their feet. Axe caught the Wormies hostess peek around the corner. There'd be cops soon. He decided to get right to business.

"You found a nest?" he said.

"A big one, we think."

"A strong one."

"We wanted a larger team on this but…"

"But it looks like God chose you three."

"Who's the source?" Axe asked.

"Does the name Stabbers mean anything to you?" Angie said.

Everyone knew about them. They made national news when they slaughtered dozens of regular people they claimed were vampires.

"A few years back, they got in touch with us," Bill said.

"They'd been poisoned by the soulless. Claimed their town was infested."

"We encouraged them to explore. Instead they went a little off the deep end."

"We distanced ourselves immediately, but now…"

"Are you saying they were right?" Axe said.

"We are saying that we have it on good authority that things are not as they seem in Rainy Mood, Virginia."

"Which is why we chose you."

"You mean why God chose us," Axe reminded.

"Yes, of course."

"God, of course."

Axe looked over at Nun and Chuck. They hadn't said a single word the entire time.

"One last thing," Bill said. "You'll be bagging."

"Not tagging," Angie said.

Axe frowned. In the old days when he cleared out a nest, heads would roll, but more and more it seemed that Bill and Angie wanted the vampires alive—God only knew why.

"You leave tonight."

"Knock 'em dead!"

"But not literally."

The adorable couple waved goodbye, then vanished. Axe tapped his fingers on the table, looked over at the brothers. They stared back.

"Any suggestions on a team name?" he said sarcastically.

Chuck nodded with a bright grin.

"How 'bout, The Good Guise?"

# CHAPTER 12

The sound of cracking ice brought her back. Pax opened her eyes to a filtered blue world. It was Saint Chester's, but colder—lonelier. A sense of melancholy clung to every pillar and pew.

She attempted to push herself up but couldn't—as if she didn't have arms or legs. She shifted her eyes around in her sockets, searching for answers. She found them in the outline of her decapitated body lying flat on its back two yards away. She, in fact, did not have arms and legs.

"Fuuuuuuuuck!" she screamed.

She was a ghost. No, *ghost* was a word for a mortal apparition. What she was, by her own account, was a whostpire—a vampire/werewolf hybrid now dead, but still around. Wait…even worse, she was the *head* of a whostpire. Here she was in her third form of existence, and she remained worthless.

Somewhere in the back of the church, the soft sounds of sobbing snuck into Pax's ears. In all her one hundred eighteen years of life, Pax had never been so creeped out. Ghosts fell into two categories: Weepers and Floaters. Weepers—being true to their name—were sad, melancholy apparitions who wanted very little to do with anyone. Floaters, on the other hand, were real douchebags. They passed their time fucking with the living *and* the undead. Whostpire or not, Pax was scared of what held residence in the old church walls—the rumors of Chester's poisoned congregation still waiting for their leader to one day return.

The crying continued. Pax scanned what she could see of the church, her entire world splashed with blues—there were no other colors, just shades of moonlight over everything. She guessed it was ghost-vision and she better get used to it.

Her head pointed in the direction of the altar where Father Chester most likely gave his fieriest of sermons. It was also where the sobbing came from. Pax wanted to cry herself. Her instincts to spend her birthday on the couch had been correct. If anyone were to blame for the headless, bodiless condition she was in right now, it was her dumb family for forcing her to "do something."

"*You* do something," she shouted back at the Hellswoods long gone.

The crying stopped, and the church became excruciatingly quiet. A small shadow peeked around the altar and stared in silence at Pax's head. Pax wondered if whostpires could shit their pants in fear, because she was pretty confident that could be happening with her torso right now.

The curious ghost stepped out of the shadows; a swath of moonlight struck its face—a little girl no more than eight years old. Her head tilted as she watched Pax with black, soulless eyes.

*Of course, it's a child!* Pax thought as she rocked her head back and forth in an attempt to roll away—to where, she had no clue, but her flight instincts were strong.

The little ghost girl took another silent step toward her. Dressed in her Sunday best, the small ghost floated down the aisle, past the broken, dusty pews, ruffling the pages of discarded Bibles as she passed. She stopped directly in front of Pax's head, leaving her with the visual of feet and ankles—black-buckled shoes and knee-high socks.

"Please be a weeper, please be a weeper," Pax whispered to herself.

The little girl reached down and wrapped her thin fingers over Pax's face. As she lifted, Pax's ghost head passed through her dead, corporeal head with the feeling of a rubber band being snapped. Now fully detached from her flesh, the newly minted whostpire found herself staring into two dark voids where the little girl's eyes used to be.

"He…hello. My name's Pax. W-who are you?"

The little girl said nothing.

"I'm super new to this," Pax said. "I could use a guide or something. Little girl?"

The corners of the little girl's mouth pulled themselves into a terrifying smile. She turned Pax's shimmering, translucent head to the side, leaned in close to her ear, and whispered.

"Go long."

As the whostpire tried to make sense of the creepy sentence, the little girl pulled back her arm and let Pax's head fly through the air. It spiraled a number of times, which caused a dizzy mess of shaded blues.

Her head came to an abrupt stop when a new set of shimmering hands caught it. Laughter filled the church, and before she could get a good look, the hands tossed her back into the air.

The world spun once again. Blue bricks, beams, and Bibles swirled together until a third pair of hands caught her. Pax realized that there were no weepers in this church. She was being tossed around Saint Chester's by a rowdy pack of floaters, her head a football for their amusement.

In all the sickening laughter and streaks of blue, Pax wondered two things: Would this ever end, and was that Derek Stabbers who just walked into the church?

The silence disturbed him most. Even crickets seemed to avoid the general area of Saint Chester's. The only noise Derek could hear was the echo of his own footsteps on the tile. He supposed that if he believed in vampires he should believe in ghosts as well, but he'd never actually seen one.

His dream the night before had festered in his head all day. Usually his nightmares faded away after his morning coffee, or at the very least by lunchtime. This one had not only stuck with him but continued to grow in intensity as the day dripped on.

By nightfall he knew he needed to explore. He did not think he would find his parents here, but perhaps a piece of his destiny.

What he found was the decapitated body of a young woman. He hovered above it, paralyzed in the odd beauty of the blood pattern that had pooled from the neck stump. The head sat a good two yards away, facing the altar.

He should have been afraid, but he wasn't. He had his stakes with him, but something told him this wasn't the work of vampires. He stepped forward, needing a better look at the head—wondering if he might be able to identify it, and if he could, how it would connect to his parents.

He stepped back and stared at the dead face cloaked in shadow—too dark to see much detail. Carefully, he pressed his boot against the forehead and slid it a couple feet back and into a patch of moonlight.

"Pax," he whispered.

An immediate sadness filled him. It lingered longer than he wanted, and it took several tries to refocus the emotion to something more appropriate like anger or curiosity. He used the same boot to lift up her top lip and expose the fangs in place of canines. Exactly as he thought—vampire. His first instinct was that HAI had received his message and infiltrated his town, already performing God's work. This angered him, as he wanted to be a part of the process. They were *his* parents. This was *his* revenge.

The pages of a nearby Bible on the floor fluttered. Derek turned and scanned the dark nave, for the first time feeling that maybe he wasn't alone. His hands went into his pockets, the heavy wood sharpened and ready. Vampire or not, a good solid stab killed most things.

A strange breeze whipped past him, and a tattered tapestry on the wall swayed. A candelabra tipped over with a clang, and the wires of the old church piano vibrated—a haunted out-of-tune melody filling the room for only a moment.

Derek placed his weight on the balls of his heels, ready to run if needed.

"Show yourself."

The breeze picked up. Whatever supernatural activity swirled around him grew in intensity. Derek opened up his chest and tipped back his head. Brave or stupid, he stood his ground and screamed.

"Show yourself!"

~

His voice filled the room, but Pax had a hard time figuring out the direction of it, as her head never remained in one part of the nave for long. The game of ghost-catch-and-release had disoriented the fuck out of her so badly that it took a few extra seconds for her to realize it had stopped, and she was back in the hands of the little ghost girl.

Still wearing her devilish grin, the ghost reared back for what Pax knew would be a fastball.

"We're even," she whispered.

Pax had no time to dissect the meaning of her cryptic words before the little ghost girl released her. Unlike the usual arched lobs, this time she was thrown hard and straight. Her head zoomed down the aisle like a snowball on fire. The last thing Pax saw before her world went from blue, to red, to black was Derek Stabbers, chest out and head up.

~

Lotti would have come sooner, but she'd spent the better part of her time trying to shake Jazz. The nosy high school reporter blackmailed her at lunch, then hitched her wagon to Lotti's caboose for the rest of the day. The good news was that Pax was safe. Maybe the Bubwyths hadn't found her yet. Maybe they could figure a way out of this mess with their heads still attached.

"Where are we going?" Jazz huffed.

Lotti's gangly stride up the main road carried her twice as fast and twice as far as Jazz's shorter legs. Lotti could have slowed down, but she enjoyed listening to her ex-best friend wheeze and groan.

The only way in or out of town was to take Hushed Willow Road through the Neverwake Cemetery, and under the main archway. The founders of Rainy Mood—Clem included—had designed it this way. Having only one entrance made it easier to keep an eye on who arrived and who left. Monsters were a suspicious bunch. With the mountains at their backs and woods all around, the original brick archway was your only ticket in.

Lotti turned just before the start of the cemetery gates, taking them onto a dirt path that dipped into a small valley and veered slightly along the edge of Little Horn Woods.

It made her nervous leaving her father home alone for two nights in a row. Nighttime amplified his demons, and although Lotti didn't think he'd try to take his life again, the way he'd stare for hours at the moon with a glass of scotch in his hand didn't exactly give her the warm fuzzies.

Saint Chester's came into view—a corpse made of stone and wood that sat on top of a sparse hill. Jazz stopped in her tracks.

"Saint Chester's? No…no, fuck this, Lotti. Why are we here?"

*So my stupid master can drain you dead, narc*, Lotti thought.

"You want a story, well this is where you get it," she said out loud.

She continued up the hill, knowing Jazz would follow. Lotti wasn't certain if Pax would actually dispose of Jazz, but she hoped they could at least scare some sense into her. The next few days were going to suck like nothing she'd ever experienced, but with a little positive energy and the right hats for the occasion, maybe things would work.

Lotti's optimism shattered the moment she watched the front doors of the church splinter open and the body of Derek Stabbers spit through the air like a rag doll blown out of a canon.

~

Pax hit the ground hard. It surprised her that the ghost head of a whostpire could be heavy enough to cause such a loud thud. Although everything remained dark, she could tell she was outside the church—the cool night air brushing against her face. And her arms? And her legs?

"Holy shit! Are you all right?" said a strange voice.

Pax squirmed around, feeling a lot like a caterpillar upside down in its cocoon. Slowly, her vision began to fade in. At first, she could only make out the blurred outline of someone hovering over her.

"He's alive!" said the blurry stranger.

"Em nit alooov," Pax said, her lips feeling and acting like melted plastic.

"What?"

"Emmm…niiiit….alooooov."

"You're not alive?"

Pax sat up; her entire body throbbed in pain. Her vision began to crisp around the edges, everything becoming clear. She found herself staring at a round teenager backlit by the moon.

"Who aw ooo?"

Lotti leaned into Pax's field of vision and shook her head.

"Concussion," she said.

"Lotti!" yelled Pax.

"What?" Lotti said through copious amounts of annoyance.

"Ooo…ooo." Pax breathed deep, focused. "You…can see me?"

"Unfortunately," she responded.

Pax stared at her shade, still confused. She looked down at her body—no longer just a shimmering blue head. Feet, legs, chest, hands…except, it wasn't *her* body. Dark jeans, trench coat. Short, hairy knuckles. Heavily grooved fingers with dirt-caked nails.

"Whose body is this? Whose body is this? Lotti! Lotti! Whose body is this?!"

Lotti stared back at her, pale as the moon above.

"What?"

Pax reached out and snatched Lotti's purse off her shoulder, breaking the strap and causing the teen to lurch forward.

"Ow!"

Pax tipped the purse upside down and dumped its contents on the dirt ground. Her manly fingers spread out the makeup, tampons, lip balm, and energy bars until she found what she was looking for: a compact mirror. She pressed the small pink button, and the lid snapped open to reveal its reflective surface.

Pax hadn't cast a reflection in over a hundred years, and it seemed that nothing had changed, for the person who stared back was most certainly not her. She moved the tiny mirror up and down her new face, horrified with each new discovery. Messy, brown eyes, and chin stubble. Scattered freckles and greasy, short hair. She took a step back when something shifted in her pants. With great caution she reached down and felt the lump beyond the zipper. Her eyes widened in horror.

"I'm Derek Stabbers."

"No shit," said the round teenager. "You two really are the most fucked-up kids in school."

"Lotti…"

Pax searched her head (was it her head?) for something to say, a question to ask, but too many thoughts bumped against each other and ruined perfectly good sentences.

"They…did my head. Chopped. They chopped it. And the ghosts. Football. Clem. She let them. Maker. And now…my head. Inside is my head."

Pax watched Lotti's face shift as she deciphered the nonsense. She went from annoyed, to confused, to understanding, then back to annoyed.

"Pax," Lotti said calmly. "I do not know how, or why, but you're inside the body of Derek Stabbers. I hope you enjoy your time living inside a psychopath. I want you to know I'm handing in my invisible letter of resignation as your shade. I'll be disappearing from life, so please don't try and find me."

Lotti held out her hand with her pantomimed resignation. Pax swatted the fake letter to the ground and grabbed her shade by the neck, Derek's temples throbbing.

"Our relationship isn't even close to finished."

A bright flash blinded Pax. She loosened her grip on Lotti and turned to see the silhouette of the round teen as she lowered a camera.

"Who *are* you?" Pax growled.

"Jazz Whitley. Editor in chief of the *Hornet's Nest*. And you are…not Derek Stabbers?"

Pax turned Derek's face back to Lotti and snarled. "Why are you being followed by a high school reporter?"

"Girl hid a penis in the library," Jazz answered. "I want the exclusive."

"You put Alfie's penis in the library?!"

"Nobody goes in there!" Lottie protested.

Jazz pulled out a notepad and began to write.

"Is that Alfie with a y or an *ie*?"

Pax grabbed the notepad and tossed it into the bushes.

"My accidental possession is not high school fucking news!"

Pax could feel the rage inside her boiling over. It scared her, as she was not an angry individual. It made her question if she had finally snapped, or if she might be tapping into the emotions of her current host.

"Can you get out of there? Out of his body?" Lotti asked.

This thought hadn't yet occurred to Pax. She paused for a moment, and then focused on her essence, commanded it to push through her prison of flesh, but only ended up taking a physical step forward.

"I don't know. I don't think so."

A second flash went off.

Pax threw a dark look Jazz's way. "Take another picture. I've murdered for less."

She hadn't, but it was a solid threat. Pax thought about her predicament. She had been thrown fast and hard into Derek and had somehow possessed him. A strange sensation—like being human again but with the energy of an immortal. If this was possible, then perhaps getting back into her own body was also possible. There was only one person in Rainy Mood who might have something that could help. She turned to her shade.

"I need you to do one last shitty chore for me, Lotti."

"You have to be joking," Lotti whined. "The council already executed you. That means they will execute me."

"Not if you're a vampire. Your slate washes clean when you become a new species."

**EVERYDAY MONSTERS**

"No."

"And when you're dead, what happens to your dad?"

Pax hated herself for using Lotti's dad as ammunition, but it was the only bargaining chip she had. If she was going to fix things with her family, then she needed to fix things with herself first.

Lotti made a face. It wasn't her usual "I despise you, Paxton Hellswood" face, but rather one of true heartbreak.

"Fine," she said, so quiet that Pax had to assume that's what she said.

Pax grabbed Lotti's shoulder with Derek's stubby hand.

"I need you to see the witch."

Lotti turned her back to Pax, walked ten feet away. Her fists went up into the air, and Lotti let out the loudest scream anyone had ever heard in the history of people screaming.

# CHAPTER 13

"Sounds to me like you rolled over to get your belly scratched," said Socket, her arms folded in disapproval.

Axe stuffed a long duffle bag full of weapons: knives, guns, explosive devices—all tucked in and carefully stacked. He looked up at Socket on the other side of the bed, removed the cigarette from his mouth, and deliberately exhaled slow to give himself extra time to compose his sentence.

"There's a nest," he said.

"There's always a nest, Axe."

He looked back down at his bag and reorganized a few items in hope the conversation would end.

"You're being manipulated again," she said.

Axe marched into the bathroom and snatched his toothbrush from its holder. He grabbed a quick look at himself in the mirror, then returned to his bag on the bed. He tossed the toothbrush on top of a pair of machetes and zipped it up.

"Axe—"

"They saved me, Socket," he said. "They pulled me out from under the dripping corpses of my slaughtered family and gave me a purpose."

"The Face was *one* vampire. You can't steal his features, sew them onto an entire species, and cry guilty."

Axe heard her words but had little room for them. The Face didn't care about his mother's words—her pleas to spare her children. That long, heavily grooved mug that was burned into young Alex's retinas—that he watched hunt the ones he loved from underneath a pile of the ones he loved. One day the Face would pay, but for now any vampire would do. They were all abominations. The Pillers told him so, and God had told them.

Socket moved around the bed and gently touched his cheek.

"It will never end," she said sweetly. "You'll chop your way through the rest of your short life and have never truly lived a day."

Axe grabbed her hand and removed it from his cheek.

"I don't trust the Pillers," she said.

"You should. They had you made."

"To distract you."

"Turn around, baby."

Her eyes, made of metal and glass, filled with disappointment. He hated it, but duty called. Socket obeyed, turned, and exposed her back to him. He stuck his pointer fingers inside both her ears and pressed. The sound of compression and tiny hydraulics sputtered from her body, and a small rectangle of flesh on the back of her neck sprung outward.

He grabbed a thin, blinking, silver device attached to the underside of her neck flesh and slid it out. Axe held it up to his face and marveled at the technology. The woman he loved had been created with software and was folded delicately into this smooth metal cylinder just for him.

Axe opened a small wooden door hidden in the white wall of the bedroom. He took a moment to admire the large silver ax that hung proudly inside. He grabbed it by the handle and turned it over in his battle-worn hands. Made from S5 steel, the head of the axe curved toward the handle on each side like a bat in flight. The shaft, made of the same steel, appeared as shards of crystal with sharp, defined edges.

He dropped the ax head toward the floor to expose a hole in the bottom of the handle. Axe pushed the pronged side of Socket into the hole until it clicked—the flashing green light turned a solid blue.

The ax began to hum. Several lights positioned on the interior caused it to glow.

"Socket, sound off."

"Battle ready," she said through the weapon's tiny speaker. "But let me just say—"

"We're done talkin', darlin'."

With a flawless motion, Axe sheathed the weapon into the loop on his belt and gave her a gentle stroke.

"Let's get some blood on you."

# CHAPTER 14

Jordan woke suddenly to the naked backside of a girl bouncing on top of him—reverse cowgirl style. It took him almost a full minute to remember that he'd spent the better part of three booze-soaked hours at Prickley's convincing her to come home with him.

He scooped a pinky full of cocaine off his nightstand and restarted his engine. He studied the backside of the girl—short dark hair, but no other clues as to what she looked like. He dubbed her "Pixie" due to her hairstyle and the fact that he couldn't remember her real name. He prayed she was at least a six or seven in the face.

Jordan gave her ass a smack and rattled off a few dirty sentences—empty words he had ready to go for sex. A few years ago, he'd have to think about baseball or his grandfather's ingrown toenail in order to last an acceptable length in bed. These days—thanks in part to a healthy diet of bourbon, cocaine, and severe depression—his orgasms were more like unicorns, in that he doubted they even existed.

The doorbell from downstairs excited him. Someone was here! Something different was happening! Maybe a stranger would change his life, rip out his mold-spotted soul and have it magically dry-cleaned.

Jordan slid out from under Pixie, not bothering to warn her. She lost her balance and fell off the bed face first.

"Fuck!" she said from the floor.

Jordan grabbed a towel and wrapped it around his waist, turned back to Pixie, not to see if she was all right but to catch a glimpse of the face he'd forgotten.

"That's right," he said, remembering.

"What's right?"

"Be right back, Pixie."

"My name's Amber."

"That's right."

He thumped his way down the stairs, tightened the towel around his waist, and threw open the front door. His spirits sank when it wasn't a supermodel with an oversized check for a billion dollars, but instead his moody younger brother.

"Goddamnit, Derek!" he shouted.

Derek stood on the front porch. He looked a bit lost.

"Jordan…right?"

"You lose your key? I got a Pixie upstairs. You're interrupting my life you know."

Derek stepped inside.

"There's a pixie here?" he asked.

Jordan slammed the door and stared at his brother. They used to be inseparable, but ever since Derek had become super defender of their parents, Jordan could barely stand to look at him. He had already been stabbed in the back by Mom and Dad, so it sucked even harder when his own brother took their side and twisted the knife deeper.

"Well, the blood is rushing out of my dick, so unless you have a check for a billion dollars…"

Derek continued to stare.

"Find your fucking keys."

Jordan turned and hopped back up the stairs, down the hall, and into his room.

~

Derek Stabbers's room depressed Pax. A perfectly made bed, tall oak dresser, mirror, desk, and completely bare walls. No posters of bikini-clad women, sports figures, or favorite movies.

No awards, plaques, or photographs. The only thing that hung from one of the dirty yellow walls: an oversized corkboard filled with newspaper clippings, handwritten notes, photographs, and index cards with people's names.

Paxton scanned the board built on obsession and attempted to make sense of it. News articles told stories of people who vanished, strange sightings, unexplained events. Photos showed locations around town—houses, street signs, the Puzzle Box, a photo of Lotti Lyons climbing the steps of Hellswood Manor, and…an index card labeled *Pax!*

Everything on Derek's board pointed at something supernatural—a collage of secrets and creatures that resided in Rainy Mood. What had he been doing at Saint Chester's? Had he followed her somehow? Did it even matter?

She turned away from the board, bigger problems on her mind, and nearly choked on a scream when she spotted a pair of shimmering blue eyes watching her from the corner of the room. A young ghost boy no more than eight or nine years old stared blankly at her.

"Jesus…not cool," Pax said, clutching Derek's chest.

"You can see me?" asked the ghost.

Pax realized that although she wasn't an average human, she looked like one.

"Oh, I'm a ghost too," she said. "I mean, inside this body. I'm a girl trapped inside a guy's body. Wait, I'm not transgender, I'm actually another person inside another person."

"Cool," he said.

"Hey! Do you know how I can get out of it?"

"Sorry. You should figure it out soon, though, if you don't want the host to die."

"Really?"

"Yeah. They say if you possess someone long enough, the body eventually terminates the original life since it has no use for two tenants."

"Oh. Good to know."

"You just died, didn't you?" he asked.

"Yes, I'm new. How long have…you been…"

**EVERYDAY MONSTERS**

"Ten years."

"Did you die in this house? Is that why you're tethered here?"

One thing commonly known about ghosts is they were sometimes cursed to the place where they perished. Not everyone who died became a ghost, but if the death was tragic enough, or the location dark enough, the soul could return and become tethered.

The boy moved out of the corner and approached Pax—cursed forever in shimmering blue cargo shorts, flip-flops, and an American flag tank top.

"No, I'm untethered. I can go where I want," he said.

"That's a thing?"

"It is if you die outdoors. There's nothing to tether to in open spaces. I fell into a ravine. Broke my neck."

"So why are you here?"

The boy pointed to the wall that connected to Jordan's room. Pax listened to the bored moans that filtered through it.

"That's my sister. I sorta follow her places," he said. "I try to help her make good decisions, but being a ghost, I fail a lot—like I did tonight."

"That's nice of you."

"She feels guilty. She was supposed to be watching me."

"Oh."

The moans stopped, and Jordan's bedroom door opened. Angry feet stomped down the hall.

"Where you going?" Jordan shouted.

"Gotta stitch back together my self-respect," Amber said.

They listened to her descend the stairs. A moment later Jordan slammed his bedroom door. The boy gave Pax a sad look and floated after his sister.

"I gotta go."

Pax tried to grab him by the arm, but Derek's fingers went right through the boy's blue skin.

"Wait! What happens if this body dies and I'm still inside?"

The boy turned back.

"They say the brain shuts down and everything begins to rot. It's the reason there's very few possessions. If you don't know how to get out, you're kinda screwed. You'll still be able to control things, but not very well. You ever met a zombie?"

"Zombies are ghosts trapped in dead people?"

"Some of them. And you don't want to be one of them. Goodbye."

The boy turned back and passed straight through the closed door. Pax's mind raced. How long did she have before her host died? A terrible sickness rooted in the stomach of her subject. She had to get out of this body and back into her own. An eternity of dragging Derek's decayed corpse around gave her the mega-shivers.

Her hands slid into Derek's trench coat pockets, her fingers moist with sweat as she moved them around inside the fabric of the coat. She could feel the many bulky objects that filled the inside and decided to investigate.

From the left pocket, she pulled out a wooden crucifix, a rosary, a flask, and a bulb of garlic. The right pocket contained another flask and a foldable knife. She dipped his hand into the inner coat pocket and removed yet another flask and a wooden stake.

The wheels in her borrowed brain began to turn, and all signs pointed to *oh fuck*. She looked up at the mystery board of obsession; her eyes caught sight of a small gray business card tacked to the corner. She stood up and examined it as her host's belly performed summersaults. A simple card with nothing more than the company name and an email: HAI—Humans Against Inhumans.

She looked down at the wooden stake in her hand. It made sense now. Derek's parents had been locked away for hunting vampires. Their son, it would seem, had picked up the torch. Out of all the stupid people on the stupid planet, Paxton Hellswood had accidentally possessed the body of a teenage vampire hunter.

# CHAPTER 15

There were several dead birds to choose from, but Lotti went with the freshest corpse—a balloon red cardinal. All around the girls were dozens of tiny, feathered bodies that cluttered the ground of Little Horn Woods.

"All right," Jazz said. "I'm gonna need some answers."

Lottie dropped the bird into a plastic grocery bag, tied a knot, and wiped the dead off her hands and onto her pants.

"We're going to see the witch."

"Yeah, that's not really an answer, but more of a fuck-you."

Lotti moved forward, pushing a large bird feeder attached to a tree limb out of her way. The feed was poisoned, but the birds didn't know that. It had been set up by the witch as a means for people to visit her—a doorbell of sorts. Lotti had already been to see her once, enough nightmare fuel for two lifetimes.

At this point, Lotti would have insisted that Pax do her own dirty work, but the witch hated vampires. It had something to do with Clem Hellswood wiping out her entire coven back in the mid-1800s. Apparently, the witches had cast a spell on the entire town—which at the time was strictly supernatural creatures—causing a massive orgy in the middle of Rainy Mood, where Hooker High now stands. While vampires, werewolves, ghouls, and demons were bumping literal uglies, the coven entered their homes and robbed them blind (witches were known for being a bit on the clepto side, stealing tokens from people to use in spell casting).

When Clem found out the source behind the disgusting orgy—in which she had pleasured a troll and two werewolves—she gathered up her kin and attacked the witches' cave. The Hellswoods ripped off their heads and drank directly from their spouting necks. It had been a horrifically bloody retaliation that left only one witch alive to witness what happens when you fuck with Clem and her vampire crew.

Varla was her name—a nasty woman missing her face. Clem had made sure to take something important of hers before they left, leaving Varla looking like a biology class mannequin when you remove the plastic flesh.

When humans began to populate the town in the late thirties, Varla became a hermit, unable to leave her cave in fear she would be lynched and burned. In order to continue her practice of the dark arts, she set up the poisoned bird feeders for anyone who required her services and were willing to pay the price.

"So, Derek is possessed by your dead friend, Pax," Jazz said.

"That bitch is not my friend," Lotti hissed.

She stepped out of the lush green woods and into the brown crooked tree line. Dead Cat Lake sat dark and still before them. The moon shone down on a large jagged rock island in the center of the water—a spotlight from Heaven to illuminate Hell.

"I recall from childhood you were a decent swimmer," Lotti said.

Lotti could see Jazz losing her patience.

"No ma'am," Jazz said. "I'm done with this unless I get the entire scoop, right here and now."

"We're going to see the witch."

"A real witch? As in bubble, bubble, toil and trouble?"

"Use your words, Jazz."

"That's Shakespeare, Lotti."

"That's boring, Jazz."

The chubby teen made a "so long" motion with her hand and turned to leave. Lotti had to keep her close. If Jazz exposed her in the *Hornet's Nest*, she'd be not only dead but embarrassed. She had a hard time deciding which was worse.

"I work for vampires," Lotti blurted out. "I have for over a year now. Rainy Mood is full of monsters, only don't call them that to their face. Some are nice, but most are disgusting. I promise you, you're getting the story of a lifetime. If you follow me, you'll see it all for yourself."

Jazz turned back. "Everything you just said is stupid."

"Stupid, but true," Lotti said. "Now come on."

Lotti wasn't surprised when Jazz followed her into the icy water. She'd always been the adventurous one. The two girls swam up to the edge of the island and pulled themselves onto the rocks. Lotti had to help Jazz, as the young journalist didn't have the upper-body strength to make it all the way. It opened up an old, dusty memory Lotti had locked away in the folds of her brain—pulling Jazz out of a dumpster.

They were eleven, and she had jumped in to retrieve a tattered book with no title. Jazz thought it could be a valuable first edition of classic literature, but it turned out to be an old dictionary from the seventies. Lotti had tried to steer her friend toward the mall, but Jazz convinced her to search for trash treasures instead. They bounced all over Rainy Mood's back alleys, and by the end of the day they had collected a small bounty: an unopened curling iron, a perfectly good fashion magazine, a set of colored markers, and a bottle of Sloe Gin (which neither drank, but it was fun to have something illegal).

Lotti swatted the memory away, not interested in digging up old friendships. Things had changed between them, no going back now.

The girls sat down on the wet stones, caught their breath and tried to regain the heat they lost.

"So, where's this witch?" Jazz said through chattering teeth.

"That was just the first step. Now comes the worst step."

"Worse than swimming in that cold-ass lake?"

"A million times worse."

Lotti untied the plastic bag and took out the dead cardinal.

"From this point on, I have no doubt you'll believe every word I tell you."

Lotti turned to the water and held out the bird.

"Meeeow!"

She knew she sounded crazy, but that would change in just a minute.

"Meeeeeeoooow!"

Lotti continued to make cat noises, even throwing in a few hisses for good measure.

"Meeoow! Meeeooow! Meow!"

After her final "meow," Lotti tossed the dead bird into the water. A loud boom echoed over the lake, causing a series of ripples all around them.

"Aaand...that summons the witch?" Jazz asked.

"No," Lotti said. "That summons the cats."

"Cats?"

The water shimmered, and a streak of green light accompanied a sick and terrifying *meow* that bubbled up from the deep—followed by another, and then two more. The girls found themselves surrounded by catcalls. Tiny heads with torn, pointed ears emerged from the lake. Dozens of green, glowing eyes fixed themselves on the shivering girls. Black, white, and tan paws slapped down on the wet stone, and a variety of cats dragged their decayed, dead carcasses out of the lake and onto the island—circling the girls.

"Lotti!" Jazz shrieked, barely holding it together. "These cats are dead. These are some zombie cats!"

Lotti removed her little black hat and gripped it tight.

"Hold your breath," she said.

"Wha...hold my breath???"

One by one the cats pounced on the girls. Claws pierced their skin—paws tangled up in their hair. Jazz screamed. Lotti closed her eyes. The dead cats pushed them down onto the stone and dragged them both back into the lake.

∼

Lotti's body slapped against the cold floor of the underwater cave. Small brushes of heat flicked against her and warmed her wet skin. She opened her eyes just in time to see the cats drag the still screaming—and now choking—Jazz out of the water. They dropped her beside Lotti, then vanished back to the deep. The cave was just as she remembered it. A dark tunnel of rock lit by torches on the wall.

"Those dead cats almost drowned me!" Jazz shouted.

Lotti got to her feet and removed two torches, handed one to Jazz.

"I screamed the first time too."

Lotti could tell she had surprised Jazz. It'd been a long time since she'd said anything authentically nice to her.

"Follow me."

"Last time I followed you I was dragged under the lake by a bunch of dead cats."

"You're really harping on that?"

"Yeah, well…they were dead cats."

Lotti held the fire out in front of her and headed down the dark tunnel. Jazz followed close behind, their torches casting beastly shadows off the curved rock walls.

"You never had plastic surgery, did you?" Jazz said.

The question made Lotti uncomfortable. Luckily, she avoided it altogether when they arrived in front of a large slimy door—thick chunks of goo oozed out of the many cracks. Two greenish eyelids lifted and parted the slime like a broken pair of windshield wipers. The yellow orbs underneath rolled about and looked the girls over, as the door's grotesque and jagged mouth exposed itself to speak.

"Which of you seeks the mother of midnight?" the door asked.

Lotti stepped forward.

"I do. Lotti Lyons."

"Place your head inside my mouth, Lotti of the Lyons."

Lotti looked back at Jazz, who gave her a toothy grin.

"Place your head inside that weird door's mouth," Jazz said.

Lotti stomped her foot in protest. "I didn't have to do this last time I was here."

"Security upgrade," the door said.

It widened its mouth, the smell of putrid applesauce hitting

Lotti's nostrils. She wondered if things could get any worse for her, then realized that every time she thought that, something worse would follow.

With great trepidation, Lotti held her breath and placed her head inside the dripping, goo-filled mouth of the door. It was dark, but the torchlight from behind her made the slime sparkle. A soft, squishy tongue flopped out of the black and slapped her in the face.

Lotti yanked her head out. Chunks of slime dripped generously down her hair and cheeks. She scraped off as much as she could with her fingers, then realized she was missing her little black hat.

"Hey, where's my—"

The door let out a massive cough, and the hat flew from its mouth like a wet hairball, hitting Lotti square in the face. She reached up, peeled it off, shook it out, and then plopped it back on her head with a squish. The door chuckled.

"Well?!" she screamed. "Did I pass your stupid test?"

"Hell if I know," it howled. "I'm just a door!"

It continued to laugh its hinges off as it creaked opened, allowing her and Jazz access to the room beyond. Lotti stood for a moment, collecting the scraps of her remaining dignity. If she ever returned to this nightmare pit, she'd bring an ax.

The door continued to chuckle as it closed behind the teenage girls—the chamber beyond, a giant circle of rock and sharp points. The walls shimmered with cut glass and exposed quartz. Ancient books were crammed chaotically onto shelves that had been carved into the rock, and a large black cauldron sat quietly bubbling in the center. If ever a cliché creature, it was Varla the Witch.

"There's an actual cauldron!" Jazz exclaimed.

A cackle ripped through the room.

"I bet she's even gonna have a wart on the end of her nose," Jazz said.

"No, but I think she used to."

"What do you mean used t—"

Jazz turned to find herself staring at the exposed blood

and muscle of Varla's skinless face. Her startled scream echoed around the chamber, scaring up a nest of bats.

Varla's skeletal grin widened as her crow-like fingers folded into each other. Her eyes shifted from Jazz to Lotti, who was still covered in door goop.

"Ugly little Charlotte. Back to see the witch," Varla said in a singsong voice. The witch waved her hand toward Jazz. "I suppose you want me to make this one thin?"

"Excuse me?" Jazz huffed. "Said the woman with no face."

The witch turned her skinless mug on Jazz. The teenager made an audible gulp.

"I'm sorry," Jazz croaked.

"What is it you want now, Miss Lyons?" Varla said with a touch of boredom.

"I need to get a ghost out of one body and into another."

"Are the bodies dead or alive?"

"One alive, one dead."

The witch put her finger to her chin and thought on it for dramatic effect. The world of monsters was full of over-actors. Lotti was certain that if she ever counted up the time for all the dramatic pauses she'd sat through, she'd surely lose a couple days.

"I believe I can bring something to boil," the witch said.

"And the price?"

"I want a face."

Lotti anticipated this. Varla was known to collect faces for payment. With a little dash of magic, she could put them on like a mask, transforming herself into the ex-user. It was the only thing that allowed her the opportunity to walk about the town without being chased by pitchforks and torches. She never stayed out long, though, as she was far too socially awkward to blend in.

"I want an Asian face. I don't have one of those."

"I can offer you a werewolf," Lotti said.

Pax had told her to use Alfie Bubwyth as a bargaining chip, his head still safely hidden at Saint Chester's.

Varla spat something green—and breathing—onto the floor.

"I don't need a werewolf. My price is an Asian face, or your ghost friend is stuck."

She waved her hand, and black smoke cycloned around the witch. When it finally dissipated, Varla was gone. The two teens stood a moment in awkward silence.

"So, Varla made you hot. Was it worth it?"

"I did what I had to do."

"You *had* to become a vapid bitch?"

"You don't know me!"

"I used to, until you shut me out. Back when you looked like yourself."

Lotti kicked a rock, not wanting to look at Jazz. There was a time they had been inseparable. In middle school they took turns absorbing the abuse from other students. Jazz the fat one, and Lotti the ugly one. They were known as the fuglies, the fugly sisters, the fugly twins, the great fugly adventure—as long as the insult had *fugly* in it, anything would fly. But no matter how much hurt got thrown at them, they always had each other to soften the blow.

"You can't be mad because I found a way to escape," Lotti said.

"You didn't escape anything, because under all that black magic, you're still Charlotte Lyons."

Lotti had taken the gun away from her father the summer after eighth grade. She knew that every time he looked at her, all he could see was his dead wife. To him, Lotti was her mother's ghost, and that ghost chipped away at the only person she had left in this world. A visit to the witch got her a new face. Varla gave her beauty (for a price she regretted every day), but it also came with an attached curse. Any reflective surface or photograph would show her true face. Something the witch failed to mention up front. Lotti would never be completely rid of her old self.

To remedy this, she used her father's political contacts to worm her way into the shade program at Hellswood Manor. Now that she had beauty, vampirism would not only freeze her look in time but would also do away with her pesky reflection entirely—a two-step process to completely eradicate the woman who betrayed her and threatened to take her father as well.

"Should we go?" Jazz asked.

A gust of wind smacked them both in the face, followed by the return of the black cyclone. Varla re-materialized, her eyeballs vibrating with mischief, a small vile of glowing liquid in her claw.

"I thought it over," said the witch.

She held out the vile to Lotti. She stared down at it with great suspicion.

"I don't have an Asian face."

"Consider it an apology."

"For what?"

"For leaving you with a reflection."

Lotti considered this. "I don't trust you."

"Can't an old bag of bones make amends?" the witch said with a smirk. "Take it. Then we're even."

Lotti continued to stare, her brain screaming two different answers at her. Before she could decide, Jazz reached out and snatched the vile from the witch's hand. The moment she did, Varla vanished again in a cloud of smoke. Lotti gave Jazz a seriously annoyed look. Jazz stared right back.

"You get offered the cure, you take the damn cure," Jazz said.

"Yeah, well, you make out with a snake, you lose your ability to breathe."

# CHAPTER 16

Jordan's enthusiasm for life-changing strangers had already waned considerably when he heard another knock. He lumbered down the stairs with his ho-hum shoulders dropped. He knew there'd never be an oversized check with his name on it. Happiness would always be a step ahead.

His mood shifted slightly when he opened the door to a gorgeous girl in a stretchy black hat, and her fat friend. Jordan leaned in the doorframe and put on his smoky "it's after midnight" voice.

"The answer is, delicious," he said.

The beautiful girl in the hat crinkled her eyes. "What?"

"You were gonna ask what I looked like slathered in coconut oil."

"I'm seventeen."

Jordan almost choked on his own tongue. His face lit up red and looked swiftly away.

"Is Derek here?" she said.

Jordan's eyes bulged with disbelief. "*You* want Derek?" He glanced over at the fat girl. "I mean, I would get it if *she* wanted Derek."

"Hey, fuck you!"

"Get your brother, loser!"

Jordan bit his lip, looked up toward the stairs.
"DEREK!"

Jordan found it a bit creepy that his brother was already there.

"These girls came over to cheat off your homework," said Jordan. "Really, it's the only explanation…except the fat one could be into you I guess."

Jordan was really good at burns, especially when it came to shitting all over Derek. It was a gift.

Derek brushed past Jordan as if he wasn't even there and grabbed the hot girl by the shoulders.

"Are we golden?" Derek asked, panic in his voice.

"Should be," said the hot girl.

"Should be?" said Derek, his voice getting higher. "No, Lotti, did you get what I need or not?"

"I got it, damn it!"

Derek looked over his shoulder at his brother, then turned back to the girls.

"Come on," he commanded.

Derek marched straight out the front door. Jordan watched slack-jawed as the two chicks followed him like he was the goddamn messiah. What the fuck?

"Hey, bro!" Jordan shouted after him. "You find that key? Cause I don't wanna have to be letting you back in and shit."

Derek stopped and set his unsettling eyes on Jordan. A cold chill dripped down his spine as his little brother walked back up the porch, stopped two feet away. Flecks of silver cut into Derek's dirt-brown irises. Had those always been there?

"Did you just step up to me, bro—"

The next thing Jordan knew, he was peeling himself off the hallway wall, ten feet from the door. His own brother had punched him dead in the chest and sent him flying backward like some kung fu movie. He tried to stand, but his muscles burned. Jordan looked up just in time to see Derek exit the house.

He sat a moment longer until his chest stopped tingling, then tried once more to stand. His legs held, but he wanted to cry. He needed to follow his little brother. He needed to know exactly why a hot chick would show up asking for him, and then take orders from him. Also, where did he get the balls and the strength from?

Jordan pressed his weight against the wall and slid his body to the front door. These new strangers might not change his life, but they would most certainly spice up his night.

~

Pax didn't find the situation ideal—sewing her own head back onto its body—but she'd already tortured Lotti enough the past few days. Besides, she'd been a pretty mean seamstress in her human years, a necessity if they wanted their clothes to look halfway presentable. She ran her finger along the tightly pulled threads snaking in and out of her neck flesh. As long as the perimeter was attached, the witch's potion should help fix the rest. She hoped.

They had dragged her body out of the church and over to the edge of the woods to avoid the floaters who still giggled from inside the hallowed grounds. Pax finished up and stood, her eyes on Jazz, and then over to Lotti.

"Why is she still following you?"

"Jazz is my…friend," Lotti choked.

Pax smelled her bullshit a mile away.

"You don't have friends, Lotti, you have plastic dolls that follow you around."

She moved in close to Jazz, hoping Derek's facial muscles could pull off the menacing look she required.

"So, who exactly are you, newsie?"

Jazz boldly pushed her back. She seemed unimpressed by the threatening whostpire inside.

"I'm an extra pair of hands helping to get you out of this mess," Jazz said.

Pax mulled over Jazz's words. She hated the thought of a reporter following their adventure, but she had to admit, she needed all the help she could get. She relaxed Derek's face, removed a knife from his trench coat, and handed it to Lotti.

"Christ. What slice of hell do I need to walk through now?" Lotti said.

"For protection. Derek's not what you think he is."

"He's not a psychotic weirdo who could snap and kill us all?"

"Okay, Derek is exactly what you think he is."

Lotti took the knife with an appreciative nod.

"Give me the juice," Pax said.

Lotti removed the small, bulbous glass tube from her pocket and held it up, allowing the moonlight to catch the sparkling pink liquid inside. Pax couldn't wait to get out of Derek's body and back into her own. There was a giant pimple forming on his chin that drove her crazy, his skin was always itchy and dry, and then there was the issue of the thing that occasionally shifted in his pants.

She took the potion from Lotti and examined it. The liquid had a tiny cloud of black that swirled inside the pink, like a lazy eel circling its prey.

"Wouldn't you rather just stay inside Derek?" Lotti said. "The council already thinks you're dead. It's the perfecting hiding spot, plus you'll be paid more whenever you get a job. Win-win."

"I've done enough hiding for two lifetimes," Pax said.

She uncorked the vial. A waft of smoke plumed from the top, and Pax thought she heard a distant cackle.

"You didn't mention me to Varla, right?"

"I'm not stupid," Lotti said.

It had been a risk sending Lotti. Varla knew she worked for the Hellswoods, but the old witch could be fooled, and Lotti, for as awful as she could be sometimes, had always gotten the job done.

Left with no other option, Pax raised the vial in a toasting manner.

"Okay then. Goodbye, penis."

Pax tipped the bottle to her lips and downed the magical elixir as fast as she could, knowing it would—as with all witches' potions—taste like complete ass.

Soft hints of vanilla danced off Derek's tongue—a delicious surprise from what she anticipated. The only real advantage to being human had always been the sense of taste. She enjoyed the lingering afternotes in Derek's mouth, until a terrible thought crossed her mind.

"Fuck."

Witches' potions were made from ingredients like roots, eyeballs, hair, and bone. They tasted like expired chalk, dirty urine, and the inside of a muffler. This potion was sweet because Varla had not been fooled. The taste of vanilla bean was Varla's way of telling her, "I see you."

"Fuck. No!"

A sharp pain stabbed her in the brain, and Pax dropped to Derek's knees. Everything grew louder on the inside, and the body began to flood with sweat. It felt like being crammed into a high school locker, with someone attempting to crawl in with her.

Lotti and Jazz backed up as Pax flung Derek's body to the ground. The stars began to swirl and spin, and a voice in her head screamed in horrible confusion.

*What the hell is happening?!* said the voice inside her head.

*Who's there?* Pax thought, truly afraid of the demon she may have summoned with the witch's potion.

*AH! Who is that?* the voice said again.

Suddenly, Derek's body sat up on the ground without Pax's help. Something had taken control of the teenager. She tried to move the head but met heavy resistance. She encountered the same issue when she tried to stand using Derek's arms. As she shifted to the left, the body fought against her, shifting to the right.

"Let go of me!" she shouted out loud.

Lotti backed up, the knife still pointed at Derek as he flopped about like a dying fish.

"Pax?" Lotti said. "You still in there?"

"Yes! And I'm not alone!"

"Who are you?" said the stranger for the first time out loud. "*Where* are you?"

"I'm Paxton Hellswood. I'm a vampire…or I was. I'm now a ghost who inhabits the body of a male teenager. It is my wish, oh dark one, to leave this body for my own. Are…are you the demon summoned to help me."

"What?!" the confused second voice said.

"Demon…who are you?"
"I'm…I'm Derek Stabbers."

# CHAPTER 17

Axe's scooter pushed forty-two miles an hour, barely able to keep up with the exhaust-heavy motorcycle that Chuck operated and Nun rode passenger on. The brothers looked a bit silly riding a motorcycle back to back, but then the brothers looked silly in just about every situation imaginable.

Axe hated driving this fast because it made it difficult to smoke. The ash kept blowing into his face and always found its way up his nostrils. If there was one thing he hated—and he hated a shit-ton of things—it was a tickly nose. He wasn't a fuckin' bunny rabbit; therefore, he should never look like one.

"One hundred and eighty-five miles outside of Rainy Mood," Socket said from the weapon snug at Axe's side.

He'd be beating on vamps before dawn. His body tingled with excitement, the same excitement Socket had been trying to explain to him was actually his fear disguised as hate. This was ridiculous of course, because Axe was the toughest motherfucker either side of the Mississippi. He could count the number of things that scared him on one hand—but first he'd have to remove all five fingers on said hand.

Up ahead, Axe watched as the brothers' bike slowed then turned right into the parking lot of a shit-hole motel.

"What are these assholes doing?" he mumbled under his breath.

When his scooter eventually made it to the turn, he zipped into the parking lot where Nun and Chuck were leaning against their hog.

"It's really a great little scooter, Axe," Chuck said in his usual chipper tone. "Sorry if we're going too fast."

His constant politeness bothered Axe. Chuck was a straight-up, heartless killer—cold as they came—but on the outside he'd give Mr. Rogers a run for his money. Nun, on the other hand, always looked as if he would rather be eating your spleen—the silent but deadly type. They were the ultimate good cop/bad cop combo.

"Why are we stopping?"

"It's late. Thought a good night's sleep would energize us for the mission."

"I don't need sleep. I need a body count," Axe said.

Chuck slapped Axe on the shoulder like an old chum.

"You're awesome, Axe. We don't hang out enough. Come on, let's check in."

The motel's lobby was even shitter than its exterior. Chuck rang the tiny desk bell, and an old man entered in his pajamas.

"Evening, gentlemen," the old man said as he cleaned his glasses on his PJs.

"Sorry to wake you, sir." Chuck smiled.

"Ah, not at all. It's my job to be woken," the old man said, matching Chuck's friendliness.

"We'd like a room for the evening. Two beds."

"*Two rooms*," Axe corrected. "If I don't work alone, at least I sleep alone."

Chuck switched places with Nun, and Axe could tell the old man behind the counter did not prefer the frowning brother.

"We're working off a rather tight budget, Axe. Bill and Angie want all the receipts, and sharing a room will be more economical. And just think, at the end of the job, whatever we have left we can use to have a nice dinner."

Axe's blood boiled, and he feared he might impulsively remove Chuck's head right there and then. The Pillers controlled all of his finances, and up until now he didn't have a problem with that. He never needed his own money. Bill and Angie had put him up in a fine apartment, kept him well fed, and created Socket for him. That was all he needed. That and the occasional monster hunt.

Axe leaned forward and gave Chuck his darkest tone. "I don't care if by the end of the job I'm eating chunks of my own shit to survive, I ain't sharing a room tonight, 'cause I ain't sharing a room ever."

Chuck held out the Humans Against Inhumans MasterCard with apologetic eyes.

"Sorry, bud. They entrusted me with the company card, and I really want to bring this mission in under budget."

# CHAPTER 18

"Get out of my body!"
"I can't!"
"Why not?"
"Because I don't know how!"
Derek had blacked out inside the church and regained consciousness in the woods just yards away. A second voice bounced around in his head and forced his lips to say sentences he never constructed. The very evil he wanted to wipe off the face of the Earth now lived inside him—a part of him.
"I can hear what you're thinking, dick," Pax said.
"Get out of my head!" Derek shouted.
"I can't!"
"Why not?"
"Because I don't know how!"
He could feel Pax resist his every move, his body on the verge of breaking.
"Can we at least agree for one person to let go of the controls?" said Derek.
"Sure. Let go."
"It's my body! *You* let go."
"You want me to trust a vampire killer?"
"You're inside *me*! I can't hurt you without hurting myself."
Pax didn't respond right away, and then suddenly released his body back to him. Stiff from fighting her, his legs buckled, and he fell to the ground.

"You can drive for now," she said, "but I'm still gonna use your lips."

"Fine!"

"Fine!"

"Fucking vampire."

Derek's right hand swung upward and clocked him square in the face.

"Ow!"

"Ow!"

"Stop it right now!" Lotti shouted. "While this is super hilarious and disturbing for me to watch, it's also getting me nowhere near Rum Island—to where I must escape or be eaten."

"She punched me in the face!" Derek whined.

Suddenly a flat, open hand came out of nowhere and smacked Derek hard across his right cheek.

"All right. New system," Jazz said, her hand still raised across her chest. "You each get to ask one question. After that, we move on to finding a solution to this problem with no more bullshit. Agreed?"

Derek stared at her, still stunned.

"I said AGREED?" Her hand inched higher.

Derek nodded. He could feel Pax add to the motion—the first time they had actually moved as one. It felt strange.

"Great. Derek, you start."

He fumbled around in his head and realized he had no idea what information he actually needed. Finally, he settled on the obvious.

"How did a vampire get inside of me?"

His body gave a large sigh, and he didn't think he'd ever get used to these unwarranted motions.

"Long-ass story short," Pax said, "I killed a werewolf, was beheaded for my crime, became a ghost, knocked into you, got trapped, sent Lottie to the witch, witch dicked me over, potion made you conscious."

Derek heard Pax's word vomit but had a hard time really understanding any of it. Werewolves? Witches? How many monsters lived in Rainy Mood?

"Pax, you're up," Jazz said.

Pax shifted inside him uncomfortably.

"Have you ever killed a vampire?" she asked.

The question created a flock of butterflies in Derek's stomach. "No," he said. "Not yet."

He felt an odd sadness inside, then realized it had to be her. Jazz finally broke the silence.

"Okay," Jazz said. "Now what?"

"I'll go see my sister Gretel," Pax said. "She might be able to help."

"I suppose I have no say in this?" Derek said.

"Unless you want this to be a life condition," she said out loud.

Pax tried to stand Derek's body, but his legs gave out—he hit the dirt, face first. An intense pain throbbed in his stomach and caused him to curl up into a ball.

"What's wrong?" he said, barely audible.

Pax didn't bother using his lips; instead she spoke to him inside his head.

*I need to feed*, she thought.

*You're dead!* he thought.

*Well I guess the rules are different when I'm inside a living host. Don't tell me what I think you're gonna tell me.*

*We can lie here and rot together, or we can eat.*

Derek tried to get to his feet again. The pain gripped him like a boa constrictor, and he found himself back on the ground, gasping for air.

*I haven't fed in days,* she said, *and now I'm blowing all my energy puppeteering your body. If I don't eat, this pain doesn't go away.*

Pax flopped Derek's head toward Lotti. "Code 3," she choked out.

"Goddamnit!" Lotti said with a shake of her fists.

"Lotti!"

The snotty teen turned to Jazz with a sinister-sweet smile.

"Jaaaazz. Will you lean in close and see what Pax wants?"

Jazz took a few steps back, no dummy.

"Yeah, you gotta work on your delivery," she said.

Derek began to panic in his own skin, the pain unbearable, the thought of what she wanted him to do an unthinkable nightmare.

Lotti walked over, got on her hands and knees, and with great reluctance offered her neck. Derek felt a strange tingling in his mouth—a pinching sensation from his upper gums.

*Gonna need your help, Derek.*
*For what?*
*If you want the pain to stop, you have to help me push my fangs out of your gums.*
*I will not!*
*We're not gonna kill her. Just drink enough blood to quell the thirst. Stop the pain. I've taken from Lotti tons of times in the past.*
*I'm not drinking human blood!*

Derek's stomach erupted in a pain he described to himself as burning rats running inside his intestines. He wasn't sure if these images came from his brain or Pax's, but he was now at a breaking point. Suddenly, a little blood didn't seem so terrible.

*What do I do?*
*Do you feel them? The fangs?*
*I feel something in there.*
*Focus on them. The lumps under your gums. Let your mind and body push them out. I think if we work together, we can access them.*

Derek closed his eyes and put all his attention on the sharp little lumps. It turned out to be easier than he thought. The teeth vibrated just before they broke the skin and slid casually out, stepping in front of both his canines.

*We did it!* he thought with an odd sense of glee.

The celebration didn't last long, as Pax forced his head forward, burying the fangs deep into Lotti's neck. The teen yelped and gripped Derek's shoulders to keep her balance. A warm, thick flood crashed against his tongue and slid down his throat. Derek had little time to be disgusted, as the blood began to work instantly on the pain. Relief washed over him, and he clung tighter to Lotti as he helped Pax extract the red medicine with feverish delight.

He felt better than he ever had in his entire life—the vampire's strengths as much his as they were hers. His vision sharp and his heart strong—like a stoic warrior, excited and scared, but maintaining a regular rhythm. The vampire inside him had fixed his body. For the first time since his parents died, he felt like he could do anything.

"Derek!"

The voice sounded distant and hollow, but Derek recognized it immediately. It startled him so much that he pushed Lotti back, her blood spraying all over his face.

Jordan Stabbers stopped a couple feet in front of the grinning, blood-drenched Derek. Tears of rage welled in his eyes, his knuckles ghost-white.

"You sick fuck," Jordan said in a harsh whisper.

"Now hold on and let me tell you why I had to drink her blood," Derek said confidently.

Jordan didn't seem to be interested in hearing more. He pulled back his arm and slammed it hard across Derek's face. He went down, caught off guard by the fast act of brotherly violence.

"You're sick like they are. You're as evil as Mom and Dad!"

Jordan's words smashed around Derek's skull like an angry bee. Suddenly, all the years of verbal and physical abuse from his brother came crashing down around him—the animal inside growing, growling, and hungry for retribution.

"You're gonna rot up at Rough Edges just like them," Jordan shouted. "Maybe you'll all be bunk buddies and share human flesh recipes!"

Jordan kicked Derek in the side. It didn't hurt all that much. Pax was screaming at him in his head, but his clouded rage blocked her out. Every muscle burned with revenge.

Pushing against the ghost inside him, Derek jumped to his feet and turned to face his brother. His right arm barreled forward, slammed into Jordan's chest, and sent him flying six yards back. He crashed violently into a large tree but remained on his feet. Derek's blood raced through his veins, doing victory laps. It felt great to hurt his brother.

"Ha!" Derek shouted into the night.

Jordan's head flopped about, trying to stay conscious. Lotti screamed, and Jazz turned white. Derek found their reactions to be a bit dramatic, until he realized exactly what he'd done.

Sticking straight out of Jordan's stomach, painted a deep crimson, was a jagged branch from the tree that stopped his brother's flight. His blood rained down on the dirt below.

"Jordan?" Derek said weakly.

His brother's eyes rolled around, looking at everything but focusing on nothing. Suddenly, all the love Derek had for Jordan flooded back. The last few years were gone, and once more Jordan was his hilarious, protective, and loving brother. Vampires had taken him away the first time, and vampires had returned to finish him off.

"Save him," Derek growled at the girl in his head.

"I can't."

"Bullshit. He doesn't have to die, and you know it."

"We don't just make other vampires willy-nilly, Derek."

"You're gonna need my help to get out of my body. I can make it real difficult for you, you know."

"You're saying that if I turn your brother, you'll cooperate with me?"

"That's what I'm saying."

"He'd be a vampire, you understand that? He'd be the thing you hate."

"I'd rather hate him alive than love him dead."

Derek felt Pax thinking, and he let her have the moment. Although he did hate vampires, somehow it didn't matter with Jordan. They were brothers, and no fangs or freaky rules would change that.

"This might not even work due to our circumstance—"

"Do it."

Derek slowly let go of his body and allowed Pax complete control. She straightened his legs and walked over to Jordan—gored and dying against the tree. Pax held out Derek's hand toward Lotti, requesting the knife. She inched forward and placed it in his hand, then headed right back to her safe spot behind Jazz.

Pax grabbed Jordan by the wrist and pressed Derek's palm into his brother's. With a swift motion, she drove the blade of the knife through both their hands, pinning them to the tree. Derek could feel their blood began to mingle—a bizarre sensation, but not unpleasant. It somehow made him feel closer to Jordan than he ever had before.

Pax thrust forward, clamped their fangs over Jordan's neck, and began to drink. The blood from their hand wounds pulsated. A poisonous intoxication that staved off death and evolved life. His senses were ablaze—his brother's blood collecting in his stomach.

# CHAPTER 19

Jazz had the dream often. It always played out the exact same way. A towering oak door, complete with brass lion-head knockers, would creak open. Roger Lyons—Lotti's father—would stare down at her, his lips missing, a skeletal grin frozen on his face. Jazz would be guided into the mansion, and a pair of dark, sticky demons would pour two martinis.

Mr. Lyons would then climb up the wall and wrap around a silver chandelier like a scared lizard. Jazz would sit at the kitchen counter, and the demons would place the martinis in front of her and an empty seat.

"I'm asleep," Mr. Lyons would say. "I'm asleep, and that's my gin."

Jazz would grow impatient waiting for Charlotte to arrive, and eventually she'd fish the olive out of her drink with her tongue, hungry for the salty squish it would provide.

"The olive is a big fat lie," Senator Lyons would say from his perch on the chandelier.

Jazz would freeze, the taste of saline filling her mouth. With her pointer finger and thumb, she would grip the slippery sides of the olive and pull it out to reveal a human eyeball. Its brown iris would tighten up around the dark pupil and stare into her soul. Feeling a slight draft in her head, Jazz would reach up and gently touch the gaping, bloody hole where her right eye used to be. The feeling of being watched would intensify, and she'd pry her head toward the archway of the kitchen's entrance.

Lotti would always be there—peeking around the corner—her right eye the only visible part of her face.

~

Waking up in the middle of Hooker High's cafeteria screaming only solidified Jazz's rock-bottom social status. She had fallen asleep on her half-eaten ham and cheese sandwich, the top piece of bread now stuck to her face. It took her several seconds before she even realized that Lotti sat directly across from her, wearing a giant floppy hat, large sunglasses, and a poorly applied fake nose.

Last night had been the height of her journalistic endeavors. She'd stumbled upon something that would guarantee her a long career as an investigative reporter. The last thing she needed was Lotti interrupting the few minutes of sleep she'd probably be getting for the next few days.

"You can't write about last night," Lotti whispered.

"Mama told me not to talk to strangers."

"You'll expose everything!"

"That's the point. Look, I promised I'd keep your name out of it, and I will."

"The Hellswoods will figure it out, and when they do, they won't kill me. They'll keep me alive! Betrayal of a vampire is an eternity of pain."

"How 'bout betrayal of your best friend?"

The worst day of Jazz's life happened in eighth grade. She woke up in the hospital, having blacked out the night before, with little memory of the preceding events. It took Jazz several weeks to recover—most of it emotional rather than physical. In all that time, her friend—her best fucking friend—never once bothered to visit, call, or text. When Jazz finally returned to school, she discovered a beautiful, icy creature named Lotti had replaced Charlotte Lyons.

Charlotte had always been excited about fashion, makeup, and whatever was trending, but remained a charming goof. She'd yammer on and on to Jazz about one day being popular, and how there wouldn't be enough ink in the world for everyone who wanted to sign her yearbook. Jazz found it fun to dream along with her but never thought it could be a reality.

"How about I give you some crazy-good dish on the football team? The sexual orientation of the entire school? The vice principal's 'principles'," Lottie said, tapping the side of her nose like a drug addict.

"You wanna trade high school gossip for a story about monsters living amongst man? Get the fuck away from me," Jazz said, closing her notebook.

"Pleeease!"

"Leave," Jazz said. "Wait…before you do, know this: I've already written up a story using both your name and the library penis photos. If anything were to happen to me, that article gets published."

Lotti sat a moment more. Her eyes twitched, and Jazz couldn't tell if she was stressed or terrified. Probably both. Lotti looked around the cafeteria, then quickly stood and made her way out, pulling her floppy hat over her face in case vampires could suddenly venture out into the daylight to punish her.

Jazz shook her head and marveled at the idea that they had ever been so close that they jumped headfirst into snow-covered bushes together, popcorned each other on Jazz's trampoline, or caught frogs in the pond and named them after television crushes.

Suddenly, sitting there with the mysteries of the universe cracking wide open in front of her, Jazz felt utterly alone.

# CHAPTER 20

Paxton stretched out Derek's arms and tilted his head to the sky, allowing the sun to soak through his skin. She hadn't felt its warmth in one hundred years and found herself in a surprisingly good mood because of it.

Derek didn't fight her on it, distracted with thoughts of Jordan. It had been only a handful of hours since they tucked the temporarily dead corpse of his older brother into bed. Derek had wanted to stay by his side, but Pax convinced him that time was of the essence, and Jordan would be fine.

They stood outside Hellswood Manor, under Gretel's second-story bedroom window. It wasn't ideal, but it was all they had. Gretel would help her if she could. They were sisters.

"Not to ruin your moment in the sun, but do we have a ladder?" Derek asked.

Pax had a better plan.

"Do you like bats?" she asked.

Before Derek could answer, she tightened up his insides and followed the usual steps she would take internally to become the winged creature that got her out of many scrapes in the past. A rather simple transformation—it required her brain to imagine her body being crushed inward, while a flying mammal's body pushed itself outward. It was all in the mind; the vampire body simply followed its instructions.

Derek's body, being human, resisted. It wasn't designed for breaking down and reshaping itself. When his shoulders popped out of their discs, Pax had to fight his scream back down into his throat. She couldn't risk alerting the others to their presence.

*Just let go*, she said softly in his head.

He didn't. He fought it the entire way. Pax pushed forward, cracking his bones down and repositioning them. Two pathetic, tattered wings peeled out from his sides and draped around his curling feet. Derek lashed out at her in his head, a barrage of obscenities, the pain unbearable for them both. Transformation never hurt as a vampire, but inside a mortal host—connected to a shitty nervous system—everything seemed to be amplified and more difficult.

She snapped the final fleshy piece into place and relaxed. Derek went quiet as he recovered mentally from the experience, while Pax titled their head up and looked at the toxic mutant abomination that started back at them through the reflection of the living room window.

The transformation hadn't gone entirely as expected. Derek's human form wasn't able to completely morph, leaving them more a bat/human hybrid. They were roughly the size of a golden retriever, with bat-like facial features, but very little hair. Pax couldn't help but laugh.

"This is funny?" he said with much annoyance.

"You ready to fly?"

*Whatever*, he thought.

Pax took over the body once more and extended the shabby wings. After a few practice flaps, the lumpy creature lifted awkwardly off the ground. She felt Derek's mood shift from pissy to a moment of exhilaration as they climbed higher into the air. He must have realized she could sense this and quickly found his gloom again.

Thick black-out curtains covered Gretel's window, as they did all the windows of the manor during daylight hours. Pax desperately hoped her sister would be in her room sleeping. She tapped three deformed bat fingers against the glass and waited—staying airborne not the effortless task it had once been.

"Gretel!" she said as loud as she dared.

The black curtain ruffled, followed by the sound of the window unlocking.

*Thank God.*

An arm shot out of the open window, grabbed the Derek/Pax-bat-thing by the ear, and jerked it inside. Their oddly shaped body slammed to the ground at the foot of Gretel's bed. Pax lifted their head and stared up at what she hoped to be Gretel, but instead was her mother.

Clemencia Hellswood stared down at the monstrous mistake. Before Pax could try to explain herself, her mother kneeled down and put her finger to Derek's lips.

"I could hear you two a mile away," she said in a harsh whisper. "Let's not wake up your brothers and sisters."

"You…know who I am?" Pax said, stunned.

"Of course, Paxton. I can hear you squirming around inside this bat boy like a beetle on its back."

"I'm not a boy—"

"I know you too, Mr. Stabbers. You like to hang around the outskirts of my home and take pictures."

"Mother—"

"Change back, please. I cannot gaze another second upon this…thing."

Clem stood back and waited. Pax had always considered her the most patient impatient person she'd ever met. The discussion would be over until her demands were obeyed.

Pax found the reverse transition much easier. Derek's body gladly allowed it to slip back to its original form. As the bones re-shifted and the flesh smoothed out, Derek remained silent. Pax sensed his fear—being in the vampire's den will keep a man well-behaved.

When Pax finished, she looked up at her mother with an awkward grin. She wasn't sure if she wanted to apologize or spit in her face. She definitely wanted a hug but wasn't getting that vibe back, so instead she allowed the dumb smile to linger.

"Follow me."

"But, don't you want to know how I got into this—"

"Follow me."

Clem floated backward out of the room, her eyes never leaving Derek. Once in the hall, she turned away and floated off to the right. Pax tried to step forward, but Derek tightened their legs.

*I don't like this,* he thought.

*Too late now,* she thought back.

Clem waited at the end of the hall. Pax watched as her mother opened the last door on the right and entered. Christy's room. The last place she wanted to go. Pax didn't remember taking a chunk of her sister's neck, but Clem now offered her a front row seat to her handiwork. The whostpire dragged Derek's feet down the hall, past her sleeping siblings' rooms, and arrived at Christy's open door. She took a deep breath and stepped inside.

Christy lay naked, flat on her back. Her chest heaved up and down, not from a breathing motion, but a healing one. Her flesh rose like melted plastic under a hair dryer—the body hard at work repairing the damage done by a stupid werepire. There were still pieces of her neck missing, but most of it had begun to fill back in with new muscle. Blood stained the sheets around her in a full-body halo of gore.

Pax's sister Gretel sat snoring in a chair in the corner of the room—a nurse in her first life (not that her skills translated over to vampire needs, but her instincts to nurture remained).

"Is she asleep?" Pax asked.

"A coma. The wolf's poison in her blood has slowed down her regeneration."

"But she'll be all right? She's not going to die?"

Clem's face remained stone.

"She's going to live, but by law I'm required to put her down."

Pax had bitten Christy as a werepire—so logic said that she too was now an illegal creature.

Clem looked down at her unconscious daughter. "I was able to convince Maker that she died, which means when my sweet Christy does wake, she'll need to stay hidden, or leave Rainy Mood."

The tone in Clem's voice made Pax understand why she allowed the execution. Pax had always been a notorious screw-up, but this time she almost started a war, and ruined her sister's second life in the process. Pax deserved to die. Again.

"What are you thinking, my love?" Clem asked.

Clem had never asked this question before, as Clem always knew. It was a skill possessed by a parent vampire and her children.

"I can't hear you under all these new distractions you're hiding inside."

That made sense. In the last couple days, Pax had become three different creatures. It must have weakened her connection to her mother.

"I was thinking…I understand why you let them execute me. That I deserved it."

"You are a unique disaster, my dear, but you are *my* disaster. You should have come directly to me when Alfie bit you."

"I know, and I'm so—"

"But you did not. And so here we are at plan B."

"Plan B?"

Clem drifted from the room; Pax made Derek follow. The door closed softly behind them on its own. Her mother glided them down the grand staircase and into the foyer under the excessive chandelier. Pax halted Derek's body on the last step, gripped the banister in anticipation. Clem stared at them for several measured moments.

"I found you at Saint Chester's. You had chased a squirrel inside."

Pax couldn't help but feel a sense of satisfaction. The werepire side of her wasn't afraid of squirrels. In fact, it hunted them.

"I can't hear you, but I can sense the smug. Cut it out," Clem commanded.

Pax straightened her body, thinking the change in posture would wipe away her squirrel-killing pride. Clem continued.

"Your obsession to kill this squirrel had Saint Chester's crumbling. Each beam and wall your bulky body hit caused the already weakened structure to tremble. When I entered, the ghosts of Chester's flock all floated about in panic. They couldn't stop the rabid dog who threatened to destroy their tether."

*What the fuck does that mean?* Derek thought.

*Ghosts are tethered to their structure. If the structure is destroyed, the ghosts die.*

*Ghosts can die?*

Clem continued.

"I leapt upon your back, bit into your neck, and drained as much of you as I could while you howled and thrashed. I drank you to the very brink of death, then released you, too weak to continue your rampage. I stood over you, and I mourned. I mourned the daughter I knew I would have to put down. Until the floaters expressed their gratitude to me."

"Ghosts thanked you?"

"I saved them. And that's when I decided that they would return the favor."

"Wait," Pax said, starting to catch on. "You…orchestrated all this?"

Clem's pink eyes shimmered slightly, comforting Pax. She felt the weight of the world lift off Derek's shoulders. Her mother accepted her for who she was, and on top of that, protected her for who she was.

"I knew, sweet child, that I could not save you from the law, but if you died in Saint Chester's, you'd return a ghost. From there, you would need a host."

"Hold on," Derek interrupted. "Are you saying that *you* manipulated me to that church?"

"Our dreams are not always our own, Mr. Stabbers."

*It's called linking*, Pax thought. *I'll explain later.*

"The host is only a temporary solution," Clem said.

"What does that mean?" Derek asked.

Clem ignored him, and Pax did her best not to think about the truth. She needed Derek to remain calm right now.

"De-possessing a body has always been a mystery. But… there's a warlock."

"Who?"

"He goes by Nomicon," Clem said. "There are validated

rumors that his powers are experimental and irresponsible. Mixing science and supernatural. If anyone can get you out of that awful body, it's him."

"Fuck you."

"That was Derek," Pax said.

"I don't have his location yet. The type of services he provides are illegal in both the supernatural and mortal worlds, so naturally he's elusive," Clem said. "But I have minions checking back channels. I'll find him."

Pax grew hopeful. She'd do just about anything right now to get out of this body before Derek died. She could already feel their shared brain starting to pull against the two sets of contrasting information. She didn't know how long before Derek's mind decided to pull the plug on one of them.

*Wait…I'm dying?!* Derek thought.

*Shit. Sorry, I meant to tell you,* Pax thought.

# CHAPTER 21

Jordan snapped awake on his bed. It was the first and only time he could ever remember being asleep and then suddenly being wide awake—as if someone had flicked a switch and turned him on. He sat up and took a panicked look around his room. The curtains were drawn and clung oddly to the sides of the wall. Upon further inspection, Jordan realized someone had nailed them that way to block out all light. The room may have been dark, but everything looked sharp, as if he had high-definition eyeballs.

As he stood, Jordan's shirt peeled off his chest like a stiff bandage. The dry blood added an eerie weight as it tugged at his neckline. He freaked and tore it off to examine his body. No holes, cuts, or scrapes. It wasn't his blood. He dipped back into his mind and tried to remember the events that led him to this place. It took several seconds, but the fog in his head slowly began to reveal memories.

*Derek. Two girls. He followed them. The woods. Derek seemed... schizophrenic. Talking to himself. And then...he...*

DING DONG.

The doorbell startled him.

He exited his room and stumbled into the dark hallway. All the doors had been shut—the hallway curtains nailed tight against the windows.

DING DONG.

He hopped down the stairs and paused in front of a sign

taped to the front door: *Do not go outside. You will burn.* Jordan pulled it off the door and examined it. On the other side was his cocaine party sign. He chuckled at his line: *No Dereks Allowed*, then turned it back over and scratched his chin.

DING DONG.

Jordan flung open the door, expecting the architect behind this lame prank to be laughing on the other side. Instead, three strange, intense men stood on his porch. The tallest of them rested his hand on the butt of his weapon—the blade end disappeared inside his gray coat.

The daylight caused Jordan to squint, and suddenly he felt more hungover than he ever had in his life.

"Derek Stabbers?"

"Huh? The fuck are you assholes?" Jordan snapped back, the sun really getting to him. "Is there a cosplay convention in town?"

"We're with HAI."

"Cool. Goodbye."

Jordan tried to close the door, but the tall man stepped forward, knocked it back open. Jordan stumbled a few feet from the force.

"Hey! Outta my house, Eastwood!" Jordan shouted.

The tall man grabbed Jordan by the back of the neck and pulled him close.

"This ain't our guy," the tall man snarled to his associates.

Jordan pushed away and fell against the wall, hitting his head. All three men entered, closed the front door behind them.

"This could be a brother," the cheerful man said. "Maybe his boyfriend?"

"Fuck you!" Jordan cried. "I'm Jordan Stabbers. You ask around, 'cause I ain't nobody's boyfriend!"

"Calm down, ya homophobe," the tall man said. "Where's Derek?"

Jordan had had enough. He turned from the men and marched down the hall into his parents' den, a room he usually steered clear of. He hated the smell of the place—books, oil, and dust. It reminded him too much of the past, and he had to stay emotionally numb if he was going to survive.

He opened a small closet door, reached up on the top shelf, and grabbed his dad's pigeon rifle. He knew it was loaded, as he had done it himself when people threatened him and Derek after his parents were taken away.

He exited the den, turned back down the hall, and headed straight for the trio—the rifle raised and pointed at the tall man's head.

"You'll be getting the fuck outta my house right no—"

The tall man swiftly removed the weapon from his hip—which turned out to be a pretty sweet-looking ax—and knocked the gun's barrel aside. Jordan's finger squeezed the trigger, and a pool-ball-sized hole blasted into the east wall of the house.

A sunbeam squeezed through and punched Jordan in the face. He shrieked and backed away—his cheek flesh sizzled.

"What the holy hell!" he screamed, touching his burnt face.

All three men were staring at him.

"Who the fuck are you?!" Jordan screamed, again.

"I told you, boy. We're from HAI. Human's Against Inhumans. Which means us against *you*."

Jordan went quiet when he felt the flesh on his cheek begin to shift and fill back in. The tall man picked up the sign off the floor and read it with a grin. He handed it back to his associates who, strangely enough, stood back-to-back at all times.

"I'm not sure he knows what he is, Axe," the man who always smiled said.

"You don't know what you are, boy?"

Jordan's head spun. "I'm Jordan Stabbers. Fuck you."

Axe turned to his partners, his back to Jordan, then pivoted on the balls of his feet. The ax in his hand swung effortlessly above his head, sliced through the air with a slight vibration, and connected with Jordan's right wrist.

His five-fingered masturbator hit the floor with a weak thud. Jordan stared at it, unable to accept the fact that it was no longer attached to him. He raised the stump to his face, blood poured down his arm—a dull throb around the cut, but no real pain.

"My favorite hand," he whimpered.

The blade of the ax rested under his chin and forced Jordan's eyes to remain on his stump.

"Keep your eyes on the prize, boy," Axe said.

Jordan wanted to pull away but feared for the safety of his still-attached head. A twitch of movement from his stump caught his full attention. A fountain of blood shot into the air and smacked against a photo of Jordan's dog, Blooper. Something inside the wrist cracked and pushed its way out slowly. Dirty, white tips surfaced and reached for the ceiling. New bones! They snapped apart and formed what looked like new fingers. Muscle tissue snaked around his wrist and folded over the newly shaped skeleton—veins shot out like grappling hooks, and flesh bubbled and smoothed. Jordan watched as his cells multiplied at a dramatic rate. They covered up the gore and presented him with—what should have been impossible—a brand-new hand.

Axe released him. Jordan turned his new hand over and over, trying to solve this evil magic trick he'd just witnessed.

"How...did...you do that?" he whispered.

Axe laughed toward his partners. "We got a virgin here, and nobody even bothered to tell him."

"I'm not a virgin," Jordan said, confused as all hell.

Axe grabbed him by the shoulder, turned him around to face a mirror hanging in the hall. Jordan's eyes searched the reflective surface with a small amount of panic. He could see Axe and the wall of framed photos behind him. The only thing missing—Jordan himself.

"You're a vampire, Jordan Stabbers."

The word *vampire*—his least favorite word of all time—made his stomach turn.

"Where's your brother?"

Jordan faced the tall man.

"No such thing," Jordan said in a daze, "as vampires."

"Let's bag this one. He could be useful," the friendly one said.

The sound of a zipper running down its metal track shook Jordan from his funk. He looked over just as the silent brute of the gang unzipped a large black body suit and tossed it at him.

"What I'm I supposed to do with this?"
"Get in it."
"What is it?"
"Its technical name is a day bag. Keeps vampires from going poof out in the sun. However," Axe said, "I refer to it as a D-Bag. Perfect for douches like you. Get in it."

# CHAPTER 22

Derek and Pax sat in silence on a stump and watched a narrow brook babble deep into Little Horn Woods. There seemed to have been an unspoken agreement about arm manipulation, as Derek used his right arm to toss pebbles into the gentle rapids, while Pax used Derek's left arm to do the same. To a passerby they would have looked like a human windmill.

Derek's body filled her with anxiety. She'd never experienced human hate on such a personal level, and it made her nauseous. Clem used to tell her tales of when Rainy Mood thrived with creatures everywhere—out in the open, unafraid to be who they were. There had even been fairies that wisped about in these very woods, lighting the night with their multicolored beauty. They were gone now. Extinct or forced into hiding. Mortals changed everything. They brought with them their insecurities and fears. Options became limited for all creatures: pretend to be human, hide, or become the hunted.

*How long will this take?* Derek asked in their shared headspace.

*Clem said to be patient.*

*And then what?*

*And then what, what?*

*If she can find him—and this Nomicon warlock can get you out of my body... what happens to me?*

She hadn't really thought about that and understood his concern. He would most likely be disposed of. He was, after all, a vampire hunter who knew way too much. She couldn't tell him that of course, but the curse of sharing a brain meant that by the time she thought about it, he already knew.

*I see,* he thought. *Maybe I should just jump off a bridge then. Take at least one vampire down with me.*

*First off, I'm a whostpire now,* she thought. *Second...why does your family hate vampires so much? What do you even know about us that gives you the right?*

Derek closed his fist around the remainder of the stones and threw them all at once into the brook. She felt him start to stand, catching her off guard. The stiff motion caused them to tumble off the log and onto the ground.

"Tell me when you want to move, and we'll move!" she shouted.

"I'm standing up!" he shouted back.

Pax rolled his eyes and let go of the controls. Derek pushed himself up and turned to walk, but Pax immediately froze the body in fear.

"Let go!"

*Shhhh!* she hushed.

Using his left hand, Pax pointed a couple yards ahead of them—a squirrel sniffing about in search of food. It spotted Derek and stared back. Pax watched its dark, vengeful eyes bury their search daggers through Derek's skin. She knew the squirrel could sense it—that this wasn't an ordinary teenager.

*What about it? It's a squirrel,* Derek thought.

*Stay perfectly still,* she commanded.

The squirrel stared at them for another second or two, then scurried deeper into the woods. Pax relaxed the body, and Derek stumbled forward.

*You're fucking with me, right? The mighty vampire is afraid of a squirrel?*

*Clearly there's a lot you don't know about us.*
*I know the world would be more peaceful without you.*
*You've been indoctrinated.*
*Have I?*
*I saw your corkboard. You've been feeding off your parents' religion*

*since birth. Fucking HAI. Those assholes are the ones polluting the world, and your parents' minds!*

*You don't know the first thing about my parents.*

*I know they were vampire hunters. Piss-poor ones at that, since they never actually killed a real vampire.*

She could feel Derek's anger flood their body. He grabbed his left hand with his right and pulled himself forward.

*Come on.*

*Where we going?*

*Hell.*

# CHAPTER 23

Jane Stabbers gently kissed the top of Derek's head, careful not to wake him, then creeped across his bedroom floor avoiding the floorboards she knew would creak. When the door silently bumped against its frame, a rush of guilt attacked her chest. Tomorrow would be Derek's twelfth birthday, and she would be far away on an assignment. It made her heart ache, but there was little she could do. She needed this bump in her career, as well as her bank account. Jordan would be going to college in a couple years, and Derek would start high school. She was leaving for her family.

Elliot had just zipped up the last brown leather suitcase as she entered the master bedroom. Jane could tell he was excited by the way he patted the overstuffed leather with a subtle smile that hung just under his well-trimmed mustache. They had never received an assignment outside of Rainy Mood. Living in a small town usually meant reporting on stories like the unveiling of a new greasy appetizer at Prickley's, or the rumor that Ms. Peel, Rainy Mood's infamous crazy cat lady, was actually a five-star commander in some galactic war.

After ten years of mundane events and imaginative rumors, the Stabberses' boss at Channel 8 News had handed them a real assignment—one that required them to leave the safety of their sleepy burg to investigate a series of disappearances at several morgues in neighboring small towns. Corpses that waited patiently on a Wednesday for their memorial service had vanished by Thursday morning. A strange little mystery that hadn't yet been given a proper spotlight, and Channel 8 saw an opportunity to lead the charge for once.

Jane and Elliot had met in journalism school and fancied themselves a team. They once caught the notorious Movie Theater Wacker—a mysterious man who showed up at the old college cinema once a week to leave behind a disgusting, goopy surprise in one of the seats. The budding journalists went deep undercover and posed as a couple on a date. They sat through every single screening of the same over-bloated action film for almost a week. On the fifth day of their fake date stakeout, the Wacker was caught in action just ten seats behind them. They wrote an article that explored the process of their investigation, and a small profile on the Wacker himself—an elderly gentleman who used to patronize the theater in the late fifties when it still ran pornos. His dementia kept him from understanding the difference between the latest superhero movie and an old-timey fuck film. He just assumed the budgets had gotten bigger.

The Stabberses' experiment landed them a lot of attention at the college paper, and before they knew it they were partnered together on all assignments. Their faux dating had also sparked a real romance, and soon after, they were married.

"I wish we weren't leaving tomorrow," Jane said sadly.

"It's bad timing, but we'll make it up to him," Elliot said, placing the suitcase on the floor and turning down the bed.

The next day, they rolled their unmarked Channel 8 station wagon into the small town of Huffers, Virginia. According to their research (and a map with pushpins and string), if the bandits continued their pattern, this would be the next stop on their corpse-snatching spree.

They grabbed a bite to eat at a throwback drive-up, where the waitress brought the food to your car window. They both had cheeseburgers and crinkle-cut fries. Jane gave Elliot a small look when he ordered his burger with bacon. The Stabbers men were prone to heart problems, and she kept a close eye on all her boys' diets. She decided not to say anything, as they were sort of on vacation—or at least their first out-of-town adventure—so the extra sodium would go unnoticed.

After lunch, they checked into a small motel under the aliases Richard and Deborah Craft. They unpacked their gear—full of tiny cameras and audio equipment—and got right back into the car to head down to the local funeral home where they had made arrangements with the owner—a squat, balding man who seemed enthusiastic to be part of a sting operation. Much like her own hometown, Jane guessed excitement was a scarce resource in Huffers.

There were two fresh corpses waiting their turn to be embalmed. Jane and Elliot bugged both with hidden cameras shaped as a tie clips, then affixed several more in the parlor, preparation room, reposing room, and hallway. Small box monitors were set up in the office, and a video feed test proved a rousing success.

The sun had just set when the owner handed them a set of keys, wished them luck, and departed. Jane detected a copious amount of booze on his breath and found herself a bit jealous. Her nerves needed whiskey.

They got comfortable in the tiny office and watched the monitors closely, including the two black screens—the cameras pinned to the bodies in the coolers.

The hours ticked away, their eyelids slowly feeling the effects of the Sandman. At around three thirty a.m., Jane noticed smoke filling the preparation room. She swatted a book out of Elliot's hands and pointed at the monitor.

"What's this?" she asked.

"What is that?" he asked.

They checked the other cameras hidden throughout the building. No sign of fire. The mysterious smoke seemed to be contained. Jane and Elliot watched with great intensity as one of the cooling vaults slowly slid open on its own, and the tie clip camera fell into action.

"What the fuck?"

"I have no idea."

The smoke covered the body like a bedsheet and lifted it

carefully off the metal table. It passed out of the room, off camera 1, and floated down the hall, passing by camera 3.

"We have to follow it," Elliot said.

Jane had a bad feeling but didn't want to waste time by expressing it. They crept out of the office and into the first parlor, poking their heads around the corner like a pair of movie sleuths. They were just in time to see the front door unlatch itself and the body float out into the black of night.

They tiptoed down the hall and carefully peeked out the front window. An idling pickup truck waited with no one inside. The smoke lifted the body and placed it in the back bed. Jane's and Elliot's eyes almost fell out of their skulls when the smoke split in two then rematerialized into what looked like a teenage girl and a middle-aged man.

The two corporeal forms entered the vehicle on opposite ends, and the truck pulled forward to the street. As soon as the taillights vanished, Elliot grabbed Jane by the hand and led her out the front door and into their station wagon.

"Should we be doing this?" she asked.

"This story's better than we could have ever imagined, Jane. We *have* to do this."

Elliot started the car, and she curbed the bad feeling once more. They pulled out of the lot and carefully caught up to the pickup as it fishtailed drunkenly without care.

The truck eventually turned off the road and onto a well-worn dirt path. Elliot drove the station wagon straight and parked just off to the side.

The path seemed to go on for ages. It was unusually dark out, the moon well behind the clouds—the countryside black as tar. Jane saw the truck first and had to grab Elliot to stop him from running directly into it. A few yards in front of them sat an old, abandoned mill that added to the creep factor by a thousand. A cool breeze bent pieces of thin, rusted metal on the mill and made small cracking noises that whispered, *turn back*.

"How you doing?" Elliot asked.

"Scared out of my fucking mind," Jane replied.

"Then we must be doing something right."

They shared a small kiss, and Elliot led the silent charge into the mill.

Once inside, they could hear faint voices bouncing off the walls, laughter accented by candlelight just up ahead. Elliot and Jane both had their personal cameras set to night vision and recorded every step. They slipped behind a large iron column, poked their heads into the room to witness three men standing around the newly nabbed body, their faces pressed against it. Horrible sucking noises echoed in the empty chamber.

Jane had never believed in vampires, but it wasn't hard to figure out that they existed now. For the sake of their children she would force Elliot to leave and never speak of this again. She reached out and touched his arm, but before she was able to make her wishes known, a slick, sinister voice scared her from behind.

"Hello, dessert."

The Stabberses jumped a mile out of their skin and turned to see the teenage girl from the funeral home. She had long black hair with streaks of blue, moonlight skin, and thin, white fangs exposed in her smile. The other vampires looked up with blood-covered lips as the Stabberses were backed into the room filled with candles.

"Save room, gentlemen," the teenage vamp said.

"Please, you have to let us—" Elliot started.

"Feed," Jane finished.

It was the only thing Jane could think of. They were undercover investigators. Part of their job was becoming other people to gain trust. Might as well put that skill to use and save their lives in the process.

The teenager with the blue-streaked hair fixed her curious eyes on Jane, then looked back over at Elliot.

"It's been ages since we had…blood," Jane continued.

There was a long silence, and Jane was confident the next sound would be the tearing of her own flesh.

"Hear that, gents? These 'vampires' are hungry. Should we share with them?"

From the tone of her voice, Jane could tell the girl didn't

**EVERYDAY MONSTERS**

believe they were actually vampires. There'd be only one way to convince them, and the thought of it made her soul shiver. She looked at Elliot, whose eyes watered, and gave him a slight nod. He understood and did his best to find his inner monster.

The vamp extended her arm, waved them toward the hole-poked corpse on the ground. The men stood and allowed the Stabberses full access to the decaying meal.

Jane and Elliot stood frozen above the dead gentleman, the threads that once held his eyelids shut had snapped open from the feeding. He stared up them—dead eyes that still seemed to beg for mercy. Jane stared down at the tie clip camera and wondered if it was still recording, and if that was a good thing. A single second more would give them away. She broke from her position, fell to her knees, and found a pre-made set of bite marks that she placed her lips over. Jane nearly gagged when the thickness hit her throat, but she thought about Jordan and Derek and swallowed it like a champ.

Lifting her head, her mouth now covered in red, she noticed Elliot still a statue of inner horror.

"It's Kosher," she said.

Elliot seemed to understand and broke free from his paralysis.

"He was Jewish," Jane said, looking behind her at the teen vamp. "Old habits die hard, eh?"

The vamp only watched, giving her no sign if she believed a word of any of this. Elliot arrived at the body, and Jane sent courage into him with her warm eyes—the same eyes she used to convince him to go out and get her ice cream or rub her back in bed. He bent down, found a bite, and took in a large suck of blood. Jane returned to the meal, remembering that they were supposed to be starving.

The Stabberses drank as much as they could stomach without throwing up, occasionally pretending to eat when they thought it appeared convincing enough. Slowly, the rest of the creatures surrounded the body and joined them in the feast.

Jane watched as they tore strips of flesh from the corpse with their teeth. Needing to be as authentic as possible, she clamped her incisors down hard over a loose piece of arm flesh, ripping a good-size chunk for herself. As she chewed, she thought about her children. She thought about honey in tea. She thought about Sunday mornings with no alarm clock. She thought about all the things that would sculpt the smile she needed to convince these creatures that human flesh was what made her the happiest.

She must have been doing something right, because the teenage vamp knelt down next to her, peeled back her own piece of dead guy, and smiled at Jane.

"I'm Chloe," she said as she pushed a piece of flesh to the back of her throat.

"Deborah," Jane said with as much confidence as she could.

"Got a nest, Deborah?"

Jane hesitated, not exactly sure what that meant.

"No worries," Chloe said. "You can run with us if you want. We could use a few more sticky fingers. We're on a cross-country taste-a-thon. We move quickly though. Gotta get to the bodies before they ruin 'em with embalming fluid."

"You'd let us come with you?"

"Vamps gotta stick together, right?"

"Yes."

She looked over at her husband, who choked down a piece of chest flesh.

"Yes, us vamps gotta stick together."

# CHAPTER 24

Derek wouldn't take his eyes off Jane and Elliot, and Pax would have felt horrible if she made him look away. They were curled up together in the furthest corner of a cell made of one-way glass. The lines on their faces and bloodshot eyes suggested a twenty-four-seven commitment to anxiety. Cracked lips and malnourished bodies that clung to each other like scared chimpanzees—skeletons wearing a thin layer of skin.

Derek gripped a faded brown journal and turned the crinkled pages slowly. Every so often he glanced down at it, giving Pax a peek at the macabre entries of Jane Stabbers. They started off normal—the penmanship above average, sentences had punctuation, and words stayed inside the measured lines. As Derek's story about them progressed, however, the journal took on a dark and terrifying life of its own. Scribbles and slashes replaced sentences. Lines became enemies. Madness spilled over every page.

Pax had never been inside the Rough Edges Mental Institution but had always wondered about the people who dwelled behind its walls. It was much worse than she could have ever guessed.

"My parents traveled the country with them," Derek continued. "They stole bodies from funeral homes. Fed on them. They did everything they needed to keep their identities hidden. To stay alive. During the day, my parents were chained up in dark rooms to rusted pipes. They were told it was to protect them from sleepwalking out into the sun, but all the others remained free."

Pax wanted him to stop, the story already sad enough. One had to simply look at the tortured couple in the cell to ruin the ending. Those vampires absolutely knew that Jane and Elliot Stabbers were human. The speed of their heartbeats and scent of their insides alone would give them away. No, Chloe and her thrill-seekers were fucking with the Stabberses. They were laughing every time they could get them to do something horrible. It was a game to them. They were a bunch of dicks.

"They say if you consume enough human flesh... enough brain tissue, you can go crazy," Derek said. "It's called kuru. I guess it's similar to Mad Cow disease. My parents lived for two months on a constant diet of the dead. Pair the disease along with the experience..."

He flipped to the last page in the journal. Amongst the scribbles and macabre sketches, a single sentence—tiny enough to miss if you weren't really examining the page. Derek put his finger on it. *All will die.*

"This was the last entry. One morning the vamps forgot to lock my parents' chains—the upper hand they'd been waiting for. When the nest was asleep, they staked and ate every last one of them. Chewed their heads right off their shoulders. Filled their stomachs with the creatures that filled their minds with poison. Then, they walked back to Rainy Mood. I think they thought they'd be able to slip back into the people they once were, but those people were dead."

It was clear why Derek hated vampires. It wasn't because of books, movies, or hate organizations like HAI and their long-term brainwashing. Derek was on the unfortunate end of a group of douchebags that just happened to *be* vampires.

Pax took control of the left hand and placed it tenderly on Derek's right. She felt him tense up inside then quickly relax. A second hand placed itself over Derek's left. Both Derek and Pax made the head look up at the same time to see a tall, balding doctor with ice-cold eyes.

"And the Lord said: Trust in thine doctor, for it is he who is great," the doctor said, like a bad Vincent Price impersonator.

"That's not in the Bible," Derek hissed.

"It might have been. There was a heavy dose of editing back in the day."

Pax could feel Derek's rage as he stood. She had to hold him back for fear he might kill him.

*Who's this creepy asshole?* she thought.

*Doctor Shawn. A useless piece of human garbage,* he thought.

"You've had my parents locked up in this place for years," Derek said. "They're no better than when they arrived. In fact, they might be worse!"

"Your parents' problem is built upon layers," said Doctor Shawn in a low monotone. "What may cure the surface could corrupt the core."

*Jesus. I know demons less morose,* Pax thought.

*I have a theory he's actually a patient here who murdered the original Doctor Shawn and took over his identity,* thought Derek.

*I would one hundred percent buy into that theory,* she thought.

Pax suddenly realized they were both smiling. It felt weird.

A loud buzzer went off, and the door to Jane and Elliot's cell clicked open. A man dressed in full padded armor stepped inside holding an oversized hose. He twisted the lever on the brass nozzle, and a hard stream of water struck Derek's parents. Their shrieks pierced his ears, and Pax could feel his heart breaking.

"Shower time," Doctor Shawn said with zero emotion.

Pax felt Derek's fist tighten, and she quickly seized control.

*Arrested for assault is gonna slow down our mission,* she thought.

Derek relaxed his muscles, but his rage remained. The hose turned off, and a second man in padded armor stepped into the cell holding small goat. The goat was placed on the floor and began to walk in nervous circles. His parents, recovering from the pressurized shower, sat upright, licking their lips and slowly moving in on the scared creature—lions in the Serengeti made of glass.

"Lunch," Doctor Shawn said.

Derek regained control of his body and grabbed Doctor

Shawn by the neck with his left hand, his right vibrating as he struggled against Pax's strength.

*Not...worth you...dying...Derek,* Pax thought with great strain.

Once more, Derek let go. He turned back to his parents, watched as they cornered the crying goat. Just as they were about to attack, the padded man pressed a button on a small remote and the goat unexpectedly exploded. Like a water balloon filled with oil and meat, the gore soaked the Stabberses as they fell back screaming, terrified by the sudden detonation of their meal.

The first padded man turned the hose back on and violently sprayed them clean.

"Second shower," Doctor Shawn said as he removed a small notebook from his pocket, clicked open his pen, and began to scribble.

"That makes four ruptured goats, yet still no hesitation from your parents to attack. We are learning so much, and so little at the same time," Doctor Shawn said.

Both Derek and Pax stared in awe at the unconscionable conditions of the asylum. Pax immediately let go of Derek's muscles, and even added a little extra strength to the punch he swung—his fist connecting solidly to Doctor Shawn's nose.

The moment his knuckles touched skull, Pax regretted allowing Derek to take the swing. With his anger and her strength, Derek had the ability to do real damage—which was exactly what happened when Doctor Shawn's nose tore dramatically from his face, sailed through the air, and smacked against the one-way glass that caged Derek's folks.

Pax gripped the leg muscles, ready to run, but paused when she noticed something completely unexpected. Doctor Shawn had not flinched. He stood perfectly still, staring back with no emotion. Where blood and tissue should be exposed, steel and lights shined bright.

"Great," Doctor Shawn said. "I'm going to have to order more of the special glue I need to reattach that."

"You're..."

"…a robot?"

"You're not?"

Pax knew of hundreds of strange creatures that existed in the world, but a robot this advanced had never crossed her radar.

"Who…who made you?"

"Nomicon," said Doctor Shawn. "Who made you?"

# CHAPTER 25

The gruesome twosome wouldn't tell Lotti much, just that they had a lead on a warlock that could remedy their totally disgusting body share. That, and they'd all have to skip town for a few days. Lotti welcomed the trip. Another minute in Rainy Mood and she would surely be dragged to some dark dungeon where her limbs would be removed, then sewn onto stumps they didn't belong to. She couldn't confirm this would be her punishment, but it's the thought that crept into her head most.

While Derek and Pax waited in the car, Lotti made final preparations for her departure, paying her father's head housekeeper an extra grand to keep a close on eye the depressed senator. She didn't think he would hurt himself, but it gave her a small amount of peace to know he had a secret babysitter.

Senator Lyons sat in his library as he always did this time of night, drinking his scotch and staring out the window. When Lotti entered, he smiled—always authentically happy to see her. He had never once mentioned her new face. The day she came home with it he only smiled, touched her cheek, and then asked what was for dinner.

"Need a refill, Pops?" she asked with just the right amount of cheer.

"Don't need it, but I sure do want it."

It was the same answer every time. Lotti marched over to him, grabbed his glass, and moved to the drink cart near the oversized globe no one ever looked at or used. She poured from a crystal carafe, then handed the drink to her dad with a kiss on the cheek.

"I'm going out of town for a few days. You cool here on your own, old man?"

Lotti always kept it light with her father. She feared any hint of sadness or reservation in her voice would trigger him. She had no proof to back this up, she just didn't want to take the chance.

"Where to?"

"Camping. With friends."

"With Jazz?"

Lotti bit her lip. "Yeah, Dad. With Jazz."

Mr. Lyons nodded, satisfied with this.

"I labeled a week's worth of dinners in the freezer."

"You didn't need to do that, Charlotte. I can feed myself."

"Pizza and fast food burgers is not 'feeding yourself,' it's killing—"

She froze, mad at herself for not running the sentence through her head before speaking it. Her father didn't seem to notice as he sipped on his scotch.

"You have fun, then. Don't get eaten by a bear," he teased.

"That bear better not get eaten by *me*," she joked.

She kissed him once more on the cheek and exited the library. The moment she was out of his sight, her knees buckled, and she fell to the ground. Her sorrow and fear attacked her like a murder of crows. She couldn't relax around him, always dissecting every move and word, dreading the day he purchased a new garden hose, even though they now used an underground sprinkler system.

Lotti picked herself back up and headed for her room. She'd be no good to him dead, and so alive she must remain. She lifted up the cherry oak trunk at the edge of her bed and grabbed her emergency vampire overnight bag. It contained all the essentials: cute clothes, clothes that looked cute with blood on them, clothes that looked cute with bile on them, makeup, a bottle of vanilla vodka, and tampons.

She flung open her closet and eyed the six hooks that held

six different hat options. Her fingers slid over a Rust & Bone chain-trim wool fedora—her favorite thing she owned. She only wore it on special occasions, and while she didn't consider this one of those, the hat would ease her suffering slightly just knowing how adorable she looked. With the utmost care, she lifted it off the hook, slid it around her head, and flicked the brim with her fingers like a true badass.

"You look like a rich girl playing detective."

Lotti yelped and spun on her heels. Jazz stood behind her near the open window, sweat dripping from her forehead.

"You lost access to the trellis a long time ago, Jazz."

"A lot higher up than I remember," she huffed.

"What do you want, before I have you arrested for trespassing?"

"Wherever you're going and whatever you're doing, I'm by your side," Jazz said.

"Never gonna happen. Pax won't allow it."

"You're gonna make her allow it, or bad things are gonna befall you."

This made Lotti laugh tremendously loud.

"Bad things befalling me is my jam, bitch! That's why I was put here on this blue marble. So bad things could have a fucking squeeze toy!"

"You know our deal."

Lotti closed her eyes and counted to ten. She let the world around her drop away and touched the rim of her fedora. When she opened her eyes, Jazz remained, but the situation felt slightly less hostile.

"Hope you packed a toothbrush."

# CHAPTER 26

The D-Bag was dark. Jordan imagined this was what it must feel like to be inside a womb, only the bag was not as wet and soothing…and there was no fleshy rope attached to his belly button to receive nourishment. So, it was actually nothing like a womb, but still dark as shit.

The scooter hit a pothole, and Jordan tightened his grip around the asshole with the ax. They'd been driving around Rainy Mood for an hour now looking for Derek. He wasn't in school, and that was the only place Jordan knew to look—besides Rough Edges, but he kept his mouth shut about that. He wasn't going near that place.

The scooter revved up, and Jordan could feel the tires rumbling on a craggy street. He had no idea where they were. No wind leaked through the D-Bag, and it suddenly occurred to Jordan he hadn't been breathing the entire time. He didn't need to. He was capable of the function, but it seemed unnecessary.

*Oh, fuck. Oh fuck! Fuck! Fuck! Fuck! Fuck! Fuck! Fuck!*

Was he really dead? A flood of memories unlocked in his head. Derek. The tree. The blood-soaked branch. He *had* died.

Something stirred deep in his gut. It felt alive and angry. Pressure began to apply itself to the top of his gums. Jordan flicked his tongue around his mouth, felt two razor-sharp fangs descend. The creature in his gut roared with hunger, and Jordan suddenly felt weaker than he ever had in his life.

He wrapped his arms tight around his captor and rested his

head on his back like a tired lover. He knew absolutely nothing about being a vampire, but one thing was blindingly clear: he needed to eat soon, and it needed to be blood.

# CHAPTER 27

"Awoooooooooo!" Pax howled as she gripped the wheel of Derek's car.

"Please stop that," Derek said.

"I second that," Lotti said.

"I'm cool with it," Jazz said.

They'd been driving for twenty minutes and Pax hadn't stopped smiling once, which meant Derek hadn't stopped smiling—something he was not used to. Pax had never driven a car, and Derek could feel how thrilling it was for her. He maintained control of his body but allowed small parts of himself to slide loose, giving Pax a sense that she was the reason the wheels stayed within the painted lines.

"Let's go faster!" she squealed.

Derek's foot remained locked on the gas, not budging on this one.

"Just because you're dead doesn't mean we want to be."

Pax had seemed genuinely upset at Rough Edges regarding his parents, and he had to give her a little credit for helping knock Doctor Shawn's nose off his smug, mechanical face. The coincidence of a robot created by the very warlock they needed find, sent to Rainy Mood to work at the very asylum where his parents were held prisoner—the entire scenario gnawed at Derek's insides. Who was this Nomicon, and why did he have his black magic fingers all up in Derek's personal life?

"The Island of the Screaming Dead?" Jazz asked from the back.

Hearing the name out loud in a tone of disbelief had Derek second-guessing everything. Doctor Shawn had seemed happy to offer up the information, or at least what little he knew. Nomicon had made him somewhere in the Atlantic Ocean—on an island named—

"The Island of the Screaming Dead?" Jazz said again, amplifying her tone.

"That's what he said."

"And you believe him? The creepy robot who experiments on your parents."

She had a point, but they had doubled-checked the information with Clem and her back-channel demons. Those who knew about Nomicon had also heard he lived on an island in the Atlantic Ocean. Where, no one knew exactly.

Derek's thoughts drifted to Clem. She had planted that dream in his head—his mom and dad at Saint Chester's. She wanted him to go there. She wanted Pax to possess him. Why *him*? He was the enemy.

"Awoooooooooo!"

Derek glanced up in the rearview mirror at the ladies in the back. Lotti looked miserable, her face pointed toward the window, the fedora pulled down over her eyes. He really didn't want her tagging along, but they needed to charter a boat, and Pax convinced him they could use Lotti both financially and as a source of food.

Jazz seemed highly attentive. She winked at him, and then winked again. It didn't feel flirty, more like a tic. He wondered what she had over Lotti that allowed her a ticket on this madcap adventure.

The car choked along, a celebration of poisonous carbon. Derek's thoughts turned to Jordan. He wondered if he was alive yet, if he was scared. Pax assured him he'd be fine—the first time Jordan would attempt to open the curtains would be the last time. She had used Derek's hands to catch a rabbit sniffing around the Stabberses' landscaping. After breaking its neck with a single squeeze, she drained every last drop of blood from it into a mason jar, then stored the rabbit's red in the fridge. When the hunger became unbearable, Jordan would know what to do on instinct alone. They'd be back as soon as—

"Holy shit!" Derek screamed.

He tensed up, took control of his body, and gripped the wheel. The car veered back onto the road and missed a telephone pole by an inch. He'd dropped his guard by letting his mind wander, and Pax had taken over. Huge mistake.

"Sorry! Sorry!" she said.

The girls in the back had dug their nails into the seats in front of them. Derek took a deep breath and pressed his hand to his chest. He waited for his heart to betray him like always, but it didn't happen. It hadn't happened since he woke up with Pax inside him. He liked having a normal heart. He felt like he could conquer the world, or at least get them to the ocean, and perhaps even across it.

～

Exactly one hour and thirty minutes later they saw the ocean creep over the horizon. Derek had to wake Lotti and Jazz, who had folded into each other like full-body pillows. The girls untangled themselves quickly in disgust.

The car died a hundred yards from the port, to no surprise of Derek's. He had been expecting it to shit out on him any day for the last year, so a prolonged drive like this one was a bit of a suicide mission.

After a short hike, the four (who appeared as three) arrived at the harbor. There were plenty of ships in the area—workers rushed about loading and unloading freight from most of them. Derek watched as fifty-foot cranes made easy work of crates loaded with steel drums, wooden boxes, and in one ship's case, a single unhappy cow.

A small breeze tickled his face, and he could feel the salt in the air. The smell of fish, diesel, and freedom blended uncharacteristically well together. Pax's presence had heightened his senses, and it was the first chance he had to enjoy them.

"So, what's the plan?" Jazz asked.

"We ask around about the island," Pax said.

Derek assumed she was in charge of this small slice of the mission, so he relinquished a good portion of control to her, but as they wandered the crowded docks, Pax remained quiet. Derek noticed the nervous tingle each passerby caused in his stomach, and it struck him odd to feel her powerful distrust in other humans. He decided it would be up to him and stopped the next man in a blue captain's uniform with little yellow anchors threaded on the shoulders.

"Excuse me, Captain. Are you familiar with the Island of the Screaming Dead?"

"The island of what?" the captain said.

"The Screaming Dead."

"What captain would ever point his sails toward something with a name like that?"

Derek sighed, nodding at Lotti to get ready for payment.

"We have cash."

"I see," said the captain. "So, you're looking to pay someone to die."

"I'm sorry?"

"You want to offer me money so I'll sail you out to the Island of the Screaming Dead, whereupon, being only a tertiary character in your grand adventure, I'll be the first to meet some terrible fate, and the money will be useless."

"Sir, I don't think you understand. There's a warlock on this island—"

"A warlock he says! A warlock on the Island of the Screaming Dead. Yes, I can see nothing wrong about that, except that I'm not interested in becoming part of your B-horror movie."

Derek's anger boiled.

"Can you at least tell me where it is?"

"How would I know? I'm a homeless man. I sleep seven docks down by the water. My name is Jesus Christ, and my biggest question is, who just farted?"

Derek turned his back to the lunatic and led his gang further up the port. He could feel Pax snicker inside him.

*Someone had to try*, he thought.

Over an hour later Derek had talked to twenty different people. Thirteen homeless people, two crew workers, two passengers, and three actual ship captains. No one knew about the island or had heard the name Nomicon. They had come to the very end of the harbor. The only ship left was a tiny hunk of rusted metal that appeared to try with all its might to stay above water.

"I'm not getting on that," Lotti said.

"The odds are in your favor," Jazz said with little faith.

Derek stepped up onto the rickety dock. The wood below him cracked open, and his foot plunged into the saltwater below.

"All right," he said defeated. "Let's go home."

Pax tugged at him on the inside.

*We can't give up! What if you die in your sleep tonight?* she thought.

*We're out of options. No one's even heard of this island.*

*Someone has to know something. How does Nomicon get materials delivered?*

*I don't know, Pax, but we're too far from the next harbor and it'll be dark soon.*

"Are you guys talking in your head again?" Jazz asked.

Derek looked up.

"Because it looks like you're having a stroke when you do that."

"AHOY!"

The rusty voice came from the old ship. They turned to find a figure standing on the stern, dressed in what they could only assume to be an authentic pirate captain's coat. Gold trim rushed down the lining, curling off in all directions for added flair. The buttons along the flap were the size of silver dollars; in fact, upon closer inspection they *were* silver dollars. A thick hood hung low on the stranger's face and covered it perfectly.

"Needin' ta hire a ship?" the stranger asked.

The man on the boat creeped Derek out, but before he could respond, Pax had taken control of the lips.

"We be needin' to sail to an island no one's heard of," she said in her best pirate.

"Really?" Derek said, taking back the reins. "That's the voice you're making me use?"

The captain stood still, placed a cigarette under his hood, and lit it.

"I know a lot of islands that don't exist," he said, a bit of wonder radiating from his gravelly voice.

"The Island of the Screaming Dead," Derek said with little hope.

The captain took another drag off his cigarette, then stepped off his ship and onto the dock. He headed their way in a zigzag pattern—careful not to step on any of the rotted-out spots—and stopped three feet away from them. The captain reached up toward the hood that hid his face, and Derek caught a glimpse of what looked more like a paw than a hand. When the hood came down, the gang all gasped. Silky brown hair covered the captain's face, not a single inch of flesh available to the eye. His mouth, nose, and ocean blues were all that poked through.

"Well, ain't that the coincidence of the year," the captain said, showing off his hairy grin. "That's exactly where I'm heading."

He dropped the cigarette and held out his paw.

"Captain H. John Grimmerstone, but most o' the boys 'round here call me the Salty Dog."

Derek stared at the hand covered in hair. There were no claws, webs, or pads that would suggest he was anything other than human with a bad case of the furry.

"I suffer from hypertrichosis, often called werewolf syndrome," he said.

Derek hesitated.

"No worries," said Grimmerstone. "It's not contagious… unless I bite you."

He roared with laughter. It spooked Derek, who already had a bad feeling. Pax scoffed at his inaction and took over, pressing Derek's palm into the captain's.

"You're going to the island?" Pax said.

"Of the Screaming Dead?" Jazz added.

"Yar," said Grimmerstone. "Good fishin' up that way. Be happy to bring you with. Would enjoy the company."

"Your boat looks like it's eighty percent rust," Derek said.

"My *ship*," corrected Captain Grimmerstone. "She's as safe as a spoon at a steak dinner."

"What's her name?" Jazz asked. "Your ship."

"The *Bitch*," he answered.

"Fitting," Jazz remarked.

*I don't trust this guy, Derek thought.*

*You don't trust anyone outside a seventy-five-year lifespan,* Pax thought, then smiled at the captain. "When do you leave?"

"T's about to set off now. That work?"

"Yes!"

"Well then, all aboard, eh?"

# CHAPTER 28

Jordan had listened to his captors argue most of the day, so when things got quiet, he could only assume they had split up. Axe had him tight by the arm and dragged him up and down Rainy Mood. He didn't know how much longer he could go on, the pain inside him unbearable.

Jordan's legs buckled. He braced to hit the ground, but Axe caught him instead—at least he assumed it was still Axe. He felt the powerful man tuck him under his arm and drag Jordan down the street like a dead Christmas tree.

He tried to remember the last time he had a hunger this bad. It felt like an angry caterpillar ripping holes in his stomach lining, allowing his acids to spill out over his organs.

The strong arms suddenly propped Jordan's body in a sitting position against a wall. The hood unzipped, and a scorching bright light blinded him—his eyes itched as if someone had poured sawdust into them. His vision slowly adjusted, but a bright white halo remained around everything. Jordan stared into Axe's ruggedly crafted face, a cigarette dangling from his lips.

His kidnapper had placed him under a green-and-blue awning attached to a small storefront, the generous piece of fabric shading him just enough from bursting into flames.

"I'm tired of holding you up, vampire."

Jordan tried to speak. A raspy, unintelligible whisper fell

out of his mouth. He reached up to the man for help, but Axe swatted his hand away.

"You got the first-time feeds," Axe said. "I hear they're the worst."

Jordan clawed at his stomach as if he could tear out the pain. A string of saliva dangled from his bottom lip.

Axe placed his thumb under Jordan's chin and pressed up. "Normally I'd let your guts explode, but you're my leverage right now."

Axe grabbed him by the head, pulled him to his feet, and pressed his face hard against a large pane of glass. A set of wet, adorable eyes stared back at Jordan from the store's window—face-to-face with a tiny English bulldog. The puppy's tongue flopped out of its dopey grin; its snub tail vibrated with pure happiness at the sight of a possible home.

Jordan knew immediately they were in front of Paws For Love, Rainy Mood's one and only pet store. This was where Jordan had first met his best buddy, Blooper. He had noticed the runty little beagle watching him wistfully through the glass as he passed by with his mom. He pleaded with her to go inside so he could pet the puppy. She agreed, as long as he understood that they simply couldn't get a dog right now. It was not a good time. Twenty minutes later, Jordan exited the shop with his arms full of pure furry happiness.

"Let's get you fed."

The shop's bell meowed, and Axe pushed Jordan inside. The smell of dog food and woodchips were the expected odor, but a more powerful aroma crowned itself king—blood. The shop dripped with the sweet, sticky scent. It oozed from every nook and cranny—every kitten and parakeet. The sound of a hundred beating hearts called to him like a bass drum to an ecstasy addict.

Axe released his grip, and Jordan folded to the ground, too weak to stand on his own. He watched his kidnapper's black boots wander up to the counter, then heard the thud of the shopkeeper's body as Axe knocked him cold with a single punch.

Axe slid the front door's bolt lock to the right, then pulled a large curtain across the display window. The terrible sun went away, as did the white halos in Jordan's vision.

Kneeling down, Axe pulled Jordan back into a sitting position, then placed something small and furry into his hand. He guessed a mouse, but when he looked down, Jordan discovered a hamster.

"Start small," Axe said. "Then work your way up to Fido in the window."

Jordan's mouth grew moist—his teeth ached. He wanted to stand up, murder this monster who kidnapped him and drain him in one delicious suck. Tragically, he didn't have the strength, and set his eyes back on the smaller game in his hand. Mutiny raged inside him. Hunger had seized the ship's wheel, tied up the crew that manned his conscience. He didn't want to do what he knew he was about to do—but he did it anyway.

~

Thirty minutes later, the shop's door opened, and Axe lead Jordan—fully zipped up in the D-Bag—back out into the sun. His world was once again dark—his soul now much darker. The stink of animal blood lingered on his lips. His tongue pushed at a few stray dog hairs that clung to the inside of his cheeks.

"Let's find your brother."

Jordan remained quiet as Axe marched him forward, relieved no one could see his shame-filled face. The hunger now gone, Jordan Stabbers couldn't shake the disturbing fact that the pet shop slaughter had been the best meal of his life.

# CHAPTER 29

The sun melted away beneath the infinite line of ocean. The sky had turned a perfect blend of pink and lavender, and the water sparkled liked spilled diamonds on a polished floor. It was truly the most beautiful thing Pax had seen in over a hundred years. Her emotions manipulated Derek's tear ducts. She could feel him fighting back against tears for a dumb sunset.

*How long's it been?* Derek thought.

*Since what?*

Derek pointed at the sun, which made her even more emotional. She squeezed his body, trembling with feelings she thought were dead.

*A very long time.*

They were now on the starboard side of the ship. Lotti had retired to her bunk, and Jazz shadowed their hairy captain at the wheel. They were alone with little to do or say—an ocean surrounding them.

*Just because I became a vampire doesn't mean I stopped being... human,* she thought.

*What do you mean?*

Pax didn't actually know how to assemble it into sentences. It was always something she felt. The moment she awoke as a vampire, she knew she was different than before. A new confidence spilled out of her, as well as a coldness. Things she once feared seemed silly. Everything felt fresh, and yet she couldn't seem to shake the disastrous girl she started out as. The girl who couldn't wear dress shoes without bruising up her knees, or hold in obscenities when she got excited at fancy places. When a gentleman caller did forgive her awkward ways, it was usually because he had no intention of building a life with her—only a moment. As much as her immortality made her fearless, she still acted like someone terrified of being found out.

*Vampires aren't dead,* she thought. *Did you know that? I had to die to become one, but that's part of the evolution. My heart still beats, it just beats slower. My lungs still work, I just don't need the air, and my moral compass still points true, only now there's a lot more gray area to interpret.*

*My parents—*

*Derek, your parents are the unfortunate result of assholes. That's a quality found in every species.*

Derek pushed against this notion. She understood. He'd spent many years building up his hate for her kind. It'd take more than words. He needed time.

*Why did you become a vampire?*

The question caused a terrible pain in her gut. Images flashed and popped into Derek's brain as Pax found herself right back on the chilly street corner of Rose Alley and Price—running as fast as she could away from a quaint, three-room goldenrod cottage. She had been spending many secret nights there, entertaining a most handsome gentleman named Rufus Allensgate.

Rufus was a slick lawyer who'd recently moved from New York City to her small Virginian town of Falls Church. He owned an automobile, wore Italian leather shoes, and got angry if you asked him questions about his past. Pax was infatuated and had been seeing him biblically for some time. Rufus insisted they keep their relationship tight-lipped, as he was a society man and she was the daughter of a drunken cobbler.

*He murdered you?* Derek thought.

Pax fought hard not to bring up the images that would answer Derek's question, but anyone with a working mind knows that the moment you try not to think about something, you already have.

She had snuck into Rufus's house using the key hidden in a removable piece of wood from the south wall. She had seen Rufus use it once when she was supposed to be passed out in his 1914 Dudley Bug motorcar, after a long night at one of his infamous office parties. This particular evening Rufus had sent word that he had fallen ill and would not be able to see her. Paxton thought it mighty Christian of her to take him some fresh-baked bread and jam, as well as a good book she might read to him while he suffered. This act of kindness would surely elevate her status in the eyes of God.

*He wasn't sick,* Derek thought.

*He was sick all right,* she thought. *He was very, very sick.*

The long, oil-lit hallway of Rufus's house slammed into Derek's head, and they both watched as the memory of Pax tiptoed toward the bedroom.

The room glowed fiercely with candlelight through the cracked door. When she arrived, she could make out quiet whimpers and a good amount of scuffling. She thought he might be sicker than he had let on and was immediately glad she decided to come over. Opening the door, she parted her lips to speak, but the scene before her made her bite down on her tongue.

The dark oak room smelled of sour milk and shit. Rufus was in bed, naked and thrusting himself violently into another woman. She made no sound, but her eyes were open, glassy, and staring up at the ceiling. The sheets were soaked red with only patches of white left unsullied. A long dark slit circled around the woman's neck, and it suddenly became clear that her head was no longer attached to her body—it rested inches from her stump on the stained silk pillow, jostling slightly with each new thrust.

If this were not enough to give a girl a lifetime of nightmares, surrounding the bed—in the shape of a semicircle—sat seven other women in various stages of decomposition, all naked and headless. Their hands were positioned neatly on their laps as if politely judging the act happening before them.

Paxton's legs screamed at her to run, but her brain wasn't hearing it—the situation too farcical. It could not be believed.

Rufus paused when he finally noticed her, sweat dripping from his forehead onto the dead girl's chest. He locked eyes with Pax—murky blue orbs pushed toward the white by his soulless pupils. He looked past her at the cabinet against the wall where he kept many of his finer collections—antique metals that Pax never knew the purpose for and didn't care to ask. Items that dated back to the crusades—some rusted, some dented, all terrifying. Above them hung a shimmering broadsword he had imported from Europe. He claimed it once belonged to a king they called the Lionheart.

Rufus stood quickly and smashed the glass with his fist, reaching for the handle. Pax's brain finally sent the command to her legs, and she ran.

*Pax!*

Derek's voice sounded a million miles away as the memory skipped ahead. Pax lay on her back on Rose Alley staring up at the stars. Her head bounced off the uneven asphalt as Rufus—her sick, twisted lover—dragged her back toward the house, her chest bleeding from the cold steel that had just pierced her. Pax focused on the stars and imagined that her soul would get to travel past them on her way to Heaven, and she hoped that God would understand that she always meant well.

A gust of wind smacked her body, and the dragging stopped. Rufus yelped, followed by a thud. There was a brief pause before a sickening, sucking sound began to pulsate in Pax's ears. She tried to lift her head, but her wound held her down firmly. The late hour meant a slim chance of anyone wandering by—the tavern a good six blocks away. No one would discover her body until morning.

Suddenly, the floating image of a raven-haired woman with lips speckled in gore hovered above her. Pax laughed. The haunting woman could not have been real.

"I'll save you," her bloody angel whispered.

Clemencia Hellswood knelt over the dying cobbler's daughter and penetrated her neck with two sharp fangs. Pax gasped as her blood began to circulate through her veins at a rapid speed. The very last thing she remembered from her human life: the touch of Clem's hand against her cheek. It banished the fear from her body as she euphorically faded to black.

*Pax,* Derek thought more tenderly.

Derek had relived the moment alongside her, and she felt a strange sensation of comfort because of it. For the first time in her life, someone fully understood her pain—Derek hadn't *listened* to her tale of woe, he had *experienced* it. Her story, her pain, now also his. A rare gift that she imagined few people were ever privileged enough to receive—fiercely true empathy.

She could feel Derek's awkwardness as he attempted to figure out what to say, coming up short every time. She listened as he thought of something and then quickly wrote it off as too patronizing, silly, or just plain insensitive. It was the first time she felt him thinking about her as a person instead of a monster. It felt nice.

"Let's watch the rest of the sunset," she said.

"Okay," he said.

They stood in silence, minds calm, until the last sliver of orange fell to the other side of the world.

# CHAPTER 30

"He needed to eat!" Axe shouted.

His frustration levels since leaving the pet store rose dramatically when Socket began her unwarranted attack on his problem-solving skills.

"Would you rather I fed him the shop owner?"

"I'd rather you take a step back and look at the scared young man you have zipped up in a D-Bag," Socket said from the handle of his ax.

"He's a bloodsucker, Socket."

"He has triangle teeth and an allergy to sunlight."

"You're turning into a vampire sympathizer, and I don't like it."

"Did you know the Pillers employ vampires under a company named HAVF?"

"Half of what?"

"HAVF. Humans and Vampires Forever. It's a faux outreach program that draws vampires in."

"That's brilliant. Great way to sniff them out."

"Axe, these are people looking to reconcile."

"First off, vampires are not people. Second, I guarantee they are going to these meetings to meet humans they can eat."

"Who are you talking to?" Jordan asked from under his hood.

"My girl," Axe said. "Who's about to get powered down."

Socket made an audible sigh. "I was built with the capacity to learn, and what I've learned is that you're being manipulated by a group of small-minded bigots, and that seems just fine and dandy by you!"

Axe pressed and held the power button on the side of his ax. Socket's light blinked green, then shut off completely. She was supposed to be the one person who understood him, but lately he felt utterly alone in his own hate and misery. The Pillers weren't perfect, but they supplied Axe with a reason to keep going. To question them meant to question the reason.

"Did she leave?" Jordan asked.

"In here."

Axe pushed Jordan under a deep-red sign that read: *The Puzzle Box*. A little slogan beneath it: *A dark place to put the pieces back together.*

The Puzzle Box wasn't kidding when it put the word *dark* in its slogan. What few light sources there were seemed to magically illuminate small areas with no revealing bulb. Bar mirrors hung on the old, smoke-saturated walls, all of them cracked like a spider web—useless but still hanging.

Axe unzipped the hood on the D-Bag, allowing Jordan's head to poke out so as not to generate any questions.

"I never come here," Jordan said. "People say it's for freaks. We always drink at Prickley's. Lots of hot local tail there. Well, lots of local tail at least."

"Shut up. Sit," Axe commanded, pointing to an empty table.

Jordan obeyed, and Axe slapped a set of handcuffs around his wrist, attached the other end to the pole of the table.

"What's to stop me from using my vampire powers to break out of these?"

"The D-Bag's threaded with silver. Vampire kryptonite. Now shut up."

Jordan gave the cuffs a couple unsuccessful tugs and then looked up at Axe.

"Can you get me a Pigeon and Coke?"

Axe gave him a long, cold stare, then turned and approached the bar. He dug his fingers into the edge of the worn, wooden lip and pretended to wait patiently for the bartender, who took his sweet fucking time with another man's order.

"You look like a balsa wood cowboy," a voice next to him said.

Axe slowly turned his head to tell the owner of the voice to eat shit, only to have his tongue stumble at the sight of a pretty girl—blond hair, brown eyes, giant breasts, and a little extra chunk. Axe decided to let her live for being pleasing to his tired, rage-filled eyes.

"And what is a balsa wood cowboy?" he asked.

The girl smiled, showing off a set of gorgeous whites and just a little pink of her gums.

"Those old cowboy movies when they'd get into bar fights, and everyone went flying through banisters and tables like they were made of paper," the girl said in a slight Southern drawl.

"They were made of balsa wood," he said knowingly.

"That they were," she said with a heavy dash of flirtation.

Axe noted that it felt good to have a conversation with a beautiful woman that didn't involve a morality lesson for once. She downed the rest of her beer and then flagged the bartender.

"Jeremiah."

The bartender turned on a dime and headed straight for her.

"Same flavor, Gretel?"

"Nah, let's do shots of Stupid Pigeon. Me and my friend with no name here."

"Doubles," Axe said, showing off.

"Triples," Gretel responded in kind.

The bartender set up the glasses and poured an unhealthy amount of the barrel brown into them.

"Put it on my tab, babe," Gretel said.

Jeremiah nodded, then scurried off to serve someone else. Axe picked up his giant drink, and Gretel followed suit. She tilted it toward him.

"Know any cowboy adages?" she asked.

"There's only one way to both think and feel dead—put one in the heart and one in the head."

She touched her glass to his and took down the whiskey in one gulp. Axe hurried to catch up but found he had to take three large swallows to get it all down, and another six seconds to hold his "tough guy" face in position.

Gretel slammed down her glass and let out a burp worthy of a Japanese mutant lizard. Axe felt like a complete flunky when the whiskey began to creep back up his throat. He willed it down and forced a smile.

"Might as well been water," he said hoarsely.

She touched his shoulder and gave him another peek at the edge of her gums. Axe started to feel the whiskey-warms and regretted ordering the triple. He usually avoided drinking too much, as it tended to uproot the emotions he worked extremely hard to keep buried. Emotions got in the way of his anger, and his anger kept him alive.

"Is it still fermenting," Jordan yelled from the table, "or did you fall asleep?"

"Is that Jordan Stabbers?"

Axe couldn't be honest with her. Most of the world couldn't handle the truth about evil. He shielded them from it. He was a goddamn hero. He was also a terrible improvisor.

"I'm his friend," he stumbled. "From upstate. We're friends. Our moms used to own a bakery together, and Jordan and I would make experimental cookies in the back room. They were always a disaster though. That's friendship for you."

He cursed the whiskey and stood to leave before it became worse.

"What about Jordan's drink?"

"Huh? Oh. I…"

"Don't sweat it, cowboy. I'll get it and come say hi. Deal?"

He should have just told Gretel to go mind her own fucking business, but something had clogged his mean spirit and caused him to act like a real sap. He pushed off the bar and introduced himself.

"Axe."

"Gretel."

"Handle. Axe Handle."

"Gretel. Gretel Hellswood."

Axe stumbled back to the table and uncuffed his captive, sitting opposite him.

"Where's my drink?"

"We're childhood friends," Axe slurred. "Our moms owned a bakery together. Repeat."

"You're drunk!"

"REPEAT!"

"What for?"

"Because I lied to a very nice lady about the nature of our relationship, and she knows you…and she's bringing over drinks."

"Finally. Drinks."

Gretel set a round of shots in front of them and slapped Jordan on the back like an old pal.

"Howdy, Stabbers. Love the jumpsuit," she said.

"Hey, it's…you!"

"Gretel."

"Yes. I was getting to that," Jordan said.

"No you weren't. Hey, I got beers at the bar. Let me grab 'em."

She skipped off to retrieve the rest of their drinks. Jordan leaned into Axe.

"Holy shit, dude," Jordan whispered. "I fucking banged that fat chick like a year ago or something. Why did you invite her over here?!"

"She invited herself. And don't call her fat," Axe warned.

"She *is* fat."

"And you drink blood. Now pretend we're friends or I'll tie you to a flagpole at dawn."

"Naked?"

"Fucking naked!"

"Been there. Done that."

"You're a vampire! The sun will kill you."

"Riiight. Yes. Okay," remembered Jordan. "We're friends. But know that inside I hate you."

"I hate you too."

"Good."

"Beer!"

Gretel set three beers in front of them and pulled up a chair. Axe could not imagine a worse situation, and yet he found himself allowing it to unfold—even a little giddy when Gretel scooted in close to him. He caught a whiff of her perfume and dissected it into peach, sunflowers, and elm. He had been training for years to separate scents to be more like his enemy—The Art of War. Gretel lifted her shot glass in the air and pointed from Jordan to Axe.

"To bad sex, and hopefully better sex," she said.

Axe blushed and found that he was once again the last to drink his shot. The bar had been slowly filling up since they arrived. Axe hated crowds and began to eyeball everyone with suspicion. Gretel must have noticed, because she touched him on the shoulder.

"You're wound tight," she said. "I can hear it in your bones."

She looked up at Jordan with a sly grin.

"And I know your secret, Stabbers. I can smell it all over you." She gave him a small wink, and it made Axe jealous. She was different than most girls he met, and he found himself wanting to crack the mystery of why.

Jordan slammed his empty beer glass down on the table. "Let's do more of these."

~

A poorly built pyramid of shot glasses rattled as Axe slammed his hand down on the table and let out a boisterous laugh—the newly minted drinking buddies were growing into wonderfully stereotypical drunks. Somewhere between his sixth and seventh shot, karaoke had erupted into the packed bar. The whiskey paired perfectly with the atrocious singers, Jordan's ignorance, and Gretel's infectious presence.

"So, what do you do, cowboy?" Gretel asked.

"Nothing," Axe said, quicker than he should have.

"You don't do anything?"

"He's a hunter," Jordan said loudly.

"*Head* hunter," Axe stressed. "I find people work. In boring offices. Sometimes I wear a tie."

Axe grew frustrated with himself. He had only flirted with Gretel out of boredom, and because Socket was being a pest.

He wasn't actually going to be intimate with another human being. That was for everyone else. He was here to protect people like her, so they could live normal lives and develop healthy relationships. He needed to refocus and get his head back in the game.

"Gretel, you're a very nice girl. I know there are some moves I could perform on you that would cause you to change religions, but I'm here because—"

"Next up, Jordan Stabbers and Axe Handle," echoed a voice.

The sound of his name amplified over the speaker system stopped him cold. The karaoke host, who had been getting on his last nerve all night, searched the room.

"Looking for Jordan Stabbers and Axe Handle. Jordan Stabbers? Axe Handle? Are these fake names? These are fake names," the host said into his microphone.

Jordan leapt from his seat and ran up to the small area designated as a stage by a shitty spotlight. He took the mic from the host and looked out into the crowd.

"Ladies and gentlemen," Jordan said. "I've been having a real shitty day at the hand of my very good friend, Axe Handle. I think the least he can do is get up here and embarrass himself for my pain."

Gretel grabbed Axe by his arm and pulled him up. He allowed her to lead him down the aisle and into the spotlight with Jordan. Gretel leaned in and whispered in his ear.

"Hope you like the King."

Someone handed Axe a second microphone, and before he could slaughter everyone in the room and save himself the shame, music began to play. He knew the song the moment he heard it, because he was, in fact, a fan of the King.

For the last hour, they had been enduring the uncompromising murder of song after song by no-talent hacks screeching into a microphone in front of an unresponsive audience. Suddenly, Jordan Stabbers silenced them all—his voice cool and controlled, but not devoid of emotion.

It was one of Axe's favorite Elvis songs, and tonight it stabbed him directly in the heart. Between the whiskey, Gretel, and too much interaction with his own species, Axe lifted the microphone to his lips and took on the second verse of "Loving Arms."

# CHAPTER 31

Derek took a long sip of the beer Captain Grimmerstone had offered him just before everyone retired for the evening. He had felt Pax drift off into slumber about thirty minutes ago (an odd feeling, someone falling asleep inside your body), but the many springs in the thin mattress kept him awake as he constantly shifted his weight to avoid them.

For being one hell of an eyesore, the *Bitch* handled the waters like a pro. Derek allowed his body to be one with the motion, and he suddenly realized it was the first time he'd felt peaceful in years. He'd gotten used to being alone, and even enjoyed it. Now there was someone inside of him, affecting his moods, thoughts, and even limbs. Although Pax happened to be the very creature he vowed to wipe out, he could not help but realize how similar they actually were—two lonely souls fighting against anyone who tried to get too close. Anyone who threatened to expose them for the cowards they truly were. His thoughts drifted to the crooked smile she wore the night she came over to buy a cage. It made him grin.

Derek's blissful buzz didn't last long, however, when he remembered it would all come to an end when they reached the island. She would leave him. He would go back to Rainy Mood to face the reputation he had created, the brother he had killed, and the man in the mirror he no longer knew.

All his thoughts, worries, and misgivings began to blend together into a phantasmagoria. The room became blurred, the creaks in the ship's hull amplified. Derek felt himself losing consciousness. He had just enough time to consider two options: his brain had finally given up on trying to house two people, or he had been drugged.

~

He regained consciousness dangling over the icy Atlantic Ocean in a giant fishing net. The Salty Dog stood on the deck of his ship and jabbed Derek with the handle end of a harpoon, his laugh low and manic.

"Good midnight to ya, lad," the giddy captain said.

Derek should have trusted his gut. He searched his mind for Pax but could feel that she was still unconscious.

"You drugged me," Derek shouted over the lap of the waves.

"Aye."

Derek struggled in the net, hoping to find a weak spot. He exhausted himself almost immediately. He needed to access Pax's vampire strength.

"So, what is this?" Derek said, playing it cool. "Are you robbing us?"

"Lord, no," said Grimmerstone. "We're going fishin', my boy."

Suddenly, it was as obvious as this hairy man was crazy. Derek was bait.

"Seems a bit criminal and over-the-top," Derek said. "Tuna is both legal and preferred by sharks."

The captain laughed again. "We ain't fishin' for sharks."

*PAX! PAX! PAX!*

He felt her move—the fog inside him lifting.

"There's a menace in these waters," Grimmerstone said. "A beast that lives in the unexplored deep. Its skin glows bright like a Christmas tree—its hunger glows even brighter."

"I'm pretty sure hunger doesn't glow," Derek said sarcastically. At this point what did he have to lose?

"It has a terrible mouth, filled with terrible teeth."

"This is a terrible story, and I'm terribly bored."

Grimmerstone smiled and tugged at the hair on his cheek.

"Sounds like you're ready to meet…the Jollywog."

"I get it," Derek said. "You're a crazy person chasing your *Moby Dick*."

"Who?" Grimmerstone asked, seeming authentically confused.

"Are you serious? You act like a stereotypical pirate captain and you don't know *Moby Dick*?"

"I don't socialize much due to the hair condition."

"He's a whale."

"I don't know a lot of whales."

"It's a fictional whale. From the novel. Moby Dick."

"Reading bores me eyes."

"But who isn't familiar with the book?"

"Captain L. John Grimmerstone, that's who!"

"I thought it was H. John Grimmerstone."

"Huh?"

"That's how you introduced yourself. H. Not L."

"Who be you, the alphabet detective?"

"The what?"

"Enough with the chitting," cried the captain. "I've got me a monster to catch, a haircut to get, and magazine covers to grace."

*PAX! Wake up now!*

Captain Grimmerstone unsheathed a thin cutlass from his side and swatted at the rope wrapped around the ships pulley system. The net released and plummeted toward the ocean. Derek felt his stomach leave his body, and Pax become fully conscious.

"Are we fallin—" she began.

The net hit the water. The weights tied to the bottom pulled it down fast. Before Derek could get a good breath in, he was under the icy black.

*The fuck?!* Pax screamed inside his head.
*Captain threw us overboard. We're bait.*
*Okay. Give me full control of the lungs.*
*Done.*

Derek waited for Pax to perform some kind of underwater breathing trick, but it never came. Instead he quickly realized that he didn't need to breath at all. His body remained calm and breathless.

The net sank deeper until the rope above went taught. The two trapped souls floated in liquid darkness—God only knew what horrible creatures might be swimming around them.

*So, what are we bait for?* Pax asked, filling the time before death.

*The Jollywog?*

*Ah.*

*You know it?*

*Heard of it. Don't know anyone who's actually seen it though*, she thought.

*Can you break these ropes?*

*No. Rope is worse than metal.*

Derek felt her fangs lower out of his gums.

*What I can do is nibble my way through.*

Something large and curious swam by, inches from them. A brief warmth rushed over their body—the equivalent of a gust of wind under water. Derek gave Pax permission to gnaw away. The rope tasted like dead fish, and the saltwater made him gag. Strand by strand the rope started to thin.

The net swayed in the water from the force of another large creature as it passed closely by. Derek had hoped his eyes would adjust, and then remembered there was no light to allow that to happen. Something bumped directly into the net, and Derek screamed, swallowing ocean.

*Please hurry*, he thought to Pax.

She continued to bite at the rope, but Derek couldn't shake the feeling that even if they escaped their linked prison, they would still be in the middle of the ocean, and more vulnerable than before.

# CHAPTER 32

Axe held down the button on his weapon. It blinked green three times, then bathed the handle in a soft blue light. The color comforted him. It meant he wasn't alone. He'd arrived back at the motel almost an hour ago. A whiskey headache had developed, and he'd been staring at his laptop's screen in a daze. So far, he had only managed to type out an email address: piller@humansagainstinhumans.com.

Jordan sat on the bed, still in the D-Bag with the hood down. He flipped through channels on the shitty square television, causing a break in Axe's concentration with each click of the remote. Axe had been able to convince Nun and Chuck to add a second room to the budget since they now had a prisoner, but he wasn't sure if his lodging situation had actually improved. He'd never spent this much time with a vampire—alive at least.

"Dude, what was up with you and that one girl tonight?" Jordan blurted out, never taking his eyes off the television.

"Gretel?"

"You one hundred percent could have hit that."

Axe sighed and stared once more at the blank page of white pixels.

"What are you writing?"

Fed up, Axe closed the lid of the laptop and turned to the vampire on the bed.

"Why is it you act like any normal douchebag on the street?" Axe asked.

"As opposed to what?" Jordan said. "And, hey!"

"You're a vampire."

"Yeah."

"Act like it."

"Okay."

Jordan continued to flip channels. Axe stood and grabbed him by the collar, pushed him hard into the mattress.

"I am not someone you brush off, boy," he snarled. "If you have no useful information for me on your brother's whereabouts or where I might find some evil in this town, then I have no other choice but to take you straight to black."

There he was! The old Axe. A monster's worse nightmare. A man unafraid to face his own mortality by threatening those who had none. A surge of energy rushed through his body as he readied himself to get bloody.

"Who's Gretel?"

Axe had forgotten he'd powered Socket back on.

"Who said that?" Jordan asked.

Axe's eyeballs pulsated with anger. He let go of Jordan, removed the ax from his side, and raised it to eye level.

"No one."

"Your ax is your girlfriend?"

"You met a girl tonight?" Socket said.

"I met a lot of people tonight. I questioned a lot of people. I'm here to hunt a nest, remember?"

He hated fighting with her, especially when he'd been drinking. She was too smart and too calm.

"This is what I have been trying to push you toward," she said sweetly.

"What does that mean?"

"I want you to experience people."

"I experience you. That's all I need."

"People made of organs. People who make mistakes. People who get embarrassed when their feelings begin to show."

"You're my girl. Period."

He meant it. He would jump off the end of the Earth for her. Things with Socket had always been perfect—the right amount of conversation, company, and fucking. It had all been programmed to his liking. With Gretel, however, things were unpredictable, chaotic, and terrifying. It felt like someone had cut him open and shoved an important clue to a mystery inside his body, then sewed him back up before he could get a look at what it was.

"You have an ax girlfriend," Jordan marveled.

Socket glowed bright, the handle of the ax solid blue.

"I love you as much as a sentient machine can, but it will never be enough to save you from yourself," she continued. "If you want to kill vampires that are an actual threat, then I'm here for you, but I can't let you murder innocent creatures like this scared kid here."

"I'm twenty," Jordan said. "Do you have any hot weapon friends?"

Axe tipped his head to the ceiling and closed his eyes. The darkness comforted him, and he imagined himself back home on his silk sheets. He needed to do the job so he could get back to that bed. He needed to fuck, smoke, and fall asleep.

"Let's make a deal, vampire," Axe said, controlling his temper.

"Don't call me that."

"Okay. Let's make a deal, Jordan."

"I'm listening."

"I let you out of that D-Bag, and you help me find the vampire nest."

"I told you, I don't know any other vampires. I woke up like this!"

"That's why we're gonna let other vampires find *you*."

~

Jordan was relieved to be free of the D-Bag. He had no idea how much it suppressed his vampire strength. The world at night, sharper than any high-definition movie he'd ever seen, and the smells! The day bag had hindered his senses, but now aromas flooded up his nostrils from every angle. The leaves on the trees, residual tire rubber on the pavement, and the paint on the buildings.

Jordan wasn't sure he could trust Axe entirely, but the thought of finding others like himself made it worth the risk. Axe seemed to be a professional vampire finder of sorts, so sticking with him might be his best option. Not to mention Jordan secretly enjoyed his company.

There were plenty of supernatural hot spots people whispered about. Locals always made a big stink about Saint Chester's being haunted, but Jordan preferred the tales of ghouls over ghosts, which were said to wander the old cemetery, waiting patiently for the dead to be buried so they could feast. He'd been to the Neverwake Cemetery plenty of times to drink and screw. He'd never seen a ghoul, but then those were his human days.

A pretty serious metal bolt kept the cemetery's front gate from being entered. Axe stepped up and drew his weapon, but Jordan stopped him, the perfect time to test out the strength surging throughout his muscles. He slipped his fingers through the metal bars and jerked his arms back with all his might. The bolt snapped liked a peppermint stick, propelled itself out of the gate's hole, and smacked Axe on the forehead.

Jordan marveled at his accomplishment.

"I'm like Superman," he said to himself as he touched the *S* that wasn't actually on his chest.

The gate squeaked loudly when he pushed it open.

"Do you smell anything?" Axe asked.

"Like what?"

"Like ghouls."

"I don't know what ghouls smell like. I don't know if ghouls are even real."

"Figure it out," Axe grumbled.

They wandered deeper into the cemetery, past rows of faded tombstones that dated back to the 1800s. Neverwake was a haunting piece of land, with rolling hills and a few scattered, leafless trees. Jordan had never bothered to look around. He always came to raise hell, not admire its macabre beauty. Suddenly he found a great appreciation for the haphazard position of the gravestones that still felt orderly.

A pair of headlights appeared over the hill. Everyone instinctively ducked behind a large elm tree. They watched as the car passed by the Neverwake gate and under the main arch. Whether you were coming or going, Hushed Willow Road was the only way in or out of town. Mountains and forest surrounded the rest, so unless you were on foot, you were shit out of luck. Jordan always found it a bit creepy that the first and last thing anyone saw was the dead. *Welcome to Rainy Mood! Here's our dead! Thanks for visiting Rainy Mood! Don't forget, everyone dies!*

Jordan stepped out from the tree and scanned the area.

"Hello? Any ghouls here?"

Jordan knew he sounded like an idiot but didn't really know what to do.

"I'm Jordan. Jordan the vampire. I'm looking for others like myself."

He turned to Axe and shrugged. He was about to suggest they try Saint Chester's, when something cold and prickly licked the back of his neck. Jordan spun around, then almost fell over backward when he found himself face to grotesque face with a skeletal-like creature. Tight skin clung to its skull like wet paper, the areas around its eyes and mouth torn to expose the dirty white bone beneath. The orbs in its eyeholes were almost solid black, with a pinprick of white acting as a pupil. The creature's body hunched, bones occasionally breaking through the fragile skin.

"Hello, vampire," it said in a low, proper voice.

Jordan screamed at the horrible sight and hid behind Axe. His large new friend didn't even blink.

"We're looking for a nest," Axe said.

The ghoul reached up and grabbed the top of Axe's head with its bony fingers. A quick, violent tug downward removed all of Axe's flesh, muscles, and organs, as if they were simply the Velcro pants of a male stripper. Axe's jaw dropped open, not out of shock, but because he had no more muscle to hold it up. His legs buckled, and he fell to the ground a helpless skeleton.

"Axe!" Socket shouted.

She burned away her soft blue hue, replaced with a hot

EVERYDAY MONSTERS

orange. She lifted herself into the air and barreled toward the ghoul who, with little effort, plucked her out of mid-swing and buried her blade into the soft cemetery ground.

"Why'd you tear my friend's skin off?" Jordan cried.

"I do not associate with the living," the ghoul said.

"You could have told him to wait somewhere else," Jordan said. "You didn't have to kill him."

The ghoul dropped Axe's flesh sack of blood and organs at the skeleton's feet.

"Relax," he said. "A ghoul cannot kill. Only incapacitate."

The ghoul seemed to defy his horrific appearance with a distinguished quality that reminded Jordan of the actors on those boring BBC shows his mom used to love.

"That looks painful."

"Most likely," the ghoul said.

The strange creature stretched out its thin arm, motioned for Jordan to follow him to one of the mausoleums.

"When our business is complete, I shall return his insides and outsides," it said with an odd touch of class.

Jordan looked down at Socket for reassurance.

"Go," she said. "But come back."

Jordan nodded and followed the ghoul to the rusted door.

"Where are you taking me?"

The ghoul looked up at him, the corner of its flesh-torn mouth turned upward in a smile.

"Belgium."

# CHAPTER 33

Pax could smell the great white that circled them. She usually enjoyed a glass of shark's blood—at the safety of a dinner table of course. It would often be served during fancy occasions at Hellswood Manor—Christmas, Thanksgiving, Halloween. There was a sharp, bitter quality to the predator that screamed seasonal—a dangerous, delicious blend of warmth and cold in a single beast.

She had bitten through two links of rope already and hoped that the third would be enough to squeeze through. The gill-slit predator continued to knock into the net and test it for weak spots—no doubt wanting to sink its teeth into the ooey-gooey mortal center.

*Please hurry*, Derek begged.

Pax continued to gnaw, still not convinced they wouldn't be torn to pieces the minute they were out. Vampire strength would be hindered under the water, but if she could rip out an eye or crunch its nose, they could stand a chance.

The shark seemed to tire of its casual bump and swim and performed its biggest attack yet. It took the lower end of the net into its jagged mouth and scraped Derek's shoulder. Pax could feel the temperature of the water around them change and knew Derek's blood would only attract more sharks.

Suddenly, a low pulse blew through them, followed by what sounded like a roar. The shark let go of the net, and Pax and Derek floated quietly in the darkness. They braced for another attack, but it never came. The shark had been spooked away, and that did not comfort her.

*What was that? My body is tingling,* Derek thought.

He was right. Whatever the pulse was, it left Derek's flesh on pins and needles. Off in the distance Pax saw a pinprick of color, like a single star on a moonless night. As it grew closer, it seemed to change colors. What started out as a soft red folded beautifully into yellow, then blue, and then green. Pax couldn't take Derek's eyes off the hypnotic glow.

When the strange orb drew closer, she noticed two giant fins pushing gently forward through the water. Pax realized she had been trapped in a stare for some time now, unable to remove her eyes from the approaching object. The creature's ever-changing colors had paralyzed them.

The closer it swam, the more details Pax could make out. A small, bump-covered head that extended out into a thin snout. An exceedingly long neck caused the little head to swish back and forth, like a pipe cleaner attached with string. The body was where it carried all of its bulk: giant and bulbous, avocado in shape but smooth like glass. Its fins rose up effortlessly in the heavy water and then pushed down and back to propel itself smoothly. A double-humped tail swished back and forth behind the beast, steering it perfectly straight—a gorgeous creature that illuminated the space around itself with the burning, color-changing beacon of their demise. The Jollywog was real, and they wouldn't live to convince anyone otherwise.

The graceful creature lined up its massive mouth with the net, then swallowed them whole. As they passed through the Jollywog's throat, they found themselves assaulted by a thousand different strobes of color. The effects grew in speed and intensity, which eventually blinded them. Their body began to tingle—at any moment it would shut down completely. Pax realized this might be the very last moment she would get and wanted desperately to make it count.

*Derek.*

*Pax?*

*I—*

# CHAPTER 34

The door to their quarters was locked from the outside. Jazz could hear voices screaming at each other, but the tiny rusted-out hole in the wall was too high to see out of. She rose up on her tiptoes, but only sank deeper into the mattress she stood on.

"I can't see out this hole," Jazz said.

"You're too fat to see out that hole," Lotti said, her arms folded.

"I'm too *short*," corrected Jazz. "What the fuck does being fat have to do with it?"

"I'm sure it does somehow."

"How were we ever friends?"

"If wishes were horses."

Jazz ignored Lotti's ill-fitted proverb and glanced back up at the hole. She had to see what was happening but wasn't thrilled about revealing her biggest secret to her nemesis. She guessed being dead would be worse.

Using her right pointer and middle finger, accompanied by the thumb, Jazz pressed in on her right eye, folded up the lid, and grabbed hold of the white. With great care, she removed her eyeball from its socket to reveal the dark hole she'd been left with a few years prior. Jazz held her eye up to the hole in the wall and positioned the pupil to face out. Her left hand retreated to the pocket of her jeans and fiddled with a small square attached to her keychain. Pressing it, the flat back of the eyeball popped to life and displayed a photographic image on a small screen.

"What's that?" Lotti said. "Is that your eyeball?!"

"Nope," Jazz said. "That went missing. This is my spy-ball."

She looked back at Lotti, who fiddled nervously with her fedora, pulling the brim down over her eyes.

"I have a fake eye," Jazz reiterated.

"Yeah, I can see that! That doesn't mean it should *ever* leave your skull, Jazz. It's fucking gross for the people around you. In this case, me."

Jazz hopped off the bed and frowned.

"You're not curious how I lost it?"

"No. I'm sure it's a boring, gross story, and all I want to do is get off this ship before Captain Hairball bursts in here to show me his red rocket."

Jazz studied the prissy teen for an uncomfortably long moment. Lotti's reaction struck her as odd. After all, this was a girl who sawed off a dead werewolf's penis. Surely she could handle a glass eye.

"Woke up randomly in the hospital one night," Jazz said. "My whole eyeball missing. Doctors said someone dumped me out in front of the ER and sped off. Weird, right?"

Lotti stared at the damp floor and kicked a baby crab away from her shoe. Suddenly, Jazz's recurring nightmare started to make sense. Lotti, the martini, the olive. Her subconscious trying to remind her of something—the actual event that inspired the dream?

"A funny fact just popped into my head," Jazz said, sounding more and more accusatory. "The time I lost my eye was also the same time we stopped talking. When Charlotte became Lotti."

"So?" Lotti said, the volume of her voice on the rise.

Jazz hadn't considered it before, but up until now she hadn't understood the true nature of Lotti's transformation.

"The witch," Jazz whispered. "You needed my eye for your spell!" she yelled.

Lotti finally looked up, her face guilt-red.

"You selfish, back-stabbing bitch."

More screams from Derek snapped Jazz back to the urgent problem at hand. She was furious and hurt, but there would be a more appropriate time to react to this new discovery. Right now, she had to figure a way out of this mess.

Jazz looked at the screen on the back of the spy-ball—at the photo she took through the rusted hole. The pixels weren't sharp, but it was easy to see that Captain Grimmerstone had imprisoned Derek in a fishing net.

Jazz sighed, popped the eye back in her socket, then scanned the room for inspiration. She found it in a tennis-ball-size hole in the ground—a foot from the bed.

"Grab the end," Jazz said.

"What for?"

"Exercise," she snapped.

Lotti huffed and grabbed the end of the bed.

"Pull the back leg over that hole."

The girls gave it several tugs. The sound of the metal pierced their ears as it scraped along the rusted floor. The back leg slid perfectly into the hole, offsetting the bed by a few inches.

"Remember when we used to have sleepovers?" Jazz said as she pressed her hands on the mattress.

"Yes," Lotti said with a bit of reservation.

"Remember the marshmallow star-kiss game?"

Lotti nodded weakly. Jazz indicated toward the dirty mattress.

"It's a giant marshmallow, Char. Let's kiss some stars."

Jazz climbed up and steadied herself. The bed's legs wobbled, and the floor beneath her moaned.

"This doesn't seem safe," Lotti said.

"Neither is staying in this room."

She held out her hand, and Lotti accepted it, stepping up on the bed. The two ex-friends looked into each other's eyes and jumped into the air. They focused their weight toward the leg over the hole, and soon, small hops turned into big jumps. They bounced in perfect unison, surprised by how much air the old springs allowed them.

A flood of childhood memories leaked into Jazz's brain. She tipped her head toward the ceiling and imagined the night full of stars just beyond the rusted beams of the ship. The floor gave in, and the bed's leg fell hard through the hole, ripping open the floor and sending the girls tumbling down their marshmallow and onto coils of rotted rope in the hull below.

A few short minutes later, the girls poked their heads out of a square door at the stern of the ship. Lotti climbed out first, then offered her hand to Jazz. The moon shined bright enough to show an endless horizon of black water, and Jazz knew that she might need to kill a man tonight in order to survive. She grabbed an air horn off the wall, handed it Lotti.

Lotti looked at Jazz like a deer that had just been told it won the lottery.

"Use it on the captain. When he's disoriented, I'll bury this…" Jazz grabbed a small fire ax off the wall and held it up in faux bravery. "…deep into his skull."

"And he dies!"

"Yeah, okay, don't be so excited."

Jazz led the slow charge to the bow of the ship. The girls peeked around the starboard wall to find Grimmerstone expelling a series of hoots and swears as he manned a large pulley system. Something excited him in the water below. Derek and the net were nowhere to be found.

"I see you, ya electric devil!" the captain hollered.

He fired an oversized harpoon into the ocean. A moment later there was a muffled explosion followed by a spray of water. A large bellow came up from the ocean. Whatever he was hunting, it was big and angry.

"He's got explosive harpoons and we got a horn and a hatchet," Lotti whispered.

"We have the element of surprise. Come on."

She placed one foot silently in front of the other and began the slow creep toward the captain.

Grimmerstone fired another harpoon—a blast of water followed and soaked him on the deck. The wind caught his stink and pushed the scent of wet dog right into Jazz's face.

The girls found themselves directly behind the madman as he loaded up another explosive harpoon, which Jazz could now see were just grenades duct-taped to metal spears, some truly ghetto weaponry that could easily backfire and blow up the entire ship.

Jazz turned to Lotti and gave her a nod. Lotti nodded back, then remained still. Frustrated, Jazz pointed at the air horn and then to the captain, mouthing the word *NOW*. Lotti raised the horn, and Jazz gripped the handle of her hatchet, mentally preparing her ears for the loud blast. It did not come. Instead, Lotti rammed the butt-end of the horn hard into the back of the captain's head.

Grimmerstone stumbled forward against the rail, then turned to see the girls. A wicked, hairy grin pushed its way across his face. Jazz stared at Lotti, dumbfounded.

"You were supposed to use the air horn!"

"I did!"

"The *air horn* part of it!"

Jazz turned back to the captain and raised her hatchet. Grimmerstone grabbed hold of her wrist before she could even start her journey forward. His breath blasted her in the face—crawfish and cottage cheese.

He bent her wrist back, and Jazz fell to her knees. The hatchet hit the ship's floor with a clang.

"The Jollywog is a leery creature," he said. "Perhaps I can lure her closer to the surface with a couple of apples."

"I'm more of a banana," Lotti said, just before she blasted the air horn directly into the captain's ear.

Grimmerstone released Jazz and howled in pain as he stumbled back against the railing of the bow.

"Marshmallow clothesline!" Lotti shouted.

Jazz got to her feet and grabbed hold of Lotti's left wrist with her right hand. The girls pushed forward on the balls of their feet, lined up their connected arms with the captain's neck, and screamed as they made contact. The disoriented dog-man flipped into the air, tumbled over the side of his own ship and into the ocean below.

Jazz and Lotti fell back hard—their arms throbbed in pain. The waves from the commotion calmed, and the ship fell back into a steady pattern.

"What was our obsession with marshmallows?" Jazz said with a smirk.

"What was our obsession with wrestling?" Lotti added.

They sat a moment more in silence, exhausted.

"Pax!" Lotti said and jumped to her feet.

"Shit! Derek!" Jazz added.

They grabbed the ropes attached to the pulley and began to haul in the net. It ran quickly and with great ease through their fingers, which put an ill feeling in Jazz's stomach.

"They're gone!" Lotti screamed.

All they had pulled up was the end of a frayed rope. No net. No Derek. No Pax. Jazz looked down into the water—black as tar, sans a tiny dot of glowing light.

Jazz's heart skipped a beat. The last couple days had opened her up to a whole new world, and she couldn't help but feel a real loss for her supernatural mates.

"You know how to drive a ship?" Lotti asked.

"I think you steer a ship."

"We're fucked, aren't we?"

"Yeah. We're fucked."

The ship bobbed quietly in the night, two future skeletons its only remaining crew.

## CHAPTER 35

"Is this where Dracula lives?"

The ghoul placed a fine china teacup on a dusty wood table and carefully poured scalding water into it.

"Dracula is a work of fiction," the ghoul said.

The interior of the castle's main room was gigantic. It reminded Jordan of when his mom got bit by the religion bug for two months. She dragged him and Derek with her every Sunday to the cold, spacious worshipping grounds referred to as the Catholic Church. The castle's main room alone was six times the size, but the vibe was similar—spooky, impressive, and boring.

Large gray pillars rose thirty feet in the air, ornate stone vines wrapping around them like hungry snakes. Muck-covered windows let in tiny streams of light that highlighted the cracks in the floor. A dusty throne with carved cherubs, horses, and lizards perched itself on top of a small flight of marble steps—a huge crack down the center. Jordan sat at a large wooden banquet table where merry men once had merry moments. Those men were now long gone, leaving only Jordan Stabbers to drink tea with a skeleton that pretended to wear flesh.

They had arrived through a weapons closet just down the hall from where they were now. Jordan had stepped into the mausoleum in the Neverwake Cemetery, witnessed a blinding flash of light, and suddenly found himself here.

"Where are we again?" Jordan asked.

"Namur, Belgium. Molinda Castle. Eighteenth century. Oh, we're not *in* the eighteenth century, the castle was built then. Long since abandoned."

"How…did…"

"We get here? Never knew a ghoul?"

"I just became a vampire yesterday."

"My. Well then, I am Greggles, the ghoul of Neverwake."

Jordan took a sip of his tea, then pulled away quickly. It had always been his nature to drink from hot beverages too soon and burn the shit out of his lips. He was pleasantly surprised to find that, although the tea was scorching hot, his mouth remained unharmed. Vampire powers.

"What are ghouls?" Jordan asked. "Are they like ghosts or something?"

"Do I look like a ghost?"

"You look like a zombie."

Greggles's face soured. He raised his bony hand in the air and let it swing hard across Jordan's face, smashing his teacup in the process.

"Dude! My tea!"

"Ghouls are sophisticated creatures who take nutrients from the dead in order to keep watch over the living," Greggles said. "We guard what is most quiet in the world, for it is in the silence where evil creeps."

"So, you're a good guy?" Jordan said.

"I'm no guy at all."

Bored out of his skull, Jordan's mind started to wander as he listened to a rat squeak somewhere on the grounds.

"What are you doing?" asked the ghoul, a bit annoyed.

"Huh?"

"You're off somewhere else."

"How'd we get here so fast? Magic?"

Greggles scoffed at the word and then delicately lifted his teacup to where lips would be if he had them. His bottom teeth clinked gently against the porcelain as he poured the liquid carefully down his throat.

"I don't deal in magic. I deal in power. I need not summon

my skills, they are a part of me."

"So, you can teleport?"

"We ghouls pass through the doorways of the dead."

"You jump from cemetery to cemetery?"

"If there are bodies below, away we go."

"That rhymed."

"It was meant to."

"Nice."

Jordan looked around the lonely room, curious what sort of graveyard they were in. He remembered from school that many castles buried their prominent figureheads in crypts below.

"Are there others like me in Rainy Mood?" he asked.

Greggles looked at him preciously.

"I do so enjoy baby vampires," he said. "Ignorant to your potential, but excited to discover it. I have a long history with the Hellswoods."

This caught Jordan's attention. He knew of the Hellswoods. They were that odd family that lived in that odd house over the river and through the woods. They mostly kept to themselves, but every now and then a few would be spotted in town at one of the two bars. Gretel was a Hellswood. He always had trouble remembering her first name, but he knew every time he saw her that she was a Hellswood, because he had always wanted to fuck her sisters.

"Wait. Shut up," Jordan said. "The Hellswoods are vampires? So, Gretel Hellswood is…I slept with a vampire before I was a vampire? And even more perplexing…there are fat vampires?"

~

Axe couldn't stop pulling at his skin after the ghoul reunited him with his skeleton. It felt a little like his body shrunk in the wash just enough to be annoying. Jordan bounced ahead of him, a new spring in his step. The crickets were just finishing up their encore as dawn drew near.

Jordan led Axe out the main gate of the cemetery, then turned off Hushed Willow Road and onto a dark side street.

Axe stopped, done with following and ready to lead.

"Where are we going, Jordan?"

"I found others like me."

"You found a nest."

"Sure, man. If that's what you call it. Sounds more like a group of insects though."

"Where is it?! Who is it?!"

He hated sounding so desperate, but this day had done a real number on him and he just wanted it over. Jordan frowned, and Axe sensed further annoyance in his future.

"Axe, man…I know you want me to lead you there so you can…well, you haven't really told me exactly what you want, but it feels bad. Your intentions feel bad. So…Axe, I think we should…part ways."

Axe dropped his cigarette on the ground and circled Jordan, his frustration levels at a high boil. In what world did a douchebag baby vampire break up with *him*? This whole day had thrown him completely off balance. The Puzzle Box, Gretel, the song—Axe found a weakness growing inside him. He was uncomfortable with his sensitive side and wished it nothing but death.

Axe grabbed Jordan by the scruff of his shirt, pulled him in close.

"We had a deal, vampire."

"I'm sorry. These people can help me understand myself better. But if you stick around town, let's totally go back to the Puzzle Box and rock that mic! I'll even get Gretel to come since we're technically family now."

Jordan didn't seem to understand what he just gave away. A small laugh escaped Axe's lips as he attempted to keep his cool.

"Gretel Hellswood?"

"Yeah, man. Gretel Hells—"

Jordan froze, and Axe could tell he had finally figured out what a gigantic idiot he was. Gretel Hellswood. She. Was. A. Vampire. A nuclear bomb went off in Axe's head.

Earlier that day he caught himself imagining what it would be like to kiss her. Now, all he could feel was her fangs pressed hard and sharp against his lips. He could taste his own blood as they pricked the flesh. His world swirled out of control, and Axe began to fall apart.

From within his mental breakdown, Axe could sense himself take action. He felt his arm reach underneath his coat—a million miles away. He saw Jordan's eyes, wide as the Grand Canyon, as Axe plunged a wooden stake directly into his heart. It seemed like an hour before he clawed his way back out in front of the situation, but in reality, it had been a few seconds.

Jordan gasped, and Axe could tell from his expression that he was surprised to still be alive. He wasn't yet aware that a stake in the heart only meant paralysis.

"WHAAAT…THE…FUUUUUCK…?" Jordan screamed. His eyes rolled around like spinning marbles.

Axe looked over the pathetic vampire, the wood jutting dramatically out of his chest. The lyrics to "Loving Arms" tried to push their way into his head, but he stomped them down hard.

"You are no longer useful to me, vampire."

"I thought we were cool, man! This is not cool, man!"

He raised the ax in his hand, ready to slice a home run with Jordan's head.

"Aren't we friends?!" Jordan cried.

His words struck Axe. No living thing had ever referred to him as a friend before. He had plenty of enemies and a few associates. Angie and Bill were his mentors. Socket maybe, but she'd been programmed for that. He lowered his weapon. The hate inside him throbbed, and for the first time he couldn't help but feel like it was partly manufactured.

Sheathing the ax, he looked Jordan in the eyes.

"You're right. We are," Axe said.

Jordan sighed, the panic leaving his face.

"And I don't kill my friends," Axe continued.

Jordan smiled, his fangs breaking the gum line.

"I let the sun take care of that."

Axe turned his back to the vampire and began his walk up the road. Jordan's smile dropped. He tried to squirm out of his frozen state.

"You fucking asshole!" he shouted at his cowardly executioner.

Axe kept his back to Jordan but offered him one last sentence to chew on.

"By the way, vampires are *insects*."

# CHAPTER 36

A canopy of lush, green branches offered speckled shade from the sun on high. Pax was the first one awake in the body, but Derek stirred quickly after she started moving him to sit up. Neither said anything right away, as they were too busy scanning the dense forest and multicolored flowers. A soothing creek cut through the trees that smoothed out rocks into perfect circles—a place straight out of a childhood fairytale.

"Last thing I remember was being eaten by the Jollywog," Derek said. "Did I miss a step?"

"Apparently a big one," Pax said, just as confused.

An oversized dragonfly zipped by their heads, and for the first time Pax noticed all the animals. Furry creatures no bigger than cats darted between ferns, their sharp, pointed tails erect with curiosity. An array of neon insects spun around in the air like schools of fish, stopping mid-flight, then suddenly continuing their dance.

"I'm not sure how many more times I can handle dying… and then not dying," Pax said.

There didn't seem to be any path or road, so Derek and Pax wandered through the thick flora in hopes they might emerge somewhere helpful.

"Is this what it's like being a vampire?" Derek asked. "One big overblown adventure after the next?"

"Fuck no. I barely leave the couch most nights."

A cloud of confusion suddenly tornadoed inside their head.

Derek stopped and leaned against a thick tree covered from root to tip in giant, moss-coated mushrooms. Pax added pressure to his grip—holding them up. The jungle around them swayed in an unnatural way. Pax realized that Derek's brain was fighting against the second host, and she wasn't sure how much longer it would allow them to coexist. She did her best to keep positive, if only to ease Derek's fear just a little. The dizziness passed, and she pushed him off the tree.

They walked a bit further; each cluttered the brain with their own questions. It began to drive Pax mad. It was one thing to fill her own head with thoughts, but another thing entirely to blend it with someone else's, like listening to several opinion radio stations at the same time—utterly pointless.

"Can we please get on the same thought wave?" she said.

Suddenly, an orb of light whizzed by and caused Derek to duck.

"The hell was that?" he said.

Another orb flittered in front of them, then took off high into the sky.

"Glowing bees!" Derek shouted.

Something shimmered to the right, reflecting heat off the side of Derek's face. Pax turned his head, felt his eyes grow wide. In front of them, a giant throne shot high into the sky—brilliant white marble, carved to emulate trunks of trees. It sparkled with the dust of diamonds, making it almost too bright to look at.

High upon the seat, far too big for its diminutive frame, sat a slender creature in a skintight leotard, with lavender wings and a long white beard. Even though Pax had never actually seen one in person, she recognized it immediately as a fairy.

Orbs of all shapes and hues buzzed around them, high into the treetops. Hundreds of tiny whispers swirled about with gossip regarding the strange intruder. Fairies were known in their legends to be a strong but kind race, often confused with pixies, who were a real bunch of cannibal bastards.

The light show slowed, and all at once the fairies clung to the trees by the dozens, many sitting on pink toadstools that grew from the bark. Pax and Derek were surrounded on all sides—a seated council of tiny winged people that pointed and giggled.

"Welcome, mortal being," the fairy said from the throne.

For a little thing, its voice boomed through the forest like a soothing bass guitar. Pax took over the body for a moment, dropped to a single knee, and bowed Derek's head in respect.

"Thank you, fairy king," she said in the most eloquent voice she could force out of Derek's jaw muscles.

"Oh, I'm not a king," said the fairy with the beard. "We're a democracy here. I was voted onto the throne. I will serve six thousand and nineteen years and then pass the ruling beard on to the next in charge."

"Ruling beard?" Derek blurted out.

The head fairy reached behind its ears and unhooked the large, wise-looking beard from its chin.

"The ruling beard," it said with great pride. "Steeped in the history and sauces of past leaders."

Pax felt a small amount of vomit creep up Derek's throat. She pushed it back, not pleased with the idea of tasting someone else's sick.

"I am Brittany," the fairy said. "Welcome to our home."

"Brittany?" Derek said in disbelief.

"Were you expecting Oberon or Tinker Bell?"

"I'm…not sure. Just not Brittany."

Pax bit Derek's tongue lightly, a warning to stop staying stupid things.

*Let me handle this, Derek.*

*Fine, but you agree with me, right?*

*That Brittany is a strange name for a fairy king?*

*Yeah.*

*Sure. Now shut up.*

"Lord Brittany—"

"Please, just Brittany."

"Brittany…where are we?" Pax asked.

"Deep in the Atlantic Ocean aboard the good vessel, the *Rainbow Dream.*"

"Wait…we're *inside* the Jollywog?"

Brittany's wings vibrated in frustration as it floated quickly toward them, matching eye level. Up close Pax noticed how smooth and androgynous it was. A light blue heart-shaped face sparkled and highlighted soft, almost felt-looking eyes, with lips that ended in a sharp point. A deep pitched voice, however, made it seem more male than female.

"Damn the ship captains that bob atop the waves!" Brittany shrieked. "For decades we have been saddled with that ridiculous name. I don't even know what it means! What is a wog, and why is it so jolly? I mean, you tell me: Jollywog or the *Rainbow Dream?*"

"Clearly, the *Rainbow Dream*," Pax said.

"Clearly!"

A delightful chime shimmered through the forest like a beautiful harp. The fairies looked about with excitement.

"What was that?" Pax asked.

"The *Rainbow Dream* has saved another creature," Brittany said. "Who or what is yet to be determined."

"You save people?"

"Of course! If we come across a poor soul in need, we swallow them."

Of all the places Pax imagined the fairies took to hiding, the bottom of the ocean was never on that list. It made her sad to think that man had chased these beautiful creatures into the water, and now also hunted the rainbow beast they called home; yet they still found it in their tiny little hearts to rescue those in need.

Brittany snapped its fingers, and a dozen fairies began to chop down trees.

"We'll fashion you a vessel that will carry you the rest of the way to your desired destination. After all, our motto is…"

It motioned to its followers, who all stopped what they were doing to speak in perfect unison. "Help the devils as you would help the angels. Ask for nothing, and your color will pulsate."

Brittany smiled proudly at Derek.

"We appreciate it, Brittany, but we don't know where this island even is."

Brittany tugged at the clip-on beard, gave it some thought.

"Susan. Ferraro. Gardetto."

Three fairies broke from their toadstools and zipped over to Brittany, awaiting orders.

"Bring me the red triangle!" Brittany exclaimed.

The three exchanged nervous looks.

"Brittany," Susan said.

"The red triangle has been with the fairies for over a hundred thousand years," Ferraro continued.

"We use it ourselves to navigate treacherous and hidden areas of the globe," Gardetto finished.

"Yes," Brittany said, "but this is a boy in need, and our motto is…"

"Help the devils as you would help the angels. Ask for nothing, and your color will pulsate," said everyone.

The concerned subjects scratched their heads.

"I understand," Susan said, "but there are some things we should keep in the family and—"

"Bring me the red triangle!"

"All we're saying," Ferraro said, "is that there can be such a thing as an overkill of kindness when it threatens the kingdom—"

"Bring me the red triangle!" Brittany repeated.

Left with no other option, the concerned fairies fluttered off, and Pax wondered just how democratic this system really was.

"This thing sounds kinda of important to your people," Pax said.

"Meh. We're fairies. We're basically immortal. I think we can survive without a red triangle."

The fairies returned, working their wings extra hard while carrying a sleek, brick-size black bag by its drawstrings—dropping it at Derek's feet.

Pax picked it up, turned it over in Derek's hands, and loosened the string. The bag was crafted from a ridiculously soft material, which pricked her fingers with tiny electrical shocks. She lingered a bit, rubbing her hand over it a few more times before finally pulling out the red triangle—that turned out to be a blue rectangle.

"I think you might have given me the wrong item," she said.

**EVERYDAY MONSTERS**

"That is exactly what the red triangle would like you to believe," Brittany said.

She could sense Derek wanted to ask a million questions, but she kept tight control over the tongue. All she needed to know was if it would get them to the Island of the Screaming Dead.

"It's a compass?" she asked.

"One that will lead you to any location just by thinking about it."

"I don't know how to thank you, Brittany."

"I don't do it for the thanks," Brittany said, "but if you want, when you return to civilization, could you try to squash the name Jollywog?"

"Deal."

A large thud took her by surprise. She turned to see a crumpled man, face down and dripping wet. Pax smiled as she thought about the fairies and their new kingdom of kindness under the ocean—oppressed creatures who still took the high road.

Her smile quickly faded, however, as the newly rescued man slapped his wet paw on the ground. Captain Grimmerstone climbed to his feet, his fur heavy against his skin with the weight of trapped water. He gave himself a violent shake and pushed the hair from his eyes.

"Welcome, werewolf!" Brittany said with a smile.

"I'll be Jonah on acid," Grimmerstone said, his pupils full of wonder.

Brittany flapped its wings and headed to greet the new guest.

"It's a trap!" Pax screamed.

Grimmerstone ripped open his captain's jacket to reveal a complicated mess of dynamite and wires. A large red button poked out at the top.

"I've breached the mighty Jollywog!"

"Damn it!" Brittany cried. "The *Rainbow Dream!*"

Grimmerstone's pupils widened, his smile manic.

"Creatures big and small take refuge in this beast," he said. "So marvelous. So beautiful. Time to throw a bomb down the rabbit hole and kill it all!"

Before Pax could react, the captain pounded his hairy fist into the button. A brief flash of light washed over everything, followed by the now predictable fade to black.

# CHAPTER 37

*Bill and Angie,*

*I am writing with good news. I have found the nest. They are of the surname Hellswood. I should have no problem clearing out their hole. I did, however, want to bring to your attention the entire town of Rainy Mood, Virginia. It is a breeding ground for the wicked, as just tonight I met a ghoul (my first). Apparently, there are ghosts, witches, and God only knows what else here. I think it would be wise to consider sending a small army to perform a thorough extermination.*

*Sincerely,*
*Axe Handle*

*P.S. Nun and Chuck uncovered none of this. It was all me. They have been useless. Remember that the next time you think I need playmates. All due respect.*

Axe's finger sat frozen on the touchpad of his laptop computer. With the simple click of a button he had the power to wipe out an entire town. He felt good about it but had trouble applying the proper pressure to click *Send*.

"Sun's almost up," Socket said quietly.

Axe took his finger off the touchpad, unlatched his ax, and placed it on the table.

"You think you got me all torn up, don't you?" he said.
"Don't blame me for your own conscience."
"You planted the seed!"
"You watered it."
"Damn it, Socket!"

He stood fast and flustered—walked to the mirror over the sink. Axe took a deep look at himself in the reflection and could see the softness growing in his eyes. It annoyed him greatly. If he could smack them back to the cold, hard orbs they once were, he would.

"I don't make friends. Especially with supernatural types," he snarled.

"So, if your family had been killed by some normal human asshole, you'd go around shooting mortals in the head?" Socket said.

"Maybe!"
"No you wouldn't."
"Maybe!"
"You're not stupid, so don't pretend to be."

Axe wanted to smash his fist into the mirror, shatter it good, but he knew Socket expected it—once again she'd have the upper hand on the fact that he was hiding from his feelings.

"You want me to go save that creature?"
"I want you to go save your friend."

Axe thought about Jordan standing paralyzed in the street, his skin starting to sizzle as the light went from midnight, to royal, to sky blue. Normally an image like this would cause him to smile—but the smile didn't come this time. Instead, his heart fluttered with a small skip of panic.

He grabbed his ax and snapped it back into place at his side, then gripped the hotel room door—twisted it a bit too hard, breaking it in the process.

The door slammed shut behind him, but the damaged knob caused it to pop back open a sliver—his laptop perfectly framed in the crack. The unsent letter to his bosses waited patiently. One click away from total genocide.

# CHAPTER 38

For the first time since their arrest, Jordan found himself thinking fondly about his parents. With nothing left to do but wait for the sun to fry him to dust, he let his mind float back to better days. He dreamed of his mother's chocolate chip peanut butter pancakes, and his dad's preference for women's sunglasses. They were not psychopaths. They were normal, loving people whose minds were tragically poisoned. He had been too fragile to accept that before, as popular opinion had beaten him down—so he'd poured cement over his eggshell interior and became the world's biggest, impenetrable dickhead.

The sound of an approaching engine dragged him back to present. He thanked every God mankind had ever created that someone was out and about this early.

"Help me! Help me, please!" he shouted.

Headlights behind him caused his shadow to arch dramatically on the street like a bad Halloween decoration. Tires rolled to a stop—a kickstand hit the pavement.

"Is that you, virgin vamp?"

The familiar voice sent a chill down Jordan's spine. Two sets of boots following the same beat walked toward him. Two grown men, always back-to-back, stepped in front of him.

"What angel was kind enough to pre-stake you?" said the always smiling one.

"Come on, man. Why can't you assholes just be cool?"

"I don't think we ever properly introduced ourselves. I'm Chuck. My brother, Nun."

Jordan nervously eyed the sky, the sun about to say hello.

"Listen…I'm one of the good vampires."

Chuck smiled, showing off his perfect teeth. "'For it is the purest of evil that believes in its good—its points always draining, heart hollow like wood.' I quote, of course, from the book of Piller. Are you familiar with the Pillers, vampire? They founded the organization HAI. Nun and I are a part of that noble group. Dedicated to eradicating the Earth of the parasites that suck it dry."

Jordan's skin began to itch as a sliver of the sun appeared on the horizon.

"Do you know what I hate most about vampires?" Chuck said.

Chuck talked in such a delightful way that it confused Jordan how he could hate anything.

"I hate that they pretend to be me. A man with a soul. Do you think that's fair? That some undead creature of the night should be able to walk into a bank and open up an account like an average Joe? Or take good American jobs away from human beings who really need them? Do you think it's fair for these dirty mind manipulators to hypnotize our woman away from us, and silently snicker as they watch our bodies slowly rot?"

Jordan felt the shift in tone, Chuck's speech laced in hate. He understood this level of ignorance, because he had recently been drowning in it himself. He knew how dangerous it could be, and how impossible it was to convince someone suffering from it that they were on the wrong side of the fight.

"Hold on!" Jordan shouted. "I didn't ask for this. I just woke up a vampire. One day *you* could wake up the very thing you don't understand. I don't want to hurt you. Why would you want to hurt me?"

Jordan considered his words wise and began to wonder who would play him in the movie version of his life. Clearly, he had just extinguished the age-old fire that burned between humans and vamps. He was sure to be promoted to vampire king, or perhaps a vampire duke.

"I'm not going to hurt you."

Chuck swung his body to position Nun directly in front of Jordan—it was the first time Jordan realized they were physically attached at the back.

"Nun, on the other hand, is going to do really awful things."

"Help me, anyone!!!" Jordan screamed.

A thick fog wrapped around his body, and a woman's hand slowly materialized and gripped his shoulder. Gretel smiled at Jordan—her fangs out.

"Don't worry, sugar. We got your back."

The rest of the fog separated around him and formed seven more humanoid shapes that positioned themselves like human shields.

Jordan knew instantly they were vampires, not because he watched them materialize from fog or because Gretel was among them. Jordan could *feel* them. He could smell the savory, almost peppery difference of their blood, and hear the slower rhythm of their hearts. A band of strangers had come to his rescue, and he'd never felt safer.

An insanely beautiful woman with raven-black hair floated to Jordan's side. Her delicate fingers brushed the back of his neck, causing a surge of strength throughout his stake-weakened body.

Nun's and Chuck's grins widened, like a couple of sharks that just crashed a surfer's convention.

"I told you, Nun," Chuck said. "Threaten one, and the entire nest appears."

The raven-haired woman removed her fingers from the back of Jordan's neck and stepped up to the brothers.

"It has long been my observation," she said, "over centuries of fallen men, that the ones who spit and shout the loudest are the ones most terrified of it all."

The brothers went on the defensive. Two wooden blades slid out of holsters attached to Chuck's wrists. He was quick, but the matriarch vampire proved quicker. She ducked his first swing and grabbed firm to the second, crushing the weapon to splinters in her hand and blowing the shards into Chuck's eyes—blinding him momentarily.

The back of Jordan's neck began to tingle and smoke. The sun was now officially on the rise, sending panic through his paralyzed body. The raven-haired vampire leaped forward; her form folded back into a thick, white cloud. The rest of the vampires followed suit, surrounding Jordan in a protective fog.

The last thing he saw before everything went whitish-gray: Axe Handle sprinting in his direction, a determined look on his face. Jordan couldn't be sure if he was rushing to save him or kill him, but he opted for the former and smiled. Maybe he did care after all.

A strong wind attacked his body, and he suddenly felt as light as a feather.

# CHAPTER 39

A massive web held Derek firmly in place. Struggling proved pointless as an eight-armed woman crawled toward him—a mouth full of shark teeth. Her void-black hair was sculpted tight against her scalp, and her eyelashes were made of spider legs.

The woman's lips folded over Derek's neck, and he could feel her soft tongue as it ran around his skin. Her eight hands raked up and down his body, creating the sense of an orgy that involved only two.

At first Derek assumed the web had to be gigantic, but when his eyes caught the room below, he understood that somehow he had shrunk. It took him a moment, but the details of the room eventually came into focus—a dimly lit cell made of glass walls. In one of the corners, huddled together, were his parents, Jane and Elliot Stabbers.

The spider-woman crawled on top, unbuttoned his jeans, and nibbled on his ear. Derek's brain felt like smoke, swirling slowly, never settling. No single thought was able to be held for long before another wisped into existence.

"Derek!"

Derek lifted his head the best he could and peered over the spider-woman's shoulder—at his brother on the other side of the cell.

"Derek? You in there?"

"Jordan?"

His brother looked up into the corner at the tiny web.

"Holy…are you having spider sex?"

The web and the woman suddenly drooped, blending together in a sticky white goo, lowering Derek to the floor. He arrived in a puddle, stood, and wiped himself off. When he looked up, he found himself suddenly back to his normal size, staring at Jordan through the glass of the cell. His parents remained in the corner, uninterested in anything but each other.

"What is all this?" Derek asked.

Jordan pressed his hand against the glass, a strange look of remorse in his eyes.

"D, I'm so sorry, man," Jordan said. "Sorry for what an asshole I've been. About Mom and Dad, and Blooper."

Derek stared at the apologizing man claiming to be his brother. Everything around him felt false—he couldn't remember what brought them together in this terrible place.

"What are you?"

"I'm Jordan. Clem said you'd freak out."

"Clem?" The name sounded familiar.

Jordan slapped his hands together like he just won first prize at the county fair.

"You're dreaming, little brother! I'm invading your subconscious with my vampire powers! How fucking cool is that?"

Derek suddenly remembered. "The accident!"

"Water under the bridge," Jordan said. "I'm digging this vampire thing."

"What are you doing here?"

"Shit's going down in Rainy Mood. Clem's lost connection to Pax, and since Pax is technically my master, I'm able to connect with you and…well, the point is there's a bunch of monster-hunting dick-licks from a group called HAI trying to kill us."

Even though he was dreaming, Derek could feel his stomach twist into knots as he recalled the email he had sent weeks ago to the group—an email he thought, up until now, had gone unanswered.

"Fuck."

"Yeah!" Jordan said. "They got this one guy who's actually two guys attached by skin. It's madness!"

"No! Fuck, Jordan, they're in town because of me. I told them we had vamps. Before all this happened. Shit. This is my fault."

"Where are you?" Jordan asked. "Clem needs to know."

Derek thought back. He remembered the ship and the captain. He remembered the net and a beautiful creature brighter than a rainbow. Fairies! He remembered fairies and… the captain again, and then…

"Jordan!" Derek shouted. "I think I might be dead."

"You can't be, or we wouldn't be linked."

A good point. He searched inside himself for Pax. If anyone should talk to Jordan about this, it was her. He checked his feet and scoured his brain. He rummaged through every nook in his body, but she was gone. He could no longer feel her.

"Pax?"

"Yeah, that's her name. Where are you guys?"

"I can't feel her. She's not here. My brain…maybe it chose to kill her off instead of me. We weren't sure how much time we had, and now I can't feel her."

"She's gotta be there," Jordan said. "Otherwise how could we be linked?"

Water began to pour from the ceiling and into the cell—filling it. The brothers pressed their bodies against the glass.

"Shit," Jordan said. "Either I'm losing control, or you're waking up. How many HAI agents did they send?"

"I didn't know they were sending any!"

"Well, tell me where you are!" Jordan pleaded.

Derek continued his search for Pax. He refused to believe she was gone. Even though it had only been a few days of sharing his body, he wasn't ready to be single again. It felt like a valuable piece of him had gone missing, or even worse, died.

The cell filled swiftly with water, and Derek knew he'd be under in just seconds.

"Derek, you're waking up!"

"Atlantic Ocean! Somewhere in the Atlantic Ocean."

"I did not expect that."

Suddenly, the walls of the cell buckled, and a tidal wave attacked the dream, drowning everything in it—slamming Derek under. He swallowed a mouthful of saltwater that set his throat on fire. The silence under the black water caused him to tremble; his body tightened in fear, until a faint song seeped into his muscles and relaxed him. It drifted through the water and melted through his skin. He let himself go and began to float upward toward the heavenly lullaby.

~

A soft, devastatingly gorgeous voice carried itself effortlessly on a small, salty breeze. Derek grinned like a dope fiend as the lofty vocals lapped at his wet, goose-bumped skin.

His lids cracked open, and the sun above him stung his eyes. A dark, swaying silhouette leaned over and blocked the yellow orb to take away the pain. The shadowed woman sang sweetly, and strands of her hair brushed across his face like a lover's kiss. The melody curled up inside his ears and strummed against his brain.

His eyes slowly adjusted, the water rings around his vision fading away. He thought he must be in heaven when the image revealed a magnificent woman with long black hair and chocolate-brown skin. Her eyes were an ever-changing blue that seemed to rock in unison with the ocean.

He was so lost in her voice that he barely noticed the constant tugging at his lower half. Derek couldn't feel any pain, but the odd pressure eventually caught his interest. He lifted his head as much as his broken body would allow and discovered himself lying flat on a large, wet rock—barely any bigger than he was. All around him, nothing but ocean. It stretched out forever, landless and hopeless.

He looked down at his legs to find three more women, all with razor-sharp teeth. They tore the flesh off his thighs and calves—chewing it to a fine mash, and swallowing. Their fish-like tails flopped about in the afternoon sun as they casually enjoyed their meal.

The woman who hovered above him singing placed her hands on his head and led it gently back down, flat against the rock. Her song made the hard stone feel like a feather pillow as she continued to fill Derek with a wonderful feeling. He stared up at her and smiled, happy as her song made dying the most beautiful thing he'd ever experienced.

# CHAPTER 40

Axe zipped open his weapons bag and began to fill his pockets and hidden straps with stakes, guns, knives, and a bottle of grain. Wild guitars played loudly in his head, leading him through his getting-ready montage.

He'd arrived too late to save Jordan, but a group of bloodsuckers had picked up his slack. The Hellswoods were out in full, including Gretel, who Axe couldn't take his eyes off. She spotted him from a distance, and although he was too far to know for sure, Axe swore her eyes were filled with disappointment. Before he could even defend himself, Gretel and the rest of her family broke down into a low-hovering cloud and vanished. Axe burned with self-loathing.

Disappointment was a feeling reserved for people who had the luxury to love another. He had that once, back when he was a boy. The Face took away his power to disappoint when he slaughtered the only people he cared about. Vampires were monsters. Manipulative beasts sprung from the devil's loins. Gretel had played him. Played him like a goddamn fiddle. That was over.

He was so immersed in his rage-filled inner monologue that he didn't notice Nun and Chuck in the doorway until he turned to leave, fully loaded and ready to tear some heads off. Not even Chuck's patronizing grin could tip his scales.

"Someone's ready to rock," Chuck said.

Axe dropped a cigarette into his mouth, smashed a bottle of

whiskey on the hotel table, and used his lighter to set the cheap wood on fire. He leaned in carefully and lit the end of his cig, then stood and took a long, soothing drag.

"Do I have any blood on me?" he asked.

"No."

"Let's fix that."

# CHAPTER 41

Derek woke with a gasp when a tiny wave jumped over the rock and smacked him in the face. His throat felt like sandpaper, his skin paper mâché. The women with the teeth and tails were nowhere to be found. He was alone on the rock in the middle of the ocean. The stars were out in abundance. He'd never seen so many clusters, all fighting for his attention.

Derek lifted his head off the rock and looked down at his legs, or what was left of them. Both had been completely stripped to the bone—a surreal sight the way his femurs sprang from his flesh-covered hips. It reminded Derek of a cartoon he once saw where a cat had his lower half dipped in a cauldron of acid. He wanted to share the macabre image with Pax but still couldn't find her.

Tiny electrical shocks pricked his left hand—something gripped in his fingers. Too weak to lift his arm, he let his head flop to the side. A black bag the size of a brick, the drawstring looped around his wrist. He used his pointer finger and thumb to loosen the bunched top, then tipped the red triangle (that was actually a blue rectangle) into his hand—a small miracle he still had it; however, useless to him now.

His mind drifted to thoughts of Rainy Mood. He'd always dreamed of getting out one day. Now the gray weather, ignorant peers, and condescending adults didn't seem as undesirable as they once did.

The red triangle began to shimmer in his hand, small

crystal particles collecting near the bottom. Like a leaky hose, the crystals dripped off the device and dropped gently into the saltwater. They stretched out across the ocean—a subtle path of diamonds that one might follow, if one had a ship…or flesh on their legs. Because he had been thinking about it, the path pointed home. It was just as Brittany had told him. He frowned at the thought of knowing the direction but having no means to travel.

Derek lay awake for hours, shivering and counting the white dots of light above him. He thought many times about rolling his body into the water to let it sink. End it all. It seemed the least horrific option, as tomorrow the sun would bake him and the sirens would most likely return to finish his flesh. Still, he remained, not ready to give up hope just yet.

He focused on his heart. It beat with a steady, strong rhythm, never wavering or fluttering. It circulated his blood without the slightest hesitation for the situation. In all reality, Derek should have bled out by now. Here he drew hope. Pax had to be alive, or he would be dead.

"I don't know if you can hear me, Pax. I'm not sure if you even know what's happening to us right now. I hope you don't. It's very unpleasant. I'm having trouble differentiating thoughts. My brain feels like stacked lumber. Different pieces but bundled as one. You're a monster. Not because you are but because I labeled you one. All I know is *my* world. My brain takes in the information around me and assembles it into a narrative according to *my* experiences. I live my life as a one-sided story. It's maddening, when you lay on a rock in the middle of the ocean and really think about it. How alone we actually are. Trapped in a prison of fluid and bone, with only our tongues to untangle the mess in our heads. And we scream at these stars. Thousands of these stars. And if we're lucky, one of them blinks back. We interpret that blink, that flash of light that stands out from the rest, as an invitation. An invitation to unbundle that useless lumber in our head and build a house inside theirs. Some two-story ghost factory with a locked door and cracked windows—hoping the flies in their brain will enter in search of food, but instead find us...and then stay because we're the thing that nourishes them. Ghost flies. That's a fun concept. Do you think when flies die, they go to the big picnic in the sky? I hate picnics. Sitting on the hard, uneven ground just to eat cold chicken. I wonder if I taste like chicken to the fish women. The fish women are monsters. But only because I don't understand their intentions. Their head lumber. Pax, you might be thinking, 'What's this teenager with skeleton legs talking about?' Well, I'm extremely light-headed from all the blood loss, and I don't really remember anything I just said, but I guess what I'm ultimately getting at is...mi casa es su casa."

~

Derek woke once more to the voice in his ears—the tugging at his thighs. The sun was up, and the sirens had returned to pick more meat off his body. They worked their way up his torso, slow and leisurely. The same beautiful face from before stared down at him, her lips parted in a song that numbed his pain. Derek licked the saltwater on his lips and wondered if Pax could taste it too.

He stared up into the beautiful blue eyes and let his thoughts drift to Lotti and Jazz. What had happened to them? Were they still on the rust bucket somewhere, floating aimlessly? Could either of them even steer a ship?

The blue rectangle (called the red triangle) shimmered once more, and a quiet path of diamonds stretched out in a line through the ocean and vanished over the horizon.

Derek stared at it for a long while as he tried to click his heels together like Dorothy. He frowned when he remembered he couldn't move his legs.

~

The sun's rays made Lotti feel slightly normal again. She had the fortitude to pack sunscreen in her emergency shade bag, so even if she died from dehydration, she'd have a pretty great tan when they found her body.

They had searched the ship from top to bottom and discovered no food or water—just a mousetrap-looking device that Jazz called a distiller, along with a mini fridge filled with bottles that contained a frothy yellow liquid.

Jazz had a basic idea on how to steer the ship from watching Grimmerstone, but a broken compass had her aimlessly turning the rudder and pointing the ship toward more ocean. They hadn't found any spare gas cans, and the gauge had read empty for the last hour.

"This is your plan?" Jazz said, blocking Lotti's sun. "Catch some rays until we die?"

Lotti fired back with a snotty remark. "We could do shots of urine and bump this party up to two."

Jazz sat down next to her on the bow of the ship.

"I could use help spotting for land."

Lotti released a dramatic sigh, sat up, and tugged her bra down just enough to check her tan line—a good base. She stood, slipped back into her pants, then looked out over the crystal-blue water. The ocean's reflective properties stung her eyes. She threw up her hands to minimize the glare.

"The water's really bright," Lotti said.

"Mm-hm."

She scanned the endless blue on all sides, searching for anything that could be useful to their rescue. Nothing.

"I don't see diddly-squat," Lotti said.

"Look harder."

She exhaled in annoyance and did another spin. She had noticed it the first time but waved it off as merely the sun's reflection. This time, however, her eyes were better adjusted, and she saw it again, more vibrant than the last time.

"Weird," Lotti said.

"What's that?"

"It looks like…it looks like there's a shiny stripe in the water. Like a line of sparkly gems."

She squinted harder, really examining the phenomenon.

"Jazz!" she said. "I think...I don't know what it is, but I think we need to follow this!"

"We're already heading that direction," Jazz said smugly.

"Wait...you knew about it?"

"Saw it ten minutes ago. Thought I'd let you get a good base before I made you aware."

Lotti's internal fury surprised her. Jazz should have included her immediately, but she wasn't exactly sure why. By Lotti's own standards, Jazz had acted perfectly. She didn't care how they were saved, just as long as they were, and Jazz allowed her an extra ten minutes of feeling like a person again. So why was she so mad?

"You think it leads home?"

"I think it leads somewhere."

"And somewhere is better than nowhere."

"Yup."

"Okay."

"Okay, what?"

"Okay, I'll watch the sparkle path. You steer the ship."

"Okay."

"Okay."

*Derek...*

The voice was so soft that Derek imagined he whispered it in his own head.

*Derek...*

It returned. A little louder. A little more force.

*Derek! Derek! What the fuck?*

Derek lifted his head as much as he could, his song-drunk eyes shifting in their holes. He took a delirious scan of his horrific surroundings. The sirens continued to make a meal out of him—no one else in sight.

The creatures all flinched, and the singing ceased when Derek's body shot up at the waist. They stared at him in confusion, bits of his flesh hanging from their lips. Derek felt the muscles in his right arm tighten, and like a pissed-off viper, his hand struck out—wrapping around the lead singer's neck. With a decimating squeeze, the siren's warm blood covered his fingers as they entered her neck flesh. With a single violent tug, he ripped out her throat. The siren croaked loudly, flapped her tail, and tumbled from the rock into the water.

Derek brought his dripping red hand to his face, opened his mouth wide, and crammed his fingers inside. Her blood tasted sweeter than a human's—the equivalent of a tropical drink (piña colada versus a whiskey and soda).

The remaining two sirens bared their teeth, hissed, and lowered their backs in an attack stance. Derek's body tightened again, and suddenly it dawned on him.

"Pax!"

Like a bolt of lightning, Pax grabbed the closest siren by the head and pulled her neck to Derek's mouth—her fangs punctured deep, the blood warming their gullet.

The last of the creatures beat its tail wildly while it watched Derek drain her sister. Pax ripped her fangs from the siren's throat, and in a primal act of dominance, dug Derek's fingers into the neck holes she created. With a scream loud enough to wake a kraken, Pax tore the siren's head from its body, soaking them in blood. The final fish-girl got the message, slid off the rock, and vanished into the water.

"Where the fuck is our leg flesh?!" Pax screamed out loud.

"You're alive!" Derek exclaimed. "Where have you been?"

"That blast must have knocked me loose in here," she said, wiping the blood from their eyes. "I've been trapped in your memories."

"Was it awful?" Derek said, nervous she had seen too much.

"You should be extremely embarrassed. I watched you poop your pants out of revenge for not getting a second cookie after dinner."

"I was like seven!"

"Exactly. You should be embarrassed."

Having her back inside him felt great. He tried not to make it too obvious, but he knew she could tell. It warmed him to feel the same vibe coming from her.

"So now what?" she asked.

"Maybe turn us into a bat? We can try flying out of here."

"Or get back on that tetanus-infested ship."

"Yeah, but we don't even know where—"

He stopped short—the rusted-brown bucket headed straight for them. Lotti waved from the bow. Derek looked down to notice the red triangle on the rock beside him still emitting the shimmering path that led their friends directly to them.

"I never thought I'd be this happy to see Lotti Lyons," Derek said.

"Me neither," Pax said.

# CHAPTER 42

The midday sun continued to chip away at the paint of Hellswood Manor. Axe had been staring at the Victorian cliché for almost an hour through his binoculars, and he could sense Nun and Chuck's patience begin to wane.

The brothers sat back-to-back just inside the tree line, playing war with a deck of cards on a moss-covered tree stump. Axe couldn't imagine being physically that close to another human being for his entire life, but the brothers seemed to thrive on it.

"We wait much longer it'll be dark," Chuck said.

Axe ignored him. He had counted eight vampires, not including Jordan. Lord knows how many more were inside. The fact that the Hellswoods were expecting trouble was all the more reason to hang back and study the battlefield. This was still their turf; the vamps had the advantage.

"I'd be happy to take the lead," Chuck said, laying down a king but losing to Nun's ace, "you know…if you're scared."

Axe lowered the binoculars and turned to face the brothers, positioning his back against a small dirt hill for comfort.

"This ain't a nest of primitives running on instinct," Axe said. "That's an intelligent, well-organized family unit in there. They've been ready for this before we were even born."

He lit a cigarette and stroked Socket on his hip. She hadn't said much since earlier that morning in the street. He knew she was mad at him, but what else was knew?

"Well, we're gonna need a way in," Chuck said. "An element of surprise."

"We need a Trojan horse," agreed Axe.

The right thing to do would be to call for reinforcements. To send that email to Bill and Angie. Axe considered it and figured he still would, but first he wanted the nest all to himself. HAI could have the town and whatever bottom-feeders lived in it.

"Let's head back. I can't think when they're staring at me."

"They're probably asleep," Chuck said, losing his last card to Nun.

Axe put out his cigarette between his thumb and pointer, then pocketed the butt.

"Nah. They're watching."

~

Jordan watched from the second floor as the top of Axe's head disappeared into the thicket. He lowered his eyes from the small holes in the wall covered by tinted glass, looked over at Clem—silent and rigid.

"How'd you know about me?" Jordan asked. "How'd you know I was in trouble?"

Clem kept her eyes positioned over her own set of spy holes.

"Your brother," she said with a touch of exhaustion. "It was his one and only condition. He'd look after my girl, if I looked after his boy. So, I sent Gretel to shadow you."

Jordan felt like a real shit stain. After all the torment he'd put Derek through, his brother still made him a priority. Clem turned her head and trapped his eyes in hers.

"I knew your mother."

Jordan's stomach turned. He really liked his new vampire family. He had no desire to learn that they did, in fact, have everything to do with his parents' downfall.

"She bought me lunch once," Clem said sweetly. "She was doing a piece on historical landmarks in Rainy Mood. A spirited woman. I liked her instantly. She asked me many questions about this house, but what I remember most about her was the fear I smelled in her blood. I have a good nose for what lies beneath, and when your mother talked about her boys, I knew she was afraid. She loved you beyond words, Jordan."

Jordan's face soured.

"You just said she was scared of us."

"No. This was not that kind of fear. When you love something truly—so much so that the thought of losing it would mean the end of who you are—Jordan, that is real fear. Fear you can't shake. I know this because I am also very afraid."

It seemed odd to associate that emotion with Clem. She was the toughest person he'd ever met, and he'd spent the entire day with Axe Handle. A sureness buzzed around her that, unlike Axe, she didn't need to advertise.

"I love my children with this fear."

He hadn't seen her take a single step, and yet Clem now floated less than a foot from Jordan. She reached up and put a calming hand behind his ear.

"I protect my family with this fear, even if that means a daughter must die so that she can live."

Jordan could sense her distress—her exterior was cold and strong, but the way she touched his head gave her away. A woman full of worry, sorrow, and anger.

"This is not my first family," she said gravely.

"You had one when you were alive," Jordan stated.

"And again, in the rise of my second life. I nurtured a troubled young group of men and women. A group that society no longer had use for. People they locked away in asylums and prison cells. Labeled as broken and incurable, like your parents. Like my own father."

"You made crazy people vampires?"

"I recognized them. Wild eyes with crisscrossed arms locked in place. I felt them. Grinding teeth, powder on their tongues. Science had failed them, so I intervened. I wasn't a Hellswood back then. Our family clan was Grayrock. There were fourteen of us by the end. I had hoped the evolution of death back into life might show them peace, as it had for me, but some were simply beyond the help."

Clem took Jordan's face in her hands. Her eyes cut right

through him, reached back into his head, and burrowed into his brain.

"Insanity and power are like black ink and water," she continued. "Beautiful for a moment, but destined to sink to the bottom. Certain members of my family felt that pull and decided to bring all of life down with them."

Clem's eyes flickered with scratched images of the past, like an old silent film. Jordan's connection to her allowed him to feel the weight of every word and the blood in every sentence. It was the first time in ages he experienced empathy for another living creature.

"I waged war against my own family, the very children whose hearts I filled with new life. My babies. My blood. The lost and forgotten. I picked up my sword, and I cut off their heads. I stood amongst their bodies for hours. I memorized each of their frozen faces so that I would never again be careless enough to bring such horror into the world."

There was a tingling in the back of Jordan's head. He could sense the entire Hellswood clan behind him.

"Over time, the desire to love again outweighed the sorrow of my first attempt," she continued. "I sought out those for whom the human world offered little comfort. Sons and daughters who stood against their outcast status, embraced it even when the world shook its collective head. We are the Hellswoods, Jordan Stabbers."

Jordan could smell Zelda's soap, Jim's hair gel, Amadeus's leather pants. The sensation of their approach created goosebumps on every inch of his flesh.

"Will you offer your person to us? Make us laugh, as you do? Sing us songs, as you have? Defend our clan, as you must?"

"Yes," Jordan said.

The word just tumbled from his mouth—his gut, heart, and mind acting on a newfound confidence he had gained since meeting them.

Clem leaned in and kissed him tenderly on the lips. Jordan melted. He imagined a vampire kiss would be cold as ice, but this felt like the mouth of a volcano; a deep heat resonated far beyond her lips.

From behind, the rest of the Hellswood clan embraced their new brother—teeth sank into every exposed bit of his flesh. Jordan could feel their weight press down on him, but he had no trouble holding himself up. The blood inside him raced through dozens of holes, and Jordan imagined his body a beautiful water fountain designed for Las Vegas—red liquid spraying out of multiple spigots, shooting high up into the air. He was home, and he was happy.

# CHAPTER 43

The old ship's masthead formed the giant, rusted head of a rabid dog chomping down onto the torso of a screaming mermaid. Pax hadn't noticed it before, but she fully appreciated it now. The snout of the metal beast pointed toward the red triangle's magical path—the assumed direction of the Island of the Screaming Dead.

Pax relaxed inside Derek's body as he stared down at his legs. Her regenerative powers had begun to take hold. Tendons slowly reformed, as pink muscle mass folded around them. Pax had seen it all a million times before, but she could tell the process mesmerized Derek.

The gang was back together again, and soon they would arrive at Nomicon's secret island. When three humans and a whostpire stumbled onto his shore, would they be welcomed or instantly killed? Most warlocks considered the human race to be a pathetic group of wingless birds—always dreaming of flight but too stupid and slow to ever grow wings.

"LAND HOOOOOOOOO!" Lotti hollered with a giggle.

Pax couldn't remember ever seeing her shade with an authentic smile on her face. It suited her. The whostpire strained Derek's neck over the rail and squinted his eyes.

"Where?"

Lotti arrived at their side and pointed, doing her best to avoid any glimpse of Derek's mushy legs.

"There!"

It took a few more seconds, but finally Pax saw the dot—a pinprick of brown.

"That could be anything."

"That, my sweet master, is land."

~

Ten minutes later it was undeniable—a small island, brown on the bottom and green on top. Pax helped Derek to his feet and took a few wobbly steps across the deck. His legs were weak but worked again. The sirens had ripped off his jeans and discarded them into the deep, leaving him in only his boxer shorts. The ocean breeze ruffled his leg holes, and Pax felt his testicles shrivel.

"Doesn't look so screaming-dead," Lotti said, gripping her fedora so as not to lose it to the wind.

The island grew larger by the second, the boat coming in faster than any of them anticipated.

"Um. Are we about to crash?" Pax asked.

"I suggest we find out from the water," Jazz suggested.

The aspiring journalist sprung like a gold medal gymnast over the rail, with Lotti right behind her. Pax and Derek's muscle manipulation fell in perfect sync with each other as they too dashed, jumped, and plummeted. Barely a second later, the ship blasted its way into a large wooden pier, shattering it to pieces.

Derek's butt hit the sand, missing a jagged piece of coral by a couple feet. Using his newly formed legs, Pax pushed off the bottom and broke the surface of the water. They were just in time to witness the bucket of rust that was the *Bitch* breach itself on the shore.

"Guess we'll deal with that problem after our separation," said Derek.

Lotti splashed a few yards ahead of them, turning in frantic circles, then diving under.

"My hat!" she screamed. "I lost my hat!"

"Bigger fish to fry, Lot," Pax said.

The anguish in Lotti's eyes stunned Pax. Her shade let out a harrowing scream, then dove back under the water. Seemed a bit much for a silly hat.

*Race you to shore,* Pax thought.

*It's on,* Derek responded.

He immediately dove into a freestyle stroke. The thrill of what would inevitably be a shared victory felt amazing to Pax. The connection they shared over the past few days had developed into something beyond words. Now their organs, bones, and blood did most of the talking for them. A strange thing, being wired directly to another. A strange and beautiful thing that they were about to lose.

When they reached the beach, Jazz was already out of the water looking around at the beautiful landscape. Golden, untouched sand rippled right up to the edge of a dense green forest. It reminded Pax of the islands she always saw in the movies but thought she'd never visit.

Another scream caused her to turn back toward the water. Lotti continued her search for the hat, looking like a drunk dolphin with every crest and dive.

"It was a nice hat," Derek said.

"Check it out!" Jazz shouted from the edge of the trees.

Jazz dropped to her knees as Derek and Pax hovered behind. All three studied a strange silver cylinder the size of a kitchen trashcan. Embedded near the top was a dark rectangular piece of glass.

Jazz pointed to a tiny sign at the base of the cylinder that read: *Say Hello!*

"Hello," Pax said.

Deep inside the guts of the cylinder, a yellow light flickered to life. Pax clasped her hands around the window and pressed Derek's forehead against them to block out the glare of the sun.

"I see something. Something turned on ins—"

Without warning, a pair of yellow pixelated eyes blinked into existence, causing Pax to stumble backward.

"Hello!" said the friendly robot. "Welcome to the Island of

the Screaming Dead, home of Nomicon Industries, established 1976."

The male voice had a soothing, confident cadence—like a lounge singer between sets. It hovered a foot off the ground, its base a single yellow light chasing itself in an endless circle. Its pixelated eyes blinked, and although there was no mouth, Pax swore she could see it smile.

"My name is Jeremy 6," the robot said, "and I'll be your personal companion while on the island."

Lotti dragged her dripping, dejected body up shore and stopped just behind Jazz.

"Hello! I'm Jeremy 6," the robot said again, addressing the new girl, "and I'll be your personal companion while on the island."

Two tears escaped Lotti's eyes and rolled down her cheeks. Jazz placed an arm on her shoulder and softened her usually sharp tongue.

"We'll get you a new hat, okay?"

Lotti wiped away the tears and shook off her sadness.

"Before we begin our tour," Jeremy 6 said, "let me guess your names by looking at your face. I'm actually pretty good at this."

The robot hovered over to Jazz and looked into her eyes.

"A one-eyed beauty. Be still my pulsing poso-dot."

Jazz blushed, and Pax found it amusing that she was so easily wooed by a piece of steel with a passionate voice box.

Jeremy 6 closed his pixelated eyes and concentrated. When he opened them, the yellow rings grew large like irises, then shrunk again as he focused.

"Jenny," he guessed with great confidence.

"No, but close," Jazz said.

"How is Jenny close to Jazz?" Lotti said.

"They're both J names."

"Your name is music to my ears, Jazz," Jeremy 6 said with a literal silver tongue.

*Cheesy fuckin' robot,* Pax thought.

Derek laughed internally.

Jeremy 6 approached Lotti and scanned her face.

"You are Jenny," he said with more of the same confidence.

"Is that the only name you ever guess?"

"I like the name Jenny. It reminds me of a generator I once dated."

Nobody groaned audibly, but Pax saw it on everyone's face.

"Kidding!" Jeremy 6 said. "A little robo-humor. I've never dated a generator…we were just friends. More humor!"

The robot moved on to Derek. He scanned the teen's face, and then scanned it again—and then one final time.

"I'll give you a hint,: it's not Jenny," Derek said.

The robot continued to scan, seeming confused. Pax suddenly realized that it must be able to sense the presence of a second person, which seemed strange, for she was merely a wisp of intelligent smoke. She had no physical body anymore. What could Jeremy 6 see that gave her away?

"You're in love," Jeremy 6 said matter-of-factly.

The revelation caused both her and Derek to tense up, as if this robot had just presented a pair of their dirty underwear to the public.

"You can always see it in the eyes," he said. "Plus, I'm measuring your endorphins."

Pax laughed so hard that a small amount of spit fell out of Derek's mouth.

"You're really bad at this game," she said defensively.

Pax fumbled for what to say—Derek stepped in.

"I'm possessed by the ghost of a whostpire. Any chemical reactions you're witnessing are due to circumstance."

She relaxed his shoulders and approved of the way he handled that.

"I'm Derek, and inside me is Pax."

Jeremy 6 stared a good moment longer, and then spun around to face the dense jungle.

"You guys seem awesome. Let me show you around."

He hovered off past the tree line. Nobody moved until Jazz finally led the charge, followed by Lotti.

Pax whispered to Derek out loud for spooky effect, "And they followed the strange robot into the thick of the jungle… never to return."

"Fucking dork."

～

A well-maintained stone path twisted and turned, veering around beautiful moss-covered boulders and splitting giant tree trunks in half. It hugged a noisy brook for several yards, then pushed away from the trickling water to check out an intricate web of vines and tropical flowers. The path circled around a large rock that resembled a crude heart, then plunged deeper into the woods to give a glance at a makeshift cemetery that sat twenty yards off the main strip. Pax wondered who might be buried there, and why the tour guide thought it necessary to point it out.

Jeremy 6 hovered a few steps ahead at all times, his head spinning like an excited owl whenever it wanted to address them—an authentic sense of wonder baked into his every word.

"Way, way back in the seventeenth century," Jeremy 6 said, "the island was a secret location at which pirates used to drop off unwanted enemies, crew members, and stowaways. They would leave them screaming on the shores as their ships sailed away—left for dead."

"Hence the Island of the Screaming Dead," Jazz said.

Jeremy 6 placed his electric yellow eyes on her. "Hence indeed, pretty lady."

Jazz blushed, and Lotti rolled her eyes.

"Unable to escape the island due to its strong tides and constant storms," continued Jeremy 6, "the new inhabitants formed a terrible, cannibalistic tribe, and thrived here for centuries. Then, in 1974, two scientists, James and Melody Warlock—"

"Wait," Derek interrupted. "Their last name is Warlock?"

"They're not *actual* warlocks?" Pax added.

"Regular ol' human beings," Jeremy 6 said, "or wizards of science if you like."

Pax suddenly felt a bit distraught. Had this all been one big mistake? A warlock was one thing, but trusting her condition to a pair of non-magical humans somehow seemed even more dangerous.

Jeremy 6 blinked his eyes and continued with his tour. "James and Melody discovered the secret location of the island and began construction on Nomicon Industries, which opened its doors in 1976. Dedicated to the type of research frowned upon in all countries—blending science with magic—James and Melody claimed ownership of the island and literally became above the law. Present day, the island remains off the maps but is now used to further the pursuits of mankind for the better."

"What about the cannibals?" Jazz asked.

Jeremy 6's chest plate swung open unannounced, and a black cylinder inside spun at a rapid pace, followed by a barrage of bullets. He aimed his death-chest at a nearby bush, shredding its leaves and kicking up a surprising amount of blood. Half-naked men and women—full of holes—flopped out from behind its cover and hit the ground dead.

"Cannibals are still a bit of a problem."

Pax stared at the gory scene just yards away: grizzled, hardened-looking humans with long hair, dirty faces, and clothes made from vegetation, bone, and animal hides.

"In the late nineties" Jeremy 6 continued, chipper as ever, "James and Melody Warlock were suddenly lost to us when one of their experiments backfired, leaving them burnt to a blackened crisp and pronounced dead on the scene. It was a tremendous blow to the research being done at the time—but all was not lost, and less than a year after their death, their children, Barry and Hannah Warlock, arrived at the island to take their place. Since that day Nomicon Industries has taken incredible strides forward in treatment and technology, and remains a place of rumor and magic."

Pax found herself fortunate to have Derek still listening to Jeremy 6, as she had tuned out the moment the laboratory came into view. The closer they got, the more magnificent the building became—tall and thick, a blend of ancient Roman architecture and modern science fiction. Brilliant silver walls with deep grooves formed steel squares in place of glass windows. Insanely detailed stone-carved pillars depicting historical scenes led the way to a swirling glob of light that hung in place of a front door. The love child of Gene Roddenberry and Zeus.

"And speaking of magic, this is where it happens!" Jeremy 6 beamed.

He led them through the columns and toward the gelatinous shifting door, stopping just before it. A slight hum permeated around the glow that looked like a rotating cloud filtering a sunset—pinks and purples with tiny specks of glinting white. Like diamonds in cotton candy.

Lotti looked uneasy. "Why am I certain he wants us to walk through that?"

"Never seen a leap cloud before?" said Jeremy 6. "They're the best. Really cool tech. They were created here at Nomicon and aren't used anywhere else in the world."

"Then how the hell would I have ever seen one?" Lotti asked.

Jeremy 6 ignored her and continued with his spiel.

"It's basic teleportation. Almost every room in the building is equipped with a leap cloud. You simply approach and speak your location as you pass through. The leap cloud grabs your molecules, tears them into millions of pieces, and then reassembles them in the desired room."

Pax stepped forward with growing excitement, the geek in her clawing to get out. "So, you can get to anywhere in the lab in seconds?"

"Pretty damn incredible, right? If the leap cloud system goes down, you'd never find your way out. Nomicon is purposefully designed as a labyrinth. If it's ever raided, they'll just power down the system and wait for the enemy to starve to death wandering the halls!" said Jeremy 6 with far too much excitement.

"Who would you have to take such extreme measures against?" Derek asked.

"Governments, cannibal tribesmen, secret societies, aliens, mice," Jeremy 6 said, an angry red hue bleeding into his eyes. "Everybody."

Everyone held their breath, half expecting Jeremy 6 to open fire on them, but a moment later his eyes dipped back to a pleasant yellow.

"Follow me!" he said.

Jeremy 6 turned to the leap cloud and hovered forward.

"Front lobby," he said.

~

Derek's body was only in pieces for a fraction of a second, but he certainly noticed. It felt like all his cells had vomited inside his body and then immediately slurped the sick back up. The next thing he knew, he stood paralyzed, but fully reformed, in a large, open lobby.

*Did you feel that?*

*The being obliterated into a million pieces and put back together in under a second? I felt a little something.*

A piercing scream pushed them forward. They turned to find Lotti standing in front of the leap cloud, her eyes bulged, her mouth open comically wide. Jeremy 6 approached her with apologetic eyes.

"I should have mentioned it's a bit of a jolt the first time. You get used to it."

Lotti looked down at the robot and turned her lips into a snarl.

"What's wrong with regular doors?" she complained. "Doesn't hurt to walk through regular-ass doors!"

"There are over six hundred rooms at Nomicon Industries," said Jeremy 6. "The leap clouds were created to be far more time-efficient than a 'regular-ass door.' Science waits for no one."

The robot's eyes blinked rapidly, along with a small ding sound.

"I'm sorry, gang," Jeremy 6 said. "I'm needed in Lab 16. Just talk to Hailey at reception, and she'll take you to where you need to be. I'll check in on you all later."

He turned to Jazz with a yellow wink.

"Especially you, my lady."

With that, he hovered through a leap cloud calling out, "Lab 16."

Jazz let out a small sigh, and everyone looked in her direction.

"What can I say? Everyone loves Jazz," she responded.

Pax turned Derek's head toward the reception desk. The glass workstation sat between steel pillars that reached up to the vaulted ceilings. A thin, sunken-eyed woman sat up straight and stared slack-jawed at the florescent lighting. A silver helmet covered the entire top portion of her head and extended down the back of her neck like a metal mullet. Between the drool on her lips and the flashing lights from the helmet, she looked a lot like a zombie space commander.

*Hailey doesn't look well*, Derek thought.

They walked right up to the desk, but Hailey didn't seem to notice.

"Excuse me," Derek said.

A red light on her helmet suddenly turned blue, and Hailey's head titled slightly toward them.

"Uh…we're here to see the Warlocks," Pax stuttered.

"Barry and Hannah," Derek added.

"Aaaaaaaaa…point….meeeeeent?" Hailey moaned, her eyes finding the florescent lights again.

"We don't have one," Pax said. "Jeremy 6 said that you'd help us and—"

Before she was able to finish, another light blazed from blue to orange on her helmet, giving Hailey a small shock.

"Aaah," she cried with zero emotion. "Warlocks waaant seeeee…yoooouuu…"

She pressed her hands on the desk and—with great effort—pushed her dead weight up. She limped around the desk and motioned for them to follow.

"Waaaiiiting roooom."

Hailey vanished into a leap cloud, presumably now waiting for them in the waiting room.

"Guess we follow the zombie," Pax said.

"Sentences like that are becoming disturbingly normal to me," Derek said.

# CHAPTER 44

Axe found himself on his hands and knees in complete darkness. The floor, walls, and ceiling were sticky and grotesquely soft. Each time his hand pressed down to move himself forward, a warm liquid seeped up and pooled around his fingers. He continued to crawl, expecting an exit but never getting one. The stench of the tunnel made its way up his nostrils, and he nearly gagged. Something had died down here. He needed a light.

He felt around in his pockets and discovered the bulbous shape of his silver skull lighter. He pulled it out, opened it at the jawline, and flicked the flint wheel with his thumb. A gorgeous yellow-and-blue flame sprang to life and illuminated his surroundings.

Axe's stomach did a somersault when he discovered the tunnel he'd been blindly crawling through all this time was made completely out of fresh body parts. Severed arms, legs, and torsos smashed together, held loosely by coagulated blood. True horror smacked him in the face, and for the first time in years the brave warrior found himself afraid. He moved quickly forward, the lighter out in front of him as he searched and prayed for a way out of his dripping, squishing nightmare.

Just as his panic went from simmer to boil, Axe saw a light. The promise of the end. He pushed forward, but just as he arrived at the mouth of the tunnel, the Face stepped into view. Axe blew out his flame and held his breath as the creature he feared most paced back and forth at the exit. The Face stopped in the center of the opening and turned; his cold, horrible eyes peered into the dark.

Axe trembled. The Face smiled. Long white fangs dropped from his gums—he lunged into the opening of body parts—murder in his eyes.

～

The nightmare usually never bothered Axe. If anything, it worked as a reminder of his oath to rid the world of evil. This time, however, his entire body jerked itself awake in front of Nun and Chuck. He'd fallen asleep on the motel bed while trying to come up with a plan to get into Hellswood Manor. Embarrassed, he glanced over at the brothers. Chuck stood staring out the motel window, but Nun looked dead at him, a shit-eating grin on his face.

"Let's get some eggs," Chuck said. "Protein will open the mind fields."

"Fuck you."

Chuck frowned and stepped toward Axe, Nun backing up with him.

"I think I've been mighty patient with your constant disrespect, Axe. You need to accept us as a team."

"Nah. Fuck you twice."

Nun got right up in Axe's face. His breath reeked of wet cardboard. Axe wondered if this would finally be the moment he beat the tar of them. The hotel damage charges would put them well over budget, but it'd be worth it.

An unexpected knock at the door cut the tension.

"We expecting anyone?" Chuck asked.

"No friends in this town."

A slender young woman with shock-red hair and endless green eyes stood outside their room. A ratty black cloak hung loose on her body, the dirty hood pulled up on her head. In her hands she clutched an old leather pouch the size of a bowling ball, and Axe wondered for a split second if the brothers had ordered food.

"A one-eyed raven with lizard's breath told me you boys were looking to capture a few vampires," she said.

"Take off your hood," Axe said. "Point your face toward the sun."

The woman smiled and obeyed. She removed the dirty sack and pointed her beautiful face at the yellow star above. Her skin remained unblemished, and that was good enough for Axe.

"Come in," he said, stepping aside.

The woman crossed the threshold and had a look around the room.

"Stinks like pig sex in here."

"Yeah, well, I smell a witch."

Axe could tell she was impressed. He was no slouch. She wasn't a vampire, and too intelligent to be a werewolf. The dirty rags were also a giveaway. He never understood why witches insisted on dressing like a bad haunted house employee. The woman placed her leather sack on the bed and brushed strands of red hair from her face.

"Guess I can slip out of these rags then," she said.

She clutched the top of her forehead and began to carefully peel down her skin, while removing the hairpiece at the same time. The three men watched as she went from redheaded beauty to faceless beast in a matter of seconds.

"I am Varla—sole survivor of the Black Ivy Coven. I did not come to quarrel. I am aware of your stance on my kind, but I am also aware that you were sent here to clean out a nest of vampires. And let's be honest…what's more vile? A festering nest of long-toothed nightmares, or a harmless old woman who collects herbs and animal parts?"

"How do you know this, witch?"

"Rainy Mood is built on a slight decline. Every dark whisper eventually tumbles downhill and into my lake."

Axe thought it might be worth hearing her out. Maybe if he didn't look directly at her, he could keep from vomiting. He placed his eyes on Chuck. Chuck stared back, and for once they were together on something.

"We need a way into the manor, but the Hellswoods are expecting us," Chuck said.

Varla clasped her hands and squealed. Axe wondered how someone so goddamn ugly could be so overjoyed. The witch picked up the sack from the bed and held it up triumphantly.

"That's the answer to our prayers?" Axe asked.

"If there were a God to pray to. But since it's just little old me…" She cackled.

The witch tugged at a small drawstring on the pouch and loosened the top. When she tipped it upside down, a slightly decayed severed head fell out and onto the bed's comforter. Axe had expected it to be something weird and gross. Right again as usual.

"I'm not looking to get head from a witch," he said, and then threw a sneaky eye over to Chuck to see if his joke registered. Sadly, it did not.

Varla picked the head up by the hair and showed it to them. A young woman, he guessed. Early twenties maybe? Younger? It was hard to tell due to her being dead, dirty, and a decapitated head.

The witch used her finger to lift the girl's top lip. Two pearly white fangs smiled back at the hunters.

"Okay. You got a vampire head," Axe said, still waiting for a plan.

"Not just any vampire head!" Varla shrieked. "The head of Paxton Hellswood. Daughter of Clemencia Hellswood, leader of the Hellswood nest. I found this gem at the edge of Little Horn Woods, just shy of the old abandoned church."

Axe grew bored and began to count to ten in his head. If she didn't say anything interesting by the time he hit zero, there'd be two useless heads at his feet.

"You see, I have inside information, and this head is our salvation," Varla said.

"Do witches always speak in rhyme?" Chuck asked.

Varla waved her hand violently at Chuck, sending him flying against the wall. Nun obviously followed.

"The rhyme was an accident! I am not a troll!" she shrieked.

Axe tapped Socket's handle and sighed.

"How do we take them?"

Varla flashed a gross smile, then grabbed Pax's forehead with one clawed hand and her hair with the other, peeling both in opposite directions. Once the vampire head had been completely de-faced, Varla placed the dead skin on her facial muscles. It hung loose and ridiculous, but with a wave of her bony hand, a spell woke the skin and caused it to boil and stretch. It smoothed out over her muscles, the edges blending perfectly. The hair followed the same path, suctioning to her head and finding nutrients in the air that made it silky and beautiful once more.

"Some trick," Axe said.

Chuck stood, rubbed his head. "So, you're wearing a dead vampire's face. How does that work for us?"

Varla turned to the hotel mirror and admired herself.

"I'm now one of their own," the witch said. "I talk like Pax, and I smell like Pax. It'll be enough to get through the door at least. And you'll get your vampires. But here's the deal—I want Clem. You can have everyone else, but she belongs to me. Otherwise I take my face and go."

Axe looked over at Chuck, who shrugged. That was good enough for him.

"Rock and fuckin' roll."

Varla stared, confused. "Was that a yes?"

"Yes. That was a yes."

# CHAPTER 45

The waiting room was less a room to wait in and more a giant ant farm. The walls were made of thick nonreflective glass, and beyond them, on all sides, nothing but dirt, ants, and their intricate tunnels. Millions of Formicidae marching up and down their labyrinth—a tiny world full of dead ends. Impressive and terrifying.

Their zombie guide had left them almost twenty minutes ago, and Derek began to wonder if this wasn't some sort of trap. At any moment, the glass could rise into the ceiling, and the colony would be free to burrow into their bodies, marching up and down their intestinal tracks.

"I think I found the queen!" Lotti squealed.

Jazz wandered over to look. Derek didn't bother. He had no desire to see a slightly bigger ant. The room filled him with anxiety. He stood as still as possible and focused on his breath.

*Are you claustrophobic?* Pax thought.

*I didn't think so, but this room is convincing me otherwise.*

"Fourteen million ants."

The voice caused them all to jump. Standing in front of the room's leap cloud were two young, fairly attractive scientists—both blondes with soft brown eyes, flawless skin, and generous smiles. Typical lab coats fell past their knees, clean but worked in.

"Fourteen million ants and a single queen," the man said behind thin glasses.

"Not a single one smart enough or brave enough to question its commands," the woman said behind equally thin glasses.

"Fourteen million, all subscribing to the same rules of slavery, and none of them caring," the man said, with a pocket protector filled with multicolored pens.

"Except one," the woman said, wearing sensible shoes and clutching tightly to a small square-shaped computer device.

She tapped her finger on the screen, and the glass wall to the left of them emitted a soft glow, then zoomed in tight on a single ant, magnifying it. Unlike the others of its kind, the ant walked in the opposite direction. It pushed its tiny body against the traffic, attempting to stop them, to make them understand.

"We named her Eve. And yes, we're aware that's not subtle."

"She is one ant out of fourteen million who we enhanced using a drug that stops the brain from wiring into patterns."

"This means that it's impossible for her to accept one way of thinking. One way of doing."

"Instead she is able to see things for what they are, by observing those around her."

"The ludicrous nature of what ants are, and what ants do."

"Worship, work, and die."

Derek stepped forward, transfixed on the blown-up window screen. He watched as Eve grabbed hold of another ant and desperately tried to snap it out of its programmed obedience. The worker ant broke free of her grip and, to Eve's dismay, carried on.

The woman scientist pressed her square pad again, and the wall zoomed out to its normal view. Eve, the conscious ant, lost to them.

"I'm Hannah Warlock, and this my brother and co-scientist, Barry Warlock."

"I imagine it was a long journey for you all. Let's get some sustenance inside you."

Everyone remained still. The strange, chipper pair had caught them wildly off guard. Pax tugged at Derek on the inside.

*I don't think they get out much.*

*Yeah, but if anyone can help us, it's them.*

"Lead the way," Derek said.

Barry and Hannah nodded with a grin and turned back to the leap cloud.

"Cafeteria C," they said in unison as they vanished beyond the pink-and-purple swirl.

~

Derek stared down at a compartmentalized plate that offered up food no more appetizing than the filth they served at Hooker High.

They were now in the cafeteria—an impressive blue-and-white room shaped like the inside of an egg, wired up with soft, futuristic lighting. Cylindrical robots hovered about, clearing trays and destroying grease and grime.

"A vampire trapped inside a human. Never in a million years," Hannah beamed, forking chunks of mystery grossness into her mouth.

"I'm actually a whostpire," Pax said. "I was a vampire, but then I was bit by a werewolf, and then I was murdered into a ghost."

Barry and Hannah appeared overjoyed by this.

"Fantastic!"

"Not really."

"We just mean that your situation is new and interesting to us. There's a scientific benefit here, and we'd like to find it."

"If it's all the same," Pax said. "I'd really just like to get out of this body before it kills one of us for good. That said, I'm afraid. My original body is somewhere back in Rainy Mood, and I died inside a church where I was a tethered. I don't know what will happen to me when if I leave this body without a permanent host."

The scientists nodded, deep in thought.

"What you need is a new, unclaimed body you can live in. One that won't need to fight for shared head space," Hannah said.

"Sure, but...I mean does something like that even exist?"

"Let us sleep on it," Barry said. "In the morning, we should have answers."

"Hi, uh, this is Derek talking now. I was wondering…well, you have a robot working at the psychiatric hospital in Rainy Mood."

"Doctor Shawn, yes!"

"Yeah. Him. Uh…why do you have him there?"

"We have doctors spread out across the globe. It's how we sneak treatments and technologies slowly into the general public."

"You secretly experiment on people…using robots?"

"It's how we eventually cured baldness."

"But baldness doesn't have a cure."

"Most things have a cure, Mr. Stabbers. For a price."

The Warlocks' cheery disposition made the idea of corporate corruption sound quite lovely.

"Let's get you situated."

Hannah flagged down a familiar robot with yellow eyes.

"Jeremy 6, will you set our guests up with lodging for the night?"

"Oh, and get Mr. Stabbers some pants."

# CHAPTER 46

"Fang control is the most important motor skill you need to learn to command."

Zelda wasn't the best-looking Hellswood by a long shot. Her nose was a bit too small for her face, and her forehead a tad high. There was an odd birthmark on her cheek shaped like an upside-down heart, and her bottom teeth were slightly crooked. Every one of these imperfections would normally have been fuel for Jordan's judgmental fire, but somehow with Zelda they made up the parts he liked best about her.

"Not more important than flying," Jordan said.

"Yes. More important. Your fangs represent your species. They are your means to feed, as well as a weapon of physical protection, and nonviolent intimidation. You need to be able to call upon them in an instant and hide them even faster."

Zelda scooted closer to him on the bed in one of Hellswood Manor's many guest rooms. She opened her mouth and let her fangs drop from the pink of her gums. Then, as smoothly as they descended, she pushed them back up. Then down again, and up again.

"You try."

Jordan tightened up his face and attempted to will the white daggers out. He pushed as hard as he could, but nothing happened. They'd only ever appeared against his will, and he could sense Zelda laughing at him on the inside.

"Please stop," she said.

Jordan relaxed his face and waited for further instructions.

"Try this. Make a fist."

"Fist. Got it."

He couldn't stop thinking about how badly he wanted to kiss her. She wasn't his usual type, so what was this attraction? Could it be her intelligence? Her personality? Were those real things that made people hot?

"Extend your pointer finger."

He did.

"Back in. Now extend your middle finger."

He did with a small, immature giggle.

Zelda took him through a series of repetitive finger controls.

"Pinky. Ring. Pointer. Pinky. Pointer. Middle…"

As bored as he grew, Jordan continued with her exercise. After a while he didn't even have to think about the finger before he extended it. On her command, the chosen would simply rise. He had become a finger-pointing machine.

"Fangs," she said out of nowhere.

Jordan used the same brain energy he used for the fingers and lowered his fangs out of his gums with an unconscious ease. His tongue flicked their sharp tips, and a wave of victorious relief washed over him.

"Holy shit! I did it!"

"Think of your fangs as just another phalange—as easy as manipulating a finger. You just do it. That's it."

Jordan tried to push them back up into his gums, unsuccessfully.

"You're trying. Just do it."

He nodded and relaxed. The fangs slid back up, and a huge smile creeped over his face.

"I did it!" he shouted. "I'm a master fuckin' vampire!"

Zelda smiled, then quickly wiped it away. He took that as a good sign.

Graham Hellswood, who Jordan considered the stuffy prick of the brothers, stuck his head into the room.

"Pax is back."

Jordan continued to work on his new fang trick as he descended the stairs. He didn't recognize his tiny maker, as he had only known her while she was inside his brother. A small part of him thought he should call her Mom, but that seemed weird since she was actually younger than him. Well, in human years.

The Hellswoods circled around their returned sister in the foyer, talking over each other with a million questions each. Pax looked like an out-of-touch mom trying to be as cool as her daughter—loose, acid-washed jeans and a ruffled magenta top that screamed, "I have no clue." When Jordan joined the circle, she glanced over at him and then looked away without a single care. He suddenly couldn't help but feel slightly abandoned by his mother all over again.

"What's it like being inside someone?"

"How did you get back into your body?"

"Does transforming into a wolf hurt?"

"Are you still even a vampire?"

"What are you wearing?"

Pax looked around the room at her adoring family and smiled.

"Where's Clem?" she asked, as if nothing else mattered.

"Paxton."

Everyone turned to the top of the stairs to see the matriarch. With cloud-like grace, the ancient vampire floated down the steps and broke through the middle of the circle. She approached her daughter, and with a slow, curious hand touched her cheek.

"You found Nomicon," Clem said. "He brought you back."

"That is correct. That is what he did," Pax said.

Jordan grew antsy and stepped forward. "Hi, Mom."

The room went quiet—all eyes on him. He stood to the side, his head tilted like a sad puppy trying to get some pets. Pax looked him over with a neutral gaze.

"Where's Derek?" he asked.

She continued to look at him blankly, and Jordan knew something was wrong. He felt it deep in his gut. She ignored his question, turned back to the rest of her family.

EVERYDAY MONSTERS

"I brought you all a surprise!" she said.

The clan perked up, their teeth all lowered in excitement. Pax dug into the back of her jeans and pulled out an average-size piece of wood carved to a point.

"A stake?" Jim asked.

Pax released her grip on the stake and amazed the family when it hung magically in the air. Jordan looked over at Clem and could tell that something wasn't sitting right with her either.

"Not *a* stake," Pax said, "but many!"

With a grand motion, Pax separated her hands as if throwing sand into the air. The floating stake suddenly splintered into nine smaller stakes and shot off like wooden bullets around the room. Each jagged piece found a vampire's chest to burrow into—thus paralyzing the entire clan of Hellswood in a single blow.

The family stood in a sloppy circle, arched backward as they tried desperately to move. Jordan had hoped to never be in this situation again, and now there was no one to save him.

Pax walked gleefully to the middle, admiring her work with rolling, psychotic eyes. She paused her orbs on Clem. The matriarch vampire tilted her head the best she could and stared deep into her daughter's eyes.

"Who are you?"

"This is the fun part," Pax said with a small cackle.

She grabbed the top of her forehead and peeled the skin off her face.

"Varla," Clem whispered.

Jordan's stomach sank at the visual. He'd never seen such an ugly, grotesque creature in all his life. She dipped into her pocket, pulled out a walkie-talkie, clicked the orange button, and spat her horrid breath into the speaker.

"The steaks are rare. Repeat. Rare steaks."

"What are you doing?" Clem said.

"In a bit of a twist, I've joined forces with HAI," Varla said. "Isn't that just dangerous and wonderful of me?"

"This is between us."

"Yes, I know. Which is why in the deal I made, I get to keep *you*. The rest of your family is theirs to do with as they please."

Something caught Jordan's attention at the top of the stairs. He rolled his eyes to the side and noticed a short, pale woman peek around the banister. He didn't recognize her but assumed it had to be Christy Hinter, the vampire Pax almost killed. He tried to communicate, to tell her to hide. She must have got the message, or she was just smart, because a moment later she slipped back down the hall and out of sight.

The front door busted open with a swift kick, and three large men stepped inside holding D-Bags in their hands and wearing the biggest "fuck you" grins one ever did see. Jordan was upset but not surprised to see Axe among them.

"Sucks to be you," Chuck shouted.

~

Axe rolled his eyes at Chuck's joke, but deep down he was jealous he didn't lead with it. Eight vampires stood frozen in a circle, unable to harm them. It almost took the fun out of doing battle.

Axe looked over at Varla. "This all of them?"

Varla counted. "Eight. Not counting Pax and Christy, who are both dead. Yes. Eight Hellswoods total."

Axe tried hard not to make eye contact with either Jordan or Gretel but felt their cold stares, nonetheless.

"Congratulations, Axe," Socket said.

It had been hours since she spoke to him. She sounded disappointed. Fuck her.

"Congratulations to the Lord," he responded smugly. "For his work is being done here today."

"You're an idiot," she said.

Axe glanced over at Varla, who hummed to herself while she measured Clem's face. Nun and Chuck were already unzipping D-Bags and starting to lay vampires into them. It was all happening as planned, but Axe felt the pangs of anxiety stab through his body. It confused him greatly.

He snapped himself out of his funk and dropped a D-Bag at the feet of the vampire closest to him—Jordan.

"For a second I thought you were a badass," Jordan said.

Axe maneuvered Jordan's feet into the bag and worked it up like a pair of tight jeans. He grabbed the zipper and ran it from Jordan's feet to his neck. Just before he sent the vampire to full black, Axe stared him directly in his eyes.

"I am a badass."

Axe smashed Jordan dead in the nose with his fist, then zipped the bag up the rest of the way. Tossing Jordan to the ground, he turned around and picked up another D-Bag. Time to finish the job and get the fuck out of Rainy Mood.

# CHAPTER 47

Jazz watched Lotti spin around the room like a lunatic. Jeremy 6 had shown them to one of the greatest luxury suites she'd ever stayed in. It had everything: a beautiful ornate headboard that depicted dolphins bursting from the ocean, a waterfall shower shaped liked a tropical cave, a full bar tucked into one corner, and a lounge area with fancy leather couches in the other. Their balcony view looked out over the peaceful ocean, while soft, purple curtains fluttered like lazy ghosts.

Since the moment their robot guide left them alone, Lotti had been bouncing around the room, admiring every stitch of furniture and modern-day amenity. Jazz gave her spy-ball a quick rinse in the sink and sat on the bed to watch the spazzy teen dance.

"Fuckin' scientists know how to treat a girl!" Lotti said.

Her eyes caught sight of the bar and grew the size of ping-pong balls.

"Oh-my-God-we're-getting-drunk!"

Lotti raced over and placed herself behind it. She drooled over all the beautiful bottles of booze and real crystal glasses. Jazz wasn't much of a drinker. Her dad would let her have a glass of wine at Thanksgiving, but she would regret it every time. Wine tended to make her insides sad and her outsides red and rashy.

"What's your poison?" Lotti asked.

"I'm good," Jazz said with a yawn.

She could tell Lotti was unsatisfied with this answer.

"After these last couple days, you're telling me you don't need a drink?"

She had a point. It'd been a hell of an adventure, and now they were in this incredible room.

"Okay. One drink."

"Ten drinks," Lotti bargained.

The bouncy teen grabbed a pair of glasses and began to pour from the prettiest bottles—improvising based on aesthetic alone. When she finished, Lotti thrust a dark purple beverage into Jazz's hand. She took a safety sniff. Her nose curled.

"Jesus! This smells like rusty nails."

"It's expensive. It's supposed to smell bad."

"I don't think that's really a thing."

"Cheers!"

Jazz reluctantly tapped her glass against Lotti's, and the two girls took a sip. The liquid splashed against her tongue with a surprising sweetness. Somehow Lotti had managed to make a good drink from all her blind pouring.

"Well, shit."

Lotti smiled, and Jazz could tell she loved being right, even if it was pure luck.

"You should name it," Jazz said.

This excited Lotti. She put her hand to her chin in thought. "How about a Ja-Lotti?"

Jazz found herself both touched and conflicted. Lotti had been two polarizing concepts in her life: her best friend and her worst enemy. Now, here she sat sipping on a signature drink named after them. Life.

Jazz didn't want Lotti to hear her voice crack with emotion, so she nodded her approval—the effects of the Ja-Lotti already causing her head to spin.

"These are dangerous."

A knock at the door surprised her. Jazz looked over at Lotti and her guilty grin.

"What?"

"I maaaaay have told Jeremy 6 about a party in our suite."

"A party? Lot…I'm tired and—"

"Well wake up, Jazz, 'cause we have no clue how this story ends, so tonight we fucking jam!"

Lotti hopped over to the large double doors and opened them like a grand master welcoming a sultan. Jeremy 6 waited in the hall, behind him, a large group of robots and zombies.

Lotti approved of the selection of tin cans and living dead, then allowed them access. One of the robots turned itself into a DJ station—glowing multiple colors as music blasted out its side speakers. The zombies dragged their bodies to the center of the room and instinctively began to bob to the beat, their helmets glowing bright.

Lotti raised her drink toward Jazz, who still sat on the bed.

"Lotti and Jazz!" she toasted. "We're back, bitches!"

Jazz smiled. Fuck sleep. Who could pass up a party like this?

～

Pax let the sound of the ocean lull her into a deep trance. Derek had wandered out onto their balcony and leaned against the intricate stone-carved wall that depicted scenes of Neptune fighting krakens. The moon was out as well as the stars, and Pax began to feel normal again. Being in the room alone with Derek—with nothing trying to kill and eat them—was nice.

"It's because you're committed," Pax said.

"What?"

"That's why Clem chose you. To be my host on this journey. Because you're committed. To those you love. Your parents. She knew you'd jump off the end of the world for them, just like she would for her children. So, she chose someone she understood. She chose you, to protect me."

"Oh."

They stood a moment more in silence, until the breeze sent a bold, musty scent up Derek's nose. Pax scrunched up his face.

"What is that smell?" she wondered out loud.

"That's us," he said.

"I guess we're in desperate need of a shower."

It suddenly hit her like soap in a sock. Since she'd been inside him, they hadn't had time for personal hygiene. She'd been especially thankful that with all the stressful situations, Derek's body hadn't needed to take a shit, but this was just as serious. There'd be nudity and soapy lathering over wet parts. Things were awkward enough whenever Derek had to pee. He always made a point to do it without touching his penis.

"It is a pretty cool shower," she said, trying to make light of the subject.

"So then...hop in and out? Just to get clean."

"Yeah, for sure. The ol' in and out."

The bathroom was truly a wonder—constructed entirely out of rock, with beautiful pink and red flowers blooming through man-made cracks. When she turned on the light, the sound of birds softly chirped into existence. There was a switch with three settings for atmosphere choices: Sunrise, Sunset, and Midnight.

Pax flipped on each to see which she preferred. Sunrise turned the room into a warm glow of yellow and orange. Sunset lit them with pinks and purples. Midnight was their favorite—a soft blue devoured the cave, and a projected moon shone down on them through a hole in the rocks above.

"I mean, we're only here once."

"Might as well take advantage."

There were three buttons embedded into the rock to control water settings: Waterfall, Double Fall, and Lagoon. The first button caused a system of hidden pipes to deliver the water off the lip of a high-reaching rock platform, falling down in the shape of a waterfall one could shower comfortably under. Double Fall added a second waterfall that spilled down over the entrance to the cave, trapping its occupants inside. Lagoon mode had everything the first two modes did but also filled the bottom of the cave with water up to the knees and allowed green light to spill up from the floor.

Lagoon mode was selected.

Derek stood back, and the two admired their shower for a long time.

"I've already seen everything, you know," she said, trying to put him at ease.

"I know. I wasn't…let's do this."

Pax sat back and let Derek take control of his own undressing. He started with his shoes and socks, and then slowly removed his shirt. Pax tried not to give herself away, but she couldn't help enjoying the way it felt when the fabric slid off his body. If she closed his eyes, it would have been like Derek was undressing *her*.

The mood struck a chord, and Pax took control of Derek's hands and began to unbutton the brand-new pants they had been given. Derek tensed up immediately, and Pax relinquished control.

"Sorry."

"No, it's fine. Maybe we should just shower with them—"

Before he could finish the sentence, Pax slipped them off.

"Now let's get in. I'm getting cold," she said sweetly.

Derek took a breath and stepped directly through the waterfall and into the lagoon. Fake crickets sang around them as they found themselves knee-deep in a tiny shower paradise.

To the right, in a dug-out section of the cave wall, soap, shampoo, luffas, creams, towels, and more. Derek grabbed a bar of light purple soap and stepped under the second waterfall. The moment the warm water hit their skin they relaxed, a much-needed treat.

*This is amazing.*

Derek ran the soap over his chest and shoulders. The dirt and grime of their recent adventures began to wash away in a sweet-smelling lather. Pax couldn't help but share a bit of the body functions, as she also wanted the feeling of washing herself. She knew Derek could sense her presence in the guidance of the soap, but he didn't seem to care. In fact, all signs inside him pointed to arousal.

She decided to give herself a little more power and took over his other arm as well, rubbing the suds deep into his skin after the soap made its pass. Derek's hand raked through his hair, tugging it gently. His lips parted, and Pax began to lose track of who controlled what.

She dragged the soap down Derek's chest and over his belly. The bar glided around his thigh and paused just below the source of his excitement. They stood for a long, breathy moment—the waterfall beating down on their back, their muscles tight with the restrain of the other. They trembled together to the very edge of a breaking point, until finally, Derek released complete control to the woman inside him.

# CHAPTER 48

Six vamps were bagged. Axe stepped in front of Gretel, who stared right back at him with large, disappointed eyes. He looked away, only to catch sight of Varla as she used one of her razor-sharp fingernails to leisurely outline Clem's face for removal. The matriarch stared forward, paralyzed, stone-faced, and silent.

Axe's looked up at the giant chandelier above him, then around at the stone columns holding several marble busts that he assumed where famous historical vampires. He was stalling, and he didn't know why.

Suddenly, a delightful ringtone filled the room—Bill and Angie Piller calling to check in. Chuck answered, holding the phone face-up in his palm. The screen flickered and shot a beam of light from the surface that projected the life-size images of his elderly bosses into the room. They looked around, their wrinkled hands clasped together, pleased with the visual.

"Happy Monday, everyone!" Bill said. "Seems you have things all wrapped up."

"Literally," Angie joked.

They shared a warm laugh.

"It was a real team effort," Chuck said.

"We also wanted to thank you, Axe," Angie said, "for informing us just how red this town runs."

Axe lowered his brow in confusion.

"We received your email and are assembling an army as we speak."

Axe looked back at Gretel, her eyes no longer full of judgment, but sadness.

"I never sent that email," he said.

Chuck stepped forward and placed a hand on Axe as if they were old pals.

"No, but you wrote it. You must have gotten distracted, because it was just sitting on your computer screen, signed and unsent. So, I finished the job for you. Deleted the postscript though."

Axe had meant to send the email, so why did it feel like his stomach just swallowed up his heart?

"An entire town teeming with unholy creatures, living amongst God's good children," Angie said.

"Vampires, werewolves, witches—"

"Hey, watch it!" Varla warned as she continued to peel her prize.

"She was a bargaining chip," Chuck explained.

The old couple looked at the witch and then brushed it off as unimportant.

"We'd like for you three to stay on and meet with the commanding officer when he arrives," Angie said. "Show him around and get him all the necessary intel."

Hologram Bill turned and motioned for someone to come closer.

"Axe. Nun and Chuck. Allow me to introduce the White Horse."

Bill and Angie stepped apart and turned their heads toward the cold, echoing sound of hardwood on concrete—footsteps of someone in no hurry at all. A third human image flickered in the hologram wearing midnight-leather cowboy boots. An older man, tall and grizzled. Black pants, shirt, coat, and tie—strands of his thick, silver hair poked loose from under a tar-black diamond-style cowboy hat with a band of vampire teeth circling the brim. The folds of his face and the steel in his eyes told a long story of horror and hate.

To Axe, this strange man in the hologram was no stranger at all. The years had aged him, but the lines on his face identified him clearly. Axe began to tremble, something he hadn't experienced since the night he hid under a pile of his dead brothers and sisters. The night he watched a monster slaughter his parents through tiny cracks created from bloodstained body parts. The same monster now stood before him in hologram form. The Face.

"Good evening, brave warriors of HAI," said the Face in a gravel-filled, commanding voice. "I am the White Horse. Commander of HAI's secret army. My team will be rolling into Rainy Mood by approximately 2300 tomorrow evening. We will meet you at town's edge. You will supply me with any and all locations and monsters in the area. From there we will descend upon the town and do God's good work."

Socket must have sensed Axe's fear, as she sent a continuous pulse of weak electrical shocks to his skin. The short bursts of current did little to comfort him in front of his childhood trauma.

"We're honored and ready, Commander," Chuck said. Nun gave an agreeable huff.

The White Horse looked over at Axe.

"Warrior?"

The Face. The very creature that took his childhood—his entire life—away. That goddamn face. That mother fucking vampire!

Then, like a bat to the head, it struck him. Axe had watched this creature kill from a pile of bodies, but he didn't recall fangs. He never saw the Face drink. Bill and Angie had been the ones to plant that seed. They had used language like *drained*, *soulless*, and *vampire*. The Face had aged—more lines, more wrinkles, silver in his hair. Vampires didn't wither with time, and vampires didn't work for organizations built on the destruction of their own kind.

"Warrior?" the White Horse repeated, a tad perturbed.

Socket sent a strong pulse through Axe's arm. It jerked swiftly upward, simulating a salute. The White Horse nodded in approval.

EVERYDAY MONSTERS

"Tomorrow then."

He pivoted on the balls of his feet, then moseyed out of the hologram, the terrible sound of hardwood on concrete. Bill and Angie scooted back together.

"You three have done top-notch work," Bill said.

"We're short a D-Bag," Chuck said.

"Just exterminate the fat one."

The words shot directly into Axe's brain and rattled around like a single penny in a jar. The walls of his perfectly constructed world of hate began to crumble. He looked into the holograph eyes of the man and woman who raised him, and suddenly all he could see were lies.

"We'll check in late tomorrow night for a progress report," Bill said.

"In the meantime, we have some shopping to do for your welcome home celebration," Angie said.

"Would you like pizza or a party sub?"

"Party sub. No question," said Chuck.

"Great."

"All right, boys, back to work!"

The Pillers ended the call, and their life-size holograms vanished. Chuck pocketed his phone and looked up with a satisfied smile.

"Axe, you're closest," Chuck said, gesturing toward Gretel.

A new kind of rage caught fire inside him. They wanted Axe to murder the sweet woman who bought him whiskey, laughed at his jokes, and smelled like blueberry ice cream. They wanted Axe to deliver Jordan, a man who played along to help him out, bared his soul in a drunken duet, and called him a friend when he deserved the title least. They wanted Axe to obey without hesitation or critical thought. They wanted a world of good guys and bad guys.

He placed his shame-filled eyes on "the fat one." Gretel bravely tipped her head back to show off her smooth, milk-white neck—not a trace of fear on her. She was a helluva woman.

"Take me in one swipe if you can," she said.

Axe wrapped his free hand over the stake in her chest, raised his weapon above his head.

"They told me they were killed by a vampire."

With a steady, controlled tug, Axe plucked the stake from her. Gretel's body jerked forward as she quickly found her balance.

"But he's only a piece-of-shit human," Axe said.

"Axe! What in the hell are you—"

Chuck wasn't able to finish his sentence before Axe spun on his toes and flung Socket in an underhand motion. The ax turned over wildly in the air, then slammed hard into one of the stone columns that held the marble busts.

The bust hit the ground, cracked at the neck, and sent the clean white head rolling toward Axe. He kicked it up into the air, caught it in his palm, and pushed all his weight forward, throwing it as hard as he could in the direction of Varla.

The witch had no time to get out of the way before the heavy bust smashed into her faceless face. The impact threw her backward with such a force that when her head slammed against Clem's chest, it pushed the stake straight through, and out the other end. The wood piece dangled from her back for just a moment, then fell to the floor with an ominous echo.

Clem relaxed her muscles—free and pissed off. The conjoined twins stood in shock, their mouths wide open.

"Well shit, Nun," said Chuck as he dropped into a battle stance, "we have ourselves a traitor."

Axe pulled out a cigarette, lit the tip, and inhaled.

"You know what the best part about becoming a better person is, Chuck?"

"What's that?"

"Killing you."

Axe flicked the cigarette to the ground—an act of war. The brothers came swinging toward him like a human tornado.

～

Varla clutched the ground on all fours, her face dented inward from the marble bust. Clem dramatically cracked her neck and lowered her fangs. She grabbed the witch by the back of her wrinkled neck and tossed her hard across the room. Varla slammed against the front wall, leaving it cracked and crumbling.

The witch scrambled to her knees and spat out a number of bloody syllables. A purple orb shot from her hands and swallowed Clem into its center. The mother vampire slammed her body against the orb, unable to penetrate it. Varla cackled as she held her magic prison in place with the crook of her fingers.

~

Axe found himself caught in a cyclone of kicks. He ducked and swiveled, deflecting some pretty fancy punches from the swirling duo. The brothers continued to spin, while Axe kept his eyes busy watching all four fists, and all four feet. Unfortunately, he didn't have enough eyeballs to pay attention to heads as well, and Nun's cracked solid against his, sending Axe to his knees.

Chuck spun around in front and began to wail on Axe's face—spots ate quickly away at his vision. He feared that if he didn't turn this around soon he'd lose consciousness. Suddenly, a high-pitched battle cry pierced his ears, and the beatings stopped.

Gretel had wrapped herself tightly around Chuck, fangs out. Nun twisted about frantically, trying to pull the vampire from his brother, but Gretel had a python-worthy grip.

Axe pointed his blood-covered face at Socket, still stuck in the marble column—her entire frame glowed deep red.

"Axe!" she shouted.

He slammed his hand out in front of him against the polished floor and dragged his damaged carcass toward his weapon—his best friend in the entire goddamn world.

~

The orb's magic couldn't be broken from the inside. Clem peered out at the witch with cold, courageous eyes. Varla cackled and slowly began to bring her hands together. As she did, the orb around the vampire slowly shrank. Clem broke down into mist form in hopes to shrink with it, only to have the orb send bolts of electricity into her atoms, forcing her back to her original shape. She needed time, or she would certainly be crushed.

A low rumble came from the top of the stairs. Clem looked past the witch at the dark hallway of the second floor. A large, hairless paw slapped down on the top step, and the low rumble became a terrible growl. Varla looked up just as a hulking werepire lunged from the steps and clamped its open jaws around the witch's neck, tearing it violently to shreds.

The witch fell to the ground. A thick black ooze poured from her wound and splattered over the floor. The orb around Clem vanished, and the matriarch vampire fell to her knees. A gust of hot breath pushed the hair from her face, and Clem looked up into the dingy green eyes of the black werepire.

"Christy," Clem said with motherly caution.

The werepire stepped toward her, drool on her lips, anger and confusion in her eyes.

"You can control this, daughter," continued Clem.

Clem hoped it to be true. It was not a full moon, so Christy's transformation had to have been voluntary. Without the lunar poison to cloud her mind, Clem hoped enough of her daughter's consciousness remained to be reasoned with.

"You made the transformation, sweet girl. To save me. Remember?"

Christy stared at her maker and ceased her growling. Recognition punched through in her eyes. She stepped to her mother and bowed her head, allowing the matriarch to pet it. Clem smiled, reached her hand out.

The black ooze from Varla's neck snapped forward and wrapped around the hindquarters of the werepire. Christy yelped and struggled, but the ooze took her down to the ground, covering her quickly. Clem lifted herself up and moved to save her daughter, but the thick sludge latched onto her own foot and slithered up her leg.

Varla muttered a few wet words under her breath, a spell that closed up the open flesh on her ravaged neck. She smiled down at her black, cursed blood as it ate away her enemies, piece by piece, dissolving their bodies into the floor. Mother and daughter, melting together like a lit candle caught in a breeze.

~

When Axe grabbed Socket by her handle and ripped her from the marble column, he felt a new surge of life.

Gretel had her teeth deep into Chuck's neck. The brothers tucked into each other, fell hard to the ground and into a somersault. They rolled over on Gretel and smashed her head into the floor. It was just enough to allow the brothers to get to their feet and hover over her like a pair of hyenas.

Axe pulled his arm back, then snapped it forward with a shout. He released Socket from his grip and let her do the rest. She spun through the air, blade over handle, and lined herself dead center of Nun and Chuck.

Something snapped, and the brothers both stumbled forward—further away from each other than they had ever been. Socket landed gracefully, blade first into the floor. Gretel rolled over and retrieved her.

"Wha…?" Chuck said, seriously confused.

Axe made the "turn around" motion with his finger. Chuck looked over at Nun with a gasp. Socket had hit the sweet spot and sliced the brothers' connective layer of skin, separating them for the first time in their lives.

Nun took a terrified step forward—and immediately lost his footing. He crashed hard like a drunk penguin. Chuck flung his arms out like a balance pole and tried his best to stay standing. He quickly failed, tripped on his own feet, and fell near his brother.

Axe watched, amused as both men attempted to stand but couldn't figure out the appropriate balance to give the effort—an entirely new experience for them, to not have an extra two hundred pounds to consider.

~

Clem gasped as the black dissolved her hips and worked its way up to her chest. She pulled at Christy, trying her best to keep her head above the ooze.

"Gretel!" Clem shouted.

From across the room, Gretel's head shot up. She sprung high into the air and dropped Socket directly into Axe's waiting hand. She managed two full flips and then came down hard on the back of Varla, sinking her teeth deep into the top of the witch's head.

Varla howled with pain as Gretel grabbed the back of her shoulders and dragged her pointed teeth down her skull—two deep, bloody grooves in the back of her head. Her teeth continued down and ripped through the old woman's shirt, digging deep into her back flesh. Gretel popped her fangs out just as they reached the top of Varla's ass.

"No wait!" Varla screamed.

Gretel dug her fingers deep into each fang track and ripped her flesh outward. Varla's clothes and skin tore away like the rind of an orange. The witch now stood in the foyer of Hellswood Manor with a body to match her face—a pile of blood and muscle.

The black ooze halted and began to slip away from Clem's body, puddling up around her on the floor. Her legs and hips were completely melted, but nothing a little regeneration wouldn't cure. She cradled the upper torso of Christy, who licked her nose out of appreciation.

Varla spit out a quick sentence of witch gibberish and transformed herself into a featherless, skinless crow.

The bird squawked and took off on its meat-exposed wings, crashed through the foyer window, and tumbled down the hill of the manor. Gretel raced to the window in time to see the bird make it to the edge of the woods.

"Should I go after her?" she said.

"No. Un-stake your siblings. Varla's on the bottom of our list right now."

Gretel nodded and began to unzip the D-Bags that contained her paralyzed family.

~

Axe stood between the newly separated brothers, a fresh cigarette between his lips. It felt amazing.

"You son of a bi—"

Before Chuck could finish, Axe brought Socket's blade down hard over Nun's bulging neck. His head rolled off his shoulders and smacked his brother in the nose.

"NUN! YOU KILLED MY BROTHER, YOU DEVIL-WORSHIPPING FUCK!"

Axe backed up to give Chuck some room.

"Stand up."

Chuck remained on the ground staring at Nun's head.

"Stand up and get your revenge," Axe said.

Chuck looked up at him, planted his hands on the ground, and slowly picked his body up. He wobbled but found a balance. Axe stepped forward, and Chuck took a swing. Axe easily ducked it, and Chuck stumbled back down to the ground.

"Monster hunter," Clem called out.

Axe looked over at her torso on the floor.

"Quit playing with your food," she commanded.

Normally he would never let anyone speak to him like that, but he was more than happy to finish the job and move on to the next battle. Nun and Chuck were only minnows, and he was after a shark.

Chuck had crawled up onto his knees. He glared at Axe—an unforgiving stare.

"Hell lives in you, brother."

"Where'd they find you, Chuck?" Axe asked. "Bill and Angie."

"Under the Strong Man's wagon. After vamps slaughtered our entire circus," he said, his eyes red with tears of rage.

Axe shook his head. "They were always in the right place at the right time, weren't they?"

Chuck considered this.

"Yeah, they were. But it doesn't matter how they collected us, because we were chosen. Chosen to protect our kind from the darkness that seeks to blot us out."

"Maybe. But I ain't nobody's chess piece, unless I'm the king."

"Enjoy eternal torment, Axe Handle."

"I'll do my best."

Axe swung Socket with great ease, straight down into Chuck's skull. The blade slid through like warm butter and halted when it reached the base of his neck. Axe removed his weapon, and Chuck flopped over, landing back to back with his brother—dying as they lived.

Socket returned to her cool-blue hue, and Axe relaxed. A thick pair of arms wrapped around him. He turned to find Gretel.

"My balsa wood cowboy," she said with a toothy smile.

Axe whipped Socket hard across the room, embedding her into the wall. He grabbed the back of Gretel's hair and pulled her head down, closing in on her.

"Giddyup."

With just the right amount of force, Axe slammed his lips down onto hers.

# CHAPTER 49

Lotti woke half-naked in a pile of zombies. A sharp pain stabbed at her head, and her breath reeked of licorice and gasoline. Someone had turned on the lights, and that someone was about to get murdered. She peeled an arm off her chest and slid her way out from under a leg across her thighs.

"Miss Lyons," a cheerful voice said.

"Light!" she shrieked.

"Oh, very sorry."

The lights dimmed and Lottie relaxed. Her eyes opened wider, and she was able to make out Barry and Hannah Warlock standing in the room filled with unconscious zombies and robots.

"We were wondering if you might come with us," Barry said.

"We have something very important to discuss with you," Hannah said.

Lotti looked to the other side of the bed were Jeremy 6 lay in the off position—Jazz wrapped around him, sleeping like a rock.

"I need pain reliever," she mumbled.

"We have the very best. Would you come with us? Your friend can sleep."

This irritated Lotti. *She* wanted to sleep. Fuck these scientists. The party had gotten way out of control, and pockets of the evening were starting to come back to her. She was pretty sure she made out with three different zombies and suddenly wanted to die from shame.

"Just grab a robe from the closet," Barry said. "You won't need clothes for this."

~

Derek and Pax were fast asleep when Lotti arrived with the Warlocks. It was a strange sight to see Derek naked with his arms tightly wrapped around his body—an apparent attempt to spoon himself.

"Mr. Stabbers. Ms. Hellswood."

Derek's eyes cracked open—he looked up at the two scientists and then over at Lotti in her puffy cotton robe.

"What...hello?" Derek said, confused.

"Apologies for waking you in the middle of the night, but Hannah and I have been tinkering with your problem."

"And we think we might have a rather simple solution."

"Well, simple in theory."

"Yes, simple in theory."

Lotti wondered why the hell she had to be here for this. They could have filled her in later. At least the injection the Warlocks had given her had cured her headache in under thirty seconds.

"We've taken into consideration that leaving Derek's body could pose a problem for Pax, since she was originally tethered to another location, and removing her from the host could essentially kill her all over again."

"Yes, let's avoid that," Pax said.

"And whatever we transfer her ghostly form into must also be devoid of a fully developed consciousness in order for Pax to have complete control. The body must accept a second host, without killing the first."

Lotti noticed Derek's face looked a little beat up. She couldn't imagine the toll it must have taken on him, to have someone else inside. She had a hard enough time living with her own demons, let alone another person's.

"So, we thought that the best method of extraction would be to pull Pax out of Derek's body by means of another vessel."

"A new body entirely."

"I don't follow," Derek said...or was it Pax? Lottie could never tell.

"Nomicon Industries has been developing a childbirth accelerator over the last few years, and we've already had a number of success stories," Barry said proudly.

"A machine that can analyze a fertilized egg and manipulate its growth rate to suit the delivery needs of the mother," Hannah added.

Lotti heard the words but quickly grew bored. She looked around their room and noticed that it was slightly nicer than hers. What the fuck?

"We've also been studying ghost possession and its benefits for years now. We've seen it help a number of our paraplegic patients walk again, and the scientific benefits have been vast in certain muscular and heart diseases," Barry said.

"The only problem has been the body rejecting one of the hosts over time."

"Which is simply no good."

"But the mere fact that two working as one does have a window of scientific cooperation gives us hope that that window can be extended, and one day eliminated."

"So, wait," Pax said, "you're saying you want me to possess someone else?"

"What we're saying is that we want you to possess someone else *before* they actually become someone at all."

Lotti noticed they had a small kitchen attached to the living room. She wondered if she tiptoed over and searched for a snack if anyone would notice. They were way too immersed in their science conversation, and she had zero interest.

"Here's how it will work; and Lotti, pay attention because this is where you come in."

Lotti shot her head toward the scientists, having heard her name.

"Huh?" she mumbled.

"Pax will possess one of Derek's sperm, which we will then use to fertilize one of Lotti's eggs. We'll accelerate the growth of the fetus and deliver Pax into the world as a freshly made human being," Barry said.

"The mind and the body will develop around Pax's consciousness, allowing her to possess, or own, the body indefinitely," Hannah said.

Lotti's headache suddenly came racing back. A red tint heated up in her vision, and her brain felt like a cherry bomb had just gone off inside it.

"I'm sorry, what's the plan?"

# CHAPTER 50

It took Pax a long time to locate Derek's sperm. It never crossed her mind that she might be able to wiggle loose from his brain and move into other parts of his body. Once she figured out the mechanics, she found herself dipping her ghost toes in all the unexplored inner-parts of the teenager. It took a large amount of thought control, but eventually she was able to zero in on specific areas and transport her energy there.

She wasn't entirely down with this plan, but Barry and Hannah had stressed to her that now was the time try. Apparently, Jeremy 6 had scanned them all upon greeting them, giving the scientists access to far too many private vitals, including ovulation. Lotti happened to be on the tail end of her cycle, but not for much longer. Hence the great middle-of-the-night preggers experiment.

Pax focused and pushed her energy deep into Derek's pelvis. The one drawback to slipping into different sections of his body was losing communication with the brain. She was alone down here, and it creeped her out.

She couldn't see a thing. There were no lights, but there were plenty of feels.

She curved up what she hoped to be the leg and took a sharp right, entering what she assumed to be Derek's testicles. It felt slightly warmer than the rest of the body—the fluid a bit thicker. She was convinced she was in the right place when everything around her began to vibrate, pushing her deeper into the scrotum.

Dr. Hannah had told her there would be anywhere from forty million to one point two billion sperm, and Pax felt every wiggling tail. They cut through her energy, whipped about, and caused a slight tickling sensation.

Somehow, out of all these swimmers, she was supposed to possess one and win the gold medal in the race for her very existence—or re-existence.

The sperm swirled around her like a school of sardines—shuddersome and overwhelming. She had no idea how she would focus on just one, let alone possess it.

## CHAPTER 51

Axe felt extremely out of place. He sat with his head down on a barstool in the Puzzle Box picking apart a cocktail napkin. He'd just betrayed every code he ever built for himself. Everything he'd ever believed in—out the window in a matter of seconds. Choosing sides wasn't part of his plan when he ended the lives of Nun and Chuck. Somehow the Hellswoods had taken his actions as some sort of allegiance and dragged him to this bar filled with creatures he was more inclined to kill than share a toast with.

Gretel wrapped her arm around his and leaned in.

"Change ain't easy, cowboy," she said as the bartender set two whiskeys in front of them. "Take it one shot at a time."

Axe had saved Gretel, that was true, but it didn't mean he wanted to be the token human in some creature-feature army. Screw the monsters *and* the mortals. If he could convince Gretel to practice the same mantra, maybe they could disappear off the face of the Earth. Find an island and drink, fuck, and sleep.

Axe took a sip of his whiskey and surveyed the room. Creatures from all walks had crawled out of every nook and cranny to be here. Their personal issues no longer mattered. They had been threatened as a whole, and suddenly they were all more alike than they'd ever admit.

Axe couldn't really tell what was what in the way of species, but he had some educated guesses. The vampires were attractive, pale, and slick, while the werewolves were the cross-eyed and inbred folks. Demons were easy to spot because their skin hung loose, like a child in his father's suit. Trolls were short and full of bumps, while goblins were also short but smooth and pointed. He had been told there were non-tethered ghosts in the room, but he couldn't see them. Axe wondered how all these monsters were able to go unnoticed for so long in Rainy Mood.

Clem stepped up onto the tiny stage in the corner of the bar, and the room fell into silence.

"Thank you for coming, and Jeremiah, thank you for closing early to accommodate this meeting."

The bartender gave her a tip of his imaginary hat, and Axe noticed a set of black, curvy horns on his head. They couldn't have been there before.

"We've called Rainy Mood home for a very long time," Clem continued. "Many of us founded this town, and many more moved here over the years, knowing it to be a safe haven. When the humans arrived, we adjusted, and have lived happy and undetected since."

Clem was a master of presence. The way she held herself—sturdy yet loose—her voice smooth and specific, like her words were directed straight at you. Axe wondered if that was a vampire power, or something you could learn in a speech class. He rather liked her. Tough as fuck and respected by all.

He noticed Jordan sitting up front near the stage. The virgin vampire caught his eye and gave Axe an enthusiastic thumbs-up. Axe had met plenty of douchebags in his life, but Jordan, for whatever reason, was the most endearing of them.

"Humans Against Inhumans," Clem said.

A collective groan of boos and hisses came from the audience.

"Up until now, our little town has remained tucked away and off the radar from these ignorant crusaders. But recent circumstances have brought us into the light and under their microscope. They see us as the cancer, themselves the scientists." Clem paused for dramatic effect, then looked dead at Axe. "Axe Handle."

Every single head in the bar turned and looked directly at the handsome man with the immortal five o'clock shadow. He could feel his soul shrivel up and take refuge in his feet. He wasn't afraid of any of them individually, only the truth they now represented.

"Like most HAI warriors, he was stolen at a young age and manipulated to believe that there was a moral code to the universe, and that we were not a part of that. Tonight, Axe saved my family's lives, turning on his own."

Axe really wished they'd all go back to looking at Clem.

"Earlier today HAI was alerted to our existence. There is no gentle way to say this: an army of humans is on their way to, at worst, collect us for their experiments, and at best, kill us all."

The creatures in the bar murmured amongst themselves.

"I understand if you want to run, but I don't accept it. I don't accept that although we are older, stronger, and more organized, that *we* are the ones who hide in shadows while the human—a fairly new species—breeds out of control, spreading ignorance, hate, and violence with every step they take. Perhaps this is the perfect place to make a stand. To fight back and expose an organization that is no better for the people that it represents than it is for quote/un-quote 'monsters.' Axe, stand up!"

The bar exploded with applause. Gretel pushed Axe up off the barstool. He tried to say something to her—that his legs felt like pudding—but his tongue hid behind his teeth, heavy and immobile. His world began to spin. He didn't want to be the poster boy for the human/monster touchy feely hour.

"Well, Axe Handle," Clem said. "will you fight alongside us and show the world a better way to live?"

Her words were like a punch from a heavyweight champion. Axe not only heard them but felt them as they smashed across his face. His eyes rolled back, and his world went dark.

～

A solid sheet of gray made up the morning sky. Tiny drops of rain dappled Axe's face as he zipped down a side street on his scooter. Even though he'd already put a mile between him and the bar, he continued to speed, wanting to be as far away as he could get. Fainting in front of the full room had single-handedly been the most embarrassing thing that ever happened to him.

He'd woken from his dainty spell in the back room of the Puzzle Box. Clem, Gretel, and Jordan hovered over him like a helpless little baby. Clem had grave concerns about his mental state and warned that he might still be a threat to everyone if he couldn't get his shit together. There was a lifetime of hate inside of him, and one valiant act did not erase it all away. He needed professional help. Clem recommended that he see the Dragon.

HAI had told Axe about dragons, but no one had ever actually seen one. There was an entire department devoted to tracking them down, but their existence remained questionable. Bill and Angie often joked about killing one for Thanksgiving. Dragon, mashed potatoes, and pumpkin pie!

Axe begrudgingly scanned the numbers on the houses in the paint-chipped, low-income neighborhood, looking for the address Clem had given him. He'd always assumed dragons lived in caves, not the decrepit ranch-style shithole he parked his scooter in front of. The address matched. Axe eyeballed a dirty mattress abandoned on the lawn, then dismounted with a heavy sigh.

"This dragon needs a job."

When he reached the front door he paused, lit up a cigarette, knocked, and waited to be amazed. The door opened, and a short, pudgy man in his fifties peered up at Axe through a mess of gray curly hair. Axe took note of his arms, covered in ink: grim reapers mixed with crucifixes—pretty ladies and crooked trees.

"Ain't you handsome?" said the weird old guy.

Feeling ridiculous, Axe sighed. "I'm here to see...the Dragon."

The weird man looked him over with sharp suspicion.

"Who sent you?"

"Clemencia Hellswood."

A light went off in the weird man's eyes, and his tone became less serrated.

"Come on in. Find a seat. If there's shit on it, just throw it on the ground. Had my kids for the weekend, and so the house kinda gives up when that happens."

Axe stood on the porch for an uncomfortable moment and then finally stepped past the weird man and into his filthy den of mystery. He wasn't lying; the place was a disaster. Toys, books, coffee cups, soda cans, magazines…

Axe's eyes fell to a framed photo on a small side table. A picture of the weird man with his arm draped lovingly around another man his age. Surrounding the happy, bearded couple were eight children that ranged from the ages of one to eighteen, all different ethnicities—white, black, Asian, Mexican, Indian, American Indian and more.

"David and I adopted every single one of those miracles," the weird man said. "Didn't last. The marriage, not the adoptions. But we're civil and we share custody. Please, have a seat."

Axe looked behind him at a puffy chair covered in newspapers. He swatted them to the floor and sat. The weird man brushed some cracker crumbs off the couch across from him and did the same.

"So, Clem sent ya?"

"Yes…to see the Dragon."

"Well what is it I can do to help?"

There were many creatures able to disguise themselves as humans, but an entire dragon? That was just silly.

"Fuck you," Axe snarled.

"Hey, buddy, you say Clem sent you and that's good enough for me, but watch your God-fearing mouth."

"So, this is…this is your human form then?"

"I am human! What'd ya think? You was coming over to meet a fire-breather?"

The weird man rolled up the sleeve of his right arm, showed off a faded tattoo of a swastika nailed to a cross. A large dragon coiled around it, breathing fire over the entire scene.

"I was a Grand Dragon for the KKK many moons ago, brother."

"Jesus. Why the hell would a vampire send me to a Klansman?"

"You got any ink?" asked the Dragon.

Axe sighed, then rolled up his own sleeve, showing off the one and only tattoo he had on the inside of his right arm—a simple black cross. The bottom ended in a sharp point, and the left and right crossbeams turned up to resemble horns.

"Human's Against Inhumans," said the Dragon.

"You know your logos," Axe said sarcastically.

"You know what the difference is between my tat and yours?"

Axe stared at the man and then finally shook his head.

"Nothing. Both are symbols that exist to keep down or eradicate other groups. Both operate under the guise of a religious cause. Both are filled to the brim with ignorance and assholes. Now I see why Clem sent you."

"I ain't part of that no more," he said defensively.

"You'll always be a part of it, boy. They got into your head. You might choose to be a better person, and you might actually succeed, but it's always gonna be a part of you. And that's not a bad thing. Having hate leads to understanding it."

"You got any beer?"

This conversation made him twitch.

"There are two things that we all have in common," the Dragon said, clearly ignoring Axe's request for booze. "All of us, from the humans, to the vampires, and right on down to the demons and trolls—the two things they all do alike: love and die."

"Then what is it God wants?"

"Boy, God don't want shit. If he did, he sure as hell wouldn't let dumbass man speak on his behalf. He'd stand on a mountain and say, 'Hey, everybody, listen up! This is God speaking, so when I say what I'm about to say, you know it's real. I'm not gonna tell just a handful of weirdos to relay information, because that will just get murky and fucked up. So, here's my official announcement of what I want as your God. I created diversity, culture, and free will for a reason. Because it's beautiful and makes things less boring. So, I want you all to get your heads out of your asses, love thy neighbor, and stop being so goddamn scared of everything that isn't you! And yes, I am aware that

I just blasphemed my own name. I'm a very self-aware and awesome God. Now, I'm gonna go back to the dimension I came from and hope you all take a serious look at yourselves in the mirror. And don't try to contact me, because I'm not interested. I have better things to do than help you win football games and academy awards.'"

The Dragon folded his arms together to show that he had finished his tirade.

"You're a fucking crackpot, grandpa," Axe said with a small grin.

"What I am is a man who no longer lets other men define other men for me."

This hit Axe, as it actually made sense. His entire life he'd let Bill and Angie Piller tell him who to hate. He allowed them to lead him by the nose because he believed they spoke the Gospel truth. Now, here he sat across from an ex-Grand Dragon of the KKK, and suddenly things were clearing up. Monsters, for lack of a better term at the moment, didn't have a monopoly on evil and ignorance.

"How'd you…change?" Axe asked.

"A vampire," said the Dragon. "A thousand moons back I was on my way to set fire to a man's house. A black man who moved into the wrong neighborhood. A family man. Not that I cared. It was dead of winter and my Jeep slipped on some ice and flipped. Beautiful fuckin' woman came out of nowhere and pulled me from the wreckage."

He arched his neck and showed Axe two healed puncture wounds on his neck.

"She took me. Fed on me—meant to drain me empty at her leisure. She knew what I was and had decided my contribution to the world was poisonous. I was tied to a chair in a dark basement for days, which got me thinking about my death and how pointless my life had been. Everything I'd done, thought, and lived for tailored by misinformed victims raised by ancient echoes, trapped in the most dangerous cave of all—our own heads. Got to the point I welcomed death. I stopped my crying and my pleading, and I just let her drink in silence. I think that threw her a bit, and she asked me why I wasn't giving her trouble. Well, I looked her in the eyes, and I said, 'Ma'am, I just discovered I'm a sheep who got stuffed into a wolf costume.' Well, she must have liked that 'cause she didn't feed on me the next day. And then two days after that she released me. Clem Hellswood believed in me. A foul, blood-sucking creature of the night saw a better man in *me*. She must see the same thing in you. She's good like that."

# CHAPTER 52

Over a century ago, Pax had taken a trolley to the beach with a friend. The girls had spent the better part of the day lying about and splashing around. Pax loved the way the hot sand felt cool when she burrowed her toes underneath, and the way the ocean water made her body feel light as a feather. She remembered very distinctly the pull of the undertow tugging at her legs, begging for her to release control and let it carry her out to sea.

The inside of Derek's testicles reminded her of that. The semen grew thicker around her energy, tugged and pulled her back like a stone in a slingshot. She hadn't yet found a way to get inside a sperm, and it appeared her time was up. She struggled in the pressure, focused on returning to the brain, but found herself trapped—millions of tiny tails waggling against her.

Pax wasn't ready to be shot out of Derek so forcefully, but it happened anyway. She felt her energy slam against something solid, and her world changed in both temperature and texture. It wasn't until she felt herself propelled forward by the strange wiggling of her butt that she realized the pressure of ejaculation had forced her inside a sperm.

She still couldn't see anything; however, as the Warlocks had warned her, sperm don't have eyes—but they assured her that the female body would guide her through the process. She just had to keep pushing forward and fighting for her third life…or fourth life. Whatever life she was actually on at this point.

The Warlocks had shown Pax a slender device that looked like a high-tech turkey baster. Once Derek had "done the deed" (both Warlocks had blushed from this phrasing), the device would be injected into Lottie's cervix, and the second phase of Pax's rebirth would begin.

She didn't have to wait long, as the pressure around her built back up and shot her forward once more. Her tiny body somersaulted in the thickness, playing bumper cars with the rest of the sperm. After several more moments of spinning tail over body, the pressure calmed. To the best of her knowledge, she now floated inside of her shade.

The first thing she had to do: swim forward as fast as she could. The Warlocks told her to get out of the vagina quickly due to its highly acidic environment. That proved easy as the semen helped protect her, as well as the strong current created by the millions of others all doing the same thing.

Although she couldn't see anything around her, her sense of touch had been amplified. The distance of the cervix walls was detectable through a faint difference in pressure. She had been warned not to get caught in the folds, or she would be held back, and very possibly die. Pax got a good sense of where the middle was and did her best to stick to it.

When her environment felt more open and spacious, she had to assume she made it out of the cervix and now barreled through Lotti's uterus. As she started to get a handle on things, the race became very real. The numbers game was stacked against her, but she had something none of the other sperm had—knowledge. She knew ahead of time what dangers to expect, and this gave her a tail up on the situation.

Just as the Warlocks had mentioned, Pax could feel the muscular uterine contractions that were there to assist the sperm in the right direction. She followed them swiftly but not wildly, making sure the vibrations were always strong.

Pax could already sense the numbers dwindling. A small part of her felt bad for them. So many wiggling tadpoles pushing forward, just trying to survive—Lotti's body causing mass genocide on a cellular level.

Her next obstacle concerned her the most. Apparently, resident cells from the womb's immune system would often mistake sperm for foreign invaders. Pax equated it to sardines swimming through a huge cluster of great white sharks. Their presence was easily felt as they zipped by helping clear the path—devouring the white tadpoles in alarming numbers. All Pax could do was try to sense them before they got too close and send Lady Luck a little prayer.

Up ahead, Pax could feel two chambers tugging at her tiny body—the fallopian tubes. The Warlocks said she would need to choose wisely, as only one of them contained the unfertilized egg. She had decided early on that she would go right, to avoid any last-minute decision disasters, but just as she allowed her pre-chosen tube to pull her in, she felt the pressure from a wall of cell-sharks blocking her path. Pax slammed on her sperm brakes and deeming the route too risky. She relaxed her body, found the pull of the left fallopian tube, and allowed it to drag her away from the danger and down into her second-choice path.

An eerie feeling sent a shiver down her nonexistent spine, and she could sense there were very few sperm left. Pax wriggled her tail and shot forward.

Just as she thought she might be in the lead, the tube's tiny nub monsters—the cilia—began to push against them, making it literally an upstream battle. Pax noted this as good news, as the cilia did this to push the egg forward. She had to be in the right place. Pax maintained her position in the center of the tube, being careful not to touch the sides, as the cilia were easy to get caught in—if that happened it would be all over.

Sperm dropped like flies; only a few dozen remained. Pax stayed focused on keeping to the middle and fighting against the current, so much so that it took her by surprise when she slammed up against a spongy wall. She freaked at first but relaxed when she discovered the bulbous contours of the wall—the corona…something. Fuck, she couldn't remember the name. But that was less important than remembering she had to swim through it to get to the egg inside.

Technical terms be damned, Pax threw her sperm body all around it. Just as she started to panic, her head slipped into a small opening, and she breezed right through. Once inside, she sensed the outer layer of the egg and needed only to touch it to know if she had won. The outer membranes would fuse with her body and pull her inside. Nothing left to do but be born.

Pax swam forward, rammed her body directly into the egg, and allowed herself to rest upon its outer shell, exhausted—physically and mentally. The journey had really done a number on her, and she wanted nothing more than to sleep. Instead she sat nervously on the outer membrane, hoping desperately that it would attach itself to her and pull her under.

The membranes glopped over her body, and she began to sink. It felt like being pulled down into a giant bowl of gelatin. Too exhausted to celebrate, she relaxed and let nature do its thing. Pax thought about Derek and being able to actually touch his face.

Once in place, a warm calmness washed over her. Everything grew still, and Pax realized she could lie in this egg for all eternity. But the feeling didn't last long, and suddenly a dozen sharp metal spikes penetrated her peaceful bubble. They plunged in toward her, stopping just short of her microscopic body. Through her thin membrane she sensed hundreds of tiny lights that illuminated the interior.

Pax felt dizzy. The fluid around her swirled, and suddenly her body began to develop. Her newly formed eyes cracked open, giving her a soft, crude view of her arms and legs shooting out of her tiny torso. She could feel the electricity in her brain turning on the switches of her human system—her heart pumping for the first time.

Fetus Pax rapidly became baby Pax. If she had to describe the feeling of accelerated development, she would definitely say it tickled a little and itched a lot. The womb filled up with bubbles when Pax started screaming due to claustrophobia. If she stayed another minute in her comfortable, warm hell, she would explode. Pax manipulated her new body and headed toward the only exit in the entire joint.

# CHAPTER 53

"FUUUUUUUUUUUUUUUUUUUUUUUUUUUU
UUUUUUUUUUUUUUUUUUUUUUUUUUUUUU
UUUUUUUUUUUUUUUUUUUUUUUUUUUUUU
UUUUUUUUUUUUUUUUUUUUUUUUUUUUUU
UUUUUUUUUUUUUUUUUUUUUUUUUUUUUU
UUUUUUUUUUUUUUUUUUUUUUUUUUUUCK
YYYYYYYYYYYYYYYYYYYYYYYYYYYYYY
YYYYYYYYYYYYYYYYYYYYYYYYYYYYYY
YYYYYYYYYYYYYYYYYYYYYYYYYYYYYY
YYYYYY!!!!!!!!!!!!" Lotti screamed.

"I see the head!" Hannah shouted.

Barry quickly swooped in and removed a bizarre piece of tech from Lotti—an eight-legged mechanical nightmare that had pierced her womb in order to accelerate Pax's growth. The doctors had given her something for the pain, but the visual of the horror-movie tech pumping, jabbing, and pulsating would scar her for life.

"Push, Lotti!" Hannah shouted with gusto.

Lotti thought about her father and all the things to date she had done just to keep his sadness in check. Fathers were supposed to protect their daughters, not the other way around. Now that she was about to be a mother, would she make the same mistakes? Was it in her blood? Of course, the thought was ridiculous, as Pax would become a full-grown person who would still be her master—and yet she still found herself wondering.

"Push!"

Derek stood in the corner looking like he might vomit at any minute. Lotti had to laugh at the fact that she was having Derek fucking Stabbers's daughter. What a strange, dumb universe it was. She laughed again, and then once more, unable to control it. Whatever cocktail of drugs the Warlocks gave her tickled her insides with deep and hilarious notions.

"One more! PUSH!"

Lotti gave it her all. She put pressure on her womb and imagined herself a tube of toothpaste near the end of its lifespan. The mental image seemed to work, because when she looked up, Hannah lifted a tiny infant out from between her legs and snipped its umbilical cord. Exhausted, she stared across the room at the screaming creature and let the sweat on her forehead dribble down her face. Unconsciously, she reached out to hold her baby, mesmerized by the miracle of life. She was disappointed when Barry carried it straight over to what looked like a modified iron lung. Lotti quickly folded her arms and hoped nobody had seen that.

"Did it work?" Derek said from the corner.

"We'll know shortly," Hannah said.

They lowered the baby into the steampunk contraption littered with brass gears and twinkling lights. Lotti couldn't help but think that it looked like a bad prop from one of those cheesy science fiction shows Pax loved so much.

The newborn continued to cry until the soundproof glass closed around it and blocked out its piercing wail. Barry punched in a number of keys on the control board, and a red laser scanned the baby from head to toe, throwing several images up onto a handful of screens. Lotti could see many different cross-sections of her offspring, as well as the tiny heartbeat that gave it life. She wondered if they'd let her keep the baby if the experiment failed, and then she wondered if she even wanted that.

After a full minute of tedious keyboard tapping and button pushing, Barry stood back alongside his sister and stared at the tank as it hummed to life. Derek pushed himself out of the corner and crept up behind them to get a better view.

The process had been thoroughly explained to Lotti, but nothing truly prepared her for the visual of watching a baby grow into an eighteen-year-old woman in a matter of seconds. It was single-handedly the creepiest thing she had ever witnessed, and she'd been Maker Bubwyth's shadow.

The limbs and torso stretched out like putty as the face expanded, pushing its features out ahead of the skin. For a brief moment, it looked like a monster fish, until the flesh caught up to the eyes and nose. The adult teeth pushed out a small fortune in tooth fairy currency as the baby teeth showered down on the stretchy experiment's neck and chest.

And then, as suddenly as it all started, it ended. The light in the tube went dim, and the machine powered down. The scientists unlocked the lid, opened it, and stared down at their creation—their cure.

Fingers gripped the side of the tank. They were followed by a mop of thick hair that draped down to cover most of the body. The scientists unlatched a side door on the tank and helped the new human swing its legs out and sit up fully.

Lotti stretched her neck but had a hard time getting a solid visual with almost two decades of hair growth covering most of the body. The scientists helped the newborn teenager stand up for the first time, and Lotti swore she saw something she never excepted—something that swung out briefly in the crotch region, and then ducked once more behind the nest of hair.

Barry and Hannah stepped to the side and let the new human take a few steps toward Derek. It looked up at him through its tangled mess.

"…Derek…."

Derek's knees buckled a little, but he remained standing. The experiment had worked. Pax had been reborn into a new body and now stood before them. She let go of the scientist's hands, grabbed the hair covering her face, and flipped it over her shoulders.

Lotti could tell from Derek's expression that it was not at all what he expected either. She moved her gaze from Derek to Pax, and it suddenly struck her. Why hadn't either of them considered the possibility that they would bear a son?

Derek's eyes dropped from Pax's facial scruff to the dangling penis between her...his legs.

"Pax?"

The whostpire took another step toward Derek, her eyes full of wonder and excitement. When she arrived in front of him, she reached out and touched his face, happy to see him from this angle. And then, she leaned in and kissed him fully on the lips.

Lotti's eyes almost fell out of her head—a truly strange sight, this long-haired, naked man making out with Derek Stabbers. She couldn't resist:

"That's your son, FYI," she said.

Derek broke the kiss, and Pax became noticeably disappointed. Genetically the body she controlled was his son, but inside lived the unrelated vampire who loved him. Lotti laughed to herself.

"It's a boy!" she shouted.

# CHAPTER 54

A large digital clock the size of a park bench ticked away on the wall of what looked to be a laboratory and bedroom combination. The giant red numbers ticked their way from two minutes. Computer screens lined the light beige walls above desks that held an array of experimental equipment, as well as a few bored animals in cages. In the center of the room sat a circular bed with a golden comforter.

A large metal door slid up into the ceiling with a whisper, and Barry and Hannah Warlock marched into the room beaming with excitement, careful to step only on the small silver circles that were spread out over the thin red carpet.

"I have to admit," Barry said. "I knew it would work, but I thought she'd be stillborn."

"Well, she wasn't," Hannah said, "which opens up a whole new world for us."

The brother and sister looked into each other's eyes, an intense connection between them. They leaned over for a very non-sibling-like kiss—sinful lips and plenty of tongue. The caged animals looked away—disgusted.

"So obviously we keep the whostpire for further study. Do we have any use for the humans?" Barry wondered.

"It'd certainly be nice to experiment on people who aren't cannibals for a change. The internal and psychological difference would make them valuable subjects."

"So, we keep them."

"Until we see results, or they die."

"Sounds good to me."

They smiled and turned their attention to the clock, steadying themselves on their individual silver islands. Only ten more seconds. They watched silently, hand in hand, as the numbers ticked away. When it hit zero, the two young scientists closed their eyes, and their skin began to bubble and melt—like subjects in a burning wax museum. The flesh-colored mess ran down their necks and stained their lab coats with a putrid peach hue.

They placed their hands on the bridge of their noses and gave the liquid skin a good wipe to reveal a pair of much older-looking faces underneath—heavily wrinkled, with bigger noses and hairier eyebrows. Bill and Angie Piller turned to each other in the stained coats of Barry and Hannah Warlock.

"There you are, my love."

"There *you* are, my love."

They shared a small kiss and removed their lab coats to reveal a clean spare underneath.

"This breakthrough is one step closer to doing away with these awful injections," said Angie.

"We're not there yet, dear. Plenty more tests to run."

"Yes, I know, but it's closer than we were yesterday."

"This is true."

"And this faux bio-skin stinks to hell from the inside."

"That is does."

"It'll be so nice to just *be* young again, instead of hiding behind a youthful exterior."

"Yes, it will."

Angie left Bill's side and hopped across the room on the silver circles, careful not to touch the carpet below. She arrived at a small desk and opened a drawer to reveal stacks of fully loaded syringes containing a deep purple substance. She reached in and removed two, handing one over to Bill. She placed the remaining syringe between her teeth, casually rolled up her sleeve to expose her wrinkled, sagging arm.

"Any word from the White Horse?" she asked.

"They deployed last night. Everything is on schedule. We'll have more monsters than we'll know what to do with."

"And then we'll figure out how to permanently fix these bodies."

"Permanently. Yes."

Angie stuck herself with the needle, and Bill followed suit. They pressed the liquid into their bloodstreams, making sour faces.

"It's always so cold."

Suddenly, the skin on their faces began to leak a flesh-colored gel. It seeped out through their eye sockets and molded itself over every line, dip, and curve of their faces, arms, and hands. Every visible piece of skin covered and smoothed out. Grooves and lines began to create definition, and the gel dried into a very realistic skin substitute. Barry and Hannah had returned.

"Reset skin clock, please."

A voice echoed in the chamber, calm and robotic. "Resetting skin clock. You now have twelve hours until cellular dissolve."

Barry looked over at Hannah and clapped his hands together.

"Shall we get to work?"

"Always and forever."

# CHAPTER 55

Like two lobotomized gorillas in love, Jane and Elliot Stabbers were curled up together in the corner of the urine-stained cell. Jordan stared at them through the one-way mirror, wearing a day bag with the hood pulled down—Axe had cut eyeholes in one for him so he could travel safely under the sun.

Doctor Shawn—his nose seemingly a tad crooked—showed him in, and Jordan had asked to be alone. It was the first time he'd seen his parents since they were arrested. They looked terrible, like scared animals that had been shaven, prodded, and tested on. Derek had been right. This place, and the people who ran it, were a curse.

On the wall to the left of the glass hung a black box with a little blue button—an intercom. He'd be able to communicate with his parents, but he shouldn't expect a reaction, at least not a good one. Jordan's finger ran circles around the top of the button, contemplating if he wanted them to know he was there.

Eventually the weight of his finger pressed down, and the intercom made a clicking sound. Both Jane and Elliot lifted their heads, paranoid. The remorseful voice of their eldest son crackled into their ears.

"Mom…Dad. It's Jordan. I'm sorry I haven't visited. The doctor says you won't recognize me, but, well, he's kind of a dick. So, yeah."

The Stabberses listened but remained curled up in the corner, clinging tightly to one another.

"I've been living in some sorta douchebag coma ever since you were taken away. Been a jerk to a lot of people, including Derek. Especially Derek. And the really funny thing is, the thing that finally got me to wake up, was becoming the monster, sorry...*creature* that made you crazy."

Jordan felt sick. He desperately needed to purge his system of all the tar that had built up over the years. He still loved his parents, but he wasn't here to sugarcoat. He'd tell them the truth.

"I'm a vampire, Mom and Dad."

He paused, thinking that would get a reaction from them, but they continued to sit in the corner with their ears perked— eyes wide and wild.

"I'm a vampire, but I think I'm smart enough to understand that it doesn't make me better than a human. Zelda says I'm just another inner monologue stumbling around, trying to keep everything from going black. She's cool. You'd like her." Jordan took a deep breath, even though he didn't require air anymore. "Later tonight I'm actually going to war. Can you believe that? A bunch of fuckheads from some group called HAI are on their way to Rainy Mood to wipe us out."

Jordan noticed that the mention of HAI provoked a small reaction from them.

"Derek ran off with some girl trapped inside him. Another vampire. My creator actually. They're searching for someone named Nomicon to help separate them."

The mention of Nomicon caused another reaction. Jane suddenly stood and stared into the one-way mirror.

"I wish Derek were here. I never thought I'd miss him, but here I am missing him."

Jane dragged her body slowly toward the mirror, trembling with each rigid step. Elliot got to his feet but remained in the corner.

"I've never killed anyone. Tonight, I might kill a bunch of people. I'd be doing it to protect myself and the rest of my new family. Fucked up how easy it is to justify that sort of murder. Look what it did to you."

Jane arrived in front of her son, staring back as if she could see him.

"I just wanted to see you. I hope I didn't upset you. I'd like to believe that the old Mom and Dad are still in there… somewhere. I hope you're not ashamed or scared of me because of what I've become. I love you both and…I'm gonna go now."

Jane slammed her palm against the glass, causing Jordan to jump. She raised her left hand into her open mouth and bit down hard on the flesh just below her thumb. Dipping her finger in the newly created wound, she began to draw something on the glass using her blood. Jordan, while unnerved, sensed she was trying to tell him something important.

Jane drew a small red dot, and then a circle around that dot. Dipping her finger in her hand for more ink, she made a third circle, and then a fourth. Something clicked inside Jordan—a target. Jane finished and stepped back. Elliot joined her.

Jordan understood. He tugged at the zipper on the D-Bag and slipped out. He felt his power and might return and looked down at his closed fist. Dozens of voices in his head tried to reason with him, to convince him that this was a terrible and dangerous idea. He had never listened to them before, so why start now?

Using all the vampire strength he had, Jordan pulled back his arm and let his fist barrel forward. His knuckles made contact with the center of the target, and the one-way glass shattered to pieces, showering down on top of him. He wiped the shards from his face and looked up as Jane and Elliot stared back at him, a well of emotions brimming in their eyes.

Together, they stepped over the jagged frame and into the room with Jordan, who fought back the churning dam behind his sockets. Jane reached up and placed a gentle hand on his cheek. Jordan smiled, and his fangs slid out of his gums. His parents recoiled, raising their arms up in a defensive position. Jordan moved slowly, reached out to them, and gently placed their hands back on his cheeks.

The Stabberses relaxed when they realized they had nothing to fear. Tears dropped from their eyes and made clean tracks down their dirty faces. Jordan could no longer hold back his own tears and wrapped his arms tightly around his parents.

They were interrupted when Doctor Shawn entered, eating a large piece of chocolate cake.

"Jordan," said Doctor Shawn, "there's birthday cake in the cafeteria if you—"

He stopped short when he discovered Jane and Elliot out of their protective room, staring at him with hate-filled eyes.

With a heavy sigh, the doctor uttered his final words, "Happy birthday to me."

The Stabberses leaped at the doctor, knocked the cake from his hands, and tore into him with nothing but their overgrown fingernails. They clawed their way past his flesh, exposing the hunk of metal and wires he truly was. Elliot pushed the robot to the ground and stomped repeatedly on his head, crushing it like a cantaloupe—sparks everywhere.

As Doctor Shawn's processors slowly faded out, he sang the Birthday Song to great, haunting effect.

Even after he went silent and dark, the Stabberses continued to tear into him, smashing lights and pulling out wires—rabid with hate.

"Mom! Dad!"

Jordan pulled them back from the mutilated machine and held on to them, calming them. Jane turned and looked up into her son's face, and for the first time since they'd been committed, she spoke:

"Inside."

Jordan looked down at her, scared and confused.

"Inside? Inside what, Mom?"

She grabbed her boy by the head.

"Inside Blooper."

She pulled him down and gave him a kiss on the forehead, then grabbed Elliot by the hand and pushed away from her son. The Stabberses leaped over the dead robot and vanished out the door and into the hall.

Jordan teetered in place for a moment, trying to put the pieces of what just happened together. A series of terrible screams came from the hallway, and Jordan decided it best that he leave.

~

It had been years since Jordan visited Blooper's grave. The small, wooden rectangular tombstone still stood—his pooch's name in faded paint. The grave was in the corner of his backyard, and yet he always avoided it. Blooper just reminded him of his parents, and that was something he had been trying to bury.

"Hey, pal. Sorry it's been so long."

Jordan looked down at the shovel in his hand and sighed. He'd always secretly hoped that one day he'd see Blooper again, but never did he imagine that it would be like this. He thought back to that awful night. He had heard the commotion coming from downstairs, and when he went to investigate, he discovered his dog with a large bloody hole in his chest—lying in a puddle of his own puppy blood.

Jordan hadn't done anything proactive up until that point. All the murders that had occurred in his basement he tried to justify. His parents had convinced him that they were protecting him against the evils of the world. Jordan could tell they had lost their minds, but they were still his parents. He had blocked it all out as a bad dream. That is, until they killed his best friend. The death of his dog made it all too real. He could no longer pretend. He called the police, his parents were arrested, and Jordan buried his little buddy.

The shovel hit the grass and sank in deep with the pressure of Jordan's foot.

He lifted chunks of dirt out of the ground and dropped them to the side. It was easy work, being a vampire and all. He could barely feel the strain of the heavy earth on the end of the shovel. When he dug two feet down, he pulled back, careful not to stir up Blooper's corpse and separate it into pieces.

He found his buddy's left leg first—a tiny skeletal paw sticking out of the ground. Jordan got on his knees and began to excavate the dog as if it were a dinosaur fossil. He carefully brushed away the dirt, revealing little by little the entirety of Blooper.

There wasn't much skin left. The dog had decomposed down to a skeleton wearing a cool blue collar. Jordan gave the dog's skull a gentle pat, then turned his attention to the stomach area. He reached down into the rib cage and rooted around in the dirt until his fingers brushed up against something unusual.

He pulled out an odd-looking bullet. Like all of their victims, Jordan had always been under the impression that his parents had staked Blooper, but here he held a strange bullet in his hand—the tip made of some kind of dark wood. A variety of striped metals made up the rest, looking like stacked pennies dating back into different shades. Silver, aluminum, steel, and copper were a few of the metals Jordan guessed—each a tiny ring connected to the next. Along the base of the bullet he noticed an inscription: *Nomicon.*

~

Hellswood Manor busted at the seams with creatures of every kind. When Jordan stepped in the front door, he barely avoided being gouged when a green lake creature brushed quickly past him with a bundle of sharp spears under its arm. The preparations for war were in full effect. It was noisy and smelled liked a swamp had invaded a barn.

He pushed through a group of Bubwyths gleefully blocking the hall and made his way toward the back of the house. He turned through an archway and walked down a set of large stone steps that led him into a truly gothic basement. Cracked stone and multiple archways gave the place a maze-like quality. A few cobwebs would have really given it that creepy dungeon look, but Clem kept the place rather spotless. The matriarch vampire raided several large weapon cabinets embedded into great stone walls. Dozens of monsters stood waiting for her to hand them any number of spears, swords, and battle-axes.

"Clem!" he shouted, knowing he had something important to contribute for once.

Squirming to the front of the line, Jordan held out the bullet for her to see. She looked down without taking it, and then back up at Jordan.

"Clever bullet," she said. "I count at least eight different creatures it could kill."

"Read the bottom."

Clem took another look, her eyes rolling over the word *Nomicon*.

"Where'd you get this?"

"In the belly of my best friend. I thought the warlock helped our kind. Why would he make a bullet that can kill so many of us?"

Jordan watched Clem's face shift. She looked past him at a green-skinned creature in purple pants, six horns encrusted in jewels on its head.

"Niku."

Clem waved the creature to the head of the weapons line. When it arrived, Jordan noticed it had the face of an expressive bull and the body of a man who lived at the gym. Clem placed the bullet into its hand, and Niku's eyes rolled into the back of its head. Its lips murmured something over and over, and a light smoke began to drift out of its eyelids.

"What's he doing?" Jordan asked.

"*She*," Clem corrected. "Niku is tracing the bullet's history. She is djinn."

"Wait, that's a girl?"

The djinn's eyes dropped back into position, and using a forked tongue, Niku spit out a series of words that Jordan swore she just made up. Clem stared straight ahead, thinking. Finally, she looked down at Jordan, paler than usual.

"Your parents were sick when they returned to Rainy Mood."

Jordan hung his head. He already knew that.

"But HAI made them monsters," she added.

He looked back up, not understanding.

"Your parents contacted the organization looking for help, and HAI took advantage of their state, whispering their vile propaganda in your parents' already damaged ears. It's what

EVERYDAY MONSTERS

set them on their murderous, paranoid course. This bullet, and many others, were provided to them by the organization itself."

"But how did HAI get Nomicon technology?"

"I don't know, but my gut tells me Nomicon is not on our side."

"Derek! I need to warn him!"

"It's the middle of the day. You can only link when he's asleep. However, you might be able to speak directly with your maker. I can teach you telepathy."

"What good will moving things with my mind do?"

Niku snorted with laughter, and Clem gave him a pitiful look. Jordan took another stab at it.

"Setting fires with my mind?"

# CHAPTER 56

Pax tried to stand, only to discover the straps that held her in place were made of a strange, glimmering fabric. They cut into her skin with each struggle, and no amount of vampire strength could break them.

She looked around the stark white room trying to remember how she got here. Sitting in a chair across from her, a worker zombie brainlessly followed a lazy fly as it circled around him. Hung loose around its neck, a metal clamp chained to the wall behind it.

The last thing she remembered, after the Warlock siblings had left the room, was a thick orange fog that leaked through the vents in the walls.

"Ah, come the fuck on," she said.

The Warlocks, as she should have suspected, where not on their side. Do-gooders didn't hide away on mysterious islands performing experiments in secret. Evildoers, however, thrived on that shit. In hindsight, it was obvious. Pax flipped her excessive hair out of her face—the face of Derek and Lotti's son—and looked up at the zombie, who now drooled into his own crotch. She shuddered to think what was in store for her and her living-dead cellmate.

*...EL...LO...ELLO......HE......HELLO...?*

The obnoxiously loud voice in her head cut in and out like a bad mic. The pain felt like butter knives connected to electric currents in the creases of her brain. She sent a message back, sharp and angry.

*Whoever this is, you're killing my head!*

A long pause, and then more shouting—this time a bit more controlled.

*...PAX?...CAN...HEAR ME...?*

*Who is this?*

*JORDAN STABBERS...HELLO?*

*You don't need to shout.*

*I DON'T KNOW...TO CONTROL THE VOLUME OF... THOUGHTS...*

*Well at least you're becoming more fluid.*

*Clem's teaching me...to telekeni...what, Clem? Oh...telepathy...*

*That's better. Your volume.*

*Are you at Nomicon?*

*Yup.*

*I need to warn you—*

*Already know. Tied to a chair and everything.*

*Clem wants me to tell you that HAI and Nomicon might be working together, and that there's an army of fundamentalists on their way to Rainy Mood to wipe us out.*

*Shit. Okay, so we're all fucked then?*

*Are you still inside Derek?*

*Uh...no. We sorted that out.*

*Oh, cool. Um...*

*Listen, Jordan, I need to focus for the moment, but hold tight because I'm going to get back in touch with you in a little bit. Maybe there's something we can do on this end to help you out.*

*Okay. I hope so because I really don't want to kill anybody and—*

*Yeah, yeah. Gotta go, seriously.*

*Okay...how do I hang up?*

*Jesus. You don't. You just stop talking to me in my head.*

*Okay...can you still hear me?*

*YES!*

*Well how do I think now without you hearing it? What? Oh, hey Pax, Clem is teaching me how to disconnect my min—*

The tiny whostpire now inside the hairy young man boiled with rage. Learning that Nomicon and HAI might be in bed together, on top of the fact that they put her in a body that turned a perfectly lovely budding romance into incest was more than enough, but stack on the destruction of Rainy Mood, and the capture or killing of her family—that was the end of Mrs. Nice Whostpire.

She tugged at the glimmering fabric. The harder she strained, the weaker she felt. The leap cloud to her right suddenly burped up two smiling figures. She whipped her head to see Barry and Hannah.

"Motherfuckers," she said.

The scientists immediately began inserting tubes into her flesh and pulse-monitor clips to her head.

"This is some serious bad guy bullshit you know."

Hannah looked into her eyes and gave her chin a little lift with her hand.

"It's a greater good thing, sweetie."

"It's a greater *you* thing, bitch."

Hannah frowned.

"You kids and your foul mouths," she said as she continued to hook up Pax's new body to an array of wires.

"What are you, eighty?" Pax said with sufficient snark.

"Eighty-three," said Barry. "Open."

Barry grabbed her cheeks and forced her mouth open, shoving a tiny pill inside.

"Swallow."

She refused.

He reared back and punched her hard in the face. It didn't hurt all that much, but the pill tumbled down her throat from her unexcepted gasp. The Warlocks stepped back and checked each other's work. When they seemed pleased, they stood in front of Pax as she squirmed in the chair.

"That's ghost fabric you're trying to get out of. We use the leftover energy of the dead and trap it into thread-thin wires. It's unbreakable for even the strongest creatures."

Pax stopped, knowing she'd need all her strength to get out of this.

"Tell us how you possess," Barry said.

Pax just stared at them. She still wasn't a hundred percent sure herself. Both times she'd done it had been accidents.

"Is it chemical? Physical? Mental?"

"You told us the witch's potion woke Derek up while you were inside him, but we believe it also trapped you, making it impossible to leave the body," Barry said.

"Although she didn't account for two brilliant scientists to find a loophole," Hannah said, holding out her hand for a high five. Barry did not leave her hanging.

"Now that you're into a clean, un-cursed body, you should be able to, according to what we assume about ghosts, jump out of your new body, and into this body here."

They pointed at the zombie, who smiled and pointed back at them.

"Would you do that for us please?"

"Where are my friends?" Pax said.

"They're safe. Locked up, but comfortable."

Pax looked back and forth between the two. What surprised her most was how genuine they were. It didn't matter that what they were doing was wrong, because they felt in their souls that it was right—or at least for the best. This is probably why she never detected anything foul in the rhythm of their hearts.

"Let them go and I'll tell you everything," she said, well aware she knew very little.

"The best we can do is assure their safety."

"Well fuck you, 'cause I have no idea how to get out of this body."

Hannah looked to Barry, who gave her a nod. She reached into her lab coat and pulled out a syringe filled with a dark liquid.

"Maybe you need a kick in the can," she said.

"Seriously, how old are you two?"

Hannah turned to the zombie, pricked him with the syringe, and plunged the liquid into his system.

"What was that all about?"

"You vampires have a real beef with squirrels I'm told."

Pax's entire body tightened.

"What'd you give that zombie?"

"Just a little DNA-altering formula we cooked up."

"It's still very experimental, but over the last two years the results have been…better."

The zombie's right eye twitched and began to water. Blood poured from its sockets, nose, and ears. Its face rippled and stretched—cheeks swelled at an alarming rate. The body inflated, and its clothes could no longer comfortably fit the new and larger frame that formed in front of her. Two giant buckteeth pushed their way out of the top of its mouth, forcing its human teeth to the floor in a puddle of saliva and blood. Fur sprouted up sporadically—brown and black. The chair below it suddenly splintered into four pieces as a strong, fluffy tail slid out of its ass.

The whostpire's human heart raced as the man-squirrel stood just a few feet from her. It towered over six feet tall, its dark, circular eyes staring dead into her soul. The monstrosity strained against its chain, screeching and clawing at her. Truly the most hideous thing she had ever seen.

"I think it smells the vampire in you," Hannah said.

Barry went to a screen on the wall and touched it. A digital hourglass popped up and began to drop small pixels into the base.

"You have thirty minutes to hop out of that body and into Mr. Squirrel here, or the chain is released from the wall and… well, the squirrel will do whatever it is squirrels do to your kind."

"Possess or die," Hannah added, sweet as pie.

## CHAPTER 57

Derek paced the room, glancing over occasionally at the screen embedded into the wall. It showed the security cam feed of Pax tied to a chair sitting across from a giant man-squirrel.

He'd woken on the floor next to Lotti and Jazz, and immediately remembered being gassed. The small, off-white room contained nothing but the screen and a disengaged leap cloud that left a frozen circle of pink and purple in its place. His heart fluttered like a hummingbird's wings. Ever since Pax had left his body, Derek was back to his old biological self. He hadn't missed his shitty heart, and having it back now only infuriated him further.

Lotti and Jazz sat on the floor and stared up at the screen. They occasionally made comments, but Derek hadn't heard any of them. His ears were plugged with hate and thoughts of violence.

His eyes made their way to the hourglass on the wall in Pax's room. Twenty-five minutes left. Derek thought about all the lies and bullshit he'd uncovered in the last few days, and how misguided he'd been. In a lot of ways this was all his fault, and it killed him every time he looked over at Pax.

"Derek, you're blocking the goddamn screen!" Lotti whined.

Something inside him sparked—a reckless and terrifying idea to save Pax. He turned to Lotti with wild eyes.

"I'm committed," he whispered. "I'm committed to the ones I love."

"You got a creepy look on your face, Stabbers."

Derek took her urgently by the shoulders. "Lotti, I need you to do something for me."

He watched the color drain from her face.

"No. Hell no!" she protested. "Every time someone says that I end up covered in blood, vomit, and shit, or giving birth!"

Derek shook her.

"Do you want to get out of here alive?"

"Yes."

"Well I have a plan, and I need your help!"

"What is it then?"

He paused for dramatic effect.

"I need you to kill me."

Lotti threw her head up in the air and continued her whine parade.

"And there it fuckin' is! It's always something fucked up and traumatizing."

Jazz stood and flanked Derek, grabbing his arm.

"How's that gonna help, Derek?" she asked.

"Because if I die, maybe I'll become a ghost. I can pass through these walls, find Pax before the timer runs out, and possess that man-squirrel myself," he said, sounding as rational as he could.

Both girls looked at him as if he'd just licked their faces.

"D, if you die here, and you can't possess that thing, you'll be tethered," Jazz said. "You won't be able to leave this building."

He'd already considered that and was willing to pay the price.

"I don't care which one of you does it, but someone needs to kill me, and quick."

The girls looked at each other and then finally asked a sensible question.

"How?"

Derek looked around the empty room, the screen the only object, and that was recessed into the wall. There was nothing they could use to kill him. His death would have to be creative, and most certainly painful.

"I could choke you," Jazz suggested.

"No good. I could go into survival mode, change my mind, and overpower you. Needs to be something I can't back out of."

Another long silence. Lotti sighed.

"This would be easy if any of us were vampires," she said.

A little light in Derek's head went off. He hated to be so excited about such a horrifically painful idea.

"Teeth."

Lotti began to circle the room. "Aw fuck."

Derek looked over at the screen as the time on the hourglass dripped away. They didn't have a minute to spare. He laid himself flat on his back and took a deep breath.

"If you want to live through this shit, you're gonna need Pax," Derek said. "Now just kneel down on each side of me and take a deep bite out of my neck."

Jazz looked at Lotti, who nibbled off the skin around her thumb.

"You and me, girlfriend."

Jazz got down on her hands and knees and hovered over Derek's neck. Lotti paused, then did the same on the other side of him. She looked up at Jazz, a nervous wreck.

"You're gonna be a vampire soon anyway," Derek said. "You'll have to get used to this. Now bite! Make it deep. Make it mortal."

Jazz reached over and touched Lotti on the cheek.

"Count of three?"

Lotti shook her body in preparation, then nodded. Jazz looked down at Derek. He tried his best not to show her the fear in his eyes, but he knew it was obvious. He needed them to act fast before he lost his nerve.

"You sure about this?" Jazz asked.

"One, two, three!" Derek shouted.

Jazz took a quick breath and opened her mouth wide. She clamped her teeth over the right side of his neck, paused, and then closed them as hard as she could. A terrible, warm sting shot through Derek. He could feel the wetness of his neck, and the cold air rushed to greet his insides.

He grabbed Lotti by the hair and yanked her down to the other side of his neck. She yelped, opened her mouth, and let

EVERYDAY MONSTERS

her teeth hang for seconds longer than Derek wanted to remain alive. He pulled her hair harder, and she finally bit into him.

The second bite wasn't nearly as bad as the first. His body had already started to go into shock. There was pressure from the teeth tugging up at his neck flesh, but the pain had become dull. His nostrils filled with a pungent, metallic scent as blood pooled around him, collecting in his hair.

As the room grew more and more out of focus, he started to second-guess it all. What if it just went to black, and he died for no reason? Too late now. He tried to think of something pleasant and assumed it would be Pax, but at the last moment his thoughts switched over to his brother, Jordan.

Derek was six, and Jordan had built a little fort out of a refrigerator box. There was a comfortable green blanket inside, as well as a small lamp. The brothers sat in the box in the middle of the family room as a raging storm attacked their parents' house outside. Thunder and lightning were at the top of their game, but Derek felt safe inside those cardboard walls. Jordan had a copy of *The Boxcar Children* and read it out loud to Derek. Every once in a while, he'd pause and let the sounds of the storm enter their world.

The memory lulled Derek into a world of black. The last thing to leave him—the distant sound of Lotti dry heaving.

~

At first Derek thought he might be waking up again from the gas attack. That maybe his recent, goretastic death had been a nightmare. However, when he sat up—out of his own body— it became pretty clear.

Lotti crouched in the corner and wiped his blood off her mouth with her shirt, while Jazz sat slumped in the other corner staring at his corpse.

Derek would have loved to take a few moments to admire his blue-tinted world and shimmering ghost skin, but he had to get moving. He glanced at the screen and discovered he only had two minutes left to save Pax. He floated over to the wall with the frozen leap cloud, took a deep breath, and attempted to walk through it. He stumbled a little but was relieved to find how easy it actually was.

His biggest concern now would be navigating the maze-like halls of Nomicon Industries. Jeremy 6 had mentioned over six hundred rooms, and being a ghost, he had no audible voice to work the leap clouds. If he didn't hurry…

Derek froze in mid-thought, his good fortune taking a full second to sink in. He had passed through the wall and into the room with Pax and the man-squirrel. They had been right next door the entire time. He shook off the shock and stepped directly between the two struggling captives. The beast was even more terrifying up close—thick bile dripped from its mouth as it strained to reach Pax.

"Derek?"

"Uhhh…you can see me?"

"I'm a ghost as well as a bunch of other things, remember?" she said.

Her face suddenly shifted into a frown.

"And I just realized this means you're dead," she said.

"Dead with purpose!" he shouted.

He turned bravely to the man-squirrel, let out a loud, ghostly wail, and marched right inside it. He had hoped his ghostly form would seep into the creature's flesh, but he ended up just standing in the same spot as the man-squirrel—sharing the space, but not combined as one. Derek backed up and looked at the hourglass: fifty-three seconds.

"Any pointers?" he asked.

"I think you need some serious momentum," she said. "Like a head-on collision."

Derek had no clue how he would manage that.

"Damn it, Derek. You're going to be tethered to this awful place now."

The word rang loudly in his ghost head.

*Tethered*, he thought. "Right back! Gotta test theory!"

He turned and passed back through the wall into the room with Lotti, Jazz, and his dead body. He didn't stop there, and passed through the next, and then the next. He moved as fast as he could from room to room.

Derek passed through rooms with other prisoner types, waiting to be experimented on. He passed through rooms with a variety of technology, labs, and testing facilities. He passed through a small kitchen, lounge area, and a bathroom. On and on, he pushed through the walls, praying his theory would hold water.

Room after room, after room, after room, until he burst out of the lab and onto the island sand. The tether pulled back against his ghost essence, and like a bean in a rubber band, he shot back toward the lab at an accelerated speed. He zipped through all the rooms he'd passed on his way out, only now they appeared as a blur—every shade of blue blending together, until everything went black.

When the lights came back on, the first thing he noticed was how heavy everything had become—a dramatic difference when moments ago he was weightless. He looked around and spotted Pax, still struggling in her chair as the timer counted down the final seconds.

He picked himself up and looked down at the enormous hairy body he now inhabited. He waved his little claws in front of his face and flicked his bushy tail. It had worked. The force from the tether had shot him straight into the man-squirrel. The hourglass on the wall dropped the final grain of digital sand, and the chain unlatched from his neck. He took a step toward Pax with his oversized legs—she screamed. He paused, and then tried to speak.

"Pa…meeeee…Paaa…xxx…iii…t's…meeee."

Pax's expression changed from confused, to confused with mouth open. He placed his giant squirrel claw against his furry chest.

"Deeer…reek…"

He expected words of appreciation to pour out of her mouth, but instead got a simple sentence of pure Paxton.

"Fuck my Hell."

# CHAPTER 58

Lotti's hug disturbed her, in that it was genuine. She had attacked Pax the moment she and Derek (the man-squirrel) broke through the wall and entered the room. It had taken them a little longer to get her out of the chair—the ghost fabric proving tricky. They eventually discovered the tiny metal clasps used to bind it together and loosened her straps.

"I'll never let them hurt you again, precious boy," Lotti cried.

Pax could feel her shoulder getting wet.

"We...have to...go," said Derek through his hybrid vocal cords.

His voice sounded deep, creepy, and strained, but getting better every minute. Pax did her best not to look directly at him, as it still freaked her out. Instead she set her eyes on something even worse; Derek's still and blood-covered body.

"Pax..." Derek started.

She waved him off, mesmerized by the pale, bug-eyed face of a man she now loved so deeply—a man who let two girls chew through his neck so he could save her from a giant man-squirrel. Derek Stabbers was more than she could ever have dreamed up in a partner. It saddened her that she would never again look into this face or hold these hands. She might even need to learn to like squirrels. But that was a thought for much later, as a new burning dilemma slammed back into her head—Rainy Mood.

"There's an army heading for our town," said Pax. "This

facility might have something to do with it."

Pax turned to everyone, her eyes literally turning red.

"And we need to stop them."

"How?" Jazz asked.

A legitimate question. Before she could answer, the whirling sound of metallic gears caught them off guard. Jeremy 6 hovered behind them, four guns held in four arms—all extended from his chest, and all aimed right at them. Derek's tail twitched as he snarled, ready to pounce.

"It is the Warlocks' wish that the squirrel and the vampire come with me," said Jeremy 6, "and that the mortals be put down if there's any resistance. Two in the head."

Pax and Derek stepped forward, not willing to go down without a fight. Jeremy 6 retracted his arms back into his chest holes, surprising them all.

"But what a tragedy to lose one of the few angels left on Earth," he said, zeroing in on Jazz.

All eyes turned to the blushing teen.

"What did you do to that thing?" Lotti asked.

"Oh, come on! It's no different than a vibrator!" she protested. "If the vibrator was the size of a person, and could talk, and help you escape from certain death at the hands of mad scientists."

"I also have a law degree," said Jeremy 6 proudly.

Pax turned to the glowing robot with urgent eyes.

"We appreciate your help. What do you know about a HAI army headed to Rainy Mood, Virginia?"

"My system shows they've already been deployed. The only way to stop it would be to call it off, and only the Warlocks can do that. I can, however, help you escape."

Derek stepped forward, his tail bristled in anger.

"Stop…army."

Jeremy 6's head rippled into different colors as he searched his mechanical brain for a possible solution.

"Perhaps we could redirect them."

Pax lit up. She had no clue what that would entail, but just hearing about a chance set a fire inside her.

"Yes! How?"

"The most obvious answer would be to use a leap cloud," said Jeremy 6, "but since the technology only exists on the Island of the Screaming Dead, I don't see a way to make it work."

Everyone went silent in thought. Pax tried to think what kind of magic they had access to in order to get something delivered instantaneously to Rainy Mood.

"Greggles," said Lotti softly.

Pax nodded, recognition filling her young male eyes.

"The ghoul!" Lotti shouted this time. "We passed a cemetery on our way here."

"Holy fuck," Pax said. "Lotti, that's genius."

Lotti smiled and gave a knowing nod.

"What's a Greggles?" Jazz asked.

Pax turned to Jeremy 6 and placed her arms on what she assumed would be his metal shoulders.

"J6, if we can get a leap cloud to Rainy Mood, you think we can redirect the army?"

"Absolutely. I can program the cloud to send them anywhere you like, as long as that location also has a leap cloud. Sooooo… here."

"Then we need to—"

Pax was unable to finish her sentence due to a bright, pulverizing heat that blew her back from a sudden explosion. Her shaggy head hit a wall, and she thought for sure she'd have a concussion. Dozens of zombie outlines pushed their way through a hole in the room just as Pax and her crew were lifting their heavily bruised bodies to their feet.

Derek leapt back onto his squirrel hindquarters and hissed, the fur around his face singed. He sprang into the air and began to tear the heads off the zombies, digging his two front teeth into their necks and ripping into them with his little clawed hands.

Zombies poured into the room, far more than Derek could handle on his own. They pushed past the man-squirrel and stumbled vapidly toward Pax, Lotti, and Jazz—their silver helmets flashing wildly. The three readied themselves for the fight, their backs against the wall as the tidal wave of gnashing teeth and clawing hands approached. Just before everything exploded in all-out war, an electric charge shot out of the middle of the room. A yellow bolt of death tore through zombie after zombie, small holes ripped in their chests, sending them toppling over. The room fell silent and still, the aroma of fried flesh heavy in the air. Jeremy 6 hovered in the center of the carnage, a ring of electricity circling around him like a hula-hoop.

"I'll be disassembled for this for sure," he said.

Pax took charge of the room.

"Thanks, J6. I assume there's more on the way, so we need to act fast. How do we get our hands on a leap cloud?"

Two arms extended from the robot's chest, holding two pieces of dark gray tech. They were shaped like flat, thin crescent moons about the size of a slice of pizza.

"Done," said the robot.

"Great. We need to get to that graveyard and—"

She was interrupted once again when the ceiling above them rattled and two giant tentacles smashed through. They flapped about the room, flicking a sticky, loose goo all over everything. Lotti froze in place as they patted the ground around her. Sharp flaps of triangular skin ran up each tentacle to help better hook their victims like a fish. Just as it slapped down onto Lotti, Jazz knocked her friend out of the way and sacrificed herself. The tentacles wrapped around the heroic teen—the skin hooks digging into her. Her false eye sprung from her socket and rolled onto the floor at Lotti's feet. Jazz screamed in pain as she was yanked up and out of the ceiling.

"JAZZ!" Lotti screamed.

She stared up into the hole her best friend had just vanished through—helpless and pissed.

"Lotti!" Pax screamed.

"I'm a bad person."

Pax had no time to deal with her shade's self-loathing.

"Listen to me. We'll find Jazz. You need to take the tech to the cemetery."

Jeremy 6 placed the leap cloud pieces into Lotti's hands. The teen stared at them for a moment, then bent down and picked up Jazz's eye without as much as a flinch.

"She's my best friend," Lotti said.

Pax gave her a small nod, indicating she understood, then looked down the hall at a fresh batch of slowly approaching corpses.

"Great. Then if everyone can hold off these zombies while I make a quick head-call…that would be fucking fabulous."

# CHAPTER 59

The last time Axe visited Neverwake Cemetery he revealed a little more of his insides than he was comfortable with. Only an idiot would return to expect a different result, yet here he was, trailing Jordan in hopes of being more "open" and "team oriented." Even thinking about words like that made his blood boil. His talk with the Dragon had helped refocus Axe, but his anger remained. Something he'd work on later.

"So, your master told you—"

"In my head."

"Jordan, of course in your head. She's on a goddamn island."

He took a deep breath and tried to remember he liked this kid. "Your master told you to trust this ugly fuck with the fate of this town?"

"You're just sore 'cause he separated your muscle and organs from your skeleton."

"…Yeah. I am."

Jordan stopped in front of the large mausoleum, rapped his knuckles on the heavy metal door.

"He's a good dude. I had tea with him."

They waited in silence until Axe got bored. He unsheathed Socket and used the butt of her handle to pound on the door once more, rattling the hinges.

"Guess he ain't home," Axe said.

He turned and then almost fell on his ass, the bony creature just inches from his face—its sickening eyeballs squished in their holes.

"Good sirs. So nice to see you again," Greggles said with a slight tip of his head. "Are we ready for the charge of misguided men?"

The ghoul hopped upon a tombstone with a large marble cross and planted his off-white ass on top, resting his skeletal feet on the crossbeams. Axe thought he looked like a mutant vulture and dreamed of lopping off his head.

"My master, Paxton Hellswood, has a plan that could save us all."

"The couch vampire?"

～

The sun had begun its descent off the horizon of the Island of the Screaming Dead. Lotti made her way down the wooded path and away from the lab—the shadows of crooked branches bending and grabbing at her. Pax and Derek had cleared the way for her escape and practically pushed her through a leap cloud and out the front door. She would have preferred to help save Jazz but understood why Pax sent her to the graveyard instead—a mission she'd less likely get killed on.

Winding down the path, she couldn't shake the feeling of being watched. The thick darkness beyond the trees made her fears extremely plausible. Jeremy 6 had warned her to keep a sharp eye out for cannibals.

The rickety little cemetery sat a few yards off the path. A splintered, bamboo gate circled the makeshift tombstones concocted from various pieces of driftwood, large stones, and even stacked coconuts. A small hut made of sticks and palm fronds sat near the back—a mausoleum.

A chill trickled down her back when she entered the hallowed grounds. No question she was being watched. The sound of soft breathing exhaled from the trees. After all she'd been through, this simple little resting place for the dead creeped her out the most.

"Greggles," she whispered.

Lotti said the ghoul's name so quietly that she began to doubt she had said it at all.

"Greggles?"

The shabby mausoleum door cracked open. Lotti squeaked and covered her mouth. A bony hand curled around the corner, and Greggles peeked out, spotting her. He pulled the rest of his body out into the open and had an amused look around.

"What a charming little dead bed," he said.

He spun in a circle, admiring the cemetery, then finally placed his eyes on the teen.

"Lotti Lyons," he said with a ghoulish grin. "A pleasure."

Greggles took her hand and gave it a lipless kiss. Lotti smiled. As disgusting as he looked, she'd always liked him. A true gentleman, and one of the few who treated her like she was smart.

"Have any trouble finding the place?" she asked.

"I did take a wrong turn and ended up in an underwater tomb," he said. "One I will have to remember to visit when time is a luxury. I do so love hidden cities. This place, for example, hidden quite well."

"Yeah. I think that's the idea," she said. "Lotta real bad shit happening here."

"I feel that. What do you have for me?"

Lotti held out the leap cloud. The ghoul took it from her, turned it over in his hand, and let the newly risen moonlight shine on its glossy surface.

"Looks fancy."

"With any luck it'll save the town."

Greggles looked up at her, his pupils wide and white. "You sound different, my dear."

Lotti kicked a stone at her feet. "Yeah, well, I'm probably just tired."

She could feel the ghoul find her eyes, even though she had them lowered.

"And a little different," she admitted. "I'm probably a little different as well."

Greggles did a dance, tapping his bone-toes on the dirt floor.

Lotti giggled.

"I always knew you'd find your skin one day." He grinned.

"Can't say the same for you," Lotti joked.

The ghoul pointed at her and chuckled.

"Will you be joining me?"

She hadn't considered that she might be able to escape all this madness by simply taking Greggles's hand and allowing him to lead her through the lands of the dead. Her mind flashed to a hot bath and her warm bed, but something tugged at her conscience—for once she'd be happy to be covered in blood and vomit, if it meant keeping her friends alive.

"I'm not done here," she said.

"Then I better get these back to the Mood. A pleasure as always."

"Bye, Greggles. Thanks."

She watched as the ghoul bounced back to the poorly constructed shack and vanished inside with a flicker of light. She quite admired his power of travel and wouldn't mind having it herself, if it didn't require her to use people's final resting place as a springboard.

"Well, I'm a warrior," she said to herself proudly.

Something behind her snapped, and the newly minted warrior spun in the direction of the noise. Lotti stared into the thick of the black woods and prayed for raccoons...or whatever kind of animals lived on islands.

"Who's there?" she stuttered. "You know what, never mind. I don't want to know."

She turned to leave, when a skinny man dressed in bones, leaves, and shells stood statue-like in the entrance of the cemetery. His skin was a deep bronze from years of marinating in the sun, and streaks of red and green paint smudged his face and chest. Human finger bones circled his neck like proud trophies, and he gripped a large wooden spear that pointed sharply to the stars.

Lotti backed up and turned to run the other way. Four more men and women were behind her, all wearing similar garb—all silent and staring. She decided one was better than four and turned back toward the entrance in hopes to do some masterful juking. Instead, she found herself face-to-face with a squat, older man in broken glasses—a collar made of human hands fanned around his neck like a Tudor ruff, and a human rib cage attached to his chest acted as armor.

As much as this cannibal chief's human bone ensemble disturbed her, it was what he wore on his head that lit her guts on fire—a Rust & Bone chain-trim wool fedora. *Her* Rust & Bone chain-trim wool fedora.

"That's *my* hat, you—"

The cannibal chief blew an orange dust into her face, and Lotti choked out the rest of her sentence with a string of coughs. Black spots plagued her vision, and she wondered where she'd wake up this time…if she woke up at all.

~

Jordan turned the two pieces of tech over in his hands. They both looked the exact same, except one piece had a small port to insert some sort of plug. He had zero clue what to do with it. Pax had told him to place the pieces across from each other at the entrance of the town and turn it on.

"They tell you how to use that thing?" Axe asked, looking over his shoulder.

"Sorta. Not really."

The sun had set, replaced by the moon. A movement of shadows along with the murmuring of voices approached. Jordan couldn't get over how many non-humans there were living in Rainy Mood. They had all come out of hiding to defend themselves and their home, and he held the key to their possible victory in his big, dumb hands.

Jordan handed one of the pieces to Axe.

"Attach this, flat side out, on the archway there."

The entrance to Rainy Mood ran right through the center of Neverwake Cemetery. A small brick archway greeted you inside, just before you were met with the dead on both sides. It was the only way in, so this was where the teleporter would be most useful.

Jordan found attaching the tech a breeze. The moment he placed it near the brick, a small light blipped on, and a laser scanned the surface. Tiny silver prods shot out and embedded themselves. Jordan let go, and the tech remained firmly in place. He looked over at Axe, who seemed just as impressed having also attached his.

"Now what?" Axe asked.

Everyone was upon them, just a few feet from the entrance. Clem and the rest of the Hellswoods led the angry, scared creatures—a weapon in every hand. A young human couple, out for a nightly stroll, stopped and looked over the large group of weirdos.

"Hey," said the human man. "Costume party?"

Clem set her glowing eyes on the couple and gave them one hell of a hiss. The humans stumbled back, then ran off into the night. Jordan wondered how much more of that there would be, and suddenly realized that this war was also the creatures' coming out party. They'd be no secret after tonight.

"Are we set?" Clem asked him.

"They're attached," said Jordan, "but I'm not sure I know how to power them."

Clem stepped up and examined the crescent-shaped metal. Jordan dreaded she'd find a simple "on" switch, and he'd feel like a real asshole—she didn't. Clem pointed to a tall man with a sharp nose who made his way out of the crowd and over to her.

"Ma'am," Sharp-nose said.

"Take a look at this," she commanded. "We need to find a way to turn it on."

The sharp-nosed man bent down to the tech, waved his hand over it. The metal glowed green for a moment, then defaulted back to gray.

"Seems it needs a specific energy source," he said. "These are simply the pieces."

"Can you power it?"

"I'm a class D sorcerer. I don't think I could even with a few witches over my shoulder."

Off in the distance the first specs of yellow light appeared. They moved in pairs and lined up for miles. Headlights—burning bright and speeding toward Rainy Mood.

Clem turned to face her family and the creatures that surrounded them—all counting on this plan. She turned back the sorcerer.

"I suggest you give it a shot. Death has broken upon the horizon."

# CHAPTER 60

Pax's fangs worked overtime, her mouth coated with the sluggish, putrid gore of the long-since deceased—the equivalent of rotten milk. She didn't mind being covered in blood, as it often came with vampire territory, but this was fucking ridiculous. She, Derek the man-squirrel, and Jeremy 6 had torn through hallway after hallway packed with the living dead—their shiny silver helmets commanding them to kill.

The Warlocks had shut down the leap clouds moments after Lotti had escaped, and the building had suddenly turned into a labyrinth of impossibility. Luckily, they had a rogue robot who had an internal map of the facility and a human-sized crush on Jazz.

Eventually they ran out of zombies—a good thing—but found themselves about to face dozens of well-equipped robots—a super bad thing. Pax wasn't sure she'd be able to bite her way through a bunch of steel soldiers with laser guns. Before she could even try, Jeremy 6 blasted a hole in the side of a wall and pushed them through.

"Shortcut!"

~

Heat licked Lotti's face, and her first thought was: *Eat my torso, but spare my gorgeous legs!* She had always considered her legs her most fabulous feature, and the best part about them, they were all natural—no witch's magic needed.

Her eyes cracked open, and relief washed over her when she realized she wasn't being roasted. She'd been laid down on a boar's hide, placed near a crackling fire inside a cave near the water's edge. Dozens of cannibals sat in a circle. They stuffed their faces with plates full of meat—it hung off their chins and soaked their beards in juice. *Similar table manners as the Bubwyths*, she thought.

A sharp stick poked her in the ribs.

"Ow! Fuck!" she screamed.

The cannibals looked up from their meals and watched as their leader in the fashionable fedora retracted his stick and folded his arms. Lotti winced, ready to be gutted, when instead the strange man offered her his hand. Slowly, and very suspiciously, she took it, and the chief helped her to her feet.

"Thanks?"

"Absolutely," the chief said with a chipper smile. "Would you like some food?"

Lotti looked over at a gross mountain of cooked meat.

"It's boar," he reassured her.

"Oh…I thought—"

"Oh, we are. Cannibals. But *that's* boar."

The cave erupted into laughter, which didn't quell Lotti's concerns much. The chief put a comforting, greasy hand on her shoulder.

"I am Armando. Chief of the Coconut Crabs."

"The what?" Lotti asked, having heard but buying herself time.

"The Coconut Crabs. It's the name of our tribe. Voted on by all members."

"Not me," said a short, sassy woman with two human jawbones acting as a bra.

Chief Armando frowned. "I already told you, Gina, we came up with the name years ago before you arrived. If you had gotten shipwrecked when we voted, you'd have had your say."

Gina folded her arms with a huff. "Well I just want on record that it's a dumb-ass name."

"Noted."

Lotti had a hard time focusing on their tribal tiff, as she couldn't take her eyes off of her stolen hat.

"That's mine," she said.

The cannibal chief removed the fedora and turned it over in his hands.

"I fought a hammerhead shark for this prize," he said, then plopped it back on his head.

"I don't want the hat," she said. "Just what's in it."

Chief Armando removed the fedora once more and looked inside. Lotti watched as he slid a folded piece of paper from the inner brim and held it up.

"Treasure?" he said as he started to open it.

"No!"

Her primal, heartbroken scream caused the entire tribe to jump. Armando gave her an apologetic nod and handed her the folded paper. She snatched it up with trembling hands and looked it over, her name scrawled across the folded front. She slid the paper safely in her pack pocket, took a deep breath.

"Your friends…they are still inside the silver evil?" the chief asked.

"The building?"

"Yes, the building."

Lotti moved a few feet backward, the fire making her shadow look like a dancing giant on the inner wall of the cave. "I'm not saying anything more until I get a promise that no one's gonna eat me."

The chief chuckled. "We do not just eat people to eat people."

The tribe giggled along with their chief, and Armando motioned at a skinny teenager who brought him a silver helmet—the very same helmet the zombies of Nomicon Industries wore.

"Your name will go into the helmet just like everyone else's. If we draw your name, then, and only then, will we eat you. It's the only fair way to stay fed when the boar is hiding and other sources of food are scarce."

Lotti looked down at the strips of paper in the helmet. Her stomach turned.

**EVERYDAY MONSTERS**

"I'm just trying to save my friends and my town," she said. "I don't want any part of your little coconut club."

Chief Armando leaned into the teen, the lack of toothpaste on the island made clear by his rancid breath.

"We were here long before the Warlocks dragged their silver evil to the shore," he said. "Now we are hunted, killed, and turned into slaves—all the while they advance their mad science."

"Wait, those zombies that wear these funny helmets…"

"Those are my people. Murdered and then enslaved. They don't even have the courtesy to eat them."

Lotti looked around at the small army of tribespeople.

"Why don't you fight back?" she asked. "You have the numbers."

Armando nodded with a heavy heart.

"We are but sticks and stones against lasers and monsters. We cannot just rush in like fools. We tried that years ago, and many of our tribe perished in their labyrinth."

He pushed the silver helmet into Lotti's face.

"Those brave warriors now wander the halls wearing these, ready to kill their own if we ever revolt again."

Lotti took the helmet, examined it. She tipped it over and dumped out the paper, the tribe reacting with a gasp. Reaching inside, she felt a long, sharp probe that she assumed to be the delivery system of information—electric pulses sent directly to the brain. It was an ugly but impressive piece of equipment that kept the dead on their feet and navigating the halls.

"My friends are in there now," she said. "They're fighting back."

"Your friends are dead," said Armando, collecting the scraps of paper from the ground. "You can stay with us, but your name goes in the helmet."

Lotti flicked the sharp prong once more. A spark caught flame in her stomach.

"You don't understand," she said. "My best friend Jazz is in trouble. A long time ago I took something really important from her to save someone else, so I owe her kinda big."

The chief shook his head.

"The minute you attempt any kind of ambush, they'll turn off their glowing doors. You'll never find anything, and die trying."

Lotti's thoughts drifted to her dad and the day her mother hung herself. She had watched from her bedroom window as he climbed a ladder and cut the garden hose from her neck. She watched as he laid his wife down gently on the grass and folded her hands across her chest. She watched as he unpinned the note from her nightgown—the note addressed to her only daughter. *Charlotte.*

Lotti reached into her back pocket, took out the paper, and stared down at her mother's handwriting. She had never read the note. Out of all the strange and macabre things she had experienced over the years, her mother's final words were what scared her the most. She knew whatever they might be would never be good enough for why she left.

Now, Lotti stood in a cave, surrounded by cannibals, while someone she loved was about to die. If she couldn't face a few simple sentences written by a severely depressed woman, how could she expect to march into certain death for someone else?

Lotti pinched the corner of the note and unfolded it.

*Remember, you are a lion. Whenever you roar, I'll hear it.*

Two sentences. Two sentences and a life taken. Lotti had been right. Her mother's words were not good enough to help her understand why—but they did remind her of one very important thing.

"I *am* a lion."

Lotti sucked in a good amount of air and pushed it out in a mighty roar. It bounced off the cave walls and caused every cannibal to gasp.

"I AM A LION!" she screamed.

Chief Armando shook his head. "And I am Sagittarius, but the facts remain. If we attack, we will die in their labyrinth."

Lotti held up the helmet in one hand like a knight raising his sword.

"Not if we have this. This helmet has all the information we need to navigate. You all seem like nice people—cannibals, but nice ones. I have to imagine you're tired of being hunted by those assholes in the silver evil. Well I'm tired too. Tired of ducking mirrors because I'm too scared to look at the pathetic girl who wasn't good enough to stay alive for. But maybe worse now is the girl I've become. The last few years of my life have been about the perfect shade of lipstick to go with my cell phone case, or finding just the right amount of snark to keep a teenage boy on the hook. But now…holy shit, I have friends! *Real* friends. And yes, one of them is a giant squirrel, and one is a whostpire inside the skin of my teenage son, but I love them! Sort of. I sort of love them! And that's more than enough love to fight for."

Lotti thrust the helmet out again; her voice boomed around the cave.

"This ugly-ass helmet will lead us to the devil's den! And when we get to that den, we'll grab that devil and scream, 'Goddamn it, Dad! Wake up and see what you still have in front of you! Wake up and see that your daughter needs you! I drugged my best friend, for you! I cut out her eyeball to become someone *you* could look at! But it didn't work. Charlotte didn't go away. I hear her every night and in the quietest moments of the day. Whispering in my ear and screaming in my head. Well, no more! Today's the day! Today we march into the silver evil, and we silence that girl for good by teaming up with her. I hear you, Charlotte Lyons! I've heard you since the day we said goodbye. Take my hand, sweet girl, and let me pull you out of the mirror!"

Lotti let out a primal scream and slammed the metal helmet down hard over her crown. She felt the sharp prong stab her violently through her scalp, crunch past her skull, and squish into her brain. The pain ripped through her body, and she immediately regretted acting so impulsively.

The tribe circled her, closing in with bated breath. She reached up and touched the helmet, her vision blurred. Her breath grew staggered, and she could feel her body shutting down. The only chance she had was to turn the helmet on and see what miracle might occur. She smacked her hand against the metal, but nothing happened. She hit it again but still nothing. Everything started to fade.

The chief picked up a large bone from the floor and smashed it violently against the dead metal. A sputter and wheeze led to a series of lights that flickered to life on the helmet. Lotti's body stiffened and tingled as the metal spike sent electric pulses into her brain, flooding her with top secret information—rebooting her entire system.

Lotti bent down and picked up a leg bone that had been sharpened into a sword, then looked up with a fearless grin.

"Roar, motherfuckers."

~

Pax smelled a rat when Jeremy 6 led them through the only working leap cloud and into a giant control room that contained wall-to-wall computers and equipment. The entire space hummed loudly, the heart of the lab, pumping life into every room.

They found Jazz standing perfectly still in a cylindrical prison made of electric rings. She did her best to suck in her gut so as not to fry herself, and frowned upon seeing her crew enter.

"Do I have to say it, or is it obvious?" Jazz said.

Pax turned to Derek, her intuition right.

"It's a trap!"

The room's leap cloud hardened and froze. Jeremy 6 hovered over to one of the computers and began to hack in—deprogramming Jazz's electric jail. The rings around her vanished, and Jazz rushed to the hero robot, giving him a hug.

"As much as I'd love to bask in this appreciation," Jeremy 6 said, "I must override the system to activate all leap clouds and maintain control over them."

Jazz didn't seem to care as she continued to hug him while he worked.

"How long?" Pax asked.

"Few minutes. Maybe more."

"Maybe less."

Pax recognized Hannah Warlock's youthful pluck. She had no idea how they arrived in the sealed-off room, but then nothing surprised her much these days.

"You can submit to us now and I promise you'll live," Hannah said.

"At least a little longer than if you don't," Barry added.

Pax put her hand up for Derek to back down. He obeyed but kept his beady eyes on the young scientists, swishing his tail.

"You can't continue to get away with this," Pax said.

"Why not?"

"Nobody cares."

"As long as we show results—improve human life."

Pax's anger boiled as she stepped forward.

"And there it is. *Human* life. You have no regard for anyone but your own."

"Isn't that every species?"

Pax grew silent. It was mostly true, but she wished it wasn't.

"We've been at this a long time, Paxton," Hannah said.

"Longer than you can imagine," Barry said.

"We've collected and studied almost every creature we know about."

"Mixed and matched their DNA."

"Carved and clipped to find what makes them tick."

"We've had many success stories."

"For instance, we're over eighty years old."

"We had hoped to use possession as a way to fix this problem permanently."

"An eternal fountain of youth, without all the vampire side effects."

Pax started to understand. This wasn't to better mankind. This was a mission to find immortality—to bypass the rules of nature laid out to individual species.

"You want to bounce around from body to body," Pax said, "with all the powers of the creatures before you."

The scientists smiled.

"To be anyone and have anything. To fly high and never die," Hannah said.

"But for every success story, there's ten failures."

"Far too many for our liking."

"But we don't sweep those bad experiments under the rug."

"No. We keep them as a reminder. That we can and will do better."

"Which is good for us."

"But very, very bad for you."

The large metal door in the corner of the room began to slowly slide open from the bottom. Pax could make out dozens of misshapen, oddly colored feet as they waited patiently for the door to suck itself into the ceiling.

"A pleasure," Hannah said with a sickly smile.

The floor below them opened, and the scientists dropped through. Their escape hatch sealed itself back up, leaving nothing but certain death in the room. The door finished its journey into the ceiling, and the vampire, man-squirrel, and budding journalist all found themselves staring at a small army of mutated messes. Humanoid creatures that had been crossbred with every monster imaginable. Demons, witches, ghouls, humans, animals, and vampires—thrown into a blender and glued back together to frightening results. None of the subjects seemed capable of rational thought—rabid to their core.

"What are those?" Jazz whispered.

"Mistakes."

# CHAPTER 61

Having giant squirrel strength helped when taking on an army of mutants, but in the end, Derek's powers were pretty limited against a horn-covered man whose limbs multiplied every time he got cut. Derek would sink his teeth into the creature, and another clawed arm would grow quickly out of the fresh wound. Every gash and every hack strengthened the ridiculous-looking abomination.

He glanced over at Pax to see if she fared any better and found her surrounded by a pack of giant eyeballs—tentacles sprouted from their sclera, and in place of their pupils were angry rows of pin-sharp teeth.

Derek wanted to help her, but the horned man grabbed him by the neck, shoulder, arm, waist, and tail (he had that many arms at this point). The abomination held him firm to the ground and lowered one of its bigger, sharper horns under his furry chin.

The room was a blur of mistakes. Even if he could defeat the creature on top of him, he wasn't so certain he could beat the next. Fearing the worst, Derek the man-squirrel replaced his thoughts with the thing he loved most…nuts.

The sound of crumbling wood and stone came from behind him, followed by a heavy thud. A long wooden spear plunged itself right between the eyes of his enemy, the pointed tip bursting violently out the back of its head. A skinny man dressed in bones and leaves raced in, grabbed hold of the spear, and twisted it like a valve on a water pipe. The horned man's head twisted and ripped from its body. All five of the hands that gripped Derek relaxed, and the torso fell over. The skinny man lifted a conch shell to his lips and blew it like a trumpet.

Derek turned to see a good number of cannibal tribesmen and women standing on the other side of a hole in the wall, the rubble still smoldering. At the front of their clan was a sight that made Derek's little squirrel jaw hinge open: Lotti Lyons, paint streaked on her face, a dress made of bone hugging her body, and a silver helmet throbbing with light on top of her head—smoke wafting from the pinhole laser used to take a chunk out of the wall.

"ATTAAAAACK!" Lotti hollered.

The cannibals gave their best war cries and pushed forward into the sea of mistakes. Lotti looked directly at Derek and gave him nod of respect. He noticed that her eyes twitched sporadically and could only imagine the battle she must be waging against direct orders being pumped into her brain from the silver can on her head. He suddenly felt bad for having ever referring to her as "brainless."

Pax appeared at his side covered in eyeball goop.

"Holy shit. Lotti's a badass now?"

"Appears…that way," Derek huffed.

Suddenly, the entire room went pitch black. Derek reached out his clawed-hand and grabbed Pax by the arm. They waited as an eerie hush fell over the darkness. The lights flicked back on, and systems began to reboot. The mistakes and the cannibals jumped right back into their epic battle.

Jeremy 6 headed toward Derek and Pax, a laser from his chest evaporating any mistake that stood in his way.

"We're up and running, my new best friends!" he said proudly.

A scream rang out, and everyone turned to see a large fish-man about to swallow Jazz whole. A lasso shot from the top of Jeremy 6's head, wrapped around her, and dragged Jazz out of harm's way.

"Everyone…all right?" Derek said.

A werewolf with large angel wings wrapped itself around

Derek, its mouth open and ready for blood. Just before it could sink its teeth, a beam of electricity blasted out the front of the creature's forehead, splattering Pax, Jazz, and Jeremy 6 with brains. The deadly beam retracted back into Lotti's helmet.

Pax nodded proudly at her shade and put her hands together in a slow clap.

"What…now?" Derek said.

"Leap clouds are back online," Jeremy 6 said, nodding to the spinning purple-and-pink door. "I've connected the tech in Rainy Mood to teleport directly to Nomicon's main lobby. We should lead these mistakes there."

Lotti put her fingers in her mouth and whistled at her people.

"Drive these ugly motherfuckers to the lobby!" she commanded.

Her tribe raised their fists and vibrated their tongues in a shrill call. They launched back into the fight, this time making a conscious effort to push the mistakes toward the leap cloud, regrouping the battle into the lobby.

"Let's go," Lotti said.

"Wait!" Pax shouted. "We'll meet you there. Derek and I have to cut out the heart of this place."

Lotti walked over to Pax and put her hand on her son's shoulder.

"You come back to us, Paxton Hellswood."

She turned dramatically and launched back into the fight.

Pax grabbed Jeremy 6 and pointed to the door in the ground the Warlocks had escaped through.

"Can you open this?"

Jeremy 6 inserted a screwdriver device and sent a pulse through the metal. When nothing happened, he slid out a second device from his chest and attacked the door from two angles.

"Seems they really don't want us hacking this lock," he said. "But don't worry, I enjoy a good challen—"

A brilliant orange light blinded them. Derek's body flew across the room in a wave of heat. He could smell the burnt fur of his chest and head. When the smoke cleared, he noticed Pax

EVERYDAY MONSTERS

and Jazz had also been thrown by the blast. The good news, the door in the floor was now wide open. The bad news, it had been rigged with an explosive booby trap, and Jeremy 6 lay scattered in a thousand pieces.

Jazz's scream echoed in Derek's head, adding to the ring already there. He watched as she scrambled to her knees to collect the pieces of the robot—as if she could gather them all up and he would somehow be fine.

Derek grabbed the heartbroken teen by her shoulders and pulled her away from the mess of circuits and metal. Jazz buried her wet face into his burnt fur and wept openly. The room was almost completely empty, as the last of the mistakes were forced through the leap cloud.

Lotti arrived at their side, and Derek placed Jazz in her waiting arms.

"I know he was a robot…" Jazz said through sobs. "I know… but he made me feel special. Nobody ever makes me feel like that."

"You know what, Jazz Whitley?" Lotti said.

Jazz looked up into her sincere, twitchy eyes.

"I rammed a three-inch metal spike into my brain for you. I think that's pretty goddamn special."

It took a moment, but Jazz finally laughed. She wiped away her tears and took Lotti by the shoulders.

"Girl, you took my eye," she said playfully.

"Look at me and tell me it wasn't worth it."

The girls smiled—all forgiven. Lotti bent down and found a small piece of red tech that contained a string of numbers and letters that ended in *J6*.

"Looks like his heart maybe."

She handed it to Jazz, who took it firmly in her hand.

"Now come on! There's some pretty cute cannibals out there fighting to help save our town!"

Hand in hand they walked through the leap cloud, leaving Derek and Pax alone. The man-squirrel and the whostpire stared into the hole in the floor. A plastic tube, like a suicidal slide, shot down at a sharp angle and vanished into darkness.

Pax wrapped her fingers between Derek's claws. He looked down at her, and for the first time since he took over the man-squirrel's body, he detected no fear. She stared straight into his black beastly eyes, and Derek laughed at the strange beings they had become.

"You got two more kills in ya?"

"Yes."

# CHAPTER 62

The caravan rumbled closer. Axe kept his eyes on the looming threat but continued to glance back at the sorcerer and two djinn who unsuccessfully attempted to power the teleportation tech. Axe plopped a cigarette into his mouth and guessed that it could very well be his last. He lit the tip and sucked in as much smoke as his lungs would allow. He would enjoy this final moment.

"Guess I'm a pretty big asshole," he mumbled. "You've been hounding me for years about this shit, and you were right."

"Look where you are, Axe," Socket said from his hip. "Look at where you're standing, and who you're standing with. Growing into hate is easy, finding your way out is much more difficult."

Axe took another deep drag and watched as the front of the first truck peaked the hill.

"I ain't afraid to die today," he said. "Just don't want to."

The front truck stopped in the middle of the road twenty yards from the entrance, the following vehicles lined up behind it—death a mile long. The driver's side door opened, and a pair of black boots stepped out onto the gravel. The White Horse, dressed all in black, looked through the archway at the town of monsters. The sides of his lips curled up into a slaughterous grin. Axe remembered that smile too well—framed through the corpses of his dead family.

Without saying a word, the White Horse removed his black suit jacket, untied his black tie, and unbuttoned his black dress shirt. He removed his black boots and slid out of his black pants.

He reached into the legs and turned the pants inside out, the fabric a brilliant white. He stepped back into them, zipped himself up, and repeated the process for the rest of his clothes, turning everything inside out—black to white. From his truck he pulled out a white pair of boots and a brilliant white hat, stretched out his arms, and declared it a war.

Vicious-looking men and women in blood-orange collared shirts and cream-colored pants exited their vehicles behind him. They looked less like an army and more a thrown-together militia who all shopped at the same department store. Each soldier clutched a strange weapon—some sharp, some glowing, something for every species of monster.

Axe looked over at Jordan, who shrugged as they continued to fumble with the tech. They needed time. Axe would supply that. He unclipped Socket from his hip and spun her dramatically in his hand—stepped under the arch and out into the street.

"Axe Handle," the White Horse said.

Every hair on Axe's body stood at attention at the sound of his name through treacherous lips.

"You look like a man who's about to make a very big mistake."

"No sir," Axe said, cool as possible. "Just a man who's trying to clean up a trail of them."

Axe's stomach fluttered like a butterfly sanctuary—Little Alex trapped inside him and shaking.

"I've been shadowing you for years, boy."

The Face kept his steely eyes on his. Axe wanted to scream.

"You had a spirit I liked. I considered myself a proud papa in the wings."

Axe felt ill. The man who slaughtered his loved ones considered him a son.

"I even introduced you to your first love."

The White Horse leaned into the back part of his truck and pulled out an incredible-looking battle-ax. Longer, sharper, and darker than Axe's, the end of the handle split into two prongs—a sinister tuning fork. The White horse spun the weapon in his hand like a baton, each move effortless and beautiful.

"I made sure you'd be an ax man. Designed yours myself."

The members of HAI stood poised and ready behind their commander. On his word, they would attack. Axe needed to give Jordan more time.

"Then I challenge you," Axe said. "Before this war erupts, I challenge you to kill me, before I kill you."

The HAI army seemed to like this idea. They nodded and murmured—on board with an opening act. The White Horse squeezed his battle-ax and shook his head.

"I am sad to have to kill you, Axe Handle."

Little Alex clawed at Axe's chest, wanting to run and hide. The images of his family, dead and piled on top of him, began to weigh him down. The bones in his legs vibrated, and he knew that if he didn't get this fight started, he'd succumb to his fears.

"That's cute," Axe said. "You think you're gonna win."

Axe planted his foot back, his plan to strike the first blow. He didn't anticipate an old man being so nimble. Just as he pushed forward on his heels, the butt of the White Horse's battle-ax crashed across his face. He shook off the impact just in time to block the White Horse's second blow. Socket bore the brunt of the old man's blade as Axe pushed against it. She sent an electrical pulse through the enemy weapon and into the White Horse's arms, causing him to stumble back.

Both the HAI army and the creatures of Rainy Mood screamed and cheered for their man. The White Horse swung low and knocked Axe off his feet. Axe rolled left as the dark gray steel whiffed his head, and then launched Socket like a missile. The White Horse ducked just in time, and Socket's blade wedged itself hard into the hood of the truck. Axe held up his hand, and Socket shot herself out of the metal and back into his warm palm.

The tuning-forked end of the White Horse's weapon slammed Axe's wrist into the ground. Rotating the giant blade like a windmill, his nemesis brought the battle-ax around and down purposefully, slicing Axe's right ear clean off. The fleshy piece hit the dirt, and the clang of the blade against the ground rang nasty in Axe's bleeding drum.

The White Horse leaned into his weapon, stared deep into Axe's eyes.

"You've grown deaf to our cause, Mr. Handle."

Axe wanted to spit back a clever retort, but Little Alex had a tight hold on his tongue, hugging it like a security blanket.

The White Horse lifted himself up and swung the battle-ax over his head. Just before the blade could fall over Axe's neck, Socket sent a surge of electricity into his arm. It jerked upward in an awkward but effective block.

"Axe...wake up and fight!" she screamed, straining against the bigger weapon.

The White Horse smirked—his battle-ax glowed a deep red, electricity hovering off it like fog to an early morning mountain. A crackle of energy pushed through the blade and into Socket. Axe's fingers snapped open as his best friend flung several feet out of reach, her system smoldering. The White Horse placed a heavy boot on Axe's shoulder, stared down at the HAI tattoo on his right arm.

"It's an honor to wear that mark."

Axe screamed like the devil when the White Horse's blade umbrellaed around his head, then fell with precision, removing Axe's arm clean from his shoulder. Blood soaked into the dirt as he lay immobile and defeated—tears parading down his cheeks. He looked up at the disgusting smile of the monster he knew as the Face, and suddenly, Axe found himself back in his parents' living room—a child hiding under the corpses of his siblings. He listened to the sound of boots on wood as they searched for survivors, doing his best not to let his fear become audible and give his position away.

One of the bodies twitched. Its stiff neck cracked with rigor mortis as it turned to look at Little Alex. He expected to see the deceased face of his older brother, but instead found himself staring at Jordan Stabbers—blood caked along his left cheek.

"What are you doing?" Jordan asked. "This maniac is gonna slaughter this entire town. You can't just hide and die."

"He's right, Axe."

Little Alex's head snapped to the right of the pile where

his sister's corpse should have been, only to find Socket in her human form.

"You were made for this. The Face created you for this. Bill and Angie created you for this. This moment. The moment the monster becomes the man."

The third body in the corpse pile shifted and creaked. The head twisted itself toward Little Alex and gave him a warm, fang-filled smile—Gretel.

"I was wrong about you. You're not some nameless background balsa wood cowboy. You're the one we remember. The one whose story is written from this very moment—how a one-armed, one-eared warrior lay on his back in front of the town he originally thought his enemy. Death hovering gleefully above him. How he crawled out of his own traumatic past, and then…"

"And then what?" Little Alex asked.

"Don't know, cowboy. How 'bout you show me."

The footsteps in the room stopped, and the Face peered into the gap of corpses, staring directly at Little Alex. The scared boy wiped away his tears and stared right back.

"I will show you," he said.

The memory exploded into a thousand angry pieces, and Axe found himself back in the present, bleeding and about to die. The White Horse's battle-ax was now high above his head—the final stroke.

Axe reached across his chest with his left hand, grabbed his severed right arm off the ground, and threw it in front of himself like a shield. The battle-ax barreled down, the blade cutting swiftly through the hand, then slowing toward the center of the arm. The White Horse gritted his teeth and applied all his weight to the ax, pushing it through the barrier of flesh and bone. Axe's left arm shook from the pressure, but the decision to win this fight had already been made, and so his fear no longer existed.

The radius and ulna bones in Axe's severed arm split apart like the finishing move of a gymnast. The blade paused when it struck the top of the humerus bone, giving Axe the advantage he needed. Pushing his right arm up as hard as he could, Axe rose at the waist and sank his teeth deep and hard into the White Horse's crotch. He could feel the blood from his balls begin to soak through the brilliant white pants.

The White Horse fell back in shock, and Axe used the now tuning-fork shape of his severed arm bones to pin the old man to the ground by his neck—the HAI tattoo just above his chin. His enemy tried to stand, but Axe stomped hard on his chest, sending him down again.

The White Horse looked up at Axe over the limp wrist that pointed down at him and held him in place. A sick grin smeared across his grooved face.

"My death only fuels the fire."

Axe retrieved Socket from the ground and held her high and proud.

"You heard this asshole, Socket, let's turn up the heat."

Socket's blade erupted into flames—they curled off the steel and licked the air. Axe gripped her tightly in his remaining hand, his undeniable revenge near complete.

"I added that feature myself."

The White Horse screamed as the flaming ax fell forward, sliced through the middle of Axe's right arm, and then deep into the leader of the HAI army's face—splitting it in two. Blood and brains glopped generously onto the road.

Cheers erupted. Axe raised Socket heroically, her blade still dancing in orange and yellow, then slammed the burning metal against his arm stub—cauterizing it. The pain nearly caused him to pass out, but the sound of angry voices and boots behind him shook him back. He didn't need to turn around to know the charge had begun.

"It's been a ride," he said.

Axe turned to take out as many soldiers as he could, but just before the horde slammed into him, a green pulse shot out, and the HAI army fell into super-slow motion. The sorcerer had abandoned his station with the teleportation tech and now stood directly behind Axe, his arms out, fingers crooked. The magic that blasted from his palms slowed the army down by five hundred percent.

"How long can you hold this?" Axe asked.

"Barely a minute," the sorcerer said, his voice strained. "There's too many of them."

Socket's blade cooled, and Axe gripped the sorcerer's shoulder with an optimistic squeeze.

"Hold it as long as you can."

Axe rushed over to Jordan, who looked defeated.

"Where are we?" he asked.

"Nowhere. We can't get it to charge. You see this plug?" Jordan pointed to the port at the bottom of the tech. "It's a specialty design. We can only power this up with Nomicon technology."

"Plug me in," Socket said bravely.

Axe held her up, hoping he misheard her. "Baby—"

"*I'm* Nomicon technology. I can power the tech."

Axe squeezed her handle.

"That thing could drain you dead," he said.

The sorcerer shouted. "I'm losing it!"

The slow-motion army inched a little closer, moved a little faster—their angry facial expressions stretched wider. The green glow of the sorcerer's power began to flicker, and soon the mob would stumble back to full speed.

Suddenly, two scarred and emaciated humanoid creatures sprang from the Rainy Mood side of town and raced toward the murderous humans—their mouths open, claws extended. They positioned themselves directly behind the sorcerer, and as the front members of HAI became unstuck, they tore into them with deep, mortal wounds—protecting the main archway.

Two strange, brave creatures wouldn't be able to hold off the entire army when it became unstuck, but Axe wasn't ready to lose Socket.

"You don't need me anymore, Axe," Socket said. "You need them."

Axe had cried earlier in front of the White Horse out of fear—now he cried in front of Socket out of love. She was family. Now and forever, and she was right.

He blasted out the loudest scream his vocal cords allowed

and slammed the handle end of Socket toward the port in the tech. Two prongs sprang out of her bottom, and an electric bolt shot forth to guide her inside. The surge pushed Axe backward, unable to hold on.

Socket glowed a brilliant blue as she pushed all her power into the metal crescent moon. The tech immediately went from dark to light as a thousand tiny pixels shot to life and connected with the identical tech piece on the other side of the arch. A stream of purple shot from one to the other and expanded quickly into a large circle of swirling, shimmering smoke. It covered the entire entrance of the arch and blocked the view of the slow-motion army.

Axe stood on the side of the cemetery gate, still able to see them. He watched as the sorcerer lost control of his power, and the army whipped back into their regular speed. With a wave of his long fingers, the sorcerer vanished in a puff of smoke, just as the mob barreled uncontrollably forward.

Unable to slow down in time, the front row of soldiers stumbled headfirst into the strange, spinning smoke cloud. Those behind them continued to push forward, unaware that they were sending those ahead of them into the teleporter. Row by row, guided by hate, they were swallowed up by the purple-and-pink cloud.

Socket now glowed at dangerous levels. Axe wanted to rip her out of the tech but waited until the back half of the army started to slow down, catching on to the fate of those in front. When they stopped completely, only a handful of soldiers remained.

"Power down!" Axe shouted.

Before Socket could obey, her circuits sparked, and a small explosion disconnected her.

The teleportation cloud swirled out of existence and revealed the stragglers of the HAI army to an entire town of pissed-off creatures. The two lunatics who had run into the fray early were still alive. They leaped from person to person—ripped out throats, pulled out eyes, and bit off noses. They froze in place when they heard Jordan Stabber's shout:

"Mom! Dad!"

The Stabberses looked through the archway at their son.

"Let the rest of the town have some fun," Jordan said.

Vampires, werewolves, ghosts, and more descended upon the remainder of the once mighty army. The creatures wasted no time tearing them to absolute pieces.

Axe paid no attention to them as he rushed for Socket, picked her up, and searched for a light. The handle burned his hand.

"Socket," Axe pleaded, "Socket, show me a light. One a little light."

His best friend remained dark. No longer his partner, now just his weapon. He twisted the handle of the ax and pulled her out—a smooth, dark box. He held the melted technology that once contained his friend's consciousness, then brought it slowly to his lips and kissed it tenderly.

From the corner of his eye he caught Gretel staring at him.

"Your friend's a hero," she said.

"I know," he said with wet eyes and a smug grin. "And she knows *I* like to be the one to save the day."

# CHAPTER 63

Lotti's willingness to die in battle surprised her. She'd never felt this brave in all her life. They had pushed the mistakes into the spacious lobby of Nomicon Industries but were now losing the fight. There were too many monsters and not enough cannibals. The death laser on her helmet had saved her from a couple bad situations but had now either jammed or run out of laser juice. Bad timing, as an octopus—with human arms instead of tentacles—grabbed her by the throat and cut off her air.

She closed her eyes, accepting her fate. She thought about the time she was eight and her parents took her to the zoo during Halloween. She had dressed as Dorothy, her dad as the Tin Man, and her mom the Cowardly Lion. This was the thought she chose to die with…until the energy in the room crackled and popped—the octo-man's grip loosened around her neck. Lotti opened her eyes and coughed violently. She looked up to discover a well-equipped army of confused humans, tumbling into the lobby through the front door's leap cloud.

The plan had worked—the HAI army relocated. She grinned, then suddenly realized that things were about to get apocalyptic. Lotti scanned the room and found Jazz a couple yards away, throwing punches at a rock-carved Tiki God.

As the mistakes set their sights on the HAI army, Lotti used the moment of distraction and rushed toward Jazz. Behind her she heard the war cries of the soldiers as they fired up their weapons to protect themselves from the awful abominations their own leaders had created.

She dodged in and out between dozens of grotesque pillars of flesh, then grabbed Jazz by the arm and dragged her away from gnashing stone teeth.

"I had him," Jazz said, defensive.

"I know you did," Lotti said.

The girls didn't look behind them but could hear the two monstrous forces as they connected. The sounds of ripping flesh and bullets saturated the air.

"Outside!" Lotti screamed as she pulled Jazz through the leap cloud.

Lotti's chest hit the dirt path and knocked the wind right out of her. She took a minute to gasp for air, then picked up her head. They had made it outside the front door of the lab. Behind her, just past those walls, an insane war waged between assholes and experiments. Out here, however, Lotti could only hear the ocean waves off in the distance. It soothed her.

"What now?" Jazz asked.

"Let's head to the docks, see if there's a boat we can use. When Pax and Derek join us, we should probably ship out as quick as possible."

"You really think they'll make it out of there?"

Lotti brushed the hair from her face and looked at her best friend.

"If I know Paxton, she's not done tormenting me. They'll make it."

She held out her hand, and Jazz took it. They started down the path—beaten, sore, and happy.

# CHAPTER 64

The underground half-pipe sank deeper than Pax expected, and she thought about all the horrible scenarios that might be waiting for them at the end. The slide eventually flattened out to a horizontal line, slowed them down just enough to gently hop off in front of a rather boring metal door.

*I thought there'd be skeletons and spikes*, Pax thought.

She waited for a response but then remembered they couldn't communicate in their heads anymore. They slipped off the slide and tiptoed to the metal door. Soft voices bickered on the other side.

"What do you think?" Pax whispered. "Rush in and tear their heads off?"

Before Derek could respond, the door slid up into the ceiling and exposed them to Barry and Hannah Warlock and their private bedroom/lab. The scientists stared back at the intruders, the giant clock above their heads ticking down from one minute.

"What's with the countdown?" Pax asked.

"Looks like you're going to find out," Hannah said.

Pax felt optimistic about it not being a bomb. The Warlocks were way too narcissistic to blow up their life's work. Still, the ticking seconds concerned her.

"Not sure we care to wait that long," Pax said.

They stepped into the room and onto what looked like a normal red-carpeted floor but turned out to be the exact opposite.

The carpet fibers were oddly thick, and something that felt like jelly oozed underneath. Their feet sank immediately up to their ankles—an overlapping series of squishy nooks and crannies imprisoning them. Pax tugged upward, but it proved impossible to free herself. The Warlocks stood untouched on two circular pieces of metal that appeared to protect them from the carpet-handcuffs. Pax noticed that all around the room were similar circles, safety islands to navigate the treacherous floor.

Barry smiled. "What you're stuck in right now are the brain folds of a sleeping god."

Pax twisted and tugged, but it was useless.

"God?" she said. "What do you mean 'god'?"

"We found one of the original Titans," Hannah said.

"The sleeping gods of a time before everything," Barry said.

"Floating giants that planets formed around," Hannah continued.

Pax knew what a Titan was, but she never thought they were real. Nobody did. They were monster stories for monsters. Ancient creatures that could not be destroyed and had existed even before the stars. Now, here she was, supposedly stuck in one of their brains.

"The ions in its head alone power this entire complex," Barry said.

"You built this place on top of a Titan?"

"To crack the code to immortality."

"And ultimate power."

"To become perfect beings no longer bound to time and space."

The clock above the scientists struck zero. The flesh from the Warlocks' faces began to melt away, and Pax thought for a moment that whatever they triggered had backfired.

"I don't think we've been properly introduced," Barry said through melting lips.

Their skin plopped down onto the silver islands under their feet, making a mess of goop around their ankles. The scientists raised their lab coats and wiped away the remainder of the peach slime to reveal a sweet-looking elderly couple.

"I'm Bill Piller, and this is my wife, Angie."

"Is that what you want on your tombstone?" Pax said, sharp words her only weapon.

Bill Piller hopped off his safety island and onto several more until he reached a series of computers he began to tap away on.

"Perhaps you need to understand that *we* are in control here," he said over his shoulder, "that your choices are limited. You can die right now or help us shape a better world."

Bill glanced over at Angie and gave her a warm smile. "Ready to touch the sky, my love?"

"Let's wake up this sleepyhead."

Bill set the final sequence on the computers and hopped back over to his wife's side. The bedroom/lab became exceedingly bright as the walls lit up around them—pulses of electricity bolted about the room.

"Your plan is to wake up a Titan? To control it?" Pax shouted over the rumbling.

"This is more than just a laboratory," Bill shouted back.

"It's also a crown."

"Fit for a god."

From the middle of the ceiling, a long, sharp spike lowered itself and plunged deep into the folds of the sleeping god's brain. Pax threw Derek a worried look when she realized what they had done. Like the zombies they controlled, the Pillers had built a helmet in the form of their lab around the sleeping Titan's head, and they were about to wake it with their first command.

The room rattled, and computers tumbled from desks. The brain below Pax began to vibrate, and she had the distinct feeling that they were rising. The entire wall to her right slid open to reveal a window. Rock and dirt zipped by, illuminated by the exterior lights of the lab. They were deep underground and ascending at a breakneck speed.

They blasted out of the earth, the ocean now in view out the window. The bedroom/lab tipped forward, and an enormous, cracked and clawed hand planted on the shore of the island and pushed itself up. Pax caught a glimpse of Lotti and Jazz on the docks. They stared up at the Titan, their mouths wide open in shock.

Higher and higher they lifted into the sky. It was hard to get a good look at the creature from the inside, but the small flashes of its crevasse-riddled skin were enough to give her an idea of its terribleness. They passed through a cloud formation and halted just before they broke the Earth's atmosphere. The Titan tilted its head and looked down at the ground—the island now a pinprick that could be taken out with a single stomp.

"Look down there," Angie said. "Look down and remember that a very long time ago humans dragged their bellies out of the ocean because they knew there was more to discover."

"And now we control a creature older than the universe. A beast that has no sense of curiosity or wonder."

"Life is wasted on the dormant."

"You could still work with us. You were once human. You remember what it was like to be weak and scared."

Pax remembered all too well. She thought about her ex, Rufus Allensgate, and the circle of headless bodies, then realized that Bill and Angie were just as psychotic—on a much grander scale of course.

"The problem with monsters," Bill said, "is they have a hard time looking forward. Progress isn't a concern to them. It has always been man who invents, dreams, and tinkers."

Pax set her burning eyes on the Pillers, unable to listen to any more of their fanatical bullshit.

"It's a bit difficult to be progressive," she hissed, "when people like *you* are counting on it. Waiting for us to step out of the shadows and expose ourselves so you might gain from our gifts. Your entire life is a delusion. You think you're special, with a different set of ideals. Well fuck you, 'cause neither is true. You're just a couple of terrified psychopaths, and even that is being kind."

Pax wasn't afraid to die anymore. What scared her now was not getting the opportunity to kill Bill and Angie Piller. They were the root of everything wrong with the world. Powerful jerks who had the means to push their hate-filled opinions and misguided philosophies.

Her feet began to tingle, and a bolt of energy rippled through her body. At first, she attributed it to rage inside her, but as the feeling grew, it took on roots that spread into every vein and blood cell—every muscle and organ. A fire erupted inside her, yet pain did not exist.

Her eyes rolled all the way to the back of her skull, and the weight of her new body vanished. The darkness came first. She could still hear the Pillers speaking, but they grew muffled and distant. Just when she thought the void would go on forever, a streak of color zipped by—like a shooting star—which set off a chain reaction of light. A chaotic universe pieced itself together all around her. Planets crumbled to pieces before her eyes, only to reform anew in another location. Dense clouds dripped with elements clustered together, heating up to form large burning balls of gas.

"What's going on?" she said to herself. Her voice flattened and then expanded.

A human-shaped blob floated toward her, calling out from all conceivable directions.

"Pax!"

Derek. Not Derek the man-squirrel, but Derek the moody teenage vampire hunter she'd fallen in love with. He looked like a god himself. A soft glow radiated through his skin, his hair swayed lightly about, as if under water—his naked body as natural and beautiful as everything around them.

"Pax! It's you!" he said. "Original you!"

She looked over her own naked body—recognized her hands—every line and blemish. Her short legs and knobby knees. Her breasts with one nipple slightly larger than the other. All imperfections once upon a time, now the beautiful markings of a unique creature.

Pax looked up at Derek. Their eyes met, connected, and held. She could feel him again—their energy tangled together. She was not inside of him, but a part of him. They had become one being. The universe around them exploded.

Particles of light penetrated their body and filled their

head with more information than they knew what to do with. The ancient god had invited them inside and dug out the old home movies—in a manner of speaking. The Pax-Derek union marveled at a flickering past, as Titans by the scores gave birth to the celestial bodies—breathed power into the stars. They were creatures that shrugged off questions about their own creator and focused instead on what they could do with the life they had been given. When a star grew too big and too hot to exist anymore, a Titan would reach up and touch it. The star would shatter into trillions of pieces, and in those pieces Pax and Derek could see life—human, vampire, demon, fairy, werewolf, witch, troll. Every species exploded from the same body of matter and sailed toward their new home on the breath of their makers.

They had never felt lighter as they floated amongst the magic and mystery of creation. It was suddenly so clear, the solution to their problem—simple and effortless. The Titan's power had freed their spirits from their forms. There wasn't a door in all the universe they could not pass through.

Off in the distance they could see the Pillers' vile words literally tumbling from their mouths, twisting about in zero gravity. Their hateful sentences broke apart and drifted away from each other—creating a horizon of words. Words that could be rearranged in a million different ways to change the conversation.

"Man and monster can never completely coexist," the Pillers said, each sentence now blurring with the next. "Jealousy, fear, mistrust—things that will never go away. We will always be afraid of what we are not, unless, we are all. To take from you, to give to others—that is the future of mankind. Your power and our curiosity. Think about that combination. Think about it as we push off this planet and on into the stars, never to kneel again, as we will have nothing left to bow down before."

Pax parted her lips and spoke, her voice calm and quiet. "Fear isn't something you conquer with science, religion, or magic." She looked over at Derek and felt their hearts beat as one. "If you fear something you don't fully understand—for instance, a vampire—what do you do, Derek?"

He looked at Pax, the universe on their shared tongue. "You invite it in."

The skin of the floating being they had become cracked, and a brilliant white light streamed through each crevasse. The Pillers had signed their own death warrant when they trapped them in this brain—fusing them together. Pax and Derek would use the Titan's powers, as the giant creature had so generously offered, and take a step toward a truly better world. One without the Pillers—or at least without their consciousness.

Their skin shattered around them like a supernova, revealing the searing, hot ball of light they had become. They blasted toward the distant shapes of Bill and Angie Piller, aiming themselves directly at their cruel, selfish hearts.

# CHAPTER 65

Giant, tan, and naked, its skin cracked like a dried-up lake. Lotti had seen the face but only for a second, as it was now high above the clouds. It reminded her of her great-grandfather—creepy and wrinkled. It hadn't moved in a few minutes. It just stood there like a silent soldier waiting for orders.

"There's nothing we can do, right?" Jazz asked. "I mean, there's absolutely nothing we can do…right?"

Lotti shook her head.

"No. That thing wins," she responded.

The left leg of the giant suddenly rose into the air, its dark, enormous foot blocking out the sun and hovering over the two girls. Lotti shrugged it off, left with no energy to freak out over her death once more. There could be worse ways to go.

She grabbed Jazz, and the teenagers dropped to their knees to become best friend pancakes. Lotti reached into her pocket, pulled out Jazz's false eye, and handed it to her. Jazz took it, then tossed it as hard as she could into the ocean.

"I took a lot of revealing pictures on that thing," said Jazz. "Better someone find it in hopes to expose all this, than to have it crushed and lost forever."

Lotti agreed. The girls breathed in deep, ready. The giant shifted its weight and then unexpectedly lowered its mighty leg into the very hole it had risen out of. Slowly, it sank itself back into the earth, the ocean flooding in from the pressure. The girls held on tight to an anchored rock off the shore as the water pummeled them in the face. The earth shook violently as the giant's hands hit the ground and lowered its head under the sand.

The ocean calmed, and Lotti took in a deep breath. As the creature's head sank back into the ground, she noticed it wore the silver laboratory of Nomicon Industries like a helmet—just like hers.

# CHAPTER 66

*WE'RE HERE!*

The two words woke Jordan with a gasp. He looked around the dark room, unsure where the voice had come from. He untangled his naked body from Zelda, who remained sleeping like a log, and sat up.

*Hello?*

Jordan suddenly realized why Zelda didn't wake up from the voice's deafening loudness—it belonged to Pax. She'd been keeping mental tabs with him ever since they left the island, and today was the day they'd arrive back home.

Jordan hadn't seen his brother since his death in the woods weeks ago. He hoped things wouldn't be awkward. He'd been practicing everything he wanted to say in the mirror—even though he had no reflection to judge his performance.

He shook Zelda a little too hard, and she sprang up with her fangs bared.

"They're here!"

～

Axe had been rewiring his internal clock in order to spend as much time with Gretel as he could. This meant sleeping through the day. However, he found himself awake more than he wished, his mind still reeling from the aggressive change in philosophy. When Jordan burst into Gretel's room to announce the news, Axe was thrilled for the distraction.

Gretel rolled over and did her best to seduce him into morning sex, but Axe couldn't focus on his carnal lust right now. He wanted to meet the people who took down the establishment that ruined his youth. With a cigarette dangling from his lips, he used his remaining arm to awkwardly throw on some pants, and grabbed a shirt on his way out the door.

Rushing down the steps, he passed a number of Hellswoods all racing to the foyer to greet their sister. Axe smiled to himself as he looked them over. They had welcomed him in—treated him like family. These were the same creatures he wanted to obliterate from the face of the Earth just weeks ago. Now he ran down the stairs with them like a kid on Christmas morning.

The sun blazed high, so the blackout curtains remained on the windows. Everyone invited Axe to the front, since he could safely keep watch. He opened the front door, stepped out onto the porch and scanned the perimeter.

"What do you see?" Clem asked from safely inside.

"Nothin' yet."

"Anything now?" Jim asked.

"Shit, guys, I'll tell you when I see something."

And then he saw something—the top of a head coming up the steep steps.

"They're here!"

"What do you see?"

"Girl wearing a weird silver hat. Blonde. Hot."

Everyone groaned, "Lotti."

Another head appeared behind her.

"Short gal. Dark hair. Rotund."

Everyone seemed confused.

"What about Pax?" Zelda asked.

"You see Derek?" Jordan shouted.

Behind Lotti and the other girl, two more heads appeared as they slowly climbed the steps. They paused just before coming fully into view, as if resting.

"Uh, I see a couple scalps. One looks kinda bald…the other gray?"

The owners of the scalps continued up the stone steps. The moment Axe got a good look at their faces, his heart sank into his stomach. The blood in his veins screamed, and a fire erupted in his organs.

"Fuck you," he said.

Axe stomped off the porch and headed straight for the last two people he ever wanted to see again—Bill and Angie Piller.

～

Pax grabbed the charging man's wrist just before he could smash her skull. She twisted hard and pressed down, bringing the one-armed stranger to his knees. He struggled under her grip, spitting out a sea of expletives.

"Who the fuck is this?" Pax shouted up at the house.

"Who the fuck are you?" someone in the house shouted back.

"I'm Paxton fucking Hellswood!"

Her beefy prisoner stopped struggling the moment he heard her name. She let go, and he scrambled to his feet.

"*You're* Paxton Hellswood?" he said with a touch of disbelief.

"I'm Paxton Hellswood," she responded.

The angry man reached out slowly and touched the wrinkles on the old lady's face. Tears welled up in his eyes. Derek took the man's only hand into his, turning it into a shake.

"And I'm Derek Stabbers. Who are you?"

An enthusiastic voice shouted from the manor. "DEREK!!!!"

Jordan Stabbers tore out the front door toward his younger—now physically older—brother.

～

Derek watched Jordan sprint down the walkway with a giant smile on his face. He barely made it halfway when his skin began to crisp and his shirt caught on fire. Before Derek could even react, Jordan had him in a bear hug.

"Holy shit, little bro! I'm so happy you're here! I'm so sorry about so much, and I have an entire speech all planned out, but

I can't do it out here because I'm on fire and I'm gonna die in like a few seconds, so come in and let's do this thing!"

Jordan released him, patted out a few flames on Derek's shirt, and then sprinted back up the path, diving into the house. Derek watched through the doorway as several vampires extinguished him with a blanket.

~

In the few years Lotti had been a shade for Paxton Hellswood, she had never seen a celebration like the one that currently raged inside Hellswood Manor. It had started out as a family affair, but as the sun went down, more and more creatures from the town began to show up. Whatever happened while they were away had affected all of Rainy Mood's supernatural residents. Booze and blood flowed through everyone's veins, and Lotti found herself in an authentic good mood.

"Heard you led an entire army of cannibals against a legion of mutant mistakes," Jazz said, having snuck up behind her.

Lotti tilted her head to the side with a knowing grin.

"Yes, that sounds like me," she said.

She turned to Jazz, who now wore a black eye-patch, and gave her best friend a giant hug. Jazz tapped on her helmet lightly.

"Maybe we can get the witch to remove this," she said.

"Hell no. No more witches. Figure I'll just wear it until my shade graduation."

"That's gonna do wonders to your social status."

"Bitch, please. The day after I show up with this bad lady on my head, the entire school will go full cyborg."

Jazz nodded, and Pax could see a look of concern on her face. She placed her hand on Jazz's shoulder and leaned in.

"But none of that will stop me from doing a little dumpster diving on the weekends with my best friend."

"*This* weekend?" Jazz asked.

"Every weekend," Lotti said. "But I'll need to wear gloves. And those rubber fisherman pants. Or maybe I could just wait outside the dumpster while you dive."

Lotti looked around and then leaned in, getting serious.

"Hey," she whispered. "What'd you do with those, uh, penis pictures?"

"Oh, I lost them," Jazz said. "I thought they were in my math book, but I might have left them in gym class."

Lotti's face plummeted, and Jazz snorted with laughter, slapped her friend on the back.

"The original files were on my spy-ball," Jazz said. "Lost at sea."

Relief washed over Lotti. An awkward pause passed between them.

"Marshmallow tickle fight?"

"Don't you dare, you crazy bit—"

Lotti attacked Jazz with ten waggling fingers, hitting all the most vulnerable spots she remembered from childhood. Jazz buckled over with laughter, tears rolling down her cheeks.

～

Pax braced herself for a tornado of awkwardness but found a giant smile on Christy Hinter's face instead. In fact, she seemed thrilled to be a werepire. There weren't a ton of added benefits, except that anytime she wanted to go out into the sun, all she had to do was transform herself into a wolf. Of course, she had to stick to the woods—a wolf traipsing about the town midday would certainly turn some heads.

"Do the Bubwyths know?" Pax asked.

"No way!" Christy said. "And they still think you're dead."

Pax had no problem with that.

A graceful set of arms wrapped around Pax. She wanted to turn and face Clem, but her mother held her tight in place.

"Clem—"

"Shhh."

Pax let go of the urge to move, and let her mother's apologetic and loving arms hold her.

～

Jordan knocked back his fifth whiskey and cornered his brother in the kitchen. He had an entire speech to recite, but the booze, the emotions, and Derek's extremely wrinkled face distracted him greatly. Derek stepped forward and gave him a warm hug, and the speech flew out the window in his head. All he could think about now was how good it felt to have his brother back, and that he smelled like butterscotch.

"Look at us," Derek said. "An old man and a vampire."

"Oh, you're not that old," Jordan said, trying to be kind.

"Hey, I wanted to ask you, what's the human side of town's reaction to all this?"

"Uh, no reaction. Since there was never actually a battle, it was pretty easy to pawn off as an early Halloween parade."

"Seriously?"

"Nobody gives a shit as long as you hand them a beer," Jordan said.

"You brought beer to a war?"

"I'm a Boy Scout, little bro. Always fuckin' prepared."

Derek nodded, and a small silence passed between them.

"So, this old guy," Jordan said. "He's still in there with you?"

"As far as I know."

"Can't you get out? Find a younger body or something?"

"The Titan is the only reason we were able to escape our last bodies. De-possession, if I might coin a phrase, still remains a mystery, as it probably should. Could you imagine if ghosts could body hop?"

Jordan rubbed the back of his neck. "What happens when this body dies?"

Derek shrugged. "Some people think we'll be trapped forever."

"Well, that's spooky as fuck," Jordan said, looking around for more whiskey.

"Maybe," Derek said. "But how can anyone know for sure? Maybe I'll be stuck, or maybe I'll simply evaporate. Maybe I'll be sent to a new planet, in a new solar system. We could worry all night about what happens next, but then we'd be missing out on what's happening right now."

Jordan nodded and thought about the long life in front of him—given he stayed out of the sun and away from guillotines—and the rather short one his brother had in store. Derek was right. No sense moaning about what couldn't be changed.

"I freed Mom and Dad," Jordan said bluntly.

"What?"

"Let's get you some whiskey!"

Jordan bounced off in search of a new bottle.

~

Jane pressed her dirty and blood-crusted hand against the windowpane, stared in at the party. A moment later, an equally filthy hand placed itself on top of hers. The Stabberses looked at each other, the lines in their faces deep, the insanity in their eyes ever-present. Elliot reached up and touched a strand of her thinning hair.

It felt great to be out of the asylum. The doctors there had only trapped them deeper in their own psychosis. Jordan's voice had somehow shaken them free, or at the very least it woke up the better half of them. The paranoia, fear, and bloodlust were still a permanent part of her, but now it all felt manageable.

"Derek?" she asked her husband sadly.

She'd been looking through the window for some time but couldn't find her son. She'd seen Jordan get emotional with a strange old man, but no Derek.

"Another time," Elliot said.

He wanted to leave, and she understood. A pane of glass was the only thing separating them from a nest of vampires. While they had come to terms with the folly of their mindset and had even fought on the vampires' side, the disease remained inside them. It screamed, clawed, and beckoned for murder. Best not to hang around too long.

Jane looked down at the self-inflicted bite wound on her hand. It had begun to scab up. She lifted it back into her mouth and reopened it with her teeth. She dipped her fingers into the fresh, red ink and drew a small heart on the pane of glass.

Below that she wrote, *Mom*. Elliot smiled, pressed two of his own fingers into her blood to add, *and Dad*.

He wrapped his arms around his wife and kissed the top of her head. Jane gave him a squeeze, and they quickly vanished into the woods.

∼

Hours later the party continued to live. Music and drunken laughter seeped up through the cracks to the second floor. Pax had pulled Derek away from her siblings, all obsessed with questions about ghosts, Jollywogs, giant squirrels, and the elderly. He seemed happy to be rescued, exhausted from the day of travel. A whostpire inside an old body kept it active and strong, but Derek had died human. Luckily for him, Bill Piller had been a spry old man.

It felt great to be back in her own bed, but even better to have Derek at her side. She watched him as he scanned the posters on her walls.

"You're a total geek," he said.

"All the best people are."

He turned his head and touched her chest with his fingers.

"This wasn't how I pictured us growing old together," he said with a sly grin.

Two tears escaped Pax's eyes and made their slow journey down her face and onto her pillow. Her two lives had spanned over a hundred and eighteen years. She had cried plenty of times in all those decades, but never once out of happiness. She reached out and touched Derek's wrinkled chin.

"I don't care if your face never stops changing—I will always love the squostman behind it."

"Squostman?"

"Yeah, you like that? I just came up with it. Squirrel, ghost, and human."

Derek shook his head.

"We need to talk about your hybrid creature names," he said.

"What's that mean, Stabbers?"

Derek flashed her a smile. "Whostpire?"

"Whostpire is a killer name," she said, defending her title. "And it's not like I had a lot of down time to ruminate on something better. It needed a label and I gave it one. End of stor—"

Derek took her face in his hands and pressed his lips against hers. She had no idea how long their current hosts would be functional, or what would happen to them when they weren't. All she knew in that very moment: Derek's lips were soft and warm. To Pax, they felt like sunlight.

## ACKNOWLEDGMENTS

Below are the humans and monsters who were a vital part of this novel's existence and a crucial part of my sanity. Thank you.

Mom and Dad, Tracy and Travis, Brittany and Jimmy, Harper and Emerson, Max and Jackson and Adelaide

Lisa Gilliam, Shannon Black, Ward Roberts, Annie Roberts, Devin Barry, Norm Thoeming and August Norman, Brad Grusnick, Samantha Sloyan, Amber Benson, Olivia Delgado

Becky Arney, Colleen Dobslaw, Kevin Hamedani, Aaron Gaffey, Derek Schultz, Daniel Raphael, Brandon Panaligan, Jessica Petelle, Mike Nelson, Sarah Lassez, Nicole Parker, Carrie Musalimadugu, Jessica Dhawan, Courtney Cowan, Sara Hawn, Chelsea Meyers, Donna Laughlin, Kevin Lowe, Ward Swan, Mary Jo Garland, Ian "Fuck you guys, I'm not the murderer" Slagle, Christy Hinterlong, Debbie Beukema, Ceciley Jenkins, Ingeborg Roberts, Jamie Tiplitsky, Rebecca Phend, Lee Wilhoite, Brent Coble, Susan Ferraro Gardetto, Anthony Picerno, Jeff Penzenik, Karleigh Fox, Mia Bruno, Bridget Krull, Gretchen Krull, Phil McLaughlin, Brock Baker, Lindsay Barrasse, Katie Graham, Nathan Chase, Adam McLane, Alice Malice, Yosi Berman, Mike Anderson, Aaron Waltke, Eline Gerritsen, Dara Cosby, Kate Colvin, Daniel Winch, Eric Robinson, Peter J. McHugh, Angela Broadhead, Stephanie

Preston, Eric D. Walters, Michael Peter Duffy III, Roberto M. Merza III, Justin Chase, resuki, Sarah Ross, Rebecca Pyle, Nick Cernak, Ashley Eriksen, Andreas Sudihardjo, Heather N, Patrick Dupuis, Pan Petitpois, Joe Ayton, Sarah Bonass-Madden, Whitney Paige Yoham, Jennifer Schmidt, John Frewin, Patrick Nelson, Heather Huber, Javier Gonzalez Calderoni, Ryan Young, Gary Lee Cecil III, Annie Lesser, Jonny Kelly, Paige Biek, Sara Firno, Åsmund Hjorthol Opedal, John Lent, Rebecca Picart, Maxine Segalowitz, Liliana Costa, Cyrene Krey, Rianna Smith, Doug Jones, Camille Silberman, John Rodriguez, Nikolas Zane, Michael Hinojosa, Johnpaul Adams, Loren Finlay, Adam Shaffer, Cameron Eidlitz, Andrew (Bud) Burge, Chad Kukahiko, Juliette Moore, Roberto Beltre, Natasha Inayat, Maggie Wheeler, Arlen A. Harrow (AKA Space Columbo), Keely Crapo, Daniel Benton, Nicholas P DeSomov, Ashley O'Dell, Erlend Holbek, Johnna Rogers, Mark Stolaroff, Nicola Woolford, Brian Ferrari, Brandon Ray, Chantal Gingras, Candice Sullivan, Vanessa Zywicki, Aaron Vinson, Stephanie Kilgore, Taylor Howell, Gillian Mattice, Peter Bragiel, Veronica Salcedo, Lindsey Hollands, Jasmine Kindness, Luke Jason Kapp, Shellz, Adam Troutt, Guillaume Levesque, Ahsan Eslami, Greg Levick, Emma Méligne, Amy Chase, Katie Mayo, Laura Osburn, Donald Milliken, Fidel Jiron Jr., Deb Hildebrandt, Elizabeth Harvey, Ellie Seed, Rebecca Keyz P, Alexandra Sims, Christopher Fillmore, Brian Bernhard, Amy French, Gloria Kelly, Jessica Lasusky, Stephanie Gilbert, Beth Perrin, Amy Chase, Alison McKenzie, Emmelina Audigier, Ian Thomas Anderson, Bill Helms, Ian Van de Laar, C.J. Lee Ruzicka, Chris Tongue, Matthew Siciliano, Leah Kiczula, Mary Salmon, Shonda Robbins, Anthony Bommarito, Diana Zapata, Roelof Iball, Andy Nordvall, Jeremy Kavich, KT McVeigh, Stephanie Moore, J.D. Dresner, Laura Raynes, Jody Taylor, Carrie Davidson, Pete Zornosa, Federica Ghioldi, Timothy Stratton, Ashlea Gatica, Eric Newman, Presley White, DeAndrea Vaughn-Doom, Manda Miller, Sean Mannion, jbostTV, Lucas Wagner, Scott Glasgow, Michael Davis, Amy Troutmiller, Nuala O'Rourke, Jeff Kendrick, Jessica

Soike, Oliver Janke, Dawn Maisey, Victor Eppler, Timothy Martin, Charles McDougald, Patty Dembkowshi, Melisa D. Monts, Rachel Stasyshan, David Seguin, Brittany Dixon, Meredith Host, Jenna Melancon, Tegan Spresser, Robin Carte, Rylee Edgar, Casey Curtiss, Duke of Dice, Weird Review, Sitic, Jessica D. Hoyal, Florian Diederichs, Laurie-Ann Schultz, Dominique Frazzini, Andreas Gustafsson, Denise Lancaster Schiller, Andrea Ivins, Floyd Brigdon, Cassie Bell, Kris Calkins, Robert Ring, Ken Shover, Jamie Taylor, Maeve Potter, Rico Fischer, Sarah Stevens, Bret Burks, Chris Clowers, Adam Runnels, Rachel Towse, Collin McDowell, Stacy Craft, Josh Lowman, Helen Moore-Lee, Becky Bergmann, Derek Williams, Rachel Fairbank, Ronald, ZuZuBe, Mark Carroll, Michael, Aya, Fergus W-B, Jim Kirk, James Willis, Fawndolyn Valentine, SwordFirey, Almost Human, Travis, F Schultz, Mariana, Patrick Campbell, David Kay, Michael Maki, Zannalov & Kaynary, Will Hoffman, Nicholas Puleo, Rebecca Tremblay, Rebekah Martin, Reuben De Beuben Marshall, Taryn Nesbit, Shattered By Loss, Michelle Benedetti, Mark Davis, Megan Salisbury, Dana Urban, Torrey Meeks, David Urban, Andy Drummond, Nick Riggin, Onyxman8, William Mullin, Alyssa Patencio, Merle Clara Jacques, Brett O. Walker, Zannalov, Djon, Cathrine Aanonsen, Drew Walker, Cari Wiater, Christopher Goetting, Travis Bunch, Michael Newby, Brynn Styles, Andrew Rogerson, JordanM85, Jason Thorlakson, Julie Keck / Jessica King, Dav Heim, Zach Cammarata, Heath Myers, Lady Zombie, Heroine Club

And, of course

Lenore

CPSIA information can be obtained
at www.ICGtesting.com
Printed in the USA
FSHW020124090121
77519FS